Mourning Doves

K. M. Vittetoe

Mourning Doves
by K. M. Vittetoe

K. M. Vittetoe, 2007
kmvittetoe@gmail.com

ISBN 978-0-6151-7025-1

This book is dedicated to
my mother, for painting the pictures of my childhood,
my father, for giving words to all my dreams,
and Jana Clark, mother to all her writers.

Chapter 1

Aurelio arrived in the United States twenty-nine years ago with a dream he carried under his arm. Inside the brown leather satchel that had been passed down from his great-grandfather, the manuscript of his families' stories, which slid from tongue to tongue from one generation to the next, was tied with a thin strand of cotton twine and wrapped in a hand-sewn shawl from Aurelio's mother. The manuscript, which Aurelio had spent years creating, contained spicy tales of Mexican folklore that his research told him had never been published. Disgruntled with the poverty and muck of Jimenez, the twenty-two-year-old had kissed his Mamá and Papá and four brothers and sisters, and begun the journey north.

Moving from town to town in the back of pickup trucks or teeming buses, Aurelio pinched whatever money he had, and carried nothing except the brown satchel and its feather-light cotton shawl that he wrapped around his broad shoulders on cold desert nights. For the first time in his life, he saw another part of his homeland. The dusty desert dragged itself for hundreds of miles between his desire and its reality: the U.S. border. Along the two-lane roads he traveled, he passed one small pueblo after another, each with scattered adobe homes, ramshackle barns, labyrinthine streets filled with Volkswagen Beetles, and small stores and markets. Every pueblo surrounded a large stone or adobe church. It was in these towns where Aurelio would rest at night, knocking on doors until a friendly housewife or farmer would offer him a room and a bath for a little money. One evening at a time, he tasted what it was like to be part of a different family, a big brother to toothless six-year-olds or an uncle to teenage farmhands. He shared with each family where he was going but did not share his dream. Al Norte touched the souls of so many people, so many times—all he had to say was, "Estados Unidos" and the father and mother would nod, their eyes glazing over with looks that combined both jealousy and bewilderment.

Always, in these tiny shacks where he often shared a room or even a large bed with two or three other family members, someone would tell a story of a friend or a grandfather or a brother who also had made the journey north. Aurelio listened to these stories, which often had no ending (as the comrade might still be in the U.S.), so he could begin to draw a picture in his mind of what to expect. He knew that many of the men who went there were migrant workers and never returned home, but sent monthly payments to their mothers or grandmothers or wives. Aurelio knew, as he held the satchel close to his chest, that he could not bear that destiny. His family expected more of him.

Aurelio's mother had chosen him, the oldest, to be the only one of her children to attend the costly Catholic school rather than the impoverished public school in their neighborhood. It was Aurelio who was chosen to be the first in their family to attend the university and to study English. Aurelio was not, like his two younger brothers, expected to stay in the small family store and work there until he died, as Aurelio's grandfather and father would. Living their dreams vicariously through their eldest son, his parents had held back tears of joy as they sent him on his way.

When Aurelio was two days' drive from the U.S. border, he thought of his mother's last words, words that rushed from her mouth as she pressed her round face and locks of curls against his cheek: "Don't come back without the book published in English and Spanish. Do you hear me, Mi Hijo?" She had pulled away, tears smearing the mascara away from her almond brown eyes. Her light brown skin had looked bruised as he let go and stared down at her.

"I won't, Mamá," he had told her, and closed the door behind him as he left his family home for the last time.

He was lying with three other men in the bed of a pickup truck when he thought of his mother's words. Two layers of dusty tarp covered their sweaty bodies, and a blond-haired Texas native sat at the wheel. He had been driving from town to town looking for Mexican men who wanted to work his ranch, somewhere in Texas (Aurelio didn't care), as long as the men would agree on cramped conditions and remaining silent and still for two days. He would pass through the border easily, he told them, because of his looks, and if no one moved.

It was in the pickup truck, lying so still that he became dizzy with thirst, hunger, and the ever-burning desire for freedom that Aurelio first tasted his ability to tolerate the bare-bones filth that must come before the clean, seamless happiness. It was in the pickup truck that bounced and jostled every nerve in his body that Aurelio first realized the suffering he must endure to bring the manuscript back to his mother. It was in the pickup truck where Aurelio's desire for drink moved from water to tequila.

Without warning, the pickup came to a stop and the blond man lifted the tarp and welcomed Aurelio and his compadres to the United States. "Land of the free," the man had drawled, "now let's get to work."

With a shovel in his hands and the satchel tied to his back, Aurelio started to dig.

Chapter 2

On the morning of his fifty-second birthday, Warren couldn't open his eyes. The lids were clamped around the eyeballs in a death-grip that clutched at his pupils just as chillingly as the fear that beat inside his chest. He didn't move to switch off the alarm clock in the gray light of predawn, moments before his alarm was set, as he had done every day for the past thirty years. He didn't roll to his side, eyes open, and stare at the blurry numbers that mocked his near-sightedness. He didn't breathe in those first moments of trepidation that encountered him in a state that rested between asleep and awake. Instead, he lay in bed without moving, waiting for the familiar sound to ring out.

The beeping startled him, and he felt his eyelids pop open as if drawn with pliers. He maneuvered his feet into the slippers on the floor next to the bed. Not even in the dim light did he need to look for the switch as he entered the bathroom. He relieved himself, shut the bathroom door, and strolled into the kitchen. The chrome teakettle rested upside down on the dish rack, scrubbed clean for the eightieth time that year. Warren, his eyes still adjusting to the bright fluorescent glare of the kitchen, counted to thirty-five as he stood at the sink, the cold water half-filling the teakettle. He placed the kettle on the right rear burner of the olive green stove and turned the knob to high, then entered the bedroom to continue his daily routine.

The night before, he had lain out a thin plaid shirt and freshly pressed khaki pants, as well as one each of his seven pairs of white briefs and white socks. Warren sat on the bed as he pulled off his flannel pajama pants and wool socks. He wore these items to bed, as well as sleeping under an electric blanket, to maintain the thermostat at fifty-eight degrees and save thirty dollars per month. The moment he felt the cold morning air on his legs, his eyes widened, and he quickly pulled on his clean underwear, socks, and pants. He stood up to unbutton his flannel pajama shirt, then folded it together with the pants and put the set in their empty spot in his bottom drawer before pulling on his shirt. Shivering, he walked down the hall to the foyer, where he put on his sweater and returned to the bathroom.

For just a moment, Warren looked at himself in the mirror. He almost said aloud, "Happy birthday, old man," but thought against it. He brushed what was left of his orange-colored hair toward the back of his round head. He squinted at the image of his blue eyes beneath the eyebrows that were bushy enough to be connected. He reached toward the edge of the sink vanity and felt for his glasses at the same time as he ran the electric razor up and down his cheek. Placing the glasses on his nose with his left hand, Warren continued to shave with his right. Just before he finished, he heard the whistle of the teakettle. He placed the electric razor back in its charger and shut the door to the bathroom before he walked toward the kitchen.

Pulling the plain white teacup out of the cupboard, Warren gathered a teaspoon from the drawer below. He reached into the metal Twining container and grabbed a single bag of Earl Grey, placed it in his cup, and walked to the stove, where he turned off the knob, picked up the teakettle and poured the steaming water in with the tea. Warren placed the tea on the counter to steep as he opened the refrigerator and retrieved two pieces of whole wheat bread and a stick of butter. He put the bread into the chrome toaster as he strolled to the front of the house, opened his door, and picked up that day's copy of The Denver Post. He returned to the kitchen, prepared his toast, and sat on the bar stool at the island to eat, drink his tea, and read his paper.

Warren skimmed over the headlines: "Does mainstreaming work for Colorado students?", "French President Chirac criticizes Bush", "Ft. Carson troop to depart for mid-east", "Drought beginning to dwindle?" Having read about the war enough this week, Warren decided on the article regarding the drought, although he had read similar articles three times in the past month. He tore off the crust from his toast while reading, then, bit by bit, placed the crust pieces on his tongue. In between bites, he took careful sips from his tea. When he finished the article, he folded each section of the paper back into its original place and laid it on top of the recycling pile. He then glanced outside, skimming the surrounding sidewalks before going upstairs to the unused back bedroom.

The early morning light danced across the concrete walkways and blacktop driveways. A few lights glared back at him from the windows of small ranch homes that lined his street. All of the cars belonging to his neighbors were still parked in their usual places. A cat dashed across the adjacent yard, its feet damp from the early morning dew. Birds called out to each other from treetops and the birdfeeders in Warren's backyard. He scanned the surrounding homes for several moments before settling into his chair.

No one was out yet. He was safe, at least for now.

Chapter 3

Luisa loved birds. She spent many of her childhood days wandering the fields behind her house with an old pair of binoculars, searching for any sign of a flutter, whether it came from a chickadee or a heron. She loved to watch robins search for worms in their bouncy, down-to-earth manner, and loved the elegance of hawks as they swooped about their prey in great godlike circles. She loved to see bird nests, so intricately weaved by mother birds' beaks, and would examine them if ever they were fallen or abandoned. She loved to talk about the graceful, yet delicate movements of birds when she met other bird lovers, or when she wanted someone to know her deepest passion. She loved the variety of colors and types, sizes and shapes that engulfed the world of birds. Watching them made her feel as if her own life could be filled with such vibrant changes, as the birds in her (now small) city backyard varied daily.

What Luisa loved most about birds was their freedom: they were not afraid of falling off their feeders or clinging to an electric wire, because they could lift their wings and flutter away. This secret, this desire to be like a bird, free of fear from falling, Luisa discussed with no one. She held this admiration in her heart, as if allowing it to escape from her tongue would mean that she would never know that freedom herself.

On the first day of spring, she was up at dawn, cradling Alejo as she nursed him by the back window, glancing out as the mourning doves pecked at the food on the ground below the feeder, when the feeling began. The doves haunted her periodically, but she hadn't seen them in weeks. She took a moment to focus her eyes, trying to examine the details of their features. Was it the same pair that she'd imagined following her all the way from her childhood home in Texas? She couldn't be sure. They finished their meal and were replaced by two loud-mouthed crows. She turned back toward Alejo, pushing the image of the doves out of her mind. How many mornings had she rocked him here, in the warmth of his upstairs bedroom, looking out at the birds for comfort? At nearly twelve months, she knew Alejo would have to be weaned soon, but she dreaded losing these soft moments together in the peace of early morning. She thought, that day, that it was the dread of weaning that crept into her stomach and caused her upper neck and head to ache. She rarely became sick, and somehow, she knew, this was no common illness. Luisa tried to ignore the sick feeling as she adjusted her eyes between the view outside and Alejo's hazel eyes, which, after nearly ten minutes of nursing, were finally beginning to open.

"Hey, baby," she cooed, stroking his feathery hair.

When Carter approached her nearly two years ago and said he thought it was time for them to begin having children, she was reluctant. Didn't he understand that she had just received a promotion at her job, and that all those years of school were paying off? She told him, "How can you know when we're ready?" and he moved next to her on the couch, wrapped his arms around her and whispered in her ear, "When is anyone ever ready?" He had kissed her neck and gently slid his fingers down her back. "You know I love you," he said, "and I want our love to make a family."

How could she say no?

Now, looking down into Alejo's eyes on the cold morning that brought spring into Denver, she silently thanked her husband for asking her to put her career on hold. After all, it was Carter who supported her, financially and emotionally, through her bachelor's and then her master's degrees. It was Carter who stood up to her father when they announced their engagement and told him, no, they weren't too young to get married, and if he had a problem with it, he didn't need to come to the wedding. It was Carter whose family Luisa had come to love, who had opened their arms to her, disregarding her own dysfunctional family, and accepting her into their own the way a bird wraps its wings around its young.

Luisa was glad she had given in to his desire. As soon as she became pregnant, she felt connected to Alejo. And, as if to erase any doubts of motherhood from her mind, Alejo had entered the world easily (only four hours of labor, the day before he was due) and had the personality of a satisfied prince: flirtatious, easy-going, yet always in control. She saw the pleasant joy of a full stomach and the warmth of his mother's arms as he looked at her now. Ignoring her discomfort, Luisa raised him up into her arms and buried her face into the back of his neck. "I love you, I love you, I love you," she murmured as he squealed in delight.

She didn't know that this would be the last morning that she could say those words to her son without breaking down in tears.

Alejo's room was painted with a mural of various birds that reflected the vivid colors of Luisa's imagination and the morning light that shined through the triple-paned window. On one wall, Luisa had painted a pair of bald eagles that swooped the cloudy-skied background over their mountaintop nest, where three babies, their thin gray feathers barely covering their pink skin, held their beaks ajar, waiting for food. On the opposite wall, Luisa painted a giant oak tree with a thick hoary trunk and bright green leaves that held three mysterious nests. On several branches, and flapping about the tree, were brown and white chickadees, black crows, and red-tailed swallows. The only other wall bearing no window held the mural of a tropical rainforest, with lush, giant leaves hiding the mossy trunks below, and rainbow macaws, large-beaked toucans, and yellow cockatiels resting on long limbs or lunging for food. The room had just three pieces of furniture: an oak crib, its edges carved in a circular spool, a matching chest of drawers that contained three drawers on the left and a raised portion on the right with a small drawer and cabinet, and which doubled as a changing table, and the red-cushioned glider where Luisa nursed her son. On the thick beige carpet where Luisa sunk her toes, multicolored blocks, puzzles, and stuffed animals were spread wherever Alejo had chosen to put them. Carter had put in the ornate molding that enhanced the ceiling and sharpened the corners of the room with its pale blue delicacy.

She sang to Alejo as she changed his diaper. Often, she made up songs, but this morning, she sang, "Twinkle, Twinkle, Little Star" as he gurgled. Luisa dressed him in a pair of blue overalls and a turtleneck. She placed Alejo on the floor of his room surrounded by his favorite toys and shut the door before going downstairs.

Luisa sighed as she slid her hand down the maple railing that led into the living room. The room held two sofas, one full size, one a loveseat, and a matching oversized chair. All were a simple beige, with narrow arms and coordinating pillows that bore a beige and brown funky pattern. The furniture centered itself around the stone fireplace, where the maple mantel bore silver-framed photographs of Luisa and Carter's wedding, Luisa's parents, Carter's parents, and Alejo. The light from the windows of the vaulted ceiling shone down on the pictures now, drawing a smile to Luisa's face. She trotted through the living room and the dining area, with its long, oval, maple table and matching beige-cushioned chairs, and into the large kitchen. Carter had built the maple cabinets himself, along with some of his coworkers, and Luisa had picked out the stainless steel handles on the drawers and cabinets to match the stainless steel dishwasher, microwave, oven, and refrigerator. The countertop, also chosen by Luisa and laid by Carter, was a magnificent burgundy tile that sparkled in the morning sun and matched the tile on the island in the center of the Pergo floor. The miniature greenhouse windowsill bore a small herb garden with basil and parsley, the sweet scents tickling Luisa's nose as she entered the room.

In the kitchen, she measured the coffee grounds and water, and then quickly began the pot, glancing at the clock. It was nearly seven, and Carter wasn't up yet. She darted back up the stairs and cracked the door open, tiptoeing into their dark bedroom. The hunter green curtains were pulled tight across the two large windows, and Carter slept in the four-poster king-size bed. Crawling next to him, Luisa snuggled against his warm body. "You're going to be late," she lied, "it's seven-thirty." His blue eyes popped open as if the eyelids were pulled apart by a machine. "Uh-uh," he said, trying to conceal a grin. "I just looked. It's not even seven. Ten more minutes." As usual, he hadn't heard the baby, and had remained in restful sleep until her return to the bed. Luisa squeezed an arm around his shoulder. "Five minutes," she said. She said nothing of her head or stomach, not wanting to disturb his few remaining minutes of peaceful sleep.

Lying there beneath the warmth of their rob-Peter-to-pay-Paul quilt, Luisa began to doze off herself. She was halfway between sleeping and waking, and images flooded her mind. First she was holding Alejo, and then she was dancing with Carter. They were twirling in a ballroom like the one where they had their wedding reception. Carter was spinning and spinning her around.

Luisa felt dizzy and sick but happy at the same time. He was laughing, throwing his head back and laughing, when suddenly he stopped. He pulled away and ran toward the back doorway. Luisa started to follow… and his alarm clock beeped in her ear. She jumped up, forgetting the brief dream instantly. "It's time, Car," she nudged, and then rolled out of bed herself.

When she walked down the hall to check on Alejo, he looked up at her and gurgled, as if to say, "I'm so happy to see you again, Mommy!" She looked back and said, "Mommy's going to go make Daddy's lunch, you be a good boy," and shut the door as she returned to the kitchen.

While Carter took a quick shower, Luisa packed a ham and cheese sandwich, an apple, and a little bag of carrots. Just before she tied the bag, she threw in a few of his favorite chocolate chip cookies that she had made that weekend and a note that said, "No cookies until you eat your vegetables, Lover," a name she called him to let him know that, when he came home that day, she would be wearing her red teddy and waiting in the bedroom. She poured his coffee into his travel mug, adding two spoons of sugar and some half-and-half.

Carter came down the stairs as she put the lunch bag on the maple end table by the door. "We're meeting some new clients today—could bring in enough to cover us for the rest of the year." He stood in front of the mirrored closet doors for a moment adjusting his belt and running his fingers through his blond hair. Luisa stood behind him at the mirror.

"That sounds good. I hope it goes well."

"What are your plans for today?" he asked, his blue eyes staring back at her in the mirror, an inquisitive look sitting on his freshly shaved oval face.

"Oh," she moaned, "I have to go drop off those papers for my dad today. Mom finally filed the divorce, and I'm hoping that Papá will be too out of it to care, and he'll just sign the paperwork and let her be." She paused. "I've been putting it off all week."

"Well, good luck," he cast his eyes toward the floor. Luisa knew he didn't know what to say, that he couldn't fathom what it felt like to enter that dark, filthy house where she would probably find her father half-asleep in his clothes on the living room couch.

"I'd better go say goodbye to Alejo," he said as she finished, and dashed upstairs. Luisa wiped the counter in the kitchen when he returned. "I gotta go," he told her, and leaned in for a brief hug and peck on the lips. "Love you," he said, grabbing his keys, wallet, and jacket from the end table and closet. "Love you, too," she said, and shut the door behind him.

Like a hundred tiny spiders carrying venom, her headache had expanded to include not just her upper neck, but her temples and forehead. Her stomach churned for something other than food, but she didn't know what. She went to the medicine cabinet in the upstairs bathroom and stood there surveying the various over-the-counter drugs, knowing in her heart that none of them would put this feeling to rest.

When she returned downstairs, she saw Carter's lunch bag still sitting on the table by the door. She didn't know if it was the cookies he wouldn't relish or the note he wouldn't read, but for some reason, Luisa couldn't stop staring at the lunch bag sitting on the table.

He had never before forgotten his lunch.

Chapter 4

He couldn't remember the exact date, but Warren knew he had been watching them for fourteen months. He'd first caught sight of their life on a Tuesday afternoon, his cleaning day. He had been cleaning out his upper back bedroom, a room that sat virtually empty, minus an antique walnut pie safe where he kept extra linens and an old rocking chair. When he first saw her, she was pregnant and painting the walls. She stood on a stepladder in the room directly across from his, and painted in a casual way that would suggest she did this regularly. Other than being largely pregnant, she was slender. Her thin brown arms were a stark contrast to the oversized, paint-spattered white t-shirt that engulfed her stomach. Her black hair was pulled back in a bun, but curly strands danced across her shoulders and upper arms. She wore no shoes, and stood on tiptoes to reach the highest parts of the wall, stretching the arches of her tiny feet. She bore a concentrated, calm expression on her smooth, round face that told him she carried a picture in her head of just how she wanted the walls to look.

He didn't mean to stare. Warren had little interest in his own family, let alone strangers, and prided himself on his solitary life. Yet, he was drawn to her. Inexplicably, her even movements attracted Warren, not in the way a man desires a woman, but in the way a father looks after his daughter. A slow longing began to form in his heart the day he first saw her painting various species of birds against a blue background which would become her baby's nursery. The longing came to life like a predator and devoured him as he watched her. But it also frightened him.

Warren didn't return to the upper back bedroom for nearly a week after that first view into another life, but he noticed changes in himself that he couldn't elucidate. Once, he was reading the paper, as always, in the early morning, but not reading: simply watching the words while his mind wandered. Another day he was mowing his lawn, walking the slow, meticulous pace in the patient way he had done a thousand times, only to turn off the mower and see that he had not created a straight line. That Sunday he roasted a chicken, one of his favorite meals that he enjoyed dividing up for three days of TV dinners, when he forgot to baste it and the chicken came out dry.

Tasting the parched poultry, Warren had put his plate into the sink without even clearing it and hiked up the stairs. He had looked across at the room, but it was dark and empty. Rocking in the chair, Warren had waited and fallen asleep. When he awoke in the early morning, she was painting again, and he forgot all else as he watched her through the window.

Adding a new event to his daily routine made Warren feel differently about his life. Besides the few customers who came into the small hobby shop he had owned for thirty years, Warren rarely spoke to anyone. He had chosen this life to protect himself from the possibility of pain that came with any relationship. He filled each day with a set of routines that made time pass, and he saved his money as if he planned a grandiose retirement filled with travel and luxury, when in reality he couldn't imagine his life ever changing.

He couldn't imagine another life until he viewed one from his back window. He began each new day by finishing his breakfast and taking about an hour to sit and watch. He feared what could happen: they might somehow see him, though he kept his blinds mostly closed, or someone else, someone walking by on the street, might discover his voyeurism, and report him to the police. He ran the possibilities through his mind frequently, but every day for fourteen months, as if pulled to them like an addict who must sniff his cocaine, he watched the young family laugh, cry, hug, and move with the effortlessness of ones in love with each other, themselves, and their intertwined lives.

He was there to witness the new arrival, a tiny boy, he figured, from the blue clothes that they'd wrapped around him. He saw the endless flashes of the camera on the morning they brought him home. He was there in the window, one sleepless late night of his own, as the petite brown mother and the tall blond father paced back and forth, passing the screaming baby from one set of arms to another, stopping only to release their own tears of anxiety and frustration. He was there each morning to observe the serene, expressionless face of the mother as she rocked and nursed her growing child, glancing back and forth between his tiny eyes and the birds in her backyard. He was there when the father came in each morning and raised the baby into his arms, then lifted him into the air above his head, lowered him to his face, and raised him again, the baby's expression filled with wonder and delight, before the father left for work each day.

Warren's desire to live within their life consumed his mornings and his evenings. He felt the wintriness around his heart begin to melt into a spring that bloomed with hopes and possibilities. He watched and waited as the new season began. He knew, somehow, that their lives were connected by more than a view from window to window.

Chapter 5

As with many of her daily habits, Luisa planned the trip to her father's house around Alejo's naptime. She wanted to have an excuse to leave almost as soon as she arrived. She found it difficult enough to bring Alejo there at all, to expose him to the acrid smell of the old house where she had spent the latter part of her childhood, but she knew she couldn't put it off any longer. Though her mother never bothered her about the money, when Luisa entered her mother's apartment, she would often make remarks such as, "Can you believe how outrageous the electric bills are now?" or, "I was barely able to make the rent this month," all of which were her guilt-tripping reminders of the weeks and weeks of Luisa's procrastination.

After Carter had driven away, Luisa put his lunch in the bottom drawer of the refrigerator. She went upstairs and opened Alejo's door. "Listo, Mi Hijo?" she asked. He locked eyes with her from his cross-legged perch next to the crib and let out a satisfied squeal. "We're going to see Abuelo, OK?" She walked over and reached under his arms as she lifted him. "Don't worry, we won't stay long."

Grabbing the diaper bag from the coat closet and the folder filled with pages of pre-highlighted lines for her father to sign, Luisa strapped Alejo into his car seat and began the twenty-minute drive across town to her father's house. Though the temperature was in the mid-thirties, the sky shone its usual garish blue, and the sun bore away at the remainder of the previous weekend's snowstorm. Luisa's eyes burned at the brightness of light reflected in the snow, and blamed her father for the aching feeling in her head and stomach. It was just one of many discomforts in her life for which Luisa blamed her father.

When she arrived, she popped open the trunk of her Corolla and retrieved Alejo's stroller. She didn't want him crawling around on the floor inside. Fastening him into the stroller, Luisa put the backpack on one shoulder and carried the paperwork under her arm. She stood for a moment looking at the outside of the house.

Its outward appearance maintained the presentable, well-trimmed and watered yard similar to many other houses that decorated the streets of Denver. The four ash trees her mother had planted when they bought the house fifteen years ago were now twice as high as the roof on the blond brick ranch. The irises, which at one time lined both sides of the corner lot had been replaced with mulch on one side and rocks on the other. (Luisa knew that her father paid people to mow and trim each week, and that those companies never maintained flower gardens). On the two front-facing windows, one that hid the master bedroom and one that disguised the living room, yellow curtains were pulled tight. The eight-foot wooden fence with faded gray semicircles from the sprinkler blocked off the backyard. Luisa wondered what had become of the vegetable garden and the birdfeeders, the only tastes of the country their family had brought with them to the city.

She looked at her watch. Eight-thirty. Alejo would go to sleep in an hour, and she needed to give him breakfast still. She paused a moment longer, then marched toward the front door and rang the doorbell. She waited. After a few minutes, Luisa rang the doorbell again. She waited. "Why do I even bother?" she mumbled under her breath, and cracked open the door.

"Papá? Papá, estás aquí?" She called into the living room. Her voice carried in the sparsely furnished room with the hardwood floors. "Papá, are you here?" she said again, in English. Her face felt hot. She knew he wouldn't answer.

"Here, Alejo," Luisa pushed Alejo's stroller into the center of the room, trying to maintain a calm, cheery voice. "You wait here for a minute while Mama finds Abuelo, OK?" She pulled out a couple of toys and placed them on the small tray of Alejo's stroller, and then tiptoed toward the bedroom. "Papá? Papá?" she called again as she tapped on the closed bedroom door. On the hamper lid in the small hallway was one large, half-empty bottle of Tequila.

Before entering the room, Luisa stood staring at the bottle. She had seen similar bottles throughout her childhood, but never laid out in plain view. As a girl, she had encountered these bottles, always with some or all of their liquid still inside, hidden behind towels in the linen closet, or in the corner cabinet in the kitchen, behind all the pans, or on the top shelf of tools in the garage, or underneath the wisteria bushes in the backyard. Always, Luisa had encountered the bottles by accident, when she was searching for a hammer or a towel or playing hide-n-seek with her brother, Byron. And always, Luisa remained silent. What advice or complaint could she offer to the man whose soft, sweet voice sang her to sleep every night?

She sucked in her breath and opened the door. He lay on his stomach on top of the comforter. One shoe had been kicked against the wall sometime in the night and left a faint black scuff mark above where it landed on the floor. His other shoe was half untied, but still on his left foot, which hung lopsidedly over the edge of the bed. His wavy black hair scattered itself halfway across his unshaved cheek and the red pillowcase that supported his head. His broad shoulders were slumped together and his long legs were pinched tight inside the Wrangler jeans.

Luisa leaned over and clutched his shoulder. "Aurelio, it's time to get up. I have some things for you to sign."

After twenty-five years of marriage, Luisa's mother, Reeve, had finally gained the courage to leave him. Luisa had been begging her for years to get out, from the time she was in high school and realized that, no matter how much she or Byron or her mother pleaded, Aurelio would never stop drinking. But set in stone were the vows her mother had taken in the small courthouse in southern Texas, and it took a chiseling of hate to chip them away.

Reeve had moved out two years ago, but, knowing that Aurelio, jobless and drunk, would never pay the bills, she could only afford a studio apartment on the bad side of town, as she still had to pay their mortgage and all of the other bills at the house. Fearful of creditors knocking down her door, as she had always had perfect credit, Reeve could not find the courage to file for a divorce until two years after she made her decision to leave.

Luisa shook her father again. "I'll go make coffee," she said, and returned to the living room where Alejo played with his toys. She peeked at the old leather couch, now covered in a layer of greasy grime and several days' laundry, and the pair of wingback chairs that were piled high with books and records. "Hey, sweetie, we'll be done in a little bit, OK?" Again, she masked her voice, then turned and headed for the kitchen.

The living room, with its un-swept floors and piles of junk, did not compare to the filth of the kitchen. Dishes were laid out with bits of food, some beginning to mold, so that Luisa couldn't even see the brown tile counter that had once been her mother's pride and joy. All along the wall were empty bottles of beer, Tequila, and amaretto, and there were three trash bags also filled with empty bottles on the floor. The coffee pot had a brown layer of grunge dripping down each of its white sides, and, after searching for several minutes, Luisa discovered that her father must be reusing the same ground coffee beans day after day. She gave in and started a pot, then headed back to the bedroom.

Aurelio was beginning to stir. He turned his face up to her and asked, "Donde está mi Alejo?" He always spoke Spanish when he was hung over, as if the cells in his brain couldn't work together to bring English to his tongue.

"He's in the living room, Papá. You can see him after you sign the papers."

"What papers?" Luisa wondered if this was masked innocence.

"The divorce papers, Papá. And the papers that take Mom's name off the deed to this house."

Aurelio stared up at her now, a perplexed look his face. "Do I…" he appeared to struggle to find the words inside of him. "Necesito firmar—sign—today?"

"Yes, Papá, today. You're going to sign them and see Alejo and then I have to take him home for his nap. Today. That's it." She wondered, as she sternly told him what he had to do, when she became the parent and he the child. His eyes watered a bit and he gripped his fingers around the top of his head. "OK," he conceded, "what do I have to lose?"

He was right. He had already lost everything.

Chapter 6

As if suddenly aware of the new season, clouds rolled in from the west and threatened an icy rain. Nearly hidden by the large maple tree that he had planted along the sidewalk when he first opened it, Warren's shop was a rectangular cave in the strip mall along the old city street. The large single-paned window overlooked a narrow parking area alongside the four-lane road, where a traffic light held up the congestion at every corner for miles. Painted in a red semicircle across the center of the window were the words, "York Hobbies: A Place for Collectors and Craftsmen." The glass door that opened into the shop was trimmed with pale gray aluminum and squeaked as it opened, then jangled the silver bells that hung above it. Inside, the fluorescent lights flickered over four slender aisles that were separated by ten-foot stained-pine shelves. In each aisle, the shelves ranged in width from six inches to two feet, depending on the items in their places.

One entire section consumed cardboard boxes with plastic trim of various models, including cars, boats, trains, and planes. Alongside the boxes, paint, brushes, replacement parts, and other accessories took up the remainder of shelf space. Most of the boxes had collected dust, and many had not been pulled from the shelf in several years.

In the next two aisles, Warren's passion and reason for opening the shop flourished: stacked neatly on top of one another were box after miniature box of electric train track pieces, light posts, engines, cars, cabooses, stations, trees, shrubs, miniature figurines, signal lights, grass, anvils, small plastic cargo boxes, and every other train accessory Warren could find to order. This collection, which took the center part of the store, Warren dusted off daily, for it was not only his hobby but the reason he had any business left in the shop at all.

The last aisle along the eastern side of the store contained a conglomerate of goods. Warren kept a small sewing supply, which included cross-stitching patterns and extra thread, needlepoint, and children's looms. Next to the sewing corner rested a few radio-controlled cars and boats, all top-of-the-line and difficult to find in department stores. Along the wall, Warren kept tools for woodworking, with several books ranging from how-to woodwork to specific designs. The last section of this aisle Warren had dedicated to miscellaneous, often seasonal items, such as create-your-own advent calendars at Christmas, create-your-own Halloween decorations, clay modeling, or other simple crafts that pleased families.

All along the perimeter of the store, Warren's expert hand had installed a large shelf that supported a small electric train community. He had three engines running on three separate tracks, all of which crisscrossed or moved under, through, or above each other in an intricate system of bridges, crossovers, and tunnels. Only two of the engines had whistles, and were programmed to whistle every three minutes. Warren had arranged the track, meticulously timing the distance, so that the trains whistled as they came out of tunnels, crossed over the gray-painted roads, or went over another track. The area contained a small town with multicolored old west façades on the buildings and a small train depot where the non-whistling red engine began. In the town, which rested above the glass window at the front of the shop, miniature figurines of cowboys and women carrying parasols and dressed in petticoats strolled about down the dirt road. On the opposite wall, in the dark corner at the back, Warren had built a modern city, modeling the skyscrapers of Denver. Warren handcrafted the buildings out of wood and molded plastic. The stonework on Union Station, with its red writing across the front, mimicked the reality with easy expertise. Along each of the sidewalls, Warren had included the geography of his state with clay models of the Rocky Mountains, thin strips of wheat fields made from shredded brown paper bags, and the Colorado and Arkansas Rivers made from a shiny hardened plastic. The trains hummed intermittently during business hours. Often, their methodic whistles were the only noises Warren heard throughout the day.

As the rain loomed over the city, Warren sifted through an old copy of Emerson poetry behind the counter of his shop. He looked at the clock: three-thirty. Though the sign claimed that he would be open until six, he hadn't seen a customer in nearly four hours. He thought he might just as well stay in the store and read, because what did he have to do at home but the same thing? But Warren had earned a curious heart in his months of spying, and he decided to take a break from his work, which hadn't pulled in much revenue for several years.

Warren flipped the sign that dangled in the glass front door from Open to Closed, then turned the deadbolt with his key. He looked out at the street for a moment, recalling when he opened the store thirty years ago, where it sat in the middle of TV repair shops, launderettes, and family-owned restaurants and meat shops and grocers. He used to know most of the other store owners, but as the years passed, they sold their outfits one by one to Dollar General or EZ Pawn or other money-gripping corporations that put bars on the windows and became symbols of a desire-to-be-bad neighborhood. Now, he was one of the few remaining owners from the seventies, and he couldn't compete with the low prices of the Wal-Mart with its huge parking lot in the suburbs. The street he'd bought the shop on, once the center route in and out of the city, now seemed to be congested with the foot traffic of homeless men or wanton women, and certainly not the easygoing route of the collector or eight-year-old explorer looking for a new hobby.

Warren sighed as he walked to the back of the store. He opened the back door and turned around in the alleyway to lock it. He felt colder now that the clouds disguised the brightness of the sun, and he shivered as he pulled his jacket out of the backseat of his Taurus. He turned on a classical radio station he liked to listen to in the afternoon as he drove the three miles home. The station played Debussy's "Claire de Lune", one of Warren's favorite pieces, as he turned into his neighborhood. Just when the orchestra reached its crescendo, Warren glimpsed a white police cruiser parked in front of their house. The flashers weren't on, and no officers sat in the car.

Without knowing why, Warren's entire body began to convulse. He felt a burning sensation move from the hair follicles on his head through the tips of his fingers and toes. His hands shook and his mouth drained itself of moisture as his heart rate doubled. A feeling of horror and dread came over him, as if the police were at his own doorstep, bearing the news that only policemen can bring. In one brief second, Warren tried to imagine what a police officer could say to him that would even make him shed a tear or hold his head in his hands in pain or anguish. Warren could think of nothing in his life, not any of his family members dying or his shop being burned to the ground or his bank account emptied by armed robbers, that would even cause him to flinch. But thinking, even beginning to imagine, something sad or dangerous happening to the petite brown mother, the tall blond father, or the gurgling baby boy, overtook everything inside Warren's soul. He couldn't move.

He didn't know how long he sat there in the middle of the street before a car behind him honked. Suddenly aware of the surroundings outside of that terrifying vision of the police car, Warren pressed his foot on the gas pedal and sped around the corner to his driveway. He yanked his key out of the ignition before even putting the car in first gear or pulling up the emergency parking brake, then slammed the driver's side door and dashed inside. He stood a few feet behind the blinds and looked across.

It was the baby's naptime. Warren had deduced months ago that the only time the mother closed the blinds was when she put him to sleep, either for nap or bedtime. She loved light to splash inside the large room, and loved to hold the baby in the window to look out and catch sight of their big backyard, his daily taste of the outside world.

Now, with the blinds closed, Warren didn't know how he could stand to wait. He wanted to open the window and yell across, "Is everything OK?" He wanted to run downstairs and through the back door and climb over the fence and bang on their glass patio doors, just to be sure someone would come and answer.

Warren felt inside of him something he hadn't felt in years: desire. More than anything, he wanted to know that they were OK, because he didn't have any purpose in his life anymore but their blissful presence. He wanted their happiness in the way that he had once desired his own, in his younger years when he still carried hopes and dreams like a child who carries his teddy to bed each night, never letting go of their security.

He had no choice. He sat stiff-necked in the rocking chair and stared across. He clasped and unclasped his fingers, ran his hands up and down his legs, through his thin strands of hair, and up and down the back of his neck. He bit every fingernail down until there was no white, and began chewing off his cuticles. He ground his teeth and munched on his tongue. He hummed "Claire de Lune" seven times. He looked at his watch and looked at his watch and looked at his watch. The sun started to set behind the darkening clouds. The thunderbolts screamed at each other across the sky and finally let loose their rain.

The blinds opened, but all Warren saw was an older blond woman crying as she swayed the baby back and forth in her arms.

Chapter 7

For months, a dream recurred in Luisa's mind like the rhythmical cycle of life that she now held in her arms each morning. In the dream, she flew like the eagles she so admired, her wings catching great gusts of wind as she flapped, then soared, then flapped again. She flew over all the places she knew—her adolescent home, the fields behind her childhood house outside the city, the art museum downtown where she used to work, and the home she now shared with Carter and Alejo. When she saw the house that she and Carter had saved for years to buy, she swooped down to perch on the windowsill. But every time the dream entered Luisa's subconscious, it ended the same way: with her eagle eyes looking into Alejo's room, which was dark and empty, the walls painted a blanching white. Luisa would try to fly away from the window, but would find her talons dug into the wood of the sill, caught. Terrified, she would flap her wings in the struggle of a caged bird, exhausting herself and getting nowhere.

When Luisa awoke from these dreams, often in the middle of the night, she would instantly grasp Carter's shoulder in the bed beside her. Carter, who always slept as soundly as a worn-out puppy, would barely flinch at her movements, and never take note of her desperate whispers of, "Oh, thank God." She would then hurry up the stairs and peek in on Alejo in his immobile slumber, and thank the bittersweet gift of the nightmare that wasn't real.

Luisa hadn't had the dream for several weeks, and Alejo had been sleeping soundly through the night for months. She began to think about the dream and wonder what it meant on her drive home from her father's house. The documents, each marked with his sloppy black signature, were placed in the folder in the passenger's seat. Alejo sucked on his pacifier and began to fall asleep in his car seat. Luisa felt a weight lifted as she drove further and further from her father's house; she felt the stinging headache begin to drain out of her like water released from a dam. Gushing and relieved that the dreaded task was finally over, she picked up her cell phone and dialed Carter's. The phone rang and rang until his voice mail picked up. She wondered if he was still in his meeting or had for some other reason turned off his phone. He nearly always answered his phone. Luisa pretended not to worry as she pulled into her neighborhood.

She looked at the sky as she undid Alejo's seat belt. Finally, some rain, she thought, tired of hearing about the drought and the water plight. She tried to conceal her grin as Alejo's eyes popped open; she remembered when he was first born, and would sleep even if she swung him from side to side, even if she tickled his back or clipped his fingernails or pinched his toes. Now, he woke up at the slightest movement or noise or light in his eyes.

"You're too much like me," Luisa cooed, "You should sleep more like your Daddy." She grabbed his diaper bag and carried him inside and up to his room. "Your diaper OK? I think so. Ready to go to sleep?" She laid him down in his crib and pulled the string to close the blinds and shut the door as she left the room.

She was fixing her midmorning coffee and toast when the doorbell rang. Can't they read? She thought, remembering the No Soliciting sign that Carter had searched in three stores to find when one afternoon he came home to a very grumpy wife whose nap, and the nap of her baby, had been interrupted by a realtor giving away catalogues and causing the neighbor's dog to wake them. She placed the steaming coffee on the countertop and paced across the room. Glancing up at Alejo's closed door, she slowly opened the front door.

For years afterwards, Luisa would replay in her mind the casual walk across the living room, the disgruntled feeling of answering to a door-to-door salesman, the calm, unwavering motion she made as she opened the door. She would try to picture in her mind that, perhaps if she had rushed to the door anticipating whomever stood on the step, someone different would have been standing there and her life wouldn't change from happiness to despair in the instant she caught view of their navy blue uniforms, hats in hands at their chests.

"We're sorry to bother you, Ma'am. Are you Mrs. Luisa DaSilva?" The taller of the two, whose badge read Hanson, slipped her name out in a shaky, hesitant tone, but managed, under penalty of falling over, to keep his blue eyes locked with hers as he said it.

Luisa had no time to even think of thinking. "What is it?" she said in a harsh whisper, the only words she would be able to say without weeping for hours and hours.

"Mrs. DaSilva? May we come in?"

Just before Alejo was born, Luisa imagined morbid things that she had never before experienced. Terrified of what might happen to her, her baby, or Carter, she would often lie in bed on sleepless nights imagining all the possibilities. What would she do if she forgot Alejo in the car when she went grocery shopping? How would she pay the bills if Carter lost his job? Worse, if he died? What if Alejo got some sort of disease?

Becoming a mother, though it filled her with a joy that was like living on chocolate but never getting fat, also plagued her with a world of, "What ifs." Unable to bury them from the skim of the thoughts that stirred in her head, Luisa always tried to match an unhappy thought of disaster with a happy thought of relief. At least, she told herself, she had a happy, healthy family to worry over.

She held the door open. The two police officers stepped in, but stood in the entryway spinning their hats in their hands like two little boys who were holding their pee. Luisa's heart was not where she left it—it was in her throat, her eardrums, her clenching-unclenching fists. She closed her eyelids to shut out the view of them and bit her tongue. No words in any language entered her mind.

"Mrs. DaSilva, you might want to sit down." Again, Hanson spoke, and spread apart his fingers in an attempt to make the couch look comfortable to her. Luisa stood still, her jaw tightening. The two officers also did not move, but waited with the patience of a spider examining its trapped prey in the web.

"Let me introduce myself. I'm Officer Hanson, and this is my partner, Officer O'Donnell. I'm afraid there's been an accident," Hanson began in a steady voice. He tried again to catch her eye, but her face was already buried in her hands. Forcefully and quickly, he finished his story. "Your husband, Carter DaSilva, was driving east through an intersection on Colfax when a blue Chevrolet Silverado ran a red light and crashed into the driver's side of your husband's truck. A bystander called 911 and paramedics arrived at the scene, but—" here, Hanson had to stop to breathe, the words filling his mouth like the fluoride dentists made their patients bite into. "But your husband was unable to be resuscitated."

Again, he paused. "I'm sorry to bring this news to you, Mrs. DaSilva. Is there someone you would like me to call to come over?"

The beige carpet called to her; Luisa felt her body drawn to its blandness as she slumped to the floor. In a flurry, bits and pieces of his story formed dark tunnels in her mind: an accident, resuscitated, called 911, blue Chevrolet Silverado, driver's side, husband, husband, husband. The words intermingled with images that Luisa could not suppress. Her ears rang and her mouth filled with the taste of salt; her tears were too many to control or clean from her face or her wet hands.

"My mother," she whimpered, "My mother, Reeve Lucero."

In the efficient way policemen knew, they had her number dialed before Luisa could draw it from her memory. Officer Hanson knelt on the floor beside her and tried to maintain a compassionate voice. "Mrs. DaSilva, your mother is on her way over. We're going to have to leave now. Will you be all right until she gets here?" Luisa, in the midst of her consuming grief, could only think what a stupid question that was. Still, she disliked the company of strangers, and managed to nod her head. She buried her face into her palms once again as she listened for the familiar creak of the front door and the snap of the outer security door as it shut.

Somewhere in the back of her mind, she knew that her mother lived twenty minutes away, and that was the amount of time she had to wait. But time engulfed her like a tidal wave, swallowing her air and suffocating her vision. The grief stamped on her heart and wrenched her body into convulsions that were beyond her control; everything seemed beyond her control. She thought only of sadness so that tears covered the room, tears of longing and regret, as she thought, Carter is the one who always makes me feel better when I'm sad, a thought that brought another wave of anger and despair. She tried to push the images of his bent truck, his ruined body, his fear as he saw what was to become of his life, to a place in the depths of her imagination, but these images danced in front of her like a marionette in a fantastical display of colors, mocking her survival.

Luisa began to count. How many seconds could it be? She asked herself, and envisioned her wings lifting, one, two, three, four, five times, flying higher, higher, six, seven… She concentrated on her white feathers spreading out as she looked at the world below, counting silently and then in a whisper, a frail voice, and finally, a scream.

Reeve entered the house in a frenzied rush to witness her daughter in a state of insanity. Speech hid inside her throat like a hunting cat that waited to pounce. All she could do was wrap her arms around the sobbing lump on the floor and let her own tears of regret drip down her face.

In the hours that followed, Luisa could only remember her mother's tearstained cheeks as she brought Alejo to Luisa's breast. Looking down into the hazel eyes of her son as he nursed, his innocence, both in life and to the tragedy, pervaded her thoughts. "Te quiero, Mi Hijo," Luisa murmured again and again. And, as if he sensed her sudden, uncontrollable fear, he began to squirm and fuss. Soon his face, too, gathered the pitiful moisture of her tears.

It wasn't until her best friend Clara arrived that Luisa recalled the detail that her mind allowed her to keep locked away until that moment: Carter didn't have life insurance. She would have to sell the house.

This new tidal wave of gloom allowed her to rush to the bathroom, where Luisa emptied her stomach in the porcelain bowl and trapped the outside world on the other side of the locked door. With her clammy hands pressed against the cold tile floor, she bent her head and prayed for the first time since she was twelve years old.

Chapter 8

After giving birth to three sons in four years, Warren's mother, Doris, was ready for a little girl. Doris had married Frank, her childhood sweetheart, three days after he returned home from the war. After two years of sending and receiving letters marked, "SWAK," they were finally able to seal their wedding vows with a kiss. Frank found a job at a textile mill in the industrial part of the city, and he made good money. They didn't consider whether they would have children; they didn't even consider when. Doris and Frank conceived quickly and easily, and Doris had easy deliveries. Frank Jr., Kenny, and Freddy filled their lives with a vivacious energy that almost made Frank forget the fighting in the South Pacific, and almost made Doris forget the long hours she stood at the weapons factory assembly line during the war. Almost.

Though not happy, Doris was also not sad; her mood shifted between the two like a long seaweed plant rolling side to side with the passing waves, unable to stay in one place. Doris often spent her mornings sweeping and mopping the kitchen floor, her shiny blond hair pulled into a long braid that fell down her back. On her knees, her large breasts sagged almost to the floor as she swept the daily dirt into the dustpan. Her freckled arms were nearly as thick as her ankles, and her great curvy hips swayed as she moved the mop in neat rows. Her long, oval face concentrated, her small chin almost hidden under the shadow of her high cheekbones. Her round green eyes squinted at every speck of dirt, and her strong, solid fingers clutched the mop with expertise. Her angular nose was a stark contrast to the thin red lips that remained closed most of the time to hide the world from two rows of crooked, yellow teeth.

Doris cleaned because it was what she knew, and she feared most in life that which she didn't know. So when she conceived again, to try to gain more control of the unknown, Doris began making daily trips to the Church (on her way home from the market) with her rosary. The large Catholic cathedral had been an integral part of Doris's life since her birth; here, in the hollow depths of the cavernous gothic-styled stonework of the Church that had been built barely a hundred years before, Doris and her three children had been baptized. The tile floor rang under her feet each morning, echoing the taps of her pumps, and the darkly stained wooden pews were always cold as she knelt in prayer.

"Please, please let this one be Grace or Jane," Doris would whisper, her eyes glistening in view of the large crucifix and at the candle she lit each morning. The baby, Freddy, would be sleeping in his carriage, and Frankie and Kenny would be squirming on the pew behind her.

"What are you praying for, Mama?" Frankie asked each day.

"My prayers are for me and God," Doris said, and they left the Church with their canvas sacks of food for that evening's meal.

Frank started coming home late. Sometimes he called and told Doris that there were extra shifts opening up, and they needed the money for the new arrival. Other times he wouldn't call, and Doris forced her two older boys to sit at the antique cherry table while the food stayed warm in the oven and they waited for Daddy. After an hour or more of little-boy torment, Doris fed them, and, starving herself, sat waiting for her husband's slow stumble up the carpeted steps of the apartment building, his loose jangle of keys, and the slumped shoulders of a drunken man stumbling through the creaking door. He came in slowly, as if afraid to enter, his red hair plastered in chunks around his head from wearing a hat for hours. His wide, sallow face cast shadows over his thin frame, and his brown eyes, bloodshot from secondhand smoke, bore dark circles of a man who hadn't slept. His pug nose scrunched up whenever he entered the apartment, and his thick pink lips opened to a gaping blackness inside of him, always as if prepared to say something, but words never came from the opening. He kept his small hands at the sides of his slender hips, and took his work boots off his long, narrow feet with the greatest caution. When he looked about the living room, the tight muscles in his skinny legs and arms twitched with anxiousness, and his heart palpitated underneath his bony chest with the fear of a man who knows he's done wrong.

Doris began to light two candles each morning: one for her daughter and one for the evil spirit that had crept into her husband through the gore and fear of war. She found herself calling her sister, childless and single, and asking her to come over to take the boys to the park or the zoo or anywhere away from her, two or three times a week. Sally, a perky know-it-all, would say as she left each day, "You know you can divorce him." And Doris would lock herself in the pink bathroom with the matching pink rug and towels and washcloths and cry, because she just couldn't.

When she was eight months pregnant, her heart filled with hope and she anticipated the daughter she had dreamed of. She bought pink sheets and made a lace skirt for the bassinet that sat next to their bed, and begged Frank to come home a bit earlier, in case, at the very least, she went in to labor. He listened and did for the following month, and Doris felt a relief that was genuine and lasting. She began a quilt for her daughter, and made Frank's favorite, chocolate cake, for dessert every night, and the days passed painlessly until she delivered.

Frank stood outside the delivery room pacing in the bleached whiteness of the hospital corridor waiting for the news of his daughter. Doris wanted to name her Rose Beatrice, after her two grandmothers. Frank, who had chosen only the name of his firstborn, just wanted his wife to be happy; when Doris was sad, her sadness flooded the air in the room so that the temperature dropped and any blanket of happiness or calm was washed away with the frostiness. This, and the images he couldn't conceal in his mind of the many battles he witnessed and escaped, made him wish to stay away from the two-bedroom apartment to work and drink and drink and work until he could afford a real house, one where their dreams would finally be realized.

When the doctor swung open the beige door of the delivery room and asked him to come see his new son, Frank's arms shivered with goose bumps as he marched into the room. Hot, angry tears had ransacked Doris's face as she sobbed and crossed her arms. Her hospital gown looked like a half-deflated white balloon around her shrunken body. Her hair lay in flat, limp strings around her oval face, and the freckles on her sharp nose and high cheeks appeared blurred by the tears. Her green irises shared their tears with red lines of stress, and her thin lips were puckered in a damp, pale pink frown.

"Where is the baby?" Frank asked, but the nurse was already taking him out of the room. The doctor pulled up a chair and asked Frank to sit down.

"The baby has pneumonia. We're going to keep him in the nursery and monitor him. He's very small and his lungs are a bit underdeveloped. We have to give him oxygen."

For a moment, Frank had a demented thought: Maybe Doris is crying because the baby is sick. But he knew better. He knew that the frigid sadness that encircled the room would not release itself into the warmth of happiness he had so longed for.

Doris squeezed his palm and spit out the words, "I'm done having children." And this was Warren's welcome into the world.

A number of weeks passed before Warren could come home. His pneumonia worsened after the first few days, and he became so frail that the doctors thought he might not survive. He stayed inside a warmer constantly, and Frank left work each night and went straight to the hospital. Doris had returned home after just a few days, and claimed, when he asked why she didn't go to the hospital, that she was scared she might make the baby worse, or that she had three other, healthy boys to care for, or that the nurses knew what they were doing, or any other reason she could think of to keep Frank at bay. Frank felt discouraged by her lack of interest in the child, but hoped that, once the boy came home, he would be welcomed into one of the remaining places of warmth left in Doris's heart.

Frankie Jr., now five, began asking about the baby. "When is he coming home? What's his name? How sick is he?" Every day a question, and every day Doris said the answer, "I don't know," until, after three weeks, Frankie stopped her in the middle of pounding on chicken breasts for that night's dinner and stunned her.

"Why don't you light a candle in Church for the baby?"

Doris gripped the meat tenderizer in her right palm and stared down at her son. "That's between me and God," she told him, a phrase she learned to play on her tongue quite often for the many dark days to come.

At last, all three boys, Doris, and Frank were able to make the final trip to the hospital to pick up their son, still without a name. Doris sat in the hospital waiting room with the boys as Frank went upstairs to the nursery.

"We'll need a name to sign him out," Frank told her as she settled the boys into the stiff-backed black leather chairs.

"Well, pick one," she said, her breath seeping out the words. Frank stood at the elevator and gazed at his family. Freddy was toddling around at Doris's knees while the other two squirmed in their seats. Doris sat straight up and looked absentmindedly forward, almost as if the boys didn't surround her. What Frank didn't know was that Doris was trying to act nonchalant, when really all she wanted to do was leave the boy here and never come back, that she had been dreading this day since the doctor first told her she had a son, and that suicide crossed her mind almost hourly now. She felt empty at the presence of this child in the world that she couldn't explain; she cursed God and Frank and her three other boys for not allowing her to have a girl.

The elevator doors opened, and Frank sighed as he went upstairs. He decided, since she was going to name her daughter after her grandmothers, that he would name his son after his grandfathers: Warren, from his father's side, and Gregory, from his mother's.

When he entered the glass-walled nursery, a stout blond nurse held the baby. He was wrapped in a blue blanket and wore a tiny white hat on his head. The blanket and the hat allowed a small triangular space for his pink face; his eyes were closed and his lips looked puckered.

"Good morning, Mr. York," the nurse said. "Are you happy to take your son home?"

"Yes, I think Warren Gregory will be very happy. Doris and I are going to finally be able to buy a house this summer," Frank tried to conceal his fear.

"Oh, you've picked a name? Warren Gregory. That's a good, strong name. This little guy is going to need it." The nurse, whose name was Belinda, had no idea how true those words would be.

"It's after my two grandfathers," Frank explained. He reached for his son and clutched him in the safety of his strong arms. Warren stirred and his eyes flashed open and closed.

"Are Doris and the boys downstairs?" Belinda asked. Frank's eyes darkened as he nodded.

He signed all the necessary paperwork and carried his son like a football under his arm. Even now, nearly a month after birth, Warren weighed only seven pounds. When the elevator doors opened and he entered the corridor, Frankie ran out of the waiting room.

"Is that my baby brother?" he shouted, unable to control his excitement.

"This is Warren Gregory," Frank boasted, but his pride was stopped short by Doris's stance.

"Let's go, then," she said, snatching the baby as if he were an unwanted package.

Doris sat with the baby on her lap while Frank drove the station wagon home. She stared down at her son and tried to imagine loving him, but it took everything out of her just to keep from crying. She prayed to God that the child's sickness would return and God could take him away to Heaven, because she didn't think he would have much of a life without his own mother's love. She grasped him in her arms, squeezed him against her chest so that Frank had the false pretense that she was hugging him, which made Frank feel an overwhelming sense of relief as he pulled into the apartment parking area.

What Frank didn't see was that, as Doris held the baby against her, she dug her fingernails into the bottoms of his tiny feet. Warren bore the first scar of her hate before he even arrived home from the hospital. Surrounded by a circle of love from his father and brothers, Warren would learn that he could not break through the sharp edges of the box of sorrow his mother shared with him.

Chapter 9

Clara's personality defined practicality. Her pragmatic nature first drew Luisa to her in seventh grade, when she observed the thin, straight haired, five-foot Clara setting aside half her lunch money each day to save up for a new stereo. Luisa began talking to Clara about what kind of music she liked, and when they discovered they had the same taste in music, this topic soon led on to other commonalities, and they became lifelong friends.

It was Clara's down-to-earth expediency that led Carter into Luisa's life. Clara, who defied the social norm whenever possible, wore black contacts over her green eyes for years, had her first tattoo put on the back of her skinny neck on her eighteenth birthday, regularly painted her long fingernails on her tiny fingers an atrocious neon green, married a man seven years her senior when she was just nineteen, and bought a house with him by the time her twentieth birthday arrived. Her husband, Marcus, a financial planner from Detroit, made immediate plans to remodel, explaining to Clara that they'd purchased the run-down house in the posh Park Hill neighborhood for location only, but that it needed work. Marcus had grandiose plans for a pop-up or other expansion that would put the couple into debt for half a century, but Clara reasoned with her husband and talked him into a simple refinish of the basement, which would add six hundred square feet of living space, and new floors and windows on the main level of their three-bedroom ranch. Admiring her for her sensible nature, Marcus let Clara make all the plans.

Since this was their dream home, Clara wanted everything done professionally, but only if the price was right. She called around to local architects and contractors, soon realizing that many of them had self-imposed conspiracies to work only with certain others of their counterparts. After several estimates and hours of research, she finally settled on an architect named Gillian Bright and a contractor named Carter DaSilva.

The tall, broad-shouldered, blue-eyed blond had a quiet, sensitive nature that reminded Clara of Luisa. And Clara, always thinking ahead, made sure to insist that there was a problem in the design, so she called up Carter to come for an emergency meeting at the same time Luisa would be over for afternoon tea (tea was something the two friends had shared once a week for eight years). Clara knew Carter would come, because he had just moved to Denver and was beginning his own business, and he needed hers (she knew enough about the importance of references from her two years of studying economics and management, with a focus in entrepreneurship, at college).

Clara had set up Luisa, who had infamously bad relationships, before, but Luisa had never been interested. Always she found something inherently wrong with the man, either his personality or his compatibility with her. "What were you thinking?" she would say to Clara, "that guy cared more about money than anything else," or, "He just wanted to show off, everything from dancing to drinking, the whole night," and Clara would groan and remind her of one of her recent loser boyfriends who would forget her birthday or disappear for three weeks without calling.

So, when she met Carter, Clara discreetly discovered he didn't have a girlfriend (by saying, "I bet your girlfriend's so happy that you can remodel her house," to which he said, "She would be, if I had one,"), and decided not to tell either Luisa or Carter about her matchmaking scheme.

It was early spring, the end of the semester for the state college they both attended, and, as Clara boiled the water for Luisa's Earl Grey and her own orange zinger, Luisa sat at the hand-me-down maple dining table in Clara's dining room and complained about finals.

"Do they really expect us to memorize the entire textbook? I don't know how I can even pass this semester. How will I ever become an art historian?" she groaned.

Clara said, "Oh, stop it. You know you're going to ace them all, as always." She glanced out one of her new windows. The sun glared at her through the budding branches of the gray-trunked maple in her front yard. Luisa's Corolla was parked on the street in front of her brick ranch, but no other cars, or people, stirred about, though it was an unusual seventy degrees outside.

"Why do you keep looking outside?" Luisa questioned, always with an eye out for abnormal behavior (she knew what an indoors person Clara was).

"Oh, it's such a nice day. Maybe we could go for a walk with Buca after our tea." Buca was Clara's Saint Bernard, a dog who spent most of her days lazily plodding around the house from one resting spot to another.

"Buca, take an unnecessary walk? What are you looking for, Clara?"

At that moment, Carter's truck pulled up in front of the house and Clara's heart skipped a beat.

"Oh, nothing. The water's ready. Did you try these cookies?" her face was flushed as she rushed into the kitchen to pour the tea. Putting a teabag in each cup, measuring out two spoonfuls of sugar for each of them, and pouring a dab of half and half in Luisa's, Clara couldn't understand why it took so long for Carter to move from his car to her front door. Then she heard Buca's ceremonious singular, "WOOF!" as the doorbell rang.

"I wonder who that is?" Clara mocked innocence.

"Just what are you up to?" Luisa shot her a suspicious stare.

When Clara opened the door, Carter stood on the step, unable to move, at the sight of Luisa. She sat upright in the antique dining chair with her dark brown hair pulled back into a low ponytail. A few loose curls tickled her chin, and her pale brown cheeks blushed beneath her almond eyes as she looked back. She had no makeup, but her eyebrows were plucked and shaped into perfect semicircles, and her oval face bore flawless skin. She wore a tight white t-shirt and equally formfitting blue jeans, and had her tiny legs crossed with her manicured hands resting on her thighs.

Carter was in love before he even walked through the door.

Clara banged on the door to the bathroom. She felt both desperate and responsible, fear and discouragement, the longer she stood waiting for Luisa to emerge from her four-by-four room of grief.

"Don't do this alone," she called through the door. "Let us help you get through this." She saw her words float into the air and dissipate like early morning mist being touched by the warmth of the rising sun.

Reeve was in the kitchen making the dreaded phone calls that come as a requisite to all deaths in a family. Reporting the news to Carter's parents and siblings required a stillness of voice that Reeve could only maintain after two glasses of wine. His parents had been planning a trip to visit from their small town outside of Kansas City for Alejo's first birthday, not three weeks away. Now, with the wails of grief from Carter's mother intermingled with questions that all began with, "Why?" or "How?" Reeve wondered how she could continue to make these calls. After clicking the receiver into its place, she poured another glass of wine, her bitterness streaming down her face at the very thought that she would need that substance. She sat with her shoulders slumped at the kitchen table and rolled a napkin in her hands, unrolled it, and rolled it again in a methodic way that maintained her stature for twenty minutes or more.

Clara returned to the room, her pleas unanswered. She stared down at Reeve, who seemed to be taking this as hard as Luisa. "Do you want me to make some calls?" she whispered, her pragmatism the only line drawn between her current sadness and the happiness she felt this morning.

As if coming out of a deep sleep, Reeve lifted her gray eyes, streaked with black splotches of eyeliner and mascara, and looked at Clara as if she had never seen her before. Unaware of the question Clara had asked her, Reeve's expression spoke of a distant place in her mind, a darkness unreachable by others.

"Is this my fault?" her raspy voice let loose the remark like a tiny child reluctantly letting loose his mother's legs.

"No, of course not. How could you even think such a thing?" Clara responded, but was shocked to see that Reeve reacted with another harsh multitude of sobs.

"You're right, Daddy, how could I even think such a thing?"

Clara, perplexed, couldn't answer. Instead, she pulled the address book off the table and carried it with the cordless phone over to the living room couch. She began sifting through names and dialing numbers as the two women moaned in their respective areas of despondency. She didn't know what else to do, or what she would do once she finished the calls. Clara called every name in the book as Alejo crawled around at her feet, unaware, as all children should be.

Later that night, when Marcus entered the depths of the house from his job, Clara walked him upstairs to the baby's room and whispered, "What should I do? Luisa won't come out of the bathroom and her mother seems to have lost her mind. She called me, 'Daddy' earlier. How am I supposed to help Luisa with anything if I can't even get her to open the door?"

Marcus stood in front of her rubbing his stubby fingers over the dark brown goatee on his chin. He cleared his throat and shook his head, the straight brown hairs standing still under the fluorescent light. His brown eyes darted between the sharp features of Clara's face, unable to focus on this moment.

"I don't know what to tell you, Baby. I can't imagine being in this position." Marcus reached for her and pulled her tiny body against his six-foot frame. He stroked the hair that cascaded down her back and held her as she let her own river of tears flow.

"Why don't I go get us all some dinner? Maybe Luisa and her mom will perk up a bit after they have something in their stomachs." Marcus quietly opened and closed the door to Alejo's room. Clara listened as he plodded down the stairs, opened the front door, and let the security door slam behind him. She listened still after she knew he had driven away. All she could hear were Alejo's occasional squeals and the methodical ticking of the grandfather clock that Carter had bought Luisa last Christmas. She hoped that Reeve and Luisa were asleep, because she didn't know how to face either of them another time that day.

Luisa felt a shiver rummage through her body like a homeless man searching for food: relentless and forlorn, it took over so that, even in the fetal position on top of the heat vent, she still froze. Fear consumed her. She didn't want to open the door, for fear that Carter's death was real, and if it was real, she didn't want to face Alejo, and if she had to face Alejo, she didn't want him to see her like this, and if he had to see her like this, she didn't want to have to go into the kitchen and pour some wine, and if she poured some wine, she didn't want to finish the bottle, and if she finished the bottle, she didn't want to get out another… She ran the possibilities in her mind's eye again and again, rocking back and forth and convulsing.

Whenever Luisa felt sad or frustrated in her life, whether it was her car not starting or her boyfriend breaking up with her, she had a habit of playing in her mind everything that was wrong with her life: her parents' broken marriage, her father's alcoholism, her few friends, Byron's drug problem, her stress at school or work… Like a baker placing clumpy bits of cookie dough on their sheet, Luisa would lay her problems out in front of her, unable to concentrate on anything but the gooey clusters of unbaked cookies.

But never in her life had Luisa experienced a sting of this magnitude. Now, she didn't simply replay the horrors of her past or present life, but turned her fears face forward into the future. She hadn't worked in a year, had only a few thousand dollars saved, a child to support, a mortgage to pay, and nothing but the vast emptiness of Carter's absence, the sweet-loving presence of him gone forever, to help her move from one moment, hour, day, to the next.

"He was my one perfect thing," Luisa moaned into the shivering depths of the cave she had created against her chest. "He was my one perfect thing," again and again, in a desperate mantra, Luisa repeated the words.

What she didn't want to say aloud, or even allow herself to think, and the reason she couldn't bear to open the door, shot through her like lightning, the electric shock burning her capillaries. Like the voice of a ghost, the lurid thought slithered across her mind: You put all your hopes and dreams into his place in your life, and now he's gone.

Clara banged on the door again. "Luisa, please, Marcus brought us some Chinese food. Please come and eat and let me help you."

With the last of her strength, Luisa pulled herself up against the handle of the door and unlocked it. She tumbled onto the floor in front of her friend.

"Everything, everything is gone," she whispered.

"No it's not," Clara said, "You're still here. Let's start with that." She held out her hand and waited for Luisa to grab it.

Chapter 10

The Texan who brought Aurelio to his first taste of freedom was named Seth O'Reilly. He had been traveling into Mexico for years, at the risk of being fined or imprisoned by the INS, to gain the invaluably cheap labor. Seth, a grandson of Irish immigrants who had given up the bitterness of the natives in New York and had moved west, admired the work ethic of the Mexicans. Though his success in life contrasted the direness of the men he picked up, he admired men who bore strong muscles that could match up to his own. Seth, at five foot eleven, had the body of a tri-athlete. Working the ranch involved using every muscle from his hamstrings to his biceps. His straight bleach-blond hair was kept short and hidden most of the time beneath his leather hat. He wore jeans and a long-sleeved button-down thin cotton plaid shirt over his pale white skin every day of the week except Sunday, the only day he took for his own rest. His cadet blue eyes spent most of their time squinting in the brightness of the hot Texas sun, and his hat shaded his soft round nose and perfectly shaped reddish lips. He kept a thin moustache, but shaved the rest of his skin each morning before the sun rose, his heart-shaped face reflecting the handsomeness of a dignified man. His whole body, from the calloused fingertips of his hands to the long, wide feet he squeezed into his boots each morning, lived for his family ranch.

At nearly a thousand acres, Seth's ranch expanded over the flat lands of southwestern Texas, sucking up the water from every nearby creek and irrigation canal and sprawling out field after field of corn. Seth had three barns that housed a variety of small goats and seven thoroughbred horses that he'd bought for his horse-loving late wife and kept for his horse-loving daughter. When Aurelio arrived, the ranch held over two thousand heads of cattle that roamed the fenced-off fields in search of sweet grass to please their palates. Seth's house, which was built by his grandfather, was originally a ranch, but had a popped top with two extra bedrooms where Seth's father had planned for all of his sons to sleep. The house sat on the southern edge of the property, half a mile from the main road, the only road that came near the ranch. It had an oversized kitchen at the back, facing east so the morning light could creep in on the cook as she prepared the men's breakfast each morning, and a good-sized dining room with an antique oak set of table and chairs. The sitting room at the front of the house, though small, had thinly armed antique furniture and a woodstove against one wall. Behind the wall of the living room was the tiny master bedroom, where there was barely room for Seth's double bed and a three-drawer dresser. The one bathroom in the house had been added on by Seth's father, and was adjacent to the kitchen at the back of the house. Inside, there stood a claw-footed porcelain tub, a white toilet, a narrow sink with no vanity, and no shower. The house, painted white with a black roof and matching black shutters to decorate the windows, had a white picket fence around its grassy yard and vegetable garden and a narrow stone path leading to the closest red barn. Inside this barn, which housed the horses and most of the goats, there was a hayloft that overlooked the expanse of the ranch, where one could skim his eyes over the cows standing under oak trees along the creek, or row after row of cornstalks, or simply take in the never-ending blue sky along the horizon.

Not even offering the men he drove up minimum wage, Seth tried to make up for it by having clean bunkhouses and hot meals three times a day. His cook, Paula, he happened upon during one of his trips to Mexico. Seth, drawn to the silky French braid that fell down her back and her tall, thin, milk-chocolate-skinned frame, pulled up as she begged for change on a lonely street corner in one of the impoverished desert towns, and used his broken Spanish to ask her if she could cook. After a brief trial of several Mexican and American meals that Paula expertly prepared, Seth built her a small shack of her own on the other side of the ranch, away from the burly men and his own wandering eye.

Paula made the long walk across the ranch each day, stopping to cast her eyes against the flatlands and the roaming cattle, to the large kitchen adjacent to Seth's family home. Inside this kitchen, Seth decided that his coming-of-age daughter, Reeve, could learn the skills of a rancher's wife. Seth had met Reeve's mother, Georgia, on a trip to visit his uncle in Houston twenty years before. Georgia had died of cancer when Reeve was just four, leaving Seth with the sole responsibility of raising his only child. Seth hoped that the gentle hands and heart of Paula would convince his daughter that the rancher's life was the life of freedom in its own rite:

"In what other job," he often said to his daughter as they walked the ranch, "can you move about your own land any time of day or night, and know that tomorrow, this openness will still be yours?"

Reeve cradled her father's words like a mother cradling her child, and everything her Daddy ever asked her to do, she attempted with hope for his approval. So when, at the age of sixteen, Seth asked her to abandon her studies and work full-time alongside Paula, since he had just purchased another three hundred acres of land from his neighbor and would have more men to feed, Reeve had no other answer than, "Yes, of course, Daddy."

Paula and Reeve's workday began before dawn and finished well after dusk. Reeve woke early enough to start the large kettle of coffee before Paula arrived each morning. Still in her nightgown, Reeve would slip back under the warm sheets of the bed in her upstairs bedroom and watch the first light of day touch the golden land of the ranch. She loved the stillness of the morning and relished the brief moment each day when all remained quiet. Then, she would brush the straight blond hair down her back and pull it into a French braid that began at the top of her head. She always washed her round face and tried, every morning, to scrub the freckles away from her high cheekbones. Her gray eyes hid underneath the long blond eyelashes that her father always said didn't need makeup to sparkle. Reeve dressed in blue jeans and a tight t-shirt every day but Sunday, because she had work to do inside and out, and couldn't risk hurting her tiny, delicate legs in the dangerous work of a ranch, even if the temperature rose to 110 degrees, which was common in the summer.

Paula arrived from her shack each morning wearing an apron over her cotton twill pants and linen shirt. Reeve often wondered if Paula owned any other clothes, because she never saw her wear anything but this outfit and a simple cream-colored home sewn dress she wore to church each Sunday. Paula came in each morning just as she left each night: carrying a calm, expectant expression on her face that asked for an easy day and offered a peaceful feeling to those who saw it. From Paula, Reeve learned more than just how to cook, clean, and sew: she learned how to smile when she didn't have the emotion to go with it, how to work without complaint, and how to serve men in a way that was both graceful and proud. Most of all, Reeve learned from Paula about the patience that comes with suffering, a patience Reeve would need in the dark years to come.

Just days before Reeve's eighteenth birthday, Seth made another trip to Mexico. The morning he left, Reeve stood in the kitchen and waved goodbye as his truck rumbled along the dusty road that led to Odessa. She had seen her father make many of these trips during her lifetime. He always returned several days later with a bed full of tall, lean Mexican men who usually spoke little English. These were the men that Paula and Reeve served meals to each day, the ones who knew to curb their rampant desires around the rancher's daughter.

On this morning, Reeve began stirring in forty beaten eggs that Paula had collected from the coop, mixing the eggs in with green bell peppers and chilies. Reeve, adding in salt and cilantro, moved the eggs with a plastic spatula on the giant electric skillet that stood as ground zero for most of the ranchers' meals. Reeve sang as she stirred, playing old country songs in her mind and through the beautiful intonations of her soprano voice so that anyone who was still asleep on the ranch would be wakened by the songs of her homeland.

Paula, meanwhile, prepared the beans she had set out to soak the night before, frying them alongside her apprentice with her own spices. Paula, who had never learned much English, always spoke to Reeve in Spanish, a skill she thought Reeve would need to communicate with the men. In Spanish, she asked her, "What do you want for your birthday?" her demure look disguised how much he anticipated her reply.

Reeve paused, not because she didn't understand (she adored the language so much that she had spent years studying it in school before she dropped out), but because she didn't know how to answer. Her father had never thought much about birthdays, saying, "Every day is special when you live out here," and Reeve had learned, by now, not to expect much from him. In her heart, what Reeve wished for was to fall in love and be carried away from the ranch by a tall, dark, and mysterious man, like Mr. Rochester from Jane Eyre or Heathcliff from Wuthering Heights, or one of the many other strange characters she encountered in the books she read in her bed before going to sleep each night. She loved the ranch, but had a notion that she kept sealed inside her that there was a whole world to discover out there beyond cattle and haystacks, and she often imagined that the only way she would ever discover that world would be through the arms of a stranger.

"Oh, maybe a chocolate cake would be nice," Reeve said, her face tingling with blush.

Paula shook her head and cooed, "I know you want more than that, Chiquita," Reeve wrenched at the name she had used for her since she was a small child. "You're a woman now, and I know what a woman wants." Paula's dark eyes locked with Reeve's and her braid swung from sided to side at her back as her hips rocked. Reeve, flushed with embarrassment, concentrated on the eggs.

"Where would I find it out here," she whispered, in English, hoping that Paula neither understood nor would answer.

"You be surprised," Paula said in English, humiliating Reeve further.

But Reeve didn't know what Paula and Seth had planned for her birthday. She thought that Paula just liked to tease her. She shook her head and kept her thoughts inside, a trick she had learned to master years ago when asking her father about the death of her mother and hearing only the words, "I can't talk about that, sweetie," to which Reeve had learned that silence was sometimes the best solution to a problem.

When Seth returned three days later, in the early afternoon of Reeve's birthday, a young man sat next to him in the cab of his pickup. The man wore a black leather cowboy hat that he removed upon seeing Reeve, who had come from the house to greet her father. He stood a foot taller than her and bowed his orange-haired head slightly, introducing himself as William Gordon. He held out his large, leathery hand as he brushed the sweat off his freckled forehead with the back of his plaid-shirted sleeve. His smile, which revealed itself under a thin red mustache, showed off a perfect set of white teeth, and his accent rang of somewhere north.

"William's here from New York visiting his grandfather, Ted Dawson. He thought, since he earned a bachelor's degree in agricultural engineering, that he might give his grandfather a hand at improving his ranch. And of course," Seth said, slapping his hand against William's back, "I couldn't let my neighbor get the upper hand, so I hired William on here. I thought you might enjoy the company of someone closer to your age, someone of the same kind as you."

Reeve stood in front of the two men in awkward silence. This sudden presentation of a suitor stunned her. What did her father think, that she would fall in love with this guy and marry him so that her father could finally attain the coveted Ted Dawson Ranch? (At nearly five hundred acres, Seth had been talking about it for years). She hated it when her father began saying things like, "same kind," because the gentlest, most loving person she knew was Paula, who had practically raised her like her own child, and was certainly the "same kind" of person. Reeve felt a boiling up of rebellion begin in her stomach. She saw, in the brief moment she stood there, her future life: married to William, living a few miles away from the place she'd grown up, doing the same kind of work day in and day out. She wanted to turn on her heels and run to her secret corner in the loft of the barn, where she often went to be alone and think of things she couldn't think of in front of her father. She wanted to say, "No, thanks, Daddy, I'm not interested in boys," and return to her work with Paula in the kitchen. She wanted to tell William to go back to his grandfather's ranch, that she wasn't interested in him or his bachelor's degree in agricultural engineering. But Reeve knew what she had to say.

"Hello, William, it's nice to meet you." She shook his hand and plastered a polite smile on her face. "I hope you like chocolate cake. Paula made it for dessert tonight."

"Your father tells me it's your birthday," William beamed. "I brought something for you." He returned to the truck, opened the door, and pulled out a small white box. He handed the box to Reeve, his green eyes sparkling like a cat's eyes reflecting the light of the moon. Reeve held the box in her hand and lifted the lid. Inside, on a thin gold chain, rested a small glass pendant with wildflower petals pressed around a painted letter R.

"It's beautiful," Reeve looked up at him. "Thank you." She paused, then closed the lid to the box and said, "I have to fix dinner. How many are eating tonight?" Seth nodded and went to the bed of the truck, pulling back the layers of tarp.

"Land of the free," Reeve cringed at the familiar words her father used in this ritual. "Now let's get to work."

The men climbed out, one by one, their eyes blinded by the sun they hadn't seen in days. They were dusty and dark, wearing everything from once-pressed cotton khakis to rugged blue jeans, some of them carrying nothing at all, some holding on to small packages or bags.

Reeve's expression held the patience of love and understanding. She looked at the men and said in Spanish, "I'll show you the bunkhouses where you can put your things and the well where you can get a drink, but then my father needs you to dig a new foundation for the barn he's going to build on the other side of the ranch."

Reeve had spoken to many groups of workers in her life, and they had all looked relieved the moment Spanish came pouring from her lips, but were often disoriented from dehydration and their new surroundings. Rarely had anyone ever spoken a word back to her. So it took her by surprise when the tall, broad-shouldered man with the wavy black hair touched her shoulder and said, almost in a whisper, "How long must I work here before I can move on to better things?"

Reeve had no answer for the man who carried the brown satchel under his arm like a mother would carry her child. She looked up into the dim pools of brown under the thick eyelashes, her speech caught in her throat like a dog tied to a leash. His words lingered in her mind as she turned her flushed face away and scurried toward the bunkhouse. The men followed her like schoolchildren after a strict teacher. No one spoke. Reeve's mouth filled with air and her mind went blank when she meant to say, "Here is where you can sleep."

How could she say anything at all when the man had put her deepest desire into words without even knowing her name?

Chapter 11

Doris moved with a roughness that made her appear to have a hump in her back. Her movements were sharp and sudden, as if she spent most of her time cutting giant slabs of steak with an oversized butcher knife. Warren learned to listen for her movements, the stomping on the floor above him, the sweep of her nylons as her legs rubbed together in a quick motion, and the methodical slapping of her palm against her thigh, as he sat in the cold corner of the basement on his cot. His heart palpitated with a great echo inside his chest when he heard her footsteps nearing the basement door, and always, a vast wave of relief soothed him when she continued to walk past.

The house Frank had saved for was a three-bedroom ranch on the west side of town. Built just after the war, Frank used the VA loan to purchase his first home. The brick home with the molded ceilings bore striking similarity to all the houses on the block. One developer had chosen this model for the entire neighborhood. The front door opened to a small living room with a bay window that faced the street, and adjacent to the living room was a miniature dining area that could not fit a table large enough for everyone in Frank's family to sit. The kitchen, too, was small, bearing only a three-shelved pantry, four drawers, and six cupboards, with just two narrow Formica countertops for Doris to prepare the food. The three bedrooms were all clustered in a circular row along the opposite side and back of the house, and each bore a single window and just enough room to house a bed and a chest of drawers. A single bathroom stood between the kitchen and the bedrooms, and was modern enough to include a tub with a shower. The unfinished basement held the washer and dryer, a concrete floor, and Warren's entire short life.

When Warren was four, he found the word to describe the feeling inside of him, the feeling that burned his eyes and stung his stomach, the only feeling he could think of to describe his relationship with his mother: hate. He often curled into a fetal position underneath his cot and whispered again and again, "I hate you I hate you I hate you." Like an unanswered prayer, it haunted him. He hoped that if he said the words enough times inside himself, she would hear them and leave the door shut.

Doris, despite resolving to Frank in the hospital delivery room four years earlier, was pregnant with her fifth. Warren didn't know about the pregnancy until just before the baby came. His mother moved in the same robotic way, and her fingernails still scraped his spine daily, her hands still slapped his bottom, and the old leather belt hadn't ceased to put welts into his thighs until just days before her delivery, when Doris found herself too exhausted to make the trek downstairs.

Late at night, Warren had his only taste of love. After Doris and Frank went to bed, Frankie waited until they were sound asleep before sneaking into the kitchen and retrieving cereal, carrots, a glass of milk, or whatever else he could carry in two hands. He learned where all the creaks in the floor were and made the silent journey downstairs each night to bring food to Warren, who was only allowed one meal per day. Warren, in his dream state, had to be shaken awake each night by Frankie, and was often too weak to even sit up. Weighing only twenty-five pounds, Warren gobbled down each of these secrets as if they were his last meal. He knew that they very well could be. Frankie would whisper to him in the dark, telling him to eat quickly, and that he loved him, and God blessed him. Warren, the food stuck against his tongue, never had an answer.

When Doris went to the hospital to have the baby, Warren knew, not because she didn't move above him or come stomping down the stairs, but because the room around him felt suddenly warm. Frankie came downstairs and told him that Daddy would allow him to sleep upstairs as long as Mother was away. Warren shook as he held the handrail and lifted his feet one after another up the stairs. The tears drenched his sallow cheeks as Frankie held the door open into a room with a window that poured sunlight onto the floor. Warren's face twitched as his lips involuntarily spread from side to side. It was the first moment in his life when he felt what it meant to be happy.

Doris, bitter to the last, screamed at the doctor, "Get this thing out of me!" Convinced that she could only have boys, she had already imagined the disappointment she would face when the doctor announced the gender of her baby. When the doctor told her the head was coming, and then pulled out the slimy fetus, Doris looked down at the infant and broke into a grin of shock and relief.

"It's a girl!" the doctor shouted. Doris clutched the baby against her chest when they brought her over, all wrapped in a blanket. She shed her first tears of joy in a great flood of hopeful longing.

"Hello, Rose Beatrice," she cooed into the newborn's eyes. "I've been waiting a long time for you."

When Frank came into the room and saw Doris gently cradling the baby against her chest, he swelled with pride. He wanted nothing more than for the cold-hearted touch of Doris to melt with the warmth she once had when she reached for him, when they fell in love, when they were children. He saw in her eyes now that same innocent love that he had experienced when he first laid eyes on her at the age of thirteen, when she sat on her front lawn reading a book and looked up at him, her green eyes filling with a moist hunger for the hand he held out to her. Now, with her eyes carrying the same loving moisture, his heart engulfed optimism as he walked over to behold his newborn daughter.

Frankie gave Warren the news that Mother had given birth to a girl. Perplexed, Warren asked, "What does that mean?" Frankie wrapped his arms around his brother and said, "Before you were born, when you were inside Mother's tummy, Mother took Kenny, Freddy, and I to Church with her every morning. She lit a candle each day for the prayer that she whispered to God. I asked her what she prayed for, but she wouldn't tell, so one time I crawled next to her when her eyes were closed tight, and I listened. She said again and again, 'Please God, give me a little girl.' Mother wanted a girl, but you were a boy. Do you understand?" But Warren didn't. Too many dark hours of his life were spent in an unexposed basement room, where only occasionally did he see Frankie.

"A boy?" Warren's small voice let the word form in his mouth, filling it with a bitter taste.

"Yes. You, Kenny, Freddy, Daddy, and me are all boys. Mother is a girl. Mother wanted a girl so she could have someone like her. But you weren't like her, so she got really sad, and Daddy came home so late every night, so she got angry, and that's why she didn't want you upstairs, because it reminded her of how she didn't get what she wanted from God." Frankie paused. "But now, she finally has her girl, so when she comes home, she'll be happy, and maybe leave you alone."

Warren didn't know what to think. He looked up into his brother's green eyes and forced a weak smile. "OK," he whispered, then looked down at the floor. He rocked back and forth from one foot to the next. He couldn't think of anything else to say.

Frankie put his arm over Warren's shoulders. "It'll be OK, you'll see," he reassured him. Warren sighed. Those were the only words of hope he'd heard in his lifetime.

When Doris came home two days later with her beautiful Rose, she glowed like a new fallen snow, unmarred by dirty footprints. She went to the linen closet and pulled out the quilt she had made and the lace and the pink sheets for the bassinet, and sang lullabies as she moved through the house. Warren, who had returned to the basement that morning, didn't recognize the movements he heard above him. They were smooth, like the spreading of cream on bread, and soft, like the cotton blanket that kept him warm. He thought that maybe someone took his mother away and replaced her with a new, gentler creature, one who would come down to the basement not with a belt but with a plate of cookies, and hold his hand as she walked him upstairs. Warren began to imagine a tall, blond-haired, beautiful woman singing to him as he fell asleep each night in the bed next to Frankie's. He felt himself break into a smile at the idea of her.

But Doris's sharp movements slapped against the door as she stomped downstairs late that evening. She squinted her eyes, glaring down at Warren, who shivered in a little ball on his cot.

"It's cold tonight. You sleep upstairs with your brothers," she said in a flat voice.

Warren opened his mouth to speak. He wanted to say thank you and hug her legs. Tears streamed down his face as he tiptoed toward her. Without even seeing the hand in the air, Warren felt the familiar sting that began on the cheekbone and crept down into a dull ache along his chin.

"What are you doing, boy?" her mouth spit out the word boy as if she had said scorpion. "Get your ass upstairs before I find the belt."

Warren's stomach churned. His whole body shook as he lifted one foot after another up the stairs like a soldier taking his last march into a deadly battle. Warren ground his teeth and pressed his lips together. He taught himself his first lesson in life: It's better not to talk and not to reach. He closed his arms around his chest and stood next to Frankie's bed. Frankie had to pull his stiff body onto the bed and wrap Warren under the covers. There, in the brief sanctuary of his brother's love, Warren released his first tears of reprieve.

Day after day, as Rose grew into a lovable, giggling baby, Doris's heart softened. She woke each morning with a joy, imagining all the talks she would have with her daughter, the shopping trips, and the tea parties. She began to pray again each night before going to bed, and dragged her boys along with her to the Church each morning, lighting a candle of thanks. Although she didn't plan on the pregnancy, she was glad she had given in to Frank's drunken grope in the night when she knew it would be possible to conceive.

She prayed each night for the health and happiness of Rose, and lit a candle each morning for Frank. Despite his many promises, now broken, and the fact that he managed to maintain his job at the mill and even get promoted, he still stumbled in well after dinner each evening from his local dive. He seemed unaware of what happened inside the house, for he left each morning when the children were still asleep and returned each night after they'd gone to bed. He imagined, when asking the bartender for another shot of whiskey, that his wife was coldly reprimanding one boy or another, and he didn't know how to tell her to stop, because Frank's life was governed by fear. Facing Doris was like facing the enemy at war. Instead of marching ahead and pulling one comrade after another out of danger, like many of his fellow infantrymen, Frank's tactic during the war was simple: hide. In every battle, he managed to slip away from his troop and hide behind a bush or under palm tree fronds, his face painted a ceremonial camouflage, his hands shaking as he pointed his rifle toward the unknown. He would listen to the relentless tapping of bullets, their death-drive whistling by his ears, and look out as men ran, aimed, were crippled by the pain of a grenade or a gunshot wound. Time after time, he would begin lifting his legs from their cramped, crouched position, ready to emerge from his hiding place, surprise his enemy, and become a war hero. Yet, as if some force greater than his desire held the leg muscles in place, each time Frank froze instead, his mind overflowing with images of the street where he used to play stickball with his brother, his kitchen where his mother baked him his favorite apple pie once a week, Doris standing up in her front lawn and smiling... He feared death so much during the war that he no longer knew how to live when it was over.

The good and bad recollections of his past and present life haunted him as he let his family slip through his fingers with each shot of whiskey in the bar. It wasn't until Doris went into the hospital and Frankie brought Warren upstairs that Frank realized what he had done. Brokenhearted, Frank did not know how to return home without alcohol in his blood.

At the age of four, Warren began to understand what it meant to love someone. He loved his brother Frankie for wrapping his arms around him each night—Doris had begun to pay less and less attention to Warren, allowing him to creep up the stairs at bedtime, choosing to ignore the existence of him in her life. He loved his sister Rose for bringing a softness to his mother's movements that he otherwise would not have felt. And most of all, he loved the tiny bits of freedom he experienced each day, whether it meant that he would not be touched by Mother, or he might receive, certainly by accident, two meals instead of one. Warren licked his freedom from his lips, its juice thick and sweet on his chin.

He learned quickly that if he stayed small and kept his mouth closed, Mother wouldn't notice him as much. He still spent much of his time in the basement, its dark safety wrapping around him like an invisible blanket, keeping his thoughts secure and his voice quiet. Mother's visits became less frequent, and Warren began to realize, on his late-evening marches up the basement stairs, that he also had a father.

His father, a short, thin man with bright orange hair, moved like a child who was confused about where he was. Warren often hid behind the partly open basement door, watching as his father entered the house and, with squinting eyes in the dim living room, looked about with a suspicious gawk. Each night, Frank fumbled with his coat as he struggled to find the hanger in the closet. Warren watched the way his father staggered about the room, his movements awkward and rough, but not sharp like his mother's. He began to wonder what place the man had in his life, and felt drawn to him in a way that he couldn't explain.

One night, in the warmth of Frankie's bed, Warren asked, "Frankie, what does Daddy do here?"

Frankie paused. "Here? Not much. But he goes to work and pays for our food and our house. Otherwise we wouldn't have a place to live," he whispered.

It was from his father, through his quiet late-evening entrances, that Warren learned his second lesson: It's easier to work and come home late—you'll miss the hurt. He stacked this lesson on top of the first in his mind's eye and fell into a deep, peaceful sleep.

Chapter 12

After the first day, not another went by that Luisa and Carter spent apart. They fell fast and hard into a love that engulfed both of their lives. Luisa, usually skittish with new men and unlikely to reveal family secrets, let loose her fears and dug in to the new relationship.

"You can't drink or I won't marry you," Luisa said over dinner on their third date. They sat across from each other in a booth at Chili's, their bodies separated by the intricately colored tile table and two orders of beef fajitas. Always realistic about what she wanted (right then she wanted him), she decided to bring out her emotions right from the start and either scare him away or see if he'd stay.

"Not even a beer once in a while?" Carter said with a cocky smile on his face.

Luisa's surprise at his response was reflected in the dimness that came over his eyes.

"I was just—"

"My father is an alcoholic. Maybe some day I'll take you over to my parents' house, where you can meet my distraught mother frantically trying to mop up the puke from the night before, or meet my father trying to go sober and having a seizure on the middle of the living room floor." Her look said, "I dare you," back into his eyes.

"I would love to meet your parents, cleaning or drinking or not. Everyone has their skeletons," Carter said.

To this, Luisa had no words. She knew that men were unlikely to so openly discuss such things without a few shots in their blood. She'd never met anyone like Carter before. He didn't scare easily, didn't seem to have any problem with her dysfunctional family, and held her stare as if looking away would cause the air to be sucked from his lungs.

"What else do you want to challenge me with? Don't tell me you're a lesbian, too," Carter's face glowed. Luisa couldn't help the smile from sneaking onto her face.

"No, but I'm not having kids right away, so don't think I'm going to be your housewife, and I want to travel the world before I get married, and I don't believe in living together... but sex is OK, as long as you're in love." She felt the words pour out of her mouth like the opening of a waterfall, the whitewater rushing over the side to fill the glistening pool below.

"Well, what are we waiting for, then?" Carter beamed.

"Are you saying you're in love with me after three days?" Luisa's high-pitched voice grew low at the words, dwelling in a strength she didn't know it had.

"Are you saying you're not in love with me?" He had mastered flirting as he grabbed her hand and stroked her palm with his thumb.

Luisa shivered at his touch. She wasn't afraid. "I am in love with you, Carter DaSilva. Think you can handle me and everything that comes attached?"

"I think so," he retorted, "on one condition."

"And what would that be?"

"That you'll love me till the day you die." Carter stood up from the booth where he sat across from her, pulled her up out of her seat, and wrapped his arms around her, pressing his lips against hers. "Think you can handle that?"

But Luisa was out of breath and couldn't answer.

At the funeral, because they lacked a defined religion, Luisa and Carter's families were forced to hold the ceremony in the nondenominational chapel of the cemetery, with its plain white walls, red carpet, and stiff-backed pews. The wood ceiling was flat and bore three large ceiling fans that hummed over the mourners. Carter's mother and father sat with Luisa in the chapel's front pew. Clustered together like field mice trying to stay warm on a winter night, the three sobbed as the minister read aloud a brief summary of Carter's life that Clara had composed. Alejo sat in the second row in the arms of Reeve. Aurelio sat in the far back with his eyes gazing absently at the oak rafters on the high ceiling of the small chapel. Clara and Marcus assembled next to Reeve, wrapping their arms around each other in a clutch of love.

Against the advice of her family, who claimed that all she ought to worry about was her grief, and that someone else, such as Carter's best friend, Mac, or one of his coworkers, or one of his clients, could write it, Luisa insisted on composing and presenting her eulogy.

"They don't know him like I do," her worn-out voice told them. "They can't do justice to Carter's presence on this earth."

Luisa had sat up for the past three nights in a state of insomnia as she composed draft after draft. Relentless as the image of the Silverado crashing into his truck was the image of her talons held fast at Alejo's window. At last, in the dark hours before dawn on the morning of the funeral, Luisa had the eulogy finished. She now shakily toddled up to the pulpit, the black ink burning her fingers as she squeezed the paper in her clammy palms. She started to speak in a whisper, but as her eyes moved down the page, strength entered her voice and everyone in the room could hear her.

"I dreamt of birds. I was an eagle, and Carter my mate. We flew from town to town, place to place, searching for the life that lived below. I often flapped my wings, exhausted, nearly falling to my death, but Carter knew how to slow his pace, spread his wings, and soar. Watching him, I learned to soften my flight, to let loose, and smile at the beauty of the world.

"Carter came into my life the only way a perfect match can: through love; in this case, the love of my best friend, Clara. Once we met, we were inseparable. We realized right away that we had the same dreams and that we clicked. Carter carried with him a humor and a sense of confidence that never deterred him from going for what he wanted, while at the same time allowing himself to laugh at his mistakes. He stood by me, even at the beginning when I tried to scare him off, and wanted to marry me for who I was, not for what he might get from me.

"Carter's love was like a bird's song: a constant beauty that sang me awake each morning. He knew how to be masculine, but also gentle. When he held Alejo—" Luisa's voice quavered. She clamped her eyelids together and sucked in a breath. "When he held Alejo, he was so soft and sweet, kissing his son all over his face, always trying to bring the giggle out. He knew how to love in every way: strong and lasting, calm and frequent.

"My happy memories of my husband far outweigh the sad ones. I remember when Carter asked me to marry him. He waited until we had been dating for a year, and on our anniversary, he drove me up to a bed and breakfast in Glenwood Springs, and on the sign in front, it read, 'Luisa, will you marry me? –Carter.' He was always thinking of creative and romantic ways to spice up our life. Once, I had been having a horrible week at work, and I complained to him again and again, and certainly wasn't in a good mood each night. That Friday, I came home to a house full of daffodils, my favorite flower, and a note that said, 'I just wanted you to know I love you even when you're sad.' It was so simple, yet so—" Again, Luisa paused. She knew what she wanted to say, but the words were blurred in front of her. She looked up at the chapel, where every pew was filled with mourners dressed in black. "So romantic," she said.

She paused for a moment, waiting for the right time to go on. When she felt the mood of the chapel move from tearful reminiscence to hopeful anticipation, she spoke again.

"I dreamt of birds. I was an eagle, and Carter my mate. But I know that flapping frantically won't bring him back. I know, when I picture his grinning face in my mind, that Carter would not want me to tire and fall. I know now, as Carter rests above me as I continue to fly, that I must remember to breathe, spread my wings as far as the wind will allow, and soar."

Stepping down from the pulpit, Luisa let loose her held-in grief and allowed the tears to flow, her throat trapping in the moans of agony. She returned to her seat, where she sat surrounded by a chapel full of people who couldn't help but cry along.

Chapter 13

Warren began his gardens each year just after Memorial Day. The risk of frost ended there, and June proved, year after year, to be the only month with consistent rain. He had cleared away most of his lawn years ago, so that his backyard displayed an intricate pattern of flagstone walks, flower beds filled with snow on the mountain, daffodils, sunflowers, tulips, and rose bushes, and vegetables and fruits ranging from pumpkins to raspberries to spinach.

Warren tended his garden much like he tended the remainder of his everyday life: with the care and precision of a meticulous engineer, pulling out weeds daily and standing over each section every night with the sprinkler in his hand. He installed a soaker hose that lay like a snake, slithering throughout the yard, in between tomato leaves and peony stems, letting out its slow drip of water into the parched ground. Most afternoons, the sky grew dark with clouds rolling in from the mountains, and Warren breathed in the gusty relief of moisture that crept in with the brief thunderstorms that would dump a minimal amount of water into the soil. He trimmed back excess leaves on his raspberry bushes and regularly pruned his three peach trees, so that, come August, he would have enough fruit to hand out to his neighbors and still be able to make jam.

In the center of Warren's backyard he had three large birdfeeders that he had handcrafted from pine. To keep the squirrels away, he installed a steel ring around the lower half of each narrow black pole, and spread enough seed on the ground each morning so that the squirrels remained satisfied. He filled each birdfeeder with a different variety of seeds and one to attract songbirds and one to attract hummingbirds. He loved to sit on his back patio and watch the birds come at various times of day to chirp, peck, and strew the seeds.

Warren always closed his shop the week of Memorial Day so that he could plant the majority of the garden. He determined that it was well worth his while to lose a little business with the amount of money he saved on groceries by growing enough fruits and vegetables to last half the winter. He loved to spend time outside, working with his hands, the hot spring sun at his back, as he worked the soil with the hoe or rake, and carefully placed seeds or young plants in the places he had drawn out on white paper weeks before. He loved the peace of his quiet backyard, and the way plants and birds brought multitudes of color to his ordinarily beige life.

On the Tuesday following Memorial Day, Warren crouched on his hands and knees along the fence line in the alley planting sunflower seeds when the young brown woman emerged from her garage. Trying to ignore her, though he could see her in his peripheral vision, Warren continued to plant as she rummaged through the items in the garage. Her movements were sharp and angular, causing Warren to choke on memories of his mother. The hair on his neck rose as his heart rate increased. He couldn't help but look over. She saw him planting and threw a halfhearted wave into the air.

"Need to sell anything at a garage sale?" she called across the alley. "I'm having one this weekend. I'm selling practically everything in my house, and then selling the house." Her voice trembled on the word house.

Warren stood up and looked into the dark pools of her eyes. He had read in the newspaper in March that Carter DaSilva, Luisa's husband (at last he learned their names), was killed in a car accident. The driver of the other vehicle was suspected to be driving under the influence. When Warren read the article, he was overcome with grief. He felt in some way responsible. He thought about his father's drunken stupors every night—how many times had he driven home in that state, and what had Warren, or anyone, ever done? He felt a grieving for Luisa and her infant son, whose father didn't live to see his first birthday. He felt an emptiness inside and outside of the window where the baby slept. Every night and every morning since the accident, he saw Luisa in tears as she cradled Alejo.

Now, Warren gazed into her eyes, unable to speak. So many times he had wanted to introduce himself to her, to offer his condolences, to bring over a casserole or a bouquet of flowers, and now, in her sweet, innocent voice, she called over to him.

At last, he thought of something to say. "Where are you going to live?"

Luisa squinted suspiciously. The way that he said those words traveled through her. She felt the language moving over her body, tapping at her heart and mind, whispering in her ear, "I know you."

She responded in a slow drawl, "I… haven't worked that out yet," and thought, to keep her face dry in front of a stranger, one thing at a time.

Warren sensed her discomfort and turned the conversation back. "I don't believe I have anything for a garage sale. I tend to give most things away to the Goodwill. But I would surely like to help you out. My name is Warren York." He walked towards her, brushed the dust off his gardening glove as he removed it, and held out his hand. Her tiny palm felt fragile in the grasp of his rough skin.

"I'm Luisa DaSilva," she said, "and I could use all the help I can get." She forced a weak smile and led Warren into the garage. As Warren began sifting through toolboxes, lawn equipment, and camping gear, an unencumbered smile spread across his face. He felt happy for the first time that he could remember.

After two hours of creating categorized piles and labeling individual items, Luisa wiped her brow, plopped down on top of a box, and sighed. "I really appreciate this, Warren." She gazed over at his arrow-thin frame, his balding head and clean-shaven face. A look of uneasiness crawled across his face like a poisonous spider. She wondered why he had offered to help, and what he knew about her. She had met most of the neighbors along her street, but none from the alleyway.

"Oh, it's no problem. I…" he paused, as if not sure of what to say. "I started my garden a bit early this year, with the weather being so mild, so I'm a little ahead of the game. I usually take this week off work to plant my vegetables and herbs." Suddenly aware of their absence of movement, Warren felt the eighty degrees of sunshine burn his skin. His face flushed with heat and embarrassment, the emotions within him running everywhere.

"Oh, I'd love to see your garden sometime. Right now, why don't we go inside and I can fix you some lemonade. I think my son is about to wake from his nap." Warren had said nothing about the baby monitor Luisa wore on her hip like a holster, but had heard, off and on during the afternoon, the steady breathing of the baby. He looked down at Luisa now, with her hair pulled back in a bun much like it was the first time he saw her, wearing small black shorts that barely covered her legs, and an oversized white t-shirt with the logo for the Kansas City Chiefs on the front. She sat with her hands resting on her knees in a comfortable fashion, innocent in her own rite. He felt ridiculous to think that she wanted anything to do with him. Yet, he couldn't explain why he wanted so badly to neglect the work of his own backyard so that he could taste the sweet and sour lemonade in her kitchen.

"OK, lemonade sounds good to me," he said. He followed her through the door of the garage and through her backyard. She had a large birdfeeder, now empty, in the center of the grass, and two large ash trees on either end of the yard, but not much else.

She saw him eyeing the expanse of the grass and said, "We were going to start a garden this year," but she couldn't think of the rest of the sentence. Instead she looked at her palms and walked quickly to the back patio door, where she thrust the glass door open and turned around. "Come on in."

Warren stepped inside and met a gush of cool air. He felt a twinge of jealousy at their air conditioning, already dreading the scorching summer months ahead where he would sit with fans blowing hot air in his face. The back door opened to the kitchen and dining area, which were open to each other. The kitchen, like his own, had a small area, but four decent-sized countertops, and in Luisa's kitchen, unlike his own, someone had replaced all the appliances and cabinets with newer, brighter models. Even her countertops were a fresh burgundy tile, making his Formica pale in comparison. Warren stood examining the updated kitchen for a moment, unsure of how to act in someone else's house. It had been too long since he'd been in anyone's but his own.

"Have a seat," Luisa motioned to the maple dining set that was surely an antique.

"This must be a collector's item. What a beautiful set," Warren said.

"Thanks." Luisa pulled a pitcher out of the side-by-side refrigerator and two glasses out of the cabinet. As she filled the glasses with ice from the dispenser on the freezer door, she said, "It's been passed down from my mother-in-law's mother. I don't know if it's worth anything." She felt her face redden.

Warren decided to say something about her husband to avoid the awkward moments they encountered. "I heard about your husband, Mrs.

DaSilva. I'm terribly sorry." As he said the words, his voice cracked and he couldn't look at her. Instead he focused on the beige carpet.

"Oh..." she barely whispered, "thank you." She brought over the glasses of lemonade, already collecting beads of sweat, and sat across from him at the table. She didn't want to cry today, so she changed the subject. "Please, call me Luisa. So how long have you lived here?"

"I bought my house just over thirty years ago, but I've lived in Denver all of my life. What about you? You sound like you have a touch of an accent."

"Well, my parents met in Texas, and I spent the first two years of my life living in Houston, and then we lived in various rural areas in Texas while my mom trained to be a midwife. My mom finally got a midwifery job here when I was eleven, and my dad..." Luisa sighed. "My dad started working for a printing press. So I lived over on the west side for the second part of my childhood, and I guess my accent comes from my mother."

"Is your father also from Texas?" Warren tried to hide his burning interest in her life story.

"No." She locked her eyes on him. He looked back at her with an expression of calm expectance. He sat straight-backed with his hands open on the table. She didn't know why, but she trusted him. "My father is from Jimenez, Mexico. He came to the United States in the back of my grandfather's pickup truck so that he could work on my grandfather's ranch. That's where he met my mother." Luisa recited the words like a poem she had memorized for school. She had never seen Jimenez, the pickup truck, the ranch, or her grandfather. She had only heard the story from her father, who only told her in her room at night, in Spanish, as a bedtime story. Her mother never spoke of their meeting, as if mentioning it would bring further curses to her life.

Warren's face ballooned with a warm expression. "You've got quite a lifetime of stories for someone so young. You should write a book."

Luisa's face reddened as if spattered with the juice of a blood orange. She fiddled with her wedding ring, a nervous habit she had picked up since Carter placed it on her finger six years ago. She didn't even know this man, and she wondered how he could speak to her heart. She thought of the manuscript that rested in a brown leather satchel in her parents' basement.

"I don't think writing is for me," she said in a low voice, and quickly finished with, "I'm an art historian. I've always loved art." It was true, the second part at least. Luisa's happiest childhood memories included weekend trips to the art museum, natural history museum, Colorado history museum, and countless art galleries, where her father and mother didn't argue, but convened in a peaceful acceptance of the beauty before them.

Warren shifted in his seat. "I'd better get back to my garden. I have to refill my birdfeeders for the evening. I see you like birds, too."

Just then, the monitor attached to Luisa's belt lit up with the chirping sound of Alejo, who was sitting up in his crib and playing with the closed blinds, trying to look out. Luisa felt a rush of relief. She didn't want to talk about birds with this stranger; not yet.

"Oh, Alejo's awake. Thank you again for helping me with the garage. I can't tell you how much I appreciate it."

"What are neighbors for? And I'll help you tomorrow, too. What time does your son usually take his nap?"

"You don't have to do that. My mother's coming over tomorrow afternoon."

"Six hands are better than four. I know what trouble it can be to clean out a house." Warren's voice darkened when he said this, and his face drew shadows beneath the garish afternoon light. He thought of his recent trip to his mother's house, where he and his brothers and sisters had to sort through sixty years of personal items before taking their mother to the assisted living home.

"OK then," Luisa said. "It's too bad that I have to move away from a nice neighbor."

An intricate plan developed in Warren's mind the moment she said those words. He tried to hide the details from his face as he stepped through the glass door and walked through the backyard, listening to the birds chatter at him from his own. He retrieved the heavy bags of seed from the garage and whistled as he filled each feeder. He felt satisfied as the sun began to set on the warm spring day and his once-lonely life.

Chapter 14

As if the onset of her eighteenth year brought adulthood and all its attached stress into her life for the first time, Reeve began having bouts of insomnia. She lay awake each night, staring at the popcorn-plastered ceiling, the tiny balls casting shadows against each other from the light of the moon. She imagined her life in many ways: riding horseback through the fields of her father's ranch until she was too old to ride, going away to college and studying literature, traveling the world, or even marrying William. Her father invited William to stay on at the ranch indefinitely, and every night he sat across from her at the dinner table grinning over the food she and Paula prepared, trying to make conversation that interested her. Each night, as she lay in bed, she thought about William—his strong, freckled shoulders, the tight muscles in his arms, the way his eyes sparkled with the happiness of a child when he caught a glimpse of her. His presence filled her mind with images and fear. Fear, she knew, shouldn't be what came inside her head when she thought of William, but it was fear that she tasted on her tongue each night like the sour juice of a dill pickle.

While she played pictures of William in the forefront of her brain, she saved space in the back corner of her imagination for the true object of her desire. Arriving on the same night and touching her shoulder in that gentle, sensual way, Aurelio (the name she heard passed to him from one set of Mexican lips) haunted her mind like a ghost, slipping in and out in a whisper of longing. Her meals each day began to contain spices that Paula had never used, and she referred to cookbooks instead of her memory, to prepare food that would outdo anything she had fixed before. When she served the food on the long picnic tables outside of the kitchen, she found herself leaning against Aurelio, or tapping his shoulder, as she poured beef stew or placed corn-on-the-cob on his plate. She listened when he spoke, his words thick and juicy, filled with the taste of a dreamer who hasn't yet achieved his dreams.

And when she couldn't sleep at night, she imagined that instead of leaning over and serving him dinner, she leaned over to place her lips on his mouth. She imagined that, instead of Aurelio telling his compadre that he wanted to be a writer, and that he already had a book ready, he would tell his dreams to Reeve in the dark loft of the barn, his voice rough and masculine as he made love to her. She imagined Aurelio carrying her to her favorite mare, strapping a few chosen items into her saddlebags, and galloping away from the ranch in the middle of the night, only to return two weeks later to inform her father of their blissful union.

Reeve shivered in the heat of summer when she imagined these ideas. She knew what her father wanted. Never blessed with any other children, he craved a son, and, unable to create his own, he had handpicked a beauty in William. William was the kind of man any woman would be proud to marry,

Reeve knew, and would be good to her. Yet, her heart told her everything about the match was wrong, and she belonged with Aurelio, his dark and mysterious eyes drawing her in at first sight. And so she spent many sleepless nights pondering her circumstances, waking each morning after brief periods of fitful sleep, until a month had passed.

Seth noticed the change in his daughter. "You must be in love," he cooed to her one morning. "I don't remember losing that much sleep and carrying such a crooked smile on my face since I met your mother."

Reeve hid her face from his view. "Oh, Daddy," she said, embarrassed, as William walked into the kitchen.

"What's on the menu for today, pretty lady?"

Seth interrupted. "You know, William and Reeve, I think you've been working too hard here on the ranch. You need a break. Why don't you two go in to town tonight and get you something to eat. Maybe go see a movie."

Reeve froze in the midst of pouring the batter for pancakes. She stood, her arm as stiff as that on a corpse, holding the pancake bowl in midair. Her eyes held a blank expression in the moment of intense silence.

"That sounds wonderful to me," William responded. "What do you think, Reeve?"

"What about the workers? How will they eat?" Reeve tried not to sound desperate.

"I think Paula can handle one meal on her own, Sweet Pea. You go and have yourself a good time."

"OK, Daddy," Reeve's voice let out the words like a balloon letting out its last bit of air.

Reeve had never been on a date before, and spent thirty minutes searching through the limited items in her closet for something to wear. Knowing that the three small restaurants in town had no dress code, she decided that she could get along well enough wearing khaki pants and a button-down polyester blouse that once belonged to her mother. Reeve slipped on the blue blouse, feeling its soft fabric against her skin, and brushed out her long blond hair in the mirror. She decided to wear her hair down, and it fell along her back like a horse's tail. Having no makeup, Reeve spread lip-gloss along her thin red lips until they shined. She smiled at herself. She knew how beautiful she was. She just didn't know what that beauty could bring.

William met her in the dining room at six. His smile widened when he saw the hair loosely framing her face.
"You look absolutely stunning with your hair down," he said as he reached for her arm. She felt small and weak in his clutch, like a kitten grasped by the teeth of its mother.

William didn't say anything at first as they drove down the two-lane road in the bright sun of early evening. The pickup rumbled its huge diesel engine and made an awkward stirring sound each time he shifted gears. Reeve sat with her hands in her lap and looked out at the ranches through the passenger window. She strained her neck so that she couldn't even see William's strong hand at the gear shifter, imagining, instead, that it was Aurelio's. She squinted her eyes to see rows of corn and fields of cattle, spotted with an occasional ranch home and barn, the only landmarks she knew to represent her homeland. Her mind wandered with thoughts of other places, places she had only imagined, that lay beyond the flat meadows out her window.

"I hope you enjoy steak. I've heard the steakhouse in town is pretty good," William finally spoke after fifteen minutes.

Reeve trapped in a sigh. Again, she imagined eating seafood or escargot or some gourmet dish that was served well beyond the borders of Texas.

"Of course, I'm a rancher's daughter, right?" but she didn't force a smile as she stared at her hands, which were clawing each other in nervousness.

"Have you ever been anywhere but Texas?" William asked.

"Well, no. Where else would I have reason to go?"

"You mean your father has never taken you down to Mexico with him?"

"No, of course not. It's much too dangerous in Mexico." She recited the words her father had told her time and again, not really believing them to be true.

"Your father knows nothing of danger," William said, his voice suddenly sinister. Reeve's back tickled with a chill as he said the words. He looked over at her and said, "I've been all over the world. I could tell you all about danger." He wanted to entice her, but instead, he frightened her.

"That's all right. I like it here on the ranch," Reeve pursed her lips and returned her look to the window. She squeezed her hands together, holding in the lie.

"Oh, but you ought to see other places, little girl. There's so much more to the world than Texas."

They hadn't even reached the town before Reeve decided she hated William. Little girl, I'll show you, she thought. She wanted to snap back at him, but decided to keep her mouth closed, a trick she would later regret.

After dinner, where William had a t-bone and Reeve a rib eye and they talked about working the ranch, William did not drive Reeve over to the movie theatre as she expected. Without saying a word, he continued down Main Street and drove out into the country, but not towards the ranch. Reeve gripped the handle on the door, picturing in her mind what it would feel like to jump out of a truck going fifty miles per hour. She felt an uncontrollable urge to swing open the door, roll into the pasty dirt of whatever ranch they were passing, then get up and run... run to where, she didn't know. Instead, after several minutes of driving along the flat countryside that bore no image beneath the moonless night, Reeve spoke.

"Where are we going, William?" She tried to coat the words with the curiosity of a young child, hoping that if she asked in just the right way, he would have something wonderful to say back to her. But as soon as the question poured from her mouth, she could feel the words, like miniature bubbles, popping in the air and tickling William's ears, causing him to shift in his seat. The truck felt darker now than the moment before she spoke, and a sick feeling crept over her like a black widow looking for a good place to inject its venom.

William didn't answer. His silence engulfed her, and the roaring engine burned in her ears. She pinched her eyelids together and pictured herself in the corner of the barn loft, curling up in the hay and petting one of the barn cats or reading a book in the dim light. Reeve chewed on her tongue and pressed her hands in between her legs.

He pulled onto a dirt road and drove for several miles, then, as if taken over by an outside force, careened into a cornfield. William turned the key in the ignition. Reeve listened to the clicking noises of the engine settling down, and the singsong chirping of cicadas and crickets out in the field.

"Are you a virgin, Reeve?" His shady voice echoed in her head. She felt heat rise to her hair follicles, and her palms began to sweat. She said nothing. William put his hands on the vinyl seat and scooted his body next to hers. He put his hefty hand on her thigh and squeezed. Reeve felt incapacitated. She sat like a fly trapped in a spider's web, unable to move a single muscle in her body. A craving to scream boiled up inside of her as she thought of her father, sitting on the porch smoking his cigar, so proud that his daughter might marry this man. The scream remained in her churning stomach as William's hand inched between her legs and his moist lips pressed against her cheek.

A single word came to her lips in a whisper.

"Please," she said, and William covered her mouth with his, his tongue penetrating her uvula. He pulled away for a brief moment, and she said the word again.

"Please."

In the hot dark cab of the pickup, the word rang out, meaning two different things to the speaker and listener. Reeve couldn't see a thing. She could only feel the pressure of his body against hers. In silence, she let go of the tears from the corners of her eyes, and held the word No at the tip of her tongue, too frightened to speak.

Thirty minutes later, before the truck had even stopped, Reeve opened the passenger door and moved as quickly as her aching legs would allow up the ladder into the loft of the barn. There, in the corner, curled up with a manuscript spread before him, was Aurelio, who had watched Reeve's entrance into the barn night after night, and waited for her now. When he saw her face streaked with the desperate leftover moisture of angry tears, and the dark brown area between her legs, his hands shook as he stood and opened his arms.

"You are safe with me," he whispered as she rushed into the warmth of his body. "You are safe with me."

He wrapped his love around her like a blanket. She felt hot and tired, like a newborn entering the world and being held against its mother's breast.

Chapter 15

Once they were married, Carter decided it was time for them to save up for a house. Luisa had a year left of college, and still wanted to pursue a master's degree, but Carter insisted they would be OK. His business had picked up since Luisa entered his life, as if her glowing presence alone brought referrals pouring into his phone lines. Since he worked in the construction field, Carter had a heads up on good house values around town, and Luisa had always dreamed of living in the posh Park Hill neighborhood. Most of the houses in that area, built in the 1940s after the war, were skyrocketing in price, so Carter decided they should act quickly and find a good fixer-upper.

After talking to several realtors and homeowners, Carter and Luisa put an offer on a large two-story brick home that belonged to an older couple who had lived there since 1950 and hadn't changed a thing inside. The metal-door cabinets in the kitchen were yellow with the tar and nicotine of thousands of cigarettes, the aqua carpet bore fifty years of stains and wear, and the pale blue paint with brown trim was faded and chipping off the walls. Luisa gagged every time she entered the house from the outside, its contagious, smoky smell infiltrating her nostrils. She despised narcotics of any nature, and warned Carter that he must work on the house for two weeks straight and hire every man in the business to remodel the interior. Carter, anxious to please his new bride, allowed her to handpick the wood for the new kitchen cabinets, choose the color of the carpet, and design murals for the walls in the three upstairs bedrooms. Carter claimed the downstairs walls for himself, where he believed simple white walls and white trim were the most appealing to visitors and homeowners alike. Luisa chose maple for the cabinets to go with the antique dining set and the two harmoniously stuck to a maple theme, choosing it for the new mantle over the hand-laid stonework on the fireplace and the railing on the staircase.

It was in the downstairs bathroom where Carter and Luisa disagreed and had their first fight as a married couple. Carter wanted to put an oak toilet seat on the new toilet to match the oak vanity on the sink, and wanted to decorate the bathroom with nothing but plain white paint, accessories, and towels. After discussing it for more than a week, Luisa lost her temper and locked herself in the bathroom one early morning before Carter and his crew arrived. She sat for nearly an hour before someone attempted to open the door. It was Carter, banging on the other side.

"Who's in the bathroom?" his voice carried through the door.

"It's me," she said, throwing nastiness into her voice. "I'm not coming out until you agree to let me choose the decorations for the bathroom. I refuse to sit on an oak toilet seat, and this whole house is going to reflect the Ku Klux

Klan if you choose the decorations. I need more color." She felt hot as the speech flooded out of her lips.

"Baby, don't be silly. It's just the downstairs bathroom, for guests. Don't you think it should be simple?"

"No. You don't want it to be simple. You just want it to be your decision. Just like buying this house, going to Hawaii for the honeymoon, not letting me drive your truck—you're so controlling, Carter! I can't stand it, and I can't be with someone who wants to control every decision." Luisa said. The night before she had convinced herself, when she tossed and turned in an insomniac's nightmare, that Carter was taking over her life, and that she would never be able to make her own decisions again.

"Baby, please open the door so we don't have to shout. I'm not trying to control you."

Luisa reluctantly twisted the lock. Carter came in and sat on the floor in front of her where she sat slumped on the white toilet seat.

"Luisa, I thought that we agreed that you could choose some of the colors and decorations for the house, and I could choose others. I thought you wanted to go to Hawaii for our honeymoon, and I thought you wanted to buy the house. I'm sorry, Baby, I'm just trying to do right by you." Carter put his face in his palms and let out a shallow wail. He sniffled and wiped his eyes, looking up at Luisa.

"We can decorate the bathroom however you want," he whispered. "I just want you to be happy."

Luisa's heart twisted on itself. Twangs of guilt consumed her thoughts. She allowed a few silent tears to spill onto her cheeks before saying anything aloud. She couldn't think of a good answer to the painful, loving truth Carter had revealed.

"OK, Carter. I'm sorry, I just—I just got scared, you know. I've never been married before, and my parents didn't exactly set the best example for me. I just am so afraid that…" But she couldn't say it. She couldn't say to him, as he choked away more sobs, that she was afraid that she wouldn't be happy with him, or anyone, in a marriage. Instead, she completed the sentence with, "that I won't be able to do anything for myself."

Carter took her hand and squeezed it between both of his own. "I love you more than anything, Luisa. And I know you too well. You will always be able to do anything you want." Luisa couldn't help but smile at the mysterious way that Carter knew exactly what to say.

That morning, Luisa painted her first mural on the downstairs bathroom wall: a volcano and waterfall scene from the Big Island, where they had spent their first seven nights of marital bliss.

Carter's apparition haunted Luisa's life. She didn't believe in spirits lurking about, but her imagination sang out to her that he was in the house. She would be fixing dinner, and hear herself yell to the family room, "Broccoli or corn?" She would be feeding Alejo his breakfast and hear Carter's alarm beep in her ear. She would be making the bed and hear Carter say, "Why? We're just going to mess it up again tonight." She would be checking the mail and see his name printed on bills or credit card offers, and set them on the counter for him to read. She would be crying, curled up into a tight ball beneath the covers, and feel Carter's warmth wrap around her as he crawled into bed, his voice whispering in her ear, "What's wrong, Baby?"

Her senses betrayed her. How could she taste, smell, see, hear, touch her life without feeling his presence? She woke each morning after a fitful sleep, and crankily pulled Alejo out of his crib. Always he cried now, as if her grief seeped through her skin onto his. She loved and hated him in the same moment. She hugged him and wanted to drop him at the same time. She would say, in a callous whisper as he slept, "If it weren't for you, I could go on with my life and be free." And, the guilt-ridden tears leaching through, she would hastily add, "If it weren't for you, I would not have a part of Carter to keep with me forever."

Her life became a pawn on a chessboard, always moving from black square to white, the borders stark and unforgiving. She wondered how she could feel such anger in one moment as she remembered how Carter always forgot to clear his plate, and such happiness in the next moment as she remembered how he always kissed her goodbye in the morning. She felt herself moving back and forth along the chessboard, never making it to the other side, always filling her blacks with whites, her whites with blacks, until she was dizzy with colors that wouldn't combine. She craved gray, a smooth, calm gray, the color of the sea, which would allow her to sleep at night and hold her son without remorse.

As the days passed, some taken over by black, some tinged with white, but always a combination, Luisa began to move out of her chessboard room, into the larger part of the house, the yard, and the outside world. Reality hit her when Alejo began to walk. She realized, as her child took his first wavering steps from the coffee table to her arms, that time would pass, life would go on, and she could still have great moments of happiness such as this. Yet, in that same moment of happiness, a wave of grief collided, and she cringed thinking that Carter couldn't be there to see this momentous occasion.

The next day, she decided to put her emotions to work. She began the tedious process of cleaning out the house and the garage. Because they didn't have life insurance, Luisa was unable to afford their house any longer. She had yet to find a job. Since she had been out of work for over a year and the economy lagged behind her persistence, she had only received one interview. And Luisa, her pain still too raw as she sat across from the casually-dressed curators of the museum, nearly broke down in nervousness and despair. She never received a callback, and still spent each morning scanning the want ads and tightening up her resume.

When she set out to clean the garage and prepare for a garage sale, she didn't know that she would be preparing for much more. Warren York mysteriously held out his hand and welcomed her into his straightforward life, giving her tips on ingenious ways to save money (such as taking two cold showers a day rather than run the air conditioning, or driving halfway across town to a discount grocery store, or walking places instead of driving), and offering his help with her life one day at a time. Luisa, unaccustomed to generosity and the encouraging feeling it woke her with on each sunny day that early summer, accepted his assistance with the deepest gratitude, welcoming him for dinner most nights, or if not, drinks at the I down the street (where Warren always drank Earl Grey tea). As she began the slow process of healing her desperate heart, Luisa found herself devouring the relationship she had hungered for during her childhood: the simple (yet so complex, she often reminded herself) exchange of a father and daughter.

In mid June, when the heat waves that rose from the black pavement in the mornings were still smothered in steam by brief rain showers in the afternoons, Aurelio appeared at Luisa's doorstep, drenched from a storm. When the doorbell rang, she and Warren were sifting through the relentless boxes in the basement that defined Carter's packrat lifestyle. Luisa hiked up the stairs, her heart working against her as she let dread engulf her thoughts. Who could it be? She wondered, thinking now not of solicitors, but of policemen.

When she opened the door, she could smell the fermented liquid emanating from his body in the sizzling shower. Though she thought her days as a pawn were streamlining into a gray world where she could easily maneuver from day to day, her father's presence reminded her of the black squares that could still creep into her view.

"What is it?" Her voice was a cold contrast to the searing weather.

Aurelio, who had only taken enough tequila to calm his nerves, but not enough to dampen his vision, felt injured at her icy stance.

"Luisa, please, I—" He had practiced the speech seven times the night before and three more on the drive over, but as she stood in front of him, her arms crossed like a stone statue, he stumbled over the words, unable to make them unglue in his mind. He pressed his palms against his face and let out a long, slow cry. He felt weak and incapable of movement. He wanted to say so many things, but the rain tapped on his aching head and limp body like the incessant pounding of a drum.

"Luisa…" was the only sound he could let loose from his mouth as he slumped down into the doorway, his body creating a warm, dark cave.

Warren emerged from the basement carrying a box labeled "Goodwill" with permanent black marker in his neat handwriting. When he saw the large man sprawled in front of the teary Luisa, he dropped the box, his mouth ajar, and pulled Luisa away from him. His mind flooded with images of his father. In anger, he shoved the man from the doorway.

"Is this man begging for money door to door?" he demanded of Luisa, who still stood as stiff as an inanimate being. He had tried to keep his voice level, but the question boiled up out of him like the sauce in an unattended pan.

Luisa's eyes widened. She stood so still because Aurelio had never before been to her house. Not when they bought the house three years ago, not when Alejo was born, not even for the gathering after Carter's funeral. Her blood turned cold with shock and anger as she stared down at the drunken creature below.

"He's my father," Luisa's voice was a harsh whisper.

As if programmed by a computer chip, Warren retreated into the kitchen to prepare coffee. As the coffee pot began to drip its slow brown liquid, Warren caught his breath for a moment. He looked at the glass doors that led into the yard. He considered his situation. He could so easily leave this place, leave Luisa and Alejo, and act as if he never had answered her that day in the alley. This drunken mess of a father was one of the reasons Warren lived alone, made no contact with his mother or brothers or sisters for years (unless absolutely necessary), and ignored his niece's annual invitations to the Labor Day barbecue or Christmas dinner. He tasted the bitter coffee in his mouth without ever taking a sip, the memories of his childhood inundating his brain after years of forced obstruction. I don't need this girl with two thousand pounds of baggage, he said to himself. The glass doors called to him in a quiet murmur, beckoning him to the safety of his lonesome life.

Warren poured two cups of coffee, set them on the dining table, and walked to the door. He helped the man to his feet and propped him under his arms as they made the slow walk to the dining area. He motioned for Luisa to join them. As if drawn by the strings on a marionette, she lifted each knee and moved toward the table with the angular movements of a puppet. She sat down across from her father and laced her fingers together on the tabletop. Her face reflected the shadows of the cloudy afternoon.

"Let's sit down, sober up, and have a talk," Warren said in a steady voice. He felt warm and calm and without doubt as their stories intertwined.

Chapter 16

Doris was pregnant again. In a brief stint of sobriety, Frank had attended AA for three months and promised his wife that things would change. He came home after work each night and sat with his family at the dinner table, telling his wife about work at the mill, asking his sons about their schoolwork. After dinner, he sat with Rose in his arms and read her stories on the living room couch. Then, after placing his daughter in the crib and turning out her light, Frank descended with a tray of leftover food each evening to the basement.

Frank had purchased a small bed for Warren, hung blankets around the partition where he slept, and bought him a small kerosene heater. All of these items he carried in late at night, when Doris paid no mind, and told Warren to keep his mouth closed in front of his mother. When his father came down every night, Warren jumped up from his bed, anxious to hug the warm body of his newfound hero, but Frank would stand tall and hold his hand out in warning.

"Don't go soft on me, boy," were the words that Warren heard each night.

Frank had convinced Doris that she could have another girl, and that she had better try soon, or it would be too late. Doris, content in the small area of her life that encompassed Rose, gave in to Frank. But, unlike her other conceptions, this pregnancy didn't occur instantly. When she finally conceived, her mind overtook itself with the dire possibility of another boy, and her expectant disappointment came out in the sharp, cold movements along the floorboards. Warren listened as his mother stomped about in the frighteningly familiar fashion, his heart beating with trepidation. For days, she moved about in her former way before making her move.

Doris didn't bother making the trek down the steps. She waited until the older boys were in school (where Warren should have been, if she would allow it) and Rose was taking a nap. Warren was six now, but as small and weak as a four-year-old. He still survived on one meal a day, cold and leftover hours after its preparation. Warren had yet to taste one hot meal in his short life.

She came to the door of the basement stairs like a convict dragging her ball and chain behind. Her footsteps throbbed against the floor and Warren's ears, and her hands cast a dark echo in his soul as she pounded them against the door.

"Boy, get your ass up these stairs. Don't make me come down there!" Her voice emanated through the oak like the wail of a dying mountain lion. Warren, weak from having not eaten in twenty hours or more, put his narrow bare feet on the concrete floor and took the shaky steps toward the stairs. He wore only a threadbare set of red jogging pants and orange t-shirt that Frankie had given him. Both were several sizes too big and hung on his frail body like a sheet covering a ghost. Goosebumps crawled up his spine as he placed one foot after another up the stairs, and his mouth dried from the combination of dehydration and fear.

Before he arrived at the top step, Doris swung open the door and reached her thick arm through the doorway, grasping Warren's shirt.

"Didn't I tell you to hurry, you worthless, good-for-nothing moron?" the language slithered into his ear like a snake. Warren cast his eyes to the floor, unable to move or answer. Doris yanked him through the doorway, her sharp fingernails tearing at the skin on his back. Warren's body convulsed. He knew only fear and anger.

"Get down on your knees," she spoke through her teeth. In a moment of relief, Warren let loose the muscles in his legs and crumpled to the floor like an accordion letting out its air.

"Now, clean the floor."

In a panic, Warren scanned his eyes around the floor, searching for a mop or a sponge or a bucket of soapy water. Just yesterday, he had scrubbed the hardwood clean, buffed it, and waxed it. It reflected the bright sun of early afternoon as he pressed his hands against it now. He saw no sign of cleaning supplies, and, with his face staring straight into the grains of wood, he whispered, "How?"

The unclipped toenails of her large bare foot dug into his ribs. His tiny body was flung to its side by the force of the kick. He gasped for air as if drowning in her sea of hate.

"Don't ask me how, you son-of-a-bitch. You clean the goddamn floor when I say!" Her voice took another breath from his lungs, its acrid tone sucking all air from the room. Warren shivered again. He pulled himself up to his hands and knees, using every ounce of strength left within him. Catching his breath, he began moving his calloused palms in circles on the wood. The wax squeaked against the clamminess of his hands.

For several minutes, Doris stood over him as he scrubbed. Then, as quick as a gunman in a duel, she drew her foot out and barreled it into his chest again. Warren's face was moist with snot and tears.

"Lick it," she spat out her command. "Lick the entire floor."

Again, Warren pulled himself back to a kneeling position. Again, Warren caught his breath. And like a bear cub reluctant to come out of the den, he brought his tongue out of his mouth and pressed it against the floor. For over an hour, Doris stood over him as he tasted dust mites, wax, and the bile of his stomach. She stood over him until he passed out on the floor, his body twitching with sickness as slow, labored breathing seeped from his mouth.

When Frank came home, he scooped his son into his arms, carried him to the car, and drove him to a church on the other side of town. He laid Warren on a pew and wept, his hands buried in his face. He asked God to forgive him as he covered Warren with his light jacket and walked out of the church.

When the bartender asked him what his pleasure was, he said, "Gin," in a flat, even voice.

Doris never saw Frank again, but Warren came home in a squad car that night. She explained to the police how her husband had been abusing the boy, but now he had disappeared. The police officers sat down on the couch and watched as Doris cradled her son, the tears streaming down her face. He had been given his first hot meal of chicken, corn, and mashed potatoes at the station. Warren, overcome with emotion, had no other inclination than to reach his arms around his mother's waist.

Relieved of their current duty, the officers left, putting out an unanswered warrant for the arrest of Frank York.

Chapter 17

Aurelio's mother had described love to him from the time he was a boy. In the old rocking chair that filled the tiny corner of his parents' bedroom, she sat with her son and told him stories every night before putting him to bed. Whenever Aurelio felt sad as an older child or an adult, he would draw up these soft moments with his mother, before the other children were born, when her silky arms wrapped around him and her smooth, sweet voice tickled his ear. She told stories that had been passed down from generations, the tales colored with gallant heroes, fearless heroines, and love. And each night, when she finished a tale, she would lower her voice and say, "Do you know about love, Mi Hijo?"

And always, though he heard it nightly, Aurelio would reply, "No, Mama, tell me."

"When you meet the person meant for you (like when I met your father), love will make a home in your heart. You will feel starved for that person, but not hungry for food. You will feel dizzy from the beauty of the person you love, but you will remain firm in every other part of your life. Love will carry you through the sickness it first brings to your head and stomach, because your heart will race with a new life. Love will know you before you know love, and when it reaches your eyes, you will never see anyone else for as long as you live."

And with a series of kisses spread across his face, his mother carried him to bed each night, whispering, "Love will find you, Aurelio, and with it your dreams will come true."

The brilliant words that filled his mother's stories lingered in the back of Aurelio's mind as he stepped out of the pickup truck onto the ground of the Texas ranch. His heart, which had throbbed with anxiety almost to the point of despair for days, now slowed its pace and beat in a state of relaxed alertness. The air, capped between a golden, flat horizon and an endless bright blue sky, tingled his body as he stretched the muscles in his arms and legs. With total control, a grin overtook his face, and he felt as though it swallowed him whole. Though he knew he stood at a ranch and should smell the stench of manure and the harsh scent of whole grains, his nostrils could only distinguish the sugary aroma of the flowers that lined the house. Even his tongue tasted a luxurious sweetness that he didn't recognize. But Aurelio's eyes, in the brief moment between his placement on the ground and Seth's introduction, couldn't see. He thought he must be blinded from the light after so many hours in the dark, but when he rubbed the moisture back in, blinked, and opened them, he knew. He knew that everything his mother had said was true: love had found him at last.

She stood in front of the men with her gray eyes scanning over their dusty appearance not with a look of disgust, but of comfortable familiarity. Her blond hair was pulled back in a tight ponytail on the back of her head, and swung coolly from side to side as she walked toward the group. Her thin red lips barely hid the sparkling whites as she spoke his native tongue in a soothing, natural voice, as if she had spoken the words from her birth. Her delicate nose quivered over her mouth and was drawn up just a bit at the tip. Her blond eyelashes delighted the faint freckles on her pale skin, and her heart-shaped face held a look of welcoming concentration. When she moved, her body glided across the grass like a butterfly fluttering comfortably from one flower to the next.

This brief interlude between his past and his future engulfed Aurelio's being. The other workers surrounded her like mindless ants after their queen, intently listening to her orders as if she barked them out rather than let them flow like breath from her mouth. Aurelio, the love encircling his existence, was the only one to reach for her and speak. When he placed his hand on her shoulder, electricity shot through his body, and the starvation that his mother had described overtook him.

He began his life in the United States with a new dream in mind: the hand of Reeve O'Reilly.

In secret, they watched each other. Aurelio clutched her view close to his heart. When she leaned into him at mealtimes, he struggled against every muscle inside his arms to keep them from wrapping themselves around her. During the day, the work of the ranch helped him stay away from his desire to spend countless hours beneath her bedroom window in hopes of one brief view of that beautiful face. Instead, he was busy learning how to brand cows, breed cows, feed cows, and clean up after cows. The work stole his time from dawn until dusk, at which point most of the men either fell exhausted into their bunks or stayed up late drinking, singing, and playing cards. Aurelio exalted himself above his fellow workers, and instead spent his evenings examining the stars, walking the land, and catching every sight he could of his beautiful Reeve. He learned her daily habits and saw, each morning, as Paula joined her from the other side of the ranch. He knew that every night, when Seth worked on his books in the light of the dining room window, Reeve escaped to the loft of the barn closest to the house. Like a cat, she sauntered from the kitchen door and retreated into the depths of the dark barn. Aurelio waited below each night, filling his mind with speeches for when she emerged. Always, when she emerged, he felt instead his mouth packed with hot breaths and no words.

Aurelio knew he had his odds stacked against him: he, a poor, illegal alien, from a culture so unlike hers, had little chance with the grace and beauty that swept across the land each day. And he saw, from the day he arrived, that he had stiff competition. William, a chameleon who held a saccharine tone when Seth was around, transformed into a barking monster, shouting orders at the men and threatening them with whips when Seth was elsewhere on the ranch. In the moments that Aurelio snuck away to watch his love, he saw that William watched her, too, and that Seth, his hand proudly patting the back of the red-haired beast as if he were congratulating his firstborn son on the extraordinary prize, only encouraged their courtship. From years of silent observation in his parents' small shop, Aurelio knew how to read people, and Reeve didn't care for William, though she wanted to please her father. He could tell from watching the three together through the window that cast golden light onto his dark shoulders as he crouched in darkness. When William spoke, Reeve's body tensed, her face flushed, and she fixated her eyes on her lap. After responding to him, she darted a look towards her father, her eyes searching for acceptance, then held a small, polite smile on her face when Seth nodded.

And Aurelio knew that Reeve loved him, though he realized she didn't know it herself. The gentle way her body swayed when he was near; her palms open, her smile impossible for her face to obscure; her gray, almond-shaped eyes unable to remain on the platter of eggs or the water glasses, but instead looking for his own. Without words, she spoke volumes to his heart, where love had settled and set itself on dreams.

So when the dreaded day arrived that William took her away for an evening, Aurelio panicked as the flustered Paula tried to prepare and serve the meal for all the workers. Unable to eat, he busied himself with helping her, strolling back and forth between the kitchen and the picnic tables in the backyard, pouring glasses full of water and taking away dirty plates with the efficiency of an experienced waiter. Paula, relieved to have the extra help and admirable of the man who was willing to go the extra mile, kept a note in her mind to tell Seth to offer him more money on that week's measly pay.

When the meal concluded, Aurelio paced in front of the barn, kicking up dust from the well-worn path connected to the house until all the lights and noises had resolved to the slumber of night. The moment he felt all was safe, he dashed into the womblike obscurity of the barn and climbed up the ladder to the loft, where, under the dim light of the stars that shone through the small window, he found a lantern, lit it, and discovered some of Reeve's deepest secrets.

Before she climbed the ladder herself, hours later, her pain was so palpable that it emanated from her soul, and it pinched his skin with cold chills. She staggered through the clusters of hay toward the warm light of the lantern that glowed its orange welcome across Aurelio's tearstained face. She looked small and weak, her hair in sweat-soaked streaks that dangled like prisoners down her back. Her hands were clenched in impenetrable fists and her gray eyes carried the dark clouds of a thunderstorm.

When he clutched her burning body against his own, her despair seeped into his veins. In the hollow heat of the loft, she spoke to him for the first time, her language shifting between Spanish, English, and choked-back sobs.

"I dreamt of you, before you came. Of the mountains in Mexico, of a mother I never knew, of the places you would take me... I dreamt... I dreamt that we would ride a stallion away from here, and that when we came back, my father would open his arms and hold on his face the happiest smile... I knew he couldn't see what I wanted, I was so afraid—" She lost her thoughts, her mind drunk with its high tide of mixed emotions.

"You do have a mother, Reeve. She is in Mexico now, and has curly, dark hair, and the stories of gods and angels to put you to sleep every night..." As he spoke, she felt her life becoming the dream, its surrealism spinning around her body. She experienced dizziness with the black and white emotions that colored her mind: the hate, the love; opposing pieces tumbling together in an echoing ruckus that rang into her ears and through her blood vessels. Fear snuck into the encounter, and she shivered in the heat, her body curling like a fetus in Aurelio's lap.

"William took me..." She found herself searching for the completion of the sentence: "to dinner," or "on a drive," or, "to a field," or, "in the truck," or, "on the seat." The ends of the sentence dangled in front of her mind's eye like the pendulum on her father's grandfather clock. Back and forth, back and forth, the words teased themselves in front of her, but she couldn't choose. Her voice, hoarse from the screams she had finally set free when the physical pain became unbearable, could only repeat, "William took me, William took me, William took me," in a mantra that lasted through the night.

In the shadowy light of predawn, Reeve still chewed on the beginning of the sentence that would never meet its end as Aurelio held her against his body on the back of the horse. Their dreams met on the gallop away from the ranch just as the nightmare of their encounter began.

Chapter 18

She didn't know how long she had been driving. She started off with enough sanity to pack Alejo's diaper bag with extra diapers, two extra sippy cups of warm milk, and three jars of food. But the further down the dark highway she drove, the further away her sanity drifted. She was far away from the city now, the obscure peaks and passes of the mountain wrapping their mystery around her underneath a sky full of stars that she could see without the glare of the metropolitan lights. The road wound through the mountains in a zigzagging, up-and-down way that made her sick with dizziness as she drove. She listened to an old Joni Mitchell tape that had belonged to her mother and whose songs had carried her through her softest childhood memories. She played the tape again and again, the tape player in the car showing no signs of exhaustion as it flipped from one side to the next in a mechanical daze. The songs rang in her ears, but they didn't keep Alejo awake. He had fallen asleep sometime past Golden, but she couldn't say when.

Luisa looked at the clock: 10:15. Then, she glanced at the gas gauge, which threatened her with a red E and a flashing gas pump symbol underneath. She knew she had to stop, but she didn't want to stop until she understood why she had begun, where she was going (everything that was anything to her was east, not west), and how she had reached this point in her so-carefully-planned-out life. She drove and drove until the car began to sputter like a dying cricket, just in time for an exit with an all-night gas station.

She realized she had reached the ski areas. The two-lane road that led to the gas station was lined with shops, restaurants, and ski rental outlets. She pulled into the only open station, its yellow and green sign glowing against the navy blue sky, its fluorescent lights casting a brightness equal to the sun where the gas pumps were covered. As if drawn by thirst to its fuel, her car gasped its last movement in the driveway, and she had to roll in neutral to the closest pump. She stood holding the gas pump in her hand, hot tears in her eyes, wondering if she should go back. She couldn't remember a time in her adult life when all she wanted was to stay away from home. The last time she had driven in a crazy escape like this was when she was sixteen and her first love had broken her heart, and she took her father's car down the highway at a hundred miles an hour, screaming with the rage of that first bittersweet pain. She thought of this now and cursed herself.

"You're twenty-seven," she murmured as she squeezed back into the car. "For Christ sakes, get a hold of yourself."

Luisa looked back at Alejo, who shifted his head a bit and let out a tiny sigh, but remained asleep. She watched the peace resting on his dark eyelashes and pale brown skin. His wavy brown hair curled around his round face, and his small red lips rested partially open. In his right arm, he still clutched the fleece blanket that Reeve had made for him, the blanket he needed for sleep. Luisa watched her son until she felt she could no longer stand to breathe in his relaxed beauty. She turned around and started the car, driving east, driving home.

Aurelio couldn't pay his bills. He hadn't worked in over a year and his small savings account had dried up two months before Carter died. Instead he turned to credit card debt, using the checks that came in the mail from the credit card companies to pay for utilities or the mortgage, and swiping the plastic for what little food he ate and for tequila. When he tumbled onto her living room floor, his eyes drooping from days of restless sleep, Warren managed to sober him enough to speak. He begged her to help him, to take him to AA meetings, to lend him some money for his bills, to come clean up the house so he could sell it, to forgive him. Luisa, boggled down by the duality of her pain, had asked Warren to drive him home and got in the car herself.

Clara had always known exactly what to say. Her mouth poured out most of the thoughts that entered her mind, and she never learned the importance of clapping her lips together. One of the reasons Luisa and Clara had become such good friends was Luisa's acceptance of Clara's opinionated nature, something that turned off many of their classmates. But when Carter's death took her for the shock of her life, Clara found her thoughts dazed, running through her mind like a lost child, and her mouth had no words. The time ticked by and Luisa carried on the best she could. Clara, her language vanished, instead took action. Two or three times a week for two months, she drove over to Luisa's house to vacuum, do laundry, cook dinner, feed Alejo, or pay her bills. She took care of her in the only way she knew at the time; but Luisa, who began to surface from the depths of the grief, wanted Clara to stop moving, slow down, and talk.

In high school, she and Clara had a pact. It was a promise they made their freshman year, when they were still just young enough to enjoy a sleepover. They had stayed up most of the night talking about the boys they liked and how they'd probably never go out with any of them, and the teachers at school, and their annoying parents, when a silence entered the room.

"Let's make a promise," Clara had said. "If either one of us is ever in trouble, for the rest of our lives, no matter where we live, the other one will drop everything to be there." Spoken in the early hours of the morning, they had shaken hands and held close to the words that come with the passion of youth.

Thirteen years later, the day after Aurelio came to visit, when Luisa called Clara at her editing job downtown in the early afternoon, Clara hung up the phone and told her managing editor that she had a personal emergency and had to leave. It was early summer, and the air conditioning broke in her old Honda Civic before she was halfway across town. Her back and neck were soaked with sweat, leaving a tear-shaped stain on her navy blue shirt. In the nervous habit she had when stressed, she bit off all her fingernails on the drive over. She couldn't imagine what else could have gone wrong in Luisa's life to make her cry so on the phone, but she guessed it probably had something to do with Aurelio.

When she arrived, Luisa's face puckered and held a sickly look of bewilderment. She didn't come to the door when Clara rang, but sat on the couch with her knees pulled tight against her chest, staring across the room like a person on drugs. Clara sat on the loveseat opposite her and put down her purse. Her keys jangled as the small fabric purse hit the floor. It was the only sound.

Her practicality taking over, she said in a soft voice, "Is Alejo still asleep?" Luisa nodded. They sat across from each other, avoiding eye contact, for several minutes. Finally Luisa's mouth opened.

"Do you ever think that God tests some people, but not others?" In the midst of the sentence, her voice weak as if she'd been asleep, she had to clear her throat. Clara didn't answer. In her mind, she could picture Luisa's thoughts, which could run by like images on a television screen. In one TV show was Clara's life, with her happily married parents, her ever-loving sister, her great husband, and secure job. No one had any major problems, and no one close to her had ever died. The show could line up with Leave it to Beaver; it was so sweet and perfect. And the other show, Luisa's life, her unemployed-and-often-missing brother, her distraught single mother, her alcoholic father, no extended family, and her husband killed suddenly. Her show might line up with a modern drama like Party of Five where everything went wrong for one family for years until the show was canceled because viewers just couldn't handle it anymore.

"Because what did I do? What is someone trying to prove to me? That life sucks, but I have to keep going just for the hell of it? Sometimes in the morning, just before my alarm goes off or Alejo cries for me, when I am in that half-asleep dream state that I so used to love, I think he's still there, sleeping like a log next to me. He never moved, always slept still on his side, never snored, never made a peep, never even woke up. And before I open my eyes, I swear I can feel him there, the warmth of his body within arm's reach. It's like, the feeling is so real, how can he be gone?" Luisa's eyes focused on the ashes in the fireplace. In a dull, steady, monotone she spoke, her body immovable.

"And then, as if God had to remind me of how crappy everything else in my life was outside of my wonderful marriage, my father came to the door. Just like that, one day, after all these years, he decided he needed me. Needed me. Why? Not because he wants to offer his love or do anything for himself, God no. He needs me to pay his fucking bills and drag him to the meetings he should have gone to thirty years ago and clean his house, his life, his goddamn mess." Her voice rose, trying to expunge herself of her emotions.

"And I have a son who—" she couldn't continue. She felt the need to talk about Alejo, because she knew that she hadn't given enough to him since Carter died. She had, instead, held his father's death against him in a way, and had only given him his basic needs, not wanting to be so close to all he represented, all the dreams she would never maintain, all the happiness she could have had if Carter were still here. She wanted to tell Clara how guilty she felt each day, on top of her feelings of grief, and how the combination of the two emotions caused getting out of bed or putting on clothes or cooking dinner the most draining tasks she could imagine. She wanted to tell Clara that she couldn't handle anything else, and in particular her father, or she might burst inside, lose what little threads of hope still clung together in her barely-sane mind, and go completely crazy. She wanted to tell Clara that she didn't have any answers to any of the problems that slammed her in the gut, that, for the first time in her life, she felt surrounded by injustice. But she sat on the couch with her legs tight against her chest and her lips equally tight, unable to think of how to say anything at all.

Clara spoke. "I can't begin to understand your position, because your life is so different from mine. All I can do is be here for you, and offer you my help and guidance. I'll do whatever it takes. Do you need money? Emotional support? Someone to take Alejo away for a day or two so you can stop and breathe?" Clara tried to ask the questions slowly, pausing between each one. But she didn't receive a positive or negative response until she mentioned Alejo. Then, tears inundated Luisa's eyes. Clara knew then what it was. She twirled the pieces of the sentence around in her mind before she said it. When she opened her mouth, she poured out the words as a candy maker pours sugar over his lollipops.

"Alejo reminds you too much of Carter and your previous life, and it's just too much to bear." She didn't want to change the pitch of her voice, and tried to catch Luisa's eye, but Luisa crumpled into a convulsive ball, her head buried in the depths of her thighs.

Clara loved Luisa in the way a mother loves her child, unequivocal and lasting. "Did you think I would hold that against you, or not understand? I would feel the same way if—" But she couldn't finish. Instead, hearing Alejo's intermittent sobs, she went upstairs into his bedroom, packed several days' clothes into the navy blue diaper bag, and changed his diaper. She carried him downstairs, pulled out seven jars of food and three sippy cups from the cupboard, four bibs, five towels, and three spoons from the drawer, and his jacket from the coat closet.

Luisa's head rose. Her red face held a look of confusion and hope. "He knows me almost as well as he knows you. He needs a break. You need a break. Take a few days and breathe. Try to figure things out. Call me when you're ready and I'll bring him home."

When Clara left, Luisa remained on the couch for an hour more. At first, she thought only of guilt. How could she let someone come in and take her son away? She wanted to call Clara's cell phone and tell her to turn around. But she didn't move. She thought of Alejo, who smiled and waved as she carried him out the door, unaware of their arrangement, his innocence profound and touching. She started to think that perhaps Clara had the right idea, and that they both needed a break, and that, when she saw her son after a few days, she wouldn't have the sick feeling in her heart every time she held him close to her. Then, Luisa's thoughts wandered, and she remembered when Alejo was just three weeks old and she had wanted to take an all day pottery class at the art museum that was being taught by a famous sculptor. She was so nervous about leaving Alejo with Carter that she had composed a three page note detailing his feeding, napping, and diapering schedule, when to use the pacifier, how to soothe him when he fussed, and other small tasks. When she was at the museum, she left the class every hour to go into the large entryway atrium and call Carter from her cell phone, just to make sure everything was OK. In his calm, patient way, he told her not to worry, and that Alejo could survive one day without his mother. When she returned home at twilight, Carter held Alejo on his chest as they enjoyed a peaceful sleep on the living room couch. And without knowing why, Luisa had begun to cry, not from sadness, but from the joy that can only come from a perfect picture of love.

Luisa was shaken from her reminiscence by the phone. She didn't answer it, but shifted her position on the couch, and realized that, for the first time since Carter had died, she was able to recall a single happy memory. The memory danced in front of her like the flame of a candle: she felt its warm glow on her face. Carter had shown her such love, and now Clara, acting from her heart, proved that love still existed in her life. She stood up from the couch, picked up her keys, and headed for the car. It was a long drive, but she needed to go.

Chapter 19

Underneath the rows of maple and ash trees that shed seeds on the gray pavement and that had been planted when the houses were built, the street in front of Warren's childhood home came to life after school each day. From the small porches, women sewed patches on the holes of their sons' dungarees and lace trim on the dresses for their daughters as they rocked in old wooden chairs and watched over their children. The street, which had little traffic while the fathers were still at work, caught the high-pitched laughter and yells of kids playing hide-n-seek, stickball, or kick-the-can. As if drawn to the outdoors by the warm sun that bore down over the city for most of the year, the children occupied the street and each other's lives with harmonious community. Often, the mothers would sit on neighbors' porches to chat or gossip while sharing a drink of iced tea. They all knew each other's names, the names of their children and their husbands, as most of the people in the predominantly Italian neighborhood attended the local Catholic Church. Keeping secrets wasn't easy underneath the meandering eyes of the women, but Doris had mastered the technique.

Never once did she mention Warren's name or existence, and admonished her other children follow her lead. Rose, now nearly three, scarcely knew of his presence on the cold basement floor. When Doris sat on the porch in the early afternoon, she held a calm expression on her face that reflected nothing but a relaxed family, though everyone on the block knew of her dire circumstances since her husband abandoned them. Rather than whispering behind her back, most of the women made a mission of helping the pleasant Doris with her children, offering them meals and taking care of her children when she had to see the doctor. Largely pregnant, Doris's ankles swelled so that she could barely walk by her ninth month, and the ladies didn't flinch when she no longer appeared on her porch.

Margaret Marie came into the world on Warren's seventh birthday. When Doris's water broke in the dark hours of the morning, she called her son up the stairs from the basement and ordered him to soak up the liquid with the shreds he wore for clothes. She knew that she had been cursed, and that another son would enter her life, and she planned nothing but the death of the child. Frankie, old enough now to watch over the rest, stayed home with Warren, his brothers and sister while Doris went to the hospital. Warren again was able to taste the brief relief that came with his mother's absence.

Frankie was in his last year of school. Doris had insisted that, at thirteen, he had to start working and become the new man of the house. Frankie, always thin and shorter than most of the boys in his class, had found solace in the schoolyard or in the warmth of his bed by reading books that took him to faraway lands, places where men went on wild adventures and came home to beautiful women who kissed them and gave them happy families where all the children were loved. Frankie didn't know what he would be able to do if not read, and dreaded the day he had to quit school and find a job. He cursed his father for being such a coward, and for leaving him with the responsibility of taking care of the family and trying to keep his mother's hands away from Warren. He began to look deeper into himself, trying to discover where his strengths lay, because he felt his spirit being crushed by the thick tension in the house from day to day.

When Doris was gone for three days giving birth to Margaret, Frankie carried Warren up the steps and offered him some of Kenny's old clothes. He fixed him three hot meals a day, giving him cinnamon apple oatmeal each morning, hearty dishes of pasta or vegetables and eggs for lunch, and dinners that included chicken or beef and potatoes or rice. Frankie had learned to cook when Frank left, and Doris decided that taking care of the children was not enough, and that the oldest should have the responsibility of providing for the family their daily meals. She received food stamps that barely covered the meals that the family needed, and took Frankie to the stores with her, where he became an expert bargain shopper. He learned to pick the cheapest cuts of meat and buy foods in bulk, and to avoid the popular name brands and luxuries like syrup or potato chips. Their daily trips to the stores around their neighborhood always included Doris's ritual stop at the Church, where she prayed again for another daughter. Frankie prayed, too, not for a sister, but the untouchable hope that his mother's heart would soften.

While his mother was gone, Warren, whose body came to life with food in his stomach, enjoyed common games that had been denied to him for his lifetime. He played stickball, kickball, hide-n-seek, and kick-the-can with his brothers and the boys on the street. The neighborhood kids, who hadn't ever seen Warren come out of the house, hardly knew he existed. When they saw the scrawny boy running about with a smile plastered to his face, they asked Kenny and Freddy if he was their cousin. The older boys, nonchalant about what their friends thought, answered with the truth. Most of the boys just nodded or asked one or two questions about why he didn't usually play with them, to which Freddy would reply, "Oh, he just doesn't usually like to play outside," with a quick tongue and a motion to get on with the game.

It was Bobby Giovanni who couldn't keep his curious mind from the strange arrival of the new child. It was the second day that Doris was in the hospital, and Frankie had already announced that Mother would be bringing home another daughter, when Bobby asked his mother about Warren.

"How come Freddy and Kenny's brother never plays with us or goes to school?" Bobby stood in his mother's yellow kitchen, where she kneaded the dough for that evening's bread. Bobby, a taut, tan-skinned Italian with black curly hair, at the age of eight already stood shoulder high to his mother's five-foot frame. His mother, Francine, clenched the dough between her long fingers and shifted her weight beneath the ankle-length navy blue dress. She caught her breath and used her wrist to push aside a loose, dark curl from her forehead.

"Who, Frankie? He's a bit too old to play stickball, sweetie," she said, and returned to her task.

"No, Mama, not Frankie. Warren. He just came out yesterday and I've never seen him before." Bobby's hands were coated in a layer of grime from the afternoon games, where he had pitched and scored three runs. He rubbed his hands down the sides of his tan slacks as his brown eyes searched his mother's round face for answers.

"Warren? Why..." Francine tried to recall another boy emerging from the house in the three years they had lived on the street. She knew of Frankie, Freddy, and Kenny, and the little girl, Rose, who all followed Doris around like obedient ducks in a line when she dressed them for Church each Sunday. Many times, Francine, her husband Robert, and Bobby had sat in the same pew with the family, whose life seemed tragic when their father disappeared one day. But never had Francine seen a fifth child. She thought Bobby must be confused, or worse, lying.

"I don't know what you mean, Bobby. The Yorks don't have another boy. He must be another neighborhood boy, or a relative from out of town, or you have him confused with someone else."

"No, Mama, I asked them about him, and they said he was their brother, but that he didn't like to play outside."

Francine grew impatient. She had to chop the carrots to surround the pot roast in the oven and peel the potatoes before mashing them. She knew that Bobby loved to tell stories, but she didn't see the point of this one. "Bobby," leaning over, she cupped his dimpled chin in the palm of her hand. "you know that lying is wrong. Remember what the priest said? When you lie, it's a sin. And when you sin, you—"

Bobby yanked his face away from his mother's grasp. "I'm not lying, Mama, see for yourself!" and he ran outside. Francine sighed and walked over to the window. In the street, she saw the usual neighborhood boys: Kenny and Freddy York, George and Jack DeLauro, Eric and Rudy Ciarlo, and Tommy Lapetino. Bobby had been playing with these boys for as long as she could remember, and she knew their faces, their voices, and the names and phone numbers of all their mothers. Just as she was about to walk away from the window, she noticed the tiny, emaciated child who hid behind Freddy. He stepped up to the plate with the thin stick in his hand, his body shaking, but with an anticipatory smile on his face. Without even questioning it, she knew that, with the orange hair that distinguished the Yorks from everyone else on the block, the little boy had to be part of their family. Francine's heart fluttered inside her chest as she reached for the phone. She called her husband and then Social Services. When she hung up, she waltzed outside and invited the entire York family over for supper. Warren tasted roast beef for the first time, along with his first taste of love from a mother.

The social worker, Mavis McFadden, never had a family of her own. Like a devout nun, she had committed her life to the welfare of other people's children. Mavis, a stout, blond Scottish lady who took second helpings of everything from dessert to hugs, dressed in frumpy homemade dresses from secondhand material leftover from quilts she had made. She had a singsong voice and a friendly disposition that allowed her to enter people's homes without their guards coming up. She was assigned to the York case in the early spring of 1958, when most women remained married to their husbands, and most men, who had defended their country in the war, worked in blue-collar jobs that put food on the table.

But Mavis didn't deal with most people. She dealt only with the misguided families who had fallen apart for one reason or another. Often, alcohol or childhood abuse led to the neglect and abuse she saw in the children.

When she arrived at the Yorks' house, her mind questioned the validity of the neighbor's accusations. In a detailed written statement that Mavis had read over that morning, Francine Giovanni had described a thin, poorly dressed child whom she didn't know existed until just two days ago. But as Mavis pulled her Model T Ford onto the street that contained nothing but clean-cut green lawns, well-trimmed bushes, and lush flower gardens lining each ranch house, she wondered how accurate the statement was. Usually, Mavis's work took her to the poorer areas of town where the houses were a conglomerate of thrown-together shacks leftover from the Depression and small-sided structures containing a single bedroom and an outhouse in the back. She had visited streets such as this before, but on rare occasions, and the problem almost always involved a husband who drank too much and hit his children in a drunken stupor. Mavis had never before read a statement that said an unknown child suddenly appeared when the mother went to deliver another baby. She was filled with concern, yet intrigued, as she rang the doorbell of the small ranch. A warm smile came over her face as Doris opened the door. She wanted to help the family get through the difficult time they were having, and the only way she knew to do that was to be friendly and cooperative.

"Hello, are you Mrs. York? I'm Mavis McFadden from Social Services. May I come in?" Mavis held out her hand to the tall woman who still bulged from her recent delivery. Doris, nervous and sweating, shifted the newborn Margaret from one arm to the other and reached out her bony hand.

"Please, come in," she said in a quiet voice, motioning for Mavis to sit on the peach-colored sofa. "Frankie, will you fix us some iced tea?" she asked in a steady voice.

Frankie, without saying a word, retreated into the kitchen. Kenny and Freddy stood like Swiss Army guards around Warren and Rose, who huddled together and pretended to play jacks on the hardwood floor. Doris placed Margaret in a bassinet and then sat across from Mavis in the matching peach wingback chair, her back stiff and her fingers interlaced on top of her solid black dress.

"I'm pleased to meet you, Mrs. York. Let me take a moment to discuss what's going to happen in the next few months. First of all, let me explain why I am here. We received information from a neighbor that you have a young son, perhaps four or five, whom you have been leaving home alone when you leave the house to go to church or elsewhere. I am here to verify the truth of that statement and to study your family life. I will be making six visits over the next four months, and if I determine that you are neglecting any of your children, they will be removed from the home. If I determine that there are no signs of neglect, then you may continue with your life as it is."

Warren, on his knees and wearing a new outfit that Doris had purchased for him from a thrift store that morning, tried to understand what the woman said. He knew that the boy she spoke of must be him, but Frankie told him he was seven, not four or five. He didn't know what she meant by the words "neglecting" or "removed," but her voice lowered when she said those words, so he knew it couldn't be good news. But everything else about the woman and her arrival into his life made him feel safe. His mother had not only bought him new clothes, but fed him a hot breakfast of pancakes and eggs that morning, and stroked his hair and told him she loved him. He knew she did that because the social worker was coming, but he didn't care. He wanted more than anything for his mother to love him.

Doris created an artificial life in response to Mavis's speech. "Let me introduce you to my children," she said, and held open her palms. "This is Frankie, my oldest. He's twelve. Freddy here is nearly eleven, and Kenny is nine and a half. My youngest boy, Warren, is seven, and Rose is three. And of course, the baby, Margaret, is only six days old." Doris painted a smile on her face.

When she received the call from Social Services the night before, she had called all her children into the kitchen. "A lady is going to come to our house tomorrow," she had said, placing her arms on the shoulders of Freddy and Kenny. "She isn't a nice lady. She's going to come and talk to us about our family, and she'll try to separate you from me. She will probably tell you that we're better off apart. But she'll be wrong." Doris had said a calm, steady voice as she spoke. "Now all of you know," she began, casting a look of warning at Frankie, who stood with his arms crossed as he leaned against the stove, "that Warren has to sleep in the basement because he's been sick since the day he was born. I don't want him getting everyone sick, and that's why he doesn't play with everyone or go to school." She had moved her eyes from peachy, freckled face to peachy, freckled face, making contact with each set of green eyes, stopping at last on Warren's.

"You know that, don't you, Warren?" and even as she said the words, she grasped his upper arm, digging her nails into his skin. Her children had all trapped their thoughts somewhere between their minds and their tongues, fearful that they would never be able to see each other again. They nodded at their mother.

Now, as Doris introduced her children, she could see the glint in Mavis's eye as she said Warren's name. Without losing her composure, she said,

"I know what this is about. Warren, my youngest boy, has been sick since he was born. He was born with pneumonia, and he never really got over being a thin, weak child. He has a very weak immune system, but I've never been able to afford to get him the best medical care. And my husband, Frank, took his drunken anger out on him. The police already came a few months ago, but they were unable to find Frank. And with my husband gone—" Doris put her hand to her chest and drew in a gasping breath. "With my husband gone, I can barely afford to put food on the table, and now I have another mouth to feed. Warren has stayed home because I think it is safer for him. I would hate for him to get sick and..." Doris lowered her voice as she let the sentence trail into nothing.

Mavis had a kind heart. She wanted to see the best in people. The house was clean, and all the other children looked healthy and lively. Their expressions were calm and innocent when Doris introduced them, and now the three older boys stood shoulder to shoulder in a united front. She wanted to believe that Doris cared for all her children in the same way, because she could see that the woman had love in her heart. But her job was not just to see the good in people, but also to recognize the bad and do something about it. And to Mavis, Warren looked like the smallest seven-year-old child she had ever seen. The way he cowered on the floor, avoided eye contact with his mother, and was unusually silent caused Mavis to think that Doris must be lying.

"Mrs. York, I think I would like to speak to Warren outside on the porch, if that would be all right."

Doris tried not to show the fear that burned beneath her skin. "Yes, of course," she said, the words barely audible.

Mavis crouched on the floor next to Warren and gently laid her hand on his back. "Would you like to come outside with me?" she asked. Warren nodded and stood up. His new khaki slacks swept against each other as he walked toward the door with Mavis. He caught a brief glance of his mother as he closed the door behind him. She nodded, as if to reinforce the conversation she'd had with him that morning in the thrift store. "Remember, Warren," she had said, "if you tell the lady I'm mean to you, you'll never see your brothers or sisters again." Doris knew that the only place Warren had in his heart for love was dedicated to his big brother Frankie and his sister Rose, the only two siblings who brought an inkling of peace to his life, and that he would rather die than go without either of them.

Mavis sat in the rocking chair, and Warren sat across from her in the white wicker chair where Doris's neighbors often sat to chat. Warren, his scrawny legs dangling well above the concrete floor, crossed his arms over his stomach and stared at the flowers that lined the side of the porch.

Mavis waited a few moments before speaking. "Warren, I'm going to ask you a few questions, is that all right?" Her voice, and her movements, were soft and delicate. Warren felt he could say anything to her. He nodded.

"Do you know the difference between lying and telling the truth, Warren?" she asked.

Warren was confused, and didn't know how to answer the question, so he lifted his chin in a weak nod.

"Telling a lie means you are not saying what really happens. But when you tell the truth, you tell me just what happens and how you feel about it. When you tell a lie, it is wrong. Telling the truth is always a good idea, because it will help you be a better person and have a better life." Mavis paused to see any sign of recognition in Warren's face, but he held his face away from her. "Do you think that you could tell me only the truth today, Warren?" Mavis leaned forward and tickled his chin with her fingertips. She raised his chin in her cupped palm as she looked into his eyes.

Warren loved the soft touch of her hand and felt himself smiling back. "Yes," he whispered, "I think so."

Warren and Mavis held each other's eyes for a few minutes longer before Mavis moved. When she did, she reached into her black canvas bag and pulled out a thick pad of paper and some crayons. "Do you like to draw, Warren?" she asked. Warren had never drawn anything before, so he shrugged his shoulders.

"Do you think you could draw me a picture of where you sleep, Warren?" Mavis leaned over and handed him the pad of paper and held out two crayons: red and black. The pad felt heavy and warm in his lap, and the crayons were hard and shiny as he clutched them in his palm. Holding the black crayon in the center of his palm with his fingers encircling it, Warren began to draw. He started out slowly, unsure of how to work with the crayon and paper. But once he saw how easily he was able to mark the page, he drew a detailed illustration of his cot, the dividers, the small basement window above where he slept, and the thin blanket. His hands moved with passion and vengeance as the image of his cold sleeping area flooded his mind and then his fingertips. He drew himself on the page, a tiny figurine curled in the fetal position on one corner of the cot.

When he finished, Warren lifted his freckled face up to see what Mavis would say. He didn't move the picture from his lap as she examined it, looking back and forth between his face and the drawing. She trapped in a fretful sigh and instead sucked in a long breath of air.

"Warren, do you think you could tell me about the picture?" her voice remained calm and soothing to his ears, and he wanted to tell her everything. But he thought of what his mother had said, and thought that if he never saw Frankie again he didn't know if he could ever be happy. He shook his head and cast his eyes at the flowers again.

Instead of explaining the picture, he whispered, "I know my mother loves me," and managed to keep the tears from spilling out of the corners of his eyes.

"Why don't we go inside," Mavis said, standing up and laying her hand like a feather on Warren's back, "and you can show me where you sleep?"

Warren felt incapable of motion. His voice panicky, he lifted his eyes and looked into Mavis's warm face. "Please don't take me away," he pleaded, "I like it here." All he could hope, in the brief instant between her reaction and her response, was that she would listen to him and grant him his one request.

Chapter 20

Ambushed by the army of emotions that had taken over her life in two months, Luisa entered Aurelio's house with a sneer on her face and a slam of the door. She called for her father several times, her voice carrying along the molded ceilings, through the small bedrooms and down into the finished basement where she and Byron used to play ping-pong in the rec room. He didn't acknowledge her greeting, at least not in words. When she approached his bedroom, she could hear the his heavy breaths. Infuriated, Luisa stomped to the kitchen, rustled through the various plastic containers in the bottom cabinet, yanked out a large blue pitcher, and filled it with cold water.

She marched back into the bedroom and flooded Aurelio's face and hair with the icy awakening, shouting, "I have no sympathy for you! I have no sympathy for you!" She wanted to say why, to explain that the things that had happened in his life were minor conflicts in comparison to the hurdles she was chosen to overcome, his alcoholism being her first and biggest until the horrific death of her husband, who was rumored to have been hit by a drunk driver, of all ironies. She wanted to tell him to get his sorry ass out of bed, clean up his house, and pour out every last bottle of tequila. She wanted to plead with him to go to AA, to enroll in a detox center, to pay his bills, so that he could spend time with his only grandchild. But what she wanted to say and what she expunged from her lungs were two different species.

"I hate you for ruining my life, for making me think that the only happiness I could ever have was in the arms of my husband, whom I no longer have! I hate you for taking Mom out of Texas, and making it so that I don't have any grandparents! I hate you! I hate you for drinking and ruining everyone's life!"

Taken over by sobs, Luisa crumpled down next to her wet, but very awake, father. She immediately regretted her speech because it was another example of how she felt out of control in her life, from her relationship with her father, to her guilt over raising Alejo the wrong way, to the words that escaped from her mouth. She cried, her face buried in the greasy sheets, thinking that this was it, the end of the end, the last thing she could stand before she became consumed by a depression that would swallow her whole. She cried, not wanting him to see her face, her body unable to lift the heavy weight of her broken heart. She cried, not because she wanted him to feel sorry for her, but because she couldn't think of one happy thing to dry up her tears. Instead, they flooded from her depths like a volcano erupting after hundreds of years of tortuous enclosure.

Aurelio stiffened with bewilderment. His brown hands reached for Luisa's back, where he began tickling her with his fingertips. His movements were soft and tranquil as he touched her. He had no words to fill her mind with a reply. He only held the regret of a lifetime that released itself in the gentle touch between father and daughter.

An inestimable amount of time passed in the quietude of the room, where Luisa's sobs relaxed into suppressed murmurs of pain, and Aurelio's hand began to work the tension from her back. She thought of her childhood, when her father's tender touch soothed her off to sleep each night. She wanted to capture those memories and trap them inside a jar that she could open when she felt sad, and release the happy recollections like butterflies, their brightly colored wings fluttering in beauty before her eyes. Thinking of the brief moments of happiness from her youth helped Luisa control the sobbing until, after some time, she no longer cried. Aurelio stopped touching her and she pushed herself up, her eyes a swollen red as she looked across at him. She waited, but she had nothing to say to him until he spoke. Aurelio looked back at his daughter through sober eyes for the first time in years. He commanded that his own tears stay within him as he opened his mouth to speak.

"I want you to do something for me," he began, his voice hoarse and shaky. "I've been meaning to do it for a long time. I want you to take the manuscript, type it into a word processing program, and begin sending it away to publishing agents."

Luisa's eyes widened in surprise. She had expected Aurelio to ask her for a loan, to take him to AA meetings, to take him to a detox center, to clean up his house to prepare it for selling, or to drive him to Mexico to reunite with his family. She never expected him to bring up the forbidden topic of the manuscript, the infamous manuscript that brought him to the United States, the tales that his mother and grandmothers had filled his childhood with, the manuscript that represented all of his dreams and failures. Without saying anything, Luisa knew where it was, in the brown leather satchel inside a plastic filing box with a blue lid in the far back corner of the crawl space in the basement, behind the Christmas decorations and several boxes of clothes. She knew where it was because she had discovered when she was fifteen, searching for a diary she had kept and hidden at the age of nine, and when she emerged with its beauty, the pages filled with the dark, delicate handwriting of a writer in love with his craft, Aurelio had admonished her to her room, never to mention the manuscript again. Later that night, she had asked her mother why her father was so upset, and her mother broke down and told her some of her father's history, and how important it was not to follow such a ridiculous dream, and especially not to center your life around the vague possibility of its success. More than twelve years had passed since the incident, and no one in her family had ever mentioned the manuscript again before this moment.

Luisa didn't know what to say. She held her eyes wide and her mouth closed, as if in anticipation of words that would come to her if she waited long enough. Instead, her father spoke again.

"It's too late for me. But not for you. I know you think your life is over now that Carter is gone, but the truth is, it's just beginning. My mother and I..." his voice trailed off for an instant. "My mother and I had a gift with words. You have a gift for art. I know why you didn't want to major in art in college. Because you wanted to be sure to go into a career that was safe. You wanted to be safe, and art can be so risky. I know why you needed safety, why you wanted to marry so young. I know you, Luisa, better than you think."

Luisa lowered her eyes. What he said was true, though she would never admit it to him.

"I want you to illustrate the book. There are ten beautiful stories that could use your talented hand to create their images. And when you send it away, the publishers will see what a gem it is, and they will not turn it away, not if they know what quality literature is."

Aurelio stopped, as if waiting for her to respond. But before she could think of something to say, he continued. The last sentence was the one he had practiced over and over, wanted more than anything to say it right, in a serious, determined tone, so that she would truly believe him this time.

"If you do this for me, I will stop drinking." He captured her eyes in the pools of his own. Luisa's heart fluttered, and she wanted more than anything to look away, to walk out of the room, to curse him again for lying, and to shut the door as she left, never to return. But she didn't. Instead, she reached out and took his hands into her own. She maintained eye contact and felt a small smile appear on her face.

"OK, Papa," she whispered. "Let's go get the manuscript."

They retreated into the basement storage room, where a crawl space had been built along with the house over sixty years ago. The storage room, which had been rummaged through by Reeve when she'd moved out two years ago, was once organized by category with neatly packed boxes labeled in black permanent marker. Now, coated in a layer of dust and decorated with cobwebs, disheveled piles of clothes, books, magazines, pots and pans, plates, camping equipment, and bottle after bottle of tequila lay in a scattered mess beneath the fluorescent lights. The storage room represented one more aspect of Aurelio's life that had fallen apart when Reeve took away her love and left him cold, lonely, and without the will to do anything but drink. Luisa sighed when she saw the disastrous mess.

"When you stop drinking," she said to her father, "you're going to clean up the house, right?"

Aurelio said, "I'm going to start cleaning up the house today, and stop drinking as we speak. Because I have faith that we will both succeed."

Luisa felt overwhelmed by the mess. She tried to overlook the half-opened boxes as she stumbled over them on the way to the crawl space. In the dark corner of the storage room, she saw the familiar plastic file box and placed her palms on either side, shuffling it out, side to side, until she had pulled its heaviness onto the concrete floor in front of her. She peered inside the blue corner, but could scarcely see anything.

"Papa, do you have a flashlight?" she asked as she reached in and felt the cold walls. Before her father could answer, her hands landed on the leather bag, now rough from years of stale stillness. "Never mind. I found it." The bag, too, felt heavy as she pulled it out. She clasped the handle in her right palm and rose to a standing position. The weight of the satchel strained her fingers as she walked out of the storage room into the rec room. She cleared off a lumpy pile of clothes that reeked of alcohol, reached for the floor lamp that had stood in the same place next to the couch for ten years, and turned it on. She sat with the satchel in her lap, feeling the warmth of her legs move into the leather. She stared down at it, unable to open it, as her father appeared in front of her.

"Promise me one thing?" she said, her eyes focused on the bronze clasp that held the leather strap tightly closed.

"Si, Mi Hija?" Aurelio spoke in Spanish as if the magnitude of the situation would be invalid in Luisa's native tongue.

"Promise me that you will tell me the story behind these stories, and what happened to you to make you fail, if I get this published."

"That's a hard thing to talk about, Luisa," her father whispered. "There are reasons why your mother and I—" he wanted to tell her about the night they fell in love, the same night that Reeve had her heart and body crushed by another man. But he had suppressed the truth for thirty years, and he felt himself clawing at it now like a rabid dog searching for its prey, incapable of attaining the sanity that might come with its release from his mind. He paused before he said, "There are reasons why your mother and I never told you about how we met. We wanted to protect you."

"Protect me from what?" But as she asked the question, she didn't want to know the answer. She couldn't look at her father. Her palms began to sweat against the sides of the bag that she clutched on her lap.

"It's a long story, Luisa, and I can't tell it today. I have a lot of work to do, and so do you. Where will you stay to work on this?" He wanted to ask her to come home, to help him get his life back together, but he thought it would be too much for one day.

"I have an idea," Luisa said, still avoiding his face. "But I don't want to talk about it until I'm sure."

When Warren had returned from driving Aurelio home two days before, he had come back to Luisa's house to sit down with her and tell her more about his life. In a story that lasted for the remainder of the afternoon and part of the evening, Warren admitted that he had been watching Luisa, Carter, and Alejo through the window.

"It was as if I saw a glimpse of the life I could have had, if only I hadn't held my childhood against everyone I met so that no one ever came close. Now I have virtually no contact with anyone from my life, no friends, and no family. And I have all this money—" he had stopped in mid-sentence to catch her eye, to examine her expression, to read any level of desire that she might display. And, seeing none, he had continued with ease, as if he had practiced the speech in front of the mirror that morning.

"And I want to help you get back on your feet. Don't say no. Don't. I can see in your eyes that you have been searching for a hand."

"OK, then," Aurelio said. "Would you like to open the satchel and take a look?" He pushed another pile of clothes onto the filthy carpet and pulled the strap through the buckle. He reached inside and gently untied the twine that felt like home to his hands. With the care of a surgeon reaching for his scalpel, he pulled the manuscript out of the bag. The thick, expensive, cream-colored paper rested heavily on his palms as he placed the stack on his thighs. The first page, which he had painstakingly practiced several times on scrap paper before laying out the beautiful black calligraphy that now centered itself on the paper with a delicate floral design, held the name of the manuscript and the truth to Aurelio's fears and desires. Los Suenos Olvidades: Historias Perdidos de Mexico.

Luisa gasped as she read the words, and said them aloud in English. "The Forgotten Dreams: Lost Stories of Mexico." She wondered how much of her father's life the pages contained.

Chapter 21

The summer slithered into southern Texas under the sneaky pretense that there had been a spring. The sun shone over the ranch in its burning brightness at a hundred degrees or more each day from March on. Seth couldn't remember a hotter spring or summer than the one when he lost Reeve. He spent restless nights, before and after her disappearance, tossing on top of the white sheets of his bed, the sweat sticking to every pore of his body and keeping him awake. The oscillating floor fan that stood next to his bed just reinforced the hot air again and again into his face. The work of the ranch became exhausting in the heat, and many of the workers passed out or became sick from dehydration during the day so that Seth felt he had to do most of the work himself. He rose an hour earlier each morning, trying to catch the darkest hour before the dawn in hopes that the glaring sun's absence would allow him some relief in his labor.

The night that William and Reeve returned from their date, Seth had already gone to bed, but couldn't sleep. He listened as the screen door slammed shut. He expected to hear laughter or voices, but all he heard was the water running in the bathroom below his bedroom. He wondered how the date had gone, and hoped that William and Reeve would fall in love. All he wanted was his daughter's happiness, and he couldn't see any other way for her to be happy without the love of an educated rancher. Reeve had always been a quiet girl who respected him and did as she was told, and he loved the simplicity of her personality. His life as a single father was that much easier.

That night, Seth tossed and turned even more than usual. The next morning would be important, because the local vet, Dr. Finch, would be driving out to the ranch to examine his pregnant cows. Seth had both skill and luck when it came to breeding his cows, and this year he had over a hundred young cows expecting. Dr. Finch and his assistant, a young boy named Carl, would arrive at the ranch just before dawn, and they wouldn't leave until after dark, or however long it took until all the cows had been examined. Seth always felt antsy when people came to the ranch. He spent so much of his life in the solitary work, or amongst men who didn't speak his language, that he had nearly grown into a recluse. He shuddered at the arrival of anyone new. Having William on hand had opened him up a bit. Thinking of William and Reeve and hoping that everything had gone well also kept him awake for most of the night. From the movement of the full moon across the sky that Seth watched from his small bedroom window, he knew that many hours had lapsed between his bedtime and his sleep time. When he finally began to doze, he entered a fitful sleep of vivid dreams that woke him in cold sweats but that eliminated themselves from his memory upon awakening.

In the one cool hour before the sun rose, Seth rose himself and headed downstairs to the kitchen. He began the pot of coffee before Reeve or Paula arrived because he knew he wouldn't make it long without it. He decided to sit out on the front porch for a few minutes and enjoy the quietude that could come when all were asleep on the ranch. The moon, which had fallen to the horizon, still lit up the sky, casting silver threads of light and shadow on the ranch structures and trees. Seth relaxed his aching six-foot frame into the old pine rocking chair that his grandfather had made for his grandmother years ago. The hardwood floorboards of the porch bore whitewashed scars where the rocking chair sat. Seth put his hard-bottomed cowboy boots on the floor and tapped, causing the chair to rock just slightly. He squinted his gray eyes and looked out into the dreary distance.

In the oak grove on the far side of the barn closest to the house, where the bunkhouses were built so that the men could have shade to eat under, Seth saw something. He heard it, too, though he couldn't quite place his finger on the sound. He thought he could hear the muffled breathing of one of his stallions, but it also sounded like the whimpering of a scared raccoon. He tried to focus his eyes to see better, and he realized that something large moved under the thick limbs of the hundred-year-old oaks. It moved with grace, but constricted, cautious grace, as if something, or someone, held it back. Rising from the chair and then standing immobile, he watched the strange creature with the heavy load for a few moments. It moved at the speed just between a trot and a canter, and before he could decide what to do, it disappeared out of the grove and into the open field beyond it. Seth felt a shudder run through his body, and the stillness came over him again as his eyes adjusted to the gray rising light of the summer sun.

Dr. Finch and Carl found him there, staring off into the distance like a zombie who had wandered the night and no longer knew what he was searching for. Dr. Finch had been coming to Seth's ranch for fifteen years, since he had earned his degree in large animal veterinary medicine, and he had never once seen the man stand still. He knew something must be wrong as he glanced at the bloodshot eyes of the rancher, but he hardly felt it was his place to examine Seth's psychological health. He had enough work on his hands for one day.

"Seth, should we get to work on those cows?" Dr. Finch tried to be polite and serious in his tone.

Seth, as if pulled out of a hypnotist's trance, widened his eyes and turned his head toward the vet. He reached up and lifted his cowboy hat off his blond head and wiped sweat from his brow with his handkerchief. "Yeah, I suppose we ought to," he said, and stepped off the porch onto the dusty path that led to the fields.

Reeve and Aurelio returned three days later with silver rings on their fingers that they had purchased from the department store in town. They had visited the local justice of the peace, who once held Seth in high regard and questioned their decision with sour solemnity, but all the same needed the fifty dollar fee that came with wedding vows.

Before they left the ranch in the dark hours of the morning, Reeve, in the midst of her mumbling mantra over William, had shown Aurelio her lock box with the money she'd been saving for years, for what she didn't know until the moment she saw him in the loft. Aurelio, who had just received that week's pay in cash from Seth, gathered what little he had from the bunkhouse and saddled up the largest stallion in the barn beneath where Reeve moaned in the loft. He carried his love to the horse, Stargazer, where she mounted him like a mechanical robot programmed to ride. Aurelio pulled himself up behind her and gathered the reins in his large brown palms. He had little experience with horses or animals of any kind, as he grew up on dirty city streets, and riding Stargazer scared him so much that he nearly forgot the other weight he carried. Reeve's money rested with his own in folded bills in his leather billfold, which he had placed next to the manuscript in the brown leather satchel strapped to his back. He wore tall leather cowboy boots and Wrangler jeans, a plaid button-down shirt, and a black suede cowboy hat, the common outfit of every man on the ranch. He felt uncomfortable in his clothes, and quite ready to shed them as he kicked Stargazer's lower ribs with his heels, trying to get him to run. Reeve leaned forward in front of him, a sobbing slump of a woman. Her usual outfit of jeans and a t-shirt was smeared with blood, mucus, and sweat, then coated with bits of hay and mud, like a forlorn cake decorated by a demon rather than a proud mother. Aurelio marched Stargazer through the oak grove where the trees whispered to him in the warm breeze of early morning. Already the weather spoke of another scorching day, and Aurelio had to stop Stargazer often to rest, drink water from the small canteen, and allow the heated animal a chance to catch his breath.

As the light of the sun cast its rosy fingertips across the flat expanse of the horizon, Aurelio could see the two-lane highway at the edge of the ranch. Numbness overtook his blistering hands as he let loose the reins. He felt again as if he were entering his freedom; as if the road could carry him away from all of his problems and pain, as if riding on this horse with this young woman down this road meant nothing but the journey of his dream materializing. He kicked Stargazer's ribs again, this time bringing the creature into a steady canter. He felt sudden control over everything from the speed of Stargazer to the life he now chose for himself.

Reeve, too, as if beckoned by the glow of the sun, came to life in his arms. She rose up from her crumpled mess and wiped the tears off her face as she opened her eyes to the light of the new day. She still cringed with physical and emotional pain, but she felt her heart swell with the blood of new life. She leaned her back against Aurelio's chest and listened to the methodic beating of his heart and felt comfort and love as they entered the town.

They found a small cluster of trees behind the courthouse on Main Street and tied up Stargazer. Then, walking hand in hand as if the passersby weren't all staring and whispering behind their backs at the odd pair of sullied lovebirds, Reeve and Aurelio waltzed into the town's one department store at the corner of First and Main. Anxious to shed the clothes of their former life, Aurelio picked out khaki slacks, a white button-down cotton shirt, a navy blue tie, and shiny black shoes. He chose the outfit for the wedding that neither of them spoke of but that each knew was their reason for coming, and thought it would come in handy when he went for job interviews at higher-class jobs. Reeve chose a yellow sleeveless summer dress that had lace trim along the hem and tied in the back with a satin ribbon. She tried it on in the small dressing room at the back of the store. It danced around her thin hips and her hair shined golden as it cascaded down the tight bodice.

Aurelio paid for the clothes under the squinty eyes of the cashier, and the pair retreated to Stargazer, where they rode to a stream a half mile outside of the town. Each chose a tree, changed in quiet solitude and relieved themselves, then washed their faces and hands in the cool water of the bubbling stream. Connected by love and not words, neither of them had spoken since the dark hours of the morning.

When Aurelio saw his bride-to-be, love washed over him and caused him to hold his breath. When he drew in his next inhalation, the air tasted sweet and pure in his mouth.

"You are the most beautiful woman I have ever seen," he said to her in Spanish, and finished in English, "I have loved you from the first moment I stepped onto the soil of this country. Will you do me the honor of becoming my wife?"

Reeve's face flushed with the love she both gave and received. He spoke to her heart, said little, and knew what she wanted most. "Will you do me the honor of becoming my husband?" she asked, and took his hand into her own.

The justice of the peace, Hiram Franklin, was also the town's judge and lawyer and had gone to grade school with Seth. Seth had left after eighth grade to work the ranch in the absence of his recently deceased father, but Hiram had gone on to college and then law school. Though their lives took different paths, Hiram and Seth had remained friends. Seth admired Hiram for being able to commit himself to the studies that he never accomplished himself, and Hiram admired Seth for taking care of his lonely mother and a thousand acre ranch at the age of fourteen. They spoke to each other often, and met for dinner or supper whenever they happened to see each other in town. Hiram had seen Seth bring home his beautiful bride, years ago, after traveling to a cattleman's show in Houston, and Georgia and his own wife, Cissy, had become good friends until Georgia's death. Hiram had watched as Seth raised his daughter alone, another task he felt that would be impossible for him, but came easily to the hardworking commitment of Seth.

When Reeve entered the courthouse with Aurelio in June of 1973, Hiram immediately noticed the bruises on her arms. A large hand had left purple imprints on her upper arms, and her eyes drooped into blue circles that stood only for lack of sleep. Hiram, concerned, glared at Reeve's companion whom he assumed to be one of Seth's workers.

"What happened to you, child?" he drawled in a syrupy voice that he hoped would bring out the truth.

Reeve held her face like a statue and looked up at Hiram. "I'm not a child. I'm eighteen, and I'm here to marry this man."

Hiram placed his hand on his chest, taken aback. Reeve had been raised with good southern manners. She knew to avoid eye contact and tilt her forehead towards the floor when spoken to. Now, she stood straight-backed and stared into his green eyes, his six-foot frame appearing minuscule against her five-foot-three one. She crossed her arms and waited for his response the way a mother waits for the response of a mischievous child.

"Well, does you father know about this, sweetheart?" Hiram was determined not to marry them without consulting Seth, but the reality of the situation burned at him. He desperately needed the fee to fix his pickup, and Reeve was old enough to make her own decisions.

"We'll tell him when we return home." She spoke in a level tone that was as unwavering as her stance next to the dark stranger.

"Well, I don't know about this," Hiram said, rubbing his copper beard with his right palm.

"Pardon me, sir, but I don't think it is your decision," Aurelio's accent echoed through the stonewalled courthouse.

Hiram sucked in his breath and let it out in a long, slow whistle through his teeth. "Well, then, I have some paperwork for you to complete. And we're going to need blood samples from you both. The licensing fee is $10, and my fee is $50." He lifted his eyes and rested them on the pair, hoping the amount of money would surprise and deter them.

"That's fine," Reeve said. Hiram told his secretary to get the paperwork. Aurelio and Reeve stood next to each other in the small entryway of the hundred-year-old courthouse, the backs of their hands touching,. They didn't speak as Hiram's secretary gathered the paperwork, and still said nothing as they sat in the plastic chairs next to the door filling it out.

Hiram, who had retreated behind the closed doors of his office, returned after a short while. "You'll have to go to the drugstore to get your blood types. We don't do that here."

Reeve handed him the papers and took Aurelio's hand as they left through the glass doors. They crossed the street to the drugstore, which was empty at midmorning, as all the ranchers around were either working or having coffee next door in Lois's Café. The pharmacist was new in town and didn't recognize Reeve or Aurelio, a fact that brought relief to Reeve's heart. She was sure of her decision, but she knew, in many ways, it couldn't be the best one for her, and she didn't want yet another person reinforcing her doubts. She looked up at Aurelio as the pharmacist punctured his fingertip. He didn't flinch, as if drawing blood was an everyday activity for him. She couldn't even look at her own blood, and instead squeezed Aurelio's palm with her free hand. The pharmacist tested the blood right then.

"Mr. Lucero, you are O+. Ms. O'Reilly, you are O-. A perfect balance. Good luck with your marriage," he winked at them as they paid the $7 and left. Reeve thought about what the pharmacist had said for many years to come. A perfect balance. She hoped that someday he would be right.

When they returned to the courthouse, Hiram had already donned his black robe and pulled out his black leather-bound copy of the King James Bible. Since they had no witnesses, his secretary had to stand in. During the brief ceremony, Reeve and Aurelio faced each other holding hands. In the cool air conditioning of the courthouse (the only structure in town with this luxury), Reeve shivered under her thin yellow dress. Her eyes warmed under Aurelio's gaze, and she felt safe as she spoke the vows to him. When they had exchanged the silver rings Aurelio had chosen in the department store that morning, Hiram said, "You may now kiss the bride." Aurelio reached his hand under Reeve's chin, the tips of his fingers hot and gentle, and raised her face close to his. He leaned forward and, as if his lips were the wings of an angel, kissed his newlywed wife. It was their first kiss. Reeve felt her body go limp from the love, the passion, and the pain she held inside her. She wrapped her arms around Aurelio's neck as he carried her out of the courthouse.

Knowing that her father would be busy all day with the vet, Reeve told Aurelio that they would have time to sneak back onto the property of the ranch without him noticing. She had spent the free hours of her life meandering along the creek that ran through the ranch, and knew of an elm grove on the outer boundary that the cattle, and the men, were too lazy to walk to. Aurelio held the reins again as they rode Stargazer back along the side of the road, and Reeve, revitalized, sat up with her shoulders pressing against his chest. She wore a confident smile and felt safer than ever with Aurelio's strong arms wrapped around her. Ever since his arrival at the ranch, his muscles had doubled in size, the heavy work of lifting hay bales and holding down cows to be inseminated caused him to work his body to its limit. Reeve felt his strength now as he controlled Stargazer, though she could tell he had little experience riding. She let him have the control because it was easy and comfortable, the only way she wanted to feel since... the night before? She almost said it aloud. It couldn't have been, she thought, because that was a million years previous to the undying love she felt now.

They rode along the highway late into the afternoon until Reeve could see the elm grove in the pink-sunset distance. Her father had taken her once as a child. He told her that the original ranch house had been built next to these trees over a hundred years ago, but the creek kept flooding during heavy rains, and the house was eventually demolished. As they approached the gigantic cluster of trees where the limbs stretched over them by ten stories or more, Reeve could still see remnants of the old house: bits of a stone laid foundation, old boards, and pieces of glass. She leaned in to Aurelio and told him the story.

She spoke in a whisper, and in Spanish, as if their presence on the ranch would beckon the ears of those who worked. Aurelio clicked his tongue for Stargazer to stop. He held on to the back of the saddle and slid off, then reached for Reeve, who had changed back into her jeans for the ride. As he reached for her, she felt herself falling into his arms like a sack of potatoes being thrown on the scale. Her body sagged into him as he wrapped his arms around her.

"You are the reason I am here," he whispered into her hair, tasting its sweetness on his lips as he spoke.

"Here on the ranch?"

"Here on earth," he said, and she melted into him.

They spent the night beneath the full moon, the stars, and the leaves of a grandfather elm. Aurelio, a gentle giant, took great care to touch Reeve with the soft hands of a writer, not a rancher. He kissed her with smooth, moist lips and ran his fingers through her hair. After he massaged the tension out of her back and shoulders, they lay looking at the stars and telling their dreams.

"I've always wanted to go somewhere else other than Texas. Wouldn't it be nice to travel?" Reeve felt herself opening every aspect of her soul to this man.

"When I publish my manuscript, you will come to Mexico and stay with me and my family. You will love Mexico. The people celebrate life. There isn't so much attention paid to working. And the food—oh, you will love the food. You will be the queen of the house, and my mother will always be there to help you with the children." Aurelio rambled on about his siblings, their shop, and the city where he grew up. At last he paused.

"What manuscript?" she asked, because he had mentioned it as if she already knew.

"Let me show you." Aurelio leaned over and opened the satchel. Like a waiter carrying a tray of filled-to-the-rim glasses, he lifted the manuscript out of the bag. Without undoing the twine, he told Reeve about his years of research in college, of the stories his mother told him as a boy, and the words she told him as he left.

Reeve sat back, resting her weight on her lower back and elbows. She watched his eyes shine in the light of the moon and his hands move excitedly as he told her the story. In the darkness that came with the night and her rash decision, she suffered doubts that she had not endured earlier, when the sun shone on their love. She tried not to speak, but felt herself saying, "Aurelio, what if you don't, or can't, get it published? Will your mother really not allow you to come home?"

Aurelio's face tightened when she asked the question. He, too, had doubts about their recent decision, and especially about the publication of the manuscript. His mother's words often haunted him and caused him to lose sleep at night. He wanted nothing more than support from Reeve, and felt threatened by her own impending doubts. He said nothing in reply.

Reeve squinted her eyes in the dim light. She tried to read his face, but couldn't. Instead she reached for him and pulled his head onto her lap. She ran her long, thin fingers through his curly dark hair. "Everything will be all right," she whispered. "Let's get some sleep."

They spent two nights in the grove relishing each other's company both physically and emotionally. Reeve wanted to stay forever, but the few items of food they had purchased from the grocer on their way out of town were diminishing, and she knew she had to face her father or starve. She wondered what had become of William, and whether her father had discovered her union with Aurelio, and if she would tell her father the truth.

On the third day of their love, Reeve woke early and watched the sun rising in the east. It adorned the sky with a gentle gray and painted hues of yellow and orange across the horizon. The creek sparkled in its glory. Reeve's eyes trapped the glittering light as she chewed on a granola bar. Aurelio stirred and rubbed his eyes, focusing them on his beautiful wife. Watching her sit like one meditating on a lotus flower, he felt he had never experienced more love than in that moment. He rose and scooted next to her, resting his arm across her shoulders.

"A perfect sunrise," he sighed, and Reeve nestled in to his warmth.

"We have to go back today. My father must be looking for me." Her voice was calm and even, though her insides shook with a mixture of fear and dread.

"It's OK," Aurelio assured her. "I will talk."

Reeve wore her new dress, and rode Stargazer with her legs hanging over the side. Aurelio again took the reins, his hands adjusting to the rubbing of the leather on his skin. They didn't run with Stargazer, but took a leisurely walk through the fields and dirt roads of the ranch. Reeve pointed out familiar landmarks, told Aurelio of the places she used to play as a child, and explained how she had come to hate beef. Aurelio listened as she rambled on, pleased that her mind seemed at ease. The truth was, Reeve wanted to talk about anything but the coming event, which she knew would bring sadness into their happy union.

Before they had arrived at the house, Seth caught sight of them coming through the oak grove. He had been to town the previous day and discovered her treason, and had not been able to eat, sleep, or work since her disappearance with the Mexican scum. He tried speaking to William about their evening, but when he returned from his day of work with the vet, he saw that William's things were all gone from the closet in the spare bedroom. He left without notice or a note When Seth called over to Ted Dawson's ranch, he received no answer. Infuriated, he paced on the porch for hours and hours, burning blisters into his heels and grinding his teeth. When he saw the figure coming through the trees, the image became a flashback of three mornings previous, and he cursed himself for not recognizing his daughter's escape.

Seth was a man of black and white: you were wrong, or you were right. There was no gray area. He controlled his temper most of the time, but when someone crossed him, the hot air filled his body like a child overfilling a balloon. He stood watching their approach, ready to burst.

Reeve could see her father's stony face from a hundred yards away. He stood like an Army general over his mischievous troops. Her mouth drained itself of all moisture as she listened to the clip-clop of the horse's hooves. They echoed the heartbeat that rang inside her ears.

Seth couldn't wait. Taking two steps at a time off the porch, he approached Stargazer before it reached the house.

"What in God's name have you done?" he shouted at her, his face fiery hot.

"Daddy, please let me explain," already, she sounded like a small girl.

"Did I not work my ass off all these years to raise a respectable daughter? Did I not teach you how to be a rancher's wife? Did I not show you that your own kind is the best kind? Did I not sacrifice all those years of hard work, just to have you sneak behind my back and disgrace me in front of the whole town?" Like a hurricane, his words swirled around Reeve and Aurelio. Reeve slid off Stargazer, unable to hold on to the saddle horn any longer. Aurelio, too, stepped down, and stood an inch taller than Seth. He too had dressed in his new clothes. He held a solemn look.

"Sir, I am sure we can work this out. I know that you may think what we did was wrong, but you must understand the circumstances—"

Seth's eyes bulged as he held up his hand, stopping Aurelio in mid-sentence. Seth's shock at the easy English that came from Aurelio's mouth was obvious to the pair as they stood in front of him. He paused a moment.

"I don't give a goddamn about your circumstances! I want you out of the house, Reeve, off the property, and out of my life! You're not my daughter anymore." He screamed the beginning of the speech and tapered off, nearly to a whisper, when he said the last sentence.

Reeve shrieked amidst the tears that streaked her dusty face. She ran to her father and began to hit him in the chest repeatedly with both fists. "Don't you see, Daddy? William raped me! William raped me! And it's your fault! You made me go with him!" She had practiced what she would say for three days, but she found herself saying only one part. She knew she had been raped, but she hadn't even been able to tell Aurelio. She felt the release of the sentence weakening her entire body. She wanted to run to the satchel and pull out the bloody jeans, but Seth answered before she could move.

"I know one thing. I did not raise the lying bitch that I see before me now." His voice was cool and even. As he said it, he stared at her with a plaintive expression, his eyes locked onto hers.

Reeve crumpled to the ground. She moaned and moaned the word no in a mantra similar to the one she had shared with Aurelio on their first night in the barn. Aurelio gathered Reeve into his arms and gently placed her slumped body back onto Stargazer. He turned to Seth with tears in his eyes.

"Where I come from, fathers love and respect their daughters. And when they see their daughters in pain, or if they see that their daughters need help, they hold open their arms, and they do justice on the people who hurt them. Where I come from, family is more important than pride."

Seth tried to disguise his surprise at the Aurelio's inept ability to speak English. He said, "Then why don't you go back to where you come from? No one wants you here." He paused and said, "Get your things and go, Reeve. I never want to see you again."

But all they took was Stargazer, the little money they had, the brown satchel with two bloody, dusty outfits, a shawl from Aurelio's mother, and the manuscript that would become the rotten core of their lives.

Chapter 22

Next to his train collection, Warren's second weakness was his art. Although the exterior and most of the interior of the house appeared plain, almost dreary, Warren had a special place in his heart and in his home for art. He had developed his interest in high school, when he took class after class from the greatest teacher he'd ever met, Mr. Gibbons. Mr. Gibbons, a tall, dark man with a mustache that he twisted into a greasy black curl on each side of his upper lip, started class each day with a slide of art. The students would walk in and, through some mysterious gift he bestowed upon them, they would all sit and stare at the painting that garnished the bigger part of the wall. After several minutes of silence, Mr. Gibbons would either have them write their reactions in a journal or have a round table discussion about the piece. Right from the start, students realized that they could say anything they liked about it, even that they hated it, and Mr. Gibbons would still accept them.

It was on the white walls of Mr. Gibbons' classroom that Warren discovered he had a passion for art. Sometimes he would see a slide and be nearly overcome with tears, or anger, or happiness. He relished the moments of silence at the beginning of the class, where he could drink in the view of the art and feel quenched for the rest of the day. Mr. Gibbons introduced him to Renoir, Monet, van Gogh, Picasso, Cassat, Degas, Michelangelo, da Vinci, Adams, and even Warhol. The art Mr. Gibbons placed in front of his students represented all cultures, walks of life, races, sexes, history, and religions. Warren felt he understood the world for the first time in Mr. Gibbons' class. He felt that he could use art to explain everything wrong with his life and with the rest of society. Without the art and the way in which Mr. Gibbons presented it, Warren felt he would not have been able to go on.

When he was older and had lived in a small studio apartment saving every penny from his factory job for three years, Warren bought his house. And in the house, he had furniture purchased from garage sales and maintained every aspect of the upkeep himself, from the plumbing to the lawn care to the electrical wiring. He continued to pinch his pennies until he had enough to qualify for the business loan for his shop, and when his shop business boomed in the early seventies, he began his collection.

The basement was unfinished when he purchased the house, and each night after work, Warren went to his second job of finishing the basement. But to him, finishing the basement for what he had in mind involved much more than reworking the heating vents and putting up drywall. He divided the basement into a small storage room, where the furnace, washer and dryer, and water heater were, and one large gallery. The gallery couldn't have shoddy workmanship, and Warren spent hours designing and installing intricate wood molding. He chose recessive can lighting for the ceiling, and had a contractor come in to drill through the concrete foundation for the light, beauty, and safety of egress windows. The walls, of course, had to be bright white, a perfect backdrop for the art he planned to collect.

Warren's collection was simple: he visited local art shows and galleries and spent hours and hours examining the art, buying pieces that touched him emotionally or pieces that he thought reflected the beauty of the masters that Mr. Gibbons had introduced. He was single, had early hours in his shop, had the time, and, because of the frugality of his lifestyle, the money, to invest in the splendor of his dreams. He took great care in collecting the most impacting pieces, so that it took him over twenty years to complete the walls of his gallery. He had oils, watercolors, abstracts, photographs, and even a few clay and bronze sculptures for which he had designed and built display cases. He kept his art collection in the basement so that people couldn't see it. In fact, no one ever had. Whenever he felt scared or lonely or reminiscent of his darker days, he would retreat into the artistic sanctuary and engulf himself in another world. Surrounded by the great works of art, Warren would feel as safe and warm as he had in his brother's arms as a small child.

From his view into Alejo's room, Warren knew that Luisa had a talent for art. The intricacy of the mural in the nursery had amazed him, and he justified to himself that perhaps the art was the primary reason he just couldn't keep his eyes from the room. But when he entered the main level of the house after he and Luisa's first circumstantial meeting, he was surprised to see the plain white walls, beige carpet, and mass-produced furniture, as if the couple had been trying to say to the world, "We're just average people."

Warren saw Luisa as anything but average. It wasn't until he first entered Alejo's room that the magnificence consumed him. He felt almost as if he were undergoing a heart attack. The colors jumped off the wall and blurred his vision. The birds were so detailed, from the tips of their feathers to the talons on their feet, that he could almost feel the wind underneath their wings, almost hear the songs emerging from their beaks, and almost see the swooping movements of the creatures over the earth.

"Where did you learn to do this?" Warren had asked her, holding his chest and catching his breath as if he'd been on a five-mile run.

Luisa, modest to the core, had said, "Years of schooling down the drain, just so I could paint my own house and never make any money."

Warren knew what he would do. He had already formed the idea in his mind, but only as a seed. Now, the thought grew into a sapling. Its branches reached for the sunlight that Luisa brought into his life. He felt himself still out of breath as he asked her what her plans were for the future. How would she live, pay her bills, make money? And when he confessed to his strange voyeurism, she surprised him by accepting his offer. He thought that he must have somehow come into the presence of an angel, because he had never felt so at ease with himself.

Before Luisa and Alejo moved in, Warren prepared the house as best he could. In Alejo's new room, he had an electric train set, similar to the one in his shop, that encircled all four corners of the room, and which he had designed. He decided that Alejo could bear the hum of the electric train as it whistled its way through the mountain villages and tunnels. Otherwise, he removed the scant furniture in the room—an old chest of drawers and a coffee table. He waxed and buffed the wood floor.

Luisa's room could only be the upper back bedroom, as he had run out of space. When he bought the house, he often questioned why he would ever need three bedrooms, and now, thirty years later, he couldn't help but smile as he and Luisa lifted her heavy oak bed frame up the stairs. Warren concentrated on laying the pieces on the floor where Luisa wanted the bed to sit, but Luisa became distracted by the view from the window.

"I had a dream about this," she whispered, but she couldn't continue. Instead she stared across into Alejo's room, now empty but for the lively mural on the wall. She was unable to move her body, face, or eyes from the spot.

Warren resumed with his work assembling the bed frame. He had nothing to reply, and sensed an emptiness between them as she stood there, as if a wall had been built that separated her level of pain from his level of safety. He busied himself with the work and wordlessly completed it before Luisa even moved a centimeter in any direction.

She turned to him at last and said, "This is hard for me, even with your welcoming embrace. Thank you." She cast her eyes on the hardwood floor and held her breath. She didn't want to cry, but the image of the eagle clawing at the window haunted her for the remainder of the day.

When he asked her to move in, he didn't tell her about the gallery in the basement, fearful that her expertise in art history would downplay his passion for modern art. After they had spent most of the morning loading furniture into the house while Clara watched Alejo, he decided to reveal his secret.

"There's something I'd like to show you," he said. Luisa looked back, expectant. "It's in the basement." He led her to the stairs at the back of the kitchen. The gallery had a security door that enclosed it from the stairs. It was shut and locked. Warren reached into his pocket for the key as he glanced back at Luisa, who still said nothing. She wondered what could be behind the door. From what she had seen of Warren's house, it was as plain as could be, with mismatching furniture he had gathered from garage sales over the years, plain cream-colored paint on the walls of every room, and shabby curtains that had clearly been a part of the house long before Warren moved in thirty years ago. Though the house was clean, its dullness drained her. That, and the view from the upper back bedroom window, caused Luisa to doubt the insane decision to move here.

"What is it?" she finally said as Warren fiddled with the lock.

"It's my collection," he said again, and a shiver rose up Luisa's spine. She feared that he might be a crazy man with a collection of skulls from the women he had wooed to move in. But when he opened the door, she couldn't believe what she saw.

Warren had never once mentioned his passion for art to her, though he often commented on the murals in her house. She had no idea that he spent any money on anything at all, as he had spent hours going over her budget with her and showing her how to pinch pennies wherever possible. As she stepped into the room, she realized that she knew little about his life. Better than murals, paintings on canvases of all sizes and colors adorned the walls. All were professionally framed and none were prints; and though she noticed that everything came from the twentieth century, she was amazed at Warren's exquisite selection. She felt as if she were walking through a museum of modern art at an exhibit of the finest pieces. She strolled through the large room, examining each piece, before she turned to Warren, who stood with his hands interlinked at his lower back. He swayed slightly and his eyes glistened with the view of the art. Each time he entered the basement, he felt as if he were entering it for the first time.

"How did you—" Luisa began, but she didn't know how to finish the question. Somehow she knew how he had collected the pieces—she could see him tallying up his money each month on an old cahier's calculator, determining how much he could budget in art expenditures—and that didn't matter to her now. What she really wanted to know was everything else about him. She thought she could read him so easily: his upright, solitary life a simple example of someone who just never liked being around a lot of people. Everything about him, up until the moment she stepped into the gallery, had been so predictable. He always helped her clean out her house at the same time, he always called her to tell her he'd be coming, he always said the same things to Alejo, he always drank the same kind of tea, and had a schedule for what he ate day after day. The word secret, matched up with what she knew of Warren, was like putting the word gracious in front of a bitter enemy. An overwhelming desire overcame her. She wanted to flood Warren with questions, to know every detail of his life, to sit down with him for the rest of the afternoon and discover the real reasons he had this collection.

"I'm very careful with my money, as you know. But everyone has a weakness, and mine is modern art. I had a great teacher in high school who introduced me to art. Ever since then, I haven't been able to get enough of it." He answered the cutoff question she had attempted to ask, but she stood looking back at him perplexed. He worried that she might think him strange, or that she wouldn't like his taste in art, or that she was afraid of him.

"Is something wrong, Luisa?" his voice cracked as he said her name. He wasn't in love with her, though he wanted to be. She couldn't know all the other secrets he held behind his face.

"Why aren't you married? Don't you have a family? Why do you live like this? What good does it do—" she realized the questions were coming out like a flood, and they nearly drowned him. He hadn't expected this kind of response. He wanted her to say something about the art. He wasn't ready to discuss any other aspect of his life. If he could talk about the art, he could still keep up walls, keep himself safe inside, and not have to worry about breaking down. As he stood there, he realized that it was too late. He cursed himself for showing her the room, for inviting her to stay in his house, for ever looking at her family from the window. Fear overtook him. He searched for an answer to any of her questions, but instead he turned away, facing the door.

"I'm sorry, I'm just so surprised—" she paused, waiting for him to turn back to her, but he remained with his back to her face. "I just didn't expect this from you, is all. I had no idea you had such fine taste in art. And—" she paused again, unsure of how to continue. "I thought I knew you so well. But I realize that I don't know you at all. And as long as I'm staying here, I hope I can get to know you a little better. Something tells me that you want me to get to know you a little better." She tried to roll out the words as gently as her mouth would allow.

Warren waited. He chewed on his tongue and took in several breaths. The room was so quiet that he could hear the second hand of his watch ticking. He began to count in his mind, telling himself that once he reached one hundred, he would turn to her and speak. He put a Mississippi between each number. He could hear her breathing behind him. She shifted, her sneakers rubbing the hardwood floor, making a tiny squeak. At last he turned around and looked into her eyes.

"I have two brothers and two sisters, but I rarely see any of them. I think I have twelve nieces and nephews. My father is long gone and my mother—" he sloshed the word around inside his mouth like poison, "my mother may as well be dead." His own candor surprised him. He waited for a response.

Luisa's face softened as she said, "Let's go upstairs and have some tea. Then we can talk."

Locking the door behind him, Warren followed Luisa upstairs and into the kitchen. She prepared the tea in a mechanical fashion. She placed the tea bags in two identical white teacups that rested on matching saucers, put two spoons of sugar in one and left the other empty but for the bag. She carried the saucers over to the table and sat across from Warren, whose body had stiffened as he sat on the green vinyl pads of the old metal chair. An air of expectancy hung between them.

"My family has lots of secrets," Luisa began. "When I met Carter, I told him everything I knew about myself and my family, right from the start. In a way, I was trying to scare him off," she felt herself smiling. "But in a way, I knew he was the one for me, and I wanted our relationship to be different from my parents'. Because my parents… well, they don't exactly like to talk about their past. All I know is that I have no relatives on either side of my family because of their own ignorance and stubbornness. I hope never to lead my life that way, even though you've seen how I might want to keep Alejo away from my father."

Warren had expected another miniature inquisition like the one she had bombarded him with in the gallery. Now his surprise matched hers at seeing the artwork. He realized that, in opening up to him, she was encouraging him to open up to her. He just wasn't sure if he could yet. Instead, when the teakettle whistled, he stood up to retrieve it and turn off the burner.

Luisa continued as if he still sat across from her. "My mother grew up on a ranch in southern Texas. My grandfather raised cattle, and did so by going south of the border and smuggling in illegal immigrants from Mexico. It was OK for them to work on his ranch, but it was not OK for any of them to go near his daughter. And when my mother married my father without telling her dad, he told her to leave and never come back." She paused to catch her breath, the speech having exploded out of her mouth in anxious anticipation of what was next. "Of course, the only reason I know any of this is because I read my mother's journal. She lied and told me her father was dead, but my own father told me the truth."

"So you never got to meet him? What about your grandmother?" Warren felt relieved to be discussing her life rather than his own.

"She really did die when my mother was a child, of cancer. Maybe that was the root of all the problems in her life, I don't know. It's hard being a single parent," Luisa knew she couldn't go on, not today. She was determined not to cry, because today she was moving in to Warren's house, moving on with her life, after three months of pure mourning and crying every day when she opened her eyes. She sat there sipping her tea in the yellow sun of the kitchen and said nothing more.

Finally, Warren spoke. "My mother was a single parent, too, after my father left when I was almost seven. They never did find my father," he said the last sentence in the low tone of someone making a confession to a priest. "My mother wanted a girl. She had three boys before me and she wanted me to be a girl. That, and I guess she was just—I don't know, mentally ill. I could have left, because one of the neighbors reported her, and I could have told the social worker that she abused me, and made me sleep in the basement, and gave me rags for clothes. But I didn't, because she was nice to all the other kids, and my oldest brother Frankie said that if I told the truth, the whole family would be separated. I couldn't do that to them, even then, even though I didn't understand at the time. So I lied. And from the time I was a little boy, all I could do was imagine what it might be like to live alone, to be away from everyone in my life, to never have anyone to deal with ever again. It seemed so easy, so safe, so perfect a dream." Warren held a distant look with an absentminded smile on his round, red-freckled face.

"Everyone in my family looks the same. We all got my mother's bright orange hair and freckles and green eyes." He didn't know why he moved from the most emotional events of his life to simple physical descriptions. He felt the latter so easy to say aloud, so easy to glide into a conversation as if their discussion had centered around the weather rather than skeletons in the closet.

"Your mother—did she drink?" Luisa asked, sure that it must be true because of the expertise Warren showed when Aurelio had stumbled into her living room.

"No, that was my father, and probably the reason he was too incapacitated to stand up to her. That or he was just a spineless bastard." His face reddened at the curse, and he focused on the gold-on-white design of the plastic top of the metal-legged table.

"I guess you know what it's like to be me, in a way," Luisa forced a weak smile. "Only, my mother loves me so much she could burst with it, and my brother, too. She has so much love in her heart waiting to be used that I think some of it goes to waste on lost dreams."

"I didn't know you had a brother," Warren said.

"Yeah, a younger brother, Byron. But I haven't talked to him in a while. He's kind of a... a loser, really. Maybe he learned it from my dad. Having a good role model for a father is important. Obviously you know that already."

Warren put his face in his hands and rested his head on the table. He didn't know what else to say. He felt he had already said too much.

"Why don't you ever talk to your siblings?" Luisa asked after waiting in the tangible awkwardness of his silence.

"Maybe they just remind me too much of my past." He kept his head down and answered in a slow monotone.

"Sometimes we need to be reminded," Luisa whispered, reaching for Warren's hand. She lifted his head from the table and examined the look on his face. "Sometimes the past is what can help us move into the future." She waited for a response, and, seeing nothing but an empty stare sit atop Warren's high cheekbones, told him about the deciding factor for her move into his home. She told him about the manuscript and the lost dream of her father, and the hope she had that she might finally get to meet her paternal grandparents, if they were still alive. As she spoke, her face released the tension from the earlier conversation and softened into a warm glow, like a rose blooming in the brightness of the sun. As she sat across from Warren, she realized that she could make her family's dreams come to life, but that she couldn't do it without the generosity of a stranger.

In a way, Carter's death had brought on a taste of happiness that she otherwise would never have known. A twang of guilt pinched her and she chewed on her cheek, trying to suppress it. But she knew she couldn't suppress the hope for a happy life again, and that was enough for her to finish telling Warren her story.

Chapter 23

Autumn sneaked back in to Warren's life when Mavis ceased coming once a month. The leaves changed from their various shades of green to a uniform gold throughout the city. Every day as he walked with his brothers to school, the wind whipped his face and burrowed inside his thin hand-me-down windbreaker. Soon the leaves began swirling down to the ground, their fragile skeletons crushed beneath car tires and children's feet during the morning commute. Warren drug his feet through the leaves each morning, the sensation of walking to school still new to him. The fall weather, which introduced random snowstorms in the middle of the night that would melt the next sunny day, brought a feeling of unrest to Warren's heart.

After the first visit, when it became obvious to Mavis that Warren was either neglected or sick, she kept a close eye on Doris. She thought she knew how to read people well, and was usually able to tell when a mother abused her child, but Doris had an uncanny way of tricking her. Whenever she arrived, most of the time unannounced, Doris's house was not only spotless, but she had iced tea and cookies waiting, as if she had expected her at any moment. The children would be playing outside on the street or reading, listening to the radio, or doing homework in the living room, and Frankie would often be fixing dinner. Doris enrolled Warren in school directly after Mavis's first visit, and she showed Mavis his schoolwork whenever she arrived. Mavis also saw a significant change in Warren, who began to emerge from his gaunt body into a healthy, freckled, seven-year-old. But the most important thing that Mavis noticed on her subsequent visits was that Warren smiled and sometimes laughed.

She took detailed notes on the atmosphere of the home, her interviews with Warren and the other children, and her observations of Doris. She had trouble believing that Doris had ever laid a hand on Warren, so after six months had passed and she was on her final visit, she wasn't surprised when Doris asked her to sit down so she could explain a few things.

"My husband was a drunk," she began, her brusqueness surprising Mavis, who had seen only polite smiles and happy words come from Doris's mouth. "And he used to trap Warren in the basement and hit him when he came home from the bar. You could ask around," she tried to keep her voice monotonous, "and anyone could tell you he drank too much. I was scared of him, and didn't know how to protect my son. I was so relieved when he left, but... but I didn't know how to care for Warren when he did. He had been down there so long; it was like he wasn't my child. And I was pregnant with another baby, and didn't know how I would be able to make ends meet... When you came here for the first time, I guess it wasn't the best of times for us. Can you understand that?"

A genius of deceit, Doris wiped the tears from the corners of her eyes as she lifted her lashes to look across at Mavis, who sat on the sofa munching on a chocolate chip cookie and sipping iced tea, her yellow notepad resting on her chunky legs. The children were out on the street playing one of their games; their voices carried in through the glass. Margaret slept in her bassinet in Doris's room. The only other sound was the methodical ticking of the wall clock.

"I do understand, Mrs. York. But please understand my position. The woman who reported you said that you never even mentioned that you had another son. If it was just your husband—" Mavis stopped and took another sip of her tea. "Then why had no one seen Warren until six months ago, when you went into the hospital to have the baby?"

Prepared for the inquiries, Doris responded as if she had practiced the line in front of the mirror that morning. "As I have told you before, Warren has been sickly since he was born. I was terribly afraid of losing him if I allowed him to play outside. And I didn't want all the neighbors asking about him all the time. That's why I never mentioned him to them. It was private, family business, and we had enough problems to deal with."

"But Warren seems fine now. I think all he needed were some warm clothes, a warm bed, and food in his stomach. I see you've been taking care of that." Mavis said and looked out the front window at Warren, who ran across the street, a small girl in a yellow dress in hot pursuit of him.

"Yes, we're doing the best we can with what little we have. Did I tell you I'm going to try to find a job? I know how to sew, and that's a start," Doris focused on the shakiness of her voice, trying to present herself as a fragile, frightened woman who wanted the best for her family.

Mavis finished her tea and began writing notes on her yellow pad. After writing for what seemed an interminable time to Doris, who tried to keep an innocent, yet patient face in front of the social worker, Mavis pulled out some white paperwork from her soft-sided briefcase.

"I'm going to file my report next week, Mrs. York. I am making a recommendation to Social Services that Warren stay with you. I hope," she held eye contact with Doris as she said the rest of her speech, "that if I ever happen to stop by, I will see Warren as happy and healthy as he is today."

"Yes, of course. I will do the best I can," and Doris stood to shake her hand and show her to the door. When she closed it, a grin that combined evil and relief washed over her face. She knew she was free again to do as she pleased, as long as she kept the secret behind closed doors.

Warren's abuse continued, though never to the extent it was before Mavis's arrival. Holding the threat over his head like a master holding a treat for his dog, Doris told Warren every day that if he ever complained to anyone, he would never see his brothers again. Often, she whispered it into his ear when she woke him before dawn each morning. She had proclaimed it his duty, now that he was officially part of the family, to fix breakfast every morning. She would wake him and trod back to the warmth of her own bed, sleeping for another half an hour as Warren prepared scrambled eggs, toast, and bacon for everyone. Warren never complained about his new duty, the coziness of his side of the bed he now shared with Frankie too precious a gift to give up. All he wanted to do was please his mother, and he thought that she would love him if he did everything right for a long time.

Doris pecked at her son now as if he were a mere annoyance rather than a disgrace. She stood over him as he did the house cleaning (all of which fell on his shoulders), and slapped his face for missing a piece of fuzz during vacuuming, dug her fingernails into his arm when he missed a spot on the dishes, kicked the backs of his calves when he didn't shine the hardwood floors well enough, and yanked his hair when he didn't fold the shirts in perfectly neat squares. Her abuse was not only premeditated but organized. Warren learned which parts of his body to flinch depending on the chore. He became an expert at all things domestic, so that, after a year of picking at him for his menial mistakes, Doris had to alternate to verbal abuse, calling him such phrases as, "Stupid lazy beggar," "Rotten child," and, "Good-for-nothing waste," as he neatly arranged dishes in the cabinet or dusted the shelves to the standards of a white glove test.

Still small and underfed, though he was now allowed to eat the same food as the family, even if it meant he had to sit on the floor, Warren shirked at standing up to her. He somehow felt that one day she would be satisfied, but only if he continued along the submissive lines he had remained in for his entire life. He hated his life, but hated even more the thought of another life, in a strange house, with strange parents, where he wouldn't know what to expect, and wouldn't have the strength of his brothers' love to support him. Freddy and Kenny always invited him out to play when he had finished working, though they knew better than to cross their mother by offering to help. Warren would smile at their offers and try to rush through his work, only to be disappointed again and again by dinnertime and darkness of the evening, when the two boys would come in red-faced and out of breath, their voices chipper as they argued over who should have won the last game of stickball. Frankie, who still shopped for and prepared dinner each night, always chose the amount of food for Warren's plate, and placed a gentle hand on his shoulders each night as he placed the plate in front of Warren on the floor. After dinner, when Warren had finished the dishes and worked on his homework, Frankie would come into their bedroom and talk to him about school. He sat across from Warren, whose bottom rested on the carpet in their room, and held a plaintive expression on his face as he saw the relief come in to Warren's eyes.

Warren loved school. He loved the freedom of it, how nice his teacher, Mrs. Barrett, was, how easily he picked up all of the subjects. He learned to read quickly, as if the task was borne into his mind. He excelled in every subject, finding that Mrs. Barrett's smiles far outweighed her frowns, and that she never spoke a harsh word to him, but instead had good things to say when he completed his work. He loved to watch the other children play on the playground at recess, and liked to imagine what it was like for them at home. He always pictured mothers who waited at the doorsteps with cups of hot cocoa and cookies on cold winter days and glasses of ice cold lemonade and Popsicles in the heat of the summer, offering their treats to their beloved children with a warm hug, kiss, and, "I love you." Though he still hadn't made any friends, being in their presence and watching the happiness engulf them as they swung or climbed the monkey bars allowed Warren to enjoy their contentment.

He told Frankie each night about what he had learned that day, things Mrs. Barrett had said, how many gold stars he had earned for the week, and what homework he had. Doris, who cared little about Warren's actions as long as the house remained spotless, never knew of these talks, as she spent her evenings reading the daily paper or listening to a special program on the radio. In the moments that Warren shared with his older brother, he felt that he could go on with his life as it was, realizing that in the far distant future, he would one day escape all of it and lead a solitary life. He never told Frankie about his future plans, but he hoped that, in a way, Frankie knew and would understand.

When Warren turned eight the following spring, Doris not only pulled Frankie out of school, but expected her three younger boys to begin working.

"A rat-pack of lazy boys I have, just like their father. You know your sisters need better clothes than the scraps you boys get away with wearing."

Rose would soon be starting school, and it was Doris's determination that she had to be the best-dressed in her class, not wearing rags like her brothers. So Doris pinched every penny for over a month to buy a used electric lawnmower from a neighbor who was purchasing a newer gas-powered one and sent the three boys knocking on all the doors in a six-block radius, asking if they needed their lawns mowed.

It was through this new employment that Warren learned how to lie to get what he wanted. Seeing that he was finally alone with Kenny and Freddy, before they even approached the first door, he had a plan.

"Mother told us we should charge one dollar per yard. What if we ask for one dollar thirty and keep the dimes for ourselves, and never tell Mother?" He shook as he said the words, fearful of what his brothers might think of him, but instead he saw excitement flush their faces.

"What a great idea, Warren!" Kenny pounded on his back and rang the doorbell.

That spring and summer, Warren began scrimping away every last dime from the forty yards they mowed per week, saving eighty dollars by the end of the summer. Kenny and Freddy, typical boys, spent all their dimes at the five and dime store three blocks away, sucking on lollipops or wolfing down ice cream cones in front of the store and wiping their faces clean as they viewed their sticky reflections in the pane glass window, always sure to hide the evidence of their deceit from Mother. They never questioned why Warren didn't ask to come to the store with them. He hardly had the time. After mowing the lawns, trimming the weeds and hedges, and cutting the straight-lined edges along the sidewalks, Warren had to return home to do the entire chore load of the household, minus the shopping and dinner that lay on Frankie's shoulders.

Doris sat on the porch each day that summer surrounded by patterns of summer and fall dresses and top-of-the line fabrics that she and the girls had chosen together. She never questioned the validity of the dollar amount that the boys came home with, but was pleased to have enough extra money to dress up the only two children she truly cherished. She became softer on Warren, only verbally snapping at him now, her mind too busy with the work in front of her.

Just after Labor Day, when the lawn-mowing season came to a close and all the children but Margaret were to walk to school each morning, Warren felt coolness come over the air and into his soul. He felt relaxed for the first time in his life. He could return to the school he loved, escape daily from hard labor to commit time to reading and math, and he had enough money for a plan of escape to form in his mind. A whiz at numbers, Warren figured that by the time he reached the golden age of eighteen, he would have more than enough to move out on his own. Even at eight, he worked out his future plans in his mind, his hopes keeping him alive and well during the harder times of his life. He began third grade with a smile on his face and optimism locked in his heart. He was happy, truly happy, for the first time in his life.

Chapter 24

It was the 1970s, but the Civil Rights Movement hadn't been introduced to the conservative ways of the Texas rancher. Reeve and Aurelio rode from town to town looking for work, only to be turned away again and again for being seen together, Reeve's blond hair a burning contrast to the dark eyes and skin of Aurelio. "Stick with your own kind, then maybe I'll offer you some work," Reeve often heard a rancher telling Aurelio at the doorstep of his home, the rancher's eyes looking over Aurelio's shoulder at the slumped-over Reeve, who sat on Stargazer, her mouth agape as if she were either starving for air or demented.

The summer skipped by on starry, cloudless skies and full moons that seemed to fill the horizon, the heat waves casting a blurry film even at night. Reeve and Aurelio decided the best thing to do was camp out near water every night, and they filled the canteens they had bought with the lukewarm water of streams each morning before continuing their journey. They traipsed across the land, vaguely expecting that they were headed north, though they often moved west or east to find ranches off the main road. They had to camp on people's land, but were careful to remain on the outer edges and to leave at dawn, before the workers began appearing in the fields. The smell of manure, which Reeve had grown so accustomed to, bothered Aurelio so that each day he began with, "When we get away from here, I never want to see a cow again."

For the first month, they had no real plan, and Aurelio had only been able to pick up work in the desperation of three ranchers who had each lost an employee. The season was well underway, and most of the ranchers had already hired on their help for the year. Reeve began to dread each new day, and wondered often if she had made a good decision by rushing into Aurelio's arms, but his gentle touch each night, and the thought of spending her life with William, consoled her as she fell asleep on the blankets they had purchased.

By the end of the month, they were nearly out of money, and Reeve told Aurelio they had to do something soon.

"You will never get your green card unless we have residency. We need to live somewhere or our lives will always be like this, wandering from one place to the next, never having any money or knowing where we're going." Aurelio said, but he hadn't any idea how he could remedy the situation. For two days, they argued and discussed their options, until finally Reeve remembered something. She had an aunt, her mother's sister, who still lived in Houston. She decided the best thing to do was go to her and see if she could help, so one early morning they took Stargazer into a small town with a cardboard sign hanging off its saddle reading, "For Sale." They sat on the concrete curb for the rest of the day, hoping to make enough for bus tickets, food, and a few months' rent. Stargazer was eight years old and well trained. Though it wouldn't buy them a future, it could buy them enough to get their lives going in the right direction.

For two days, Reeve and Aurelio took turns sitting on the curb next to Stargazer in front of the local diner. Ranchers streamed in and out with the consistency of the ocean tide, their work scheduled by their daily chores rather than the moon. With what little money they had left, Aurelio bought turkey sandwiches and cold jars of milk for the couple to enjoy as they waited out the heat in the shade of the diner's overhang. A few men stopped to examine Stargazer, a black bay thoroughbred with a white star between his eyes, but no one seemed serious about their examination until the morning of the third day.

It was a woman. She couldn't have been much older than twenty, but carried her petite frame like a queen. She wore tight fitting Wrangler jeans that called attention to her slender hips, a white button-down cotton blouse, and a beige leather cowboy hat that kept the strands of her black hair from her face while allowing the ends to tickle the small of her back. She had the hands of a rancher: thick with calluses, short fingernails, and rough, dry skin, and she placed her hands on her hips as she moved her icy blue eyes from Stargazer to the couple to Stargazer to the couple, back and forth like the methodical clicking of a train pulling out of the station.

"How much?" She squinted down at Reeve, who stood to greet her at the question.

"He's a great horse. Only eight years old. Nearly seventeen hands, a bay thoroughbred. He's great for riding or for doing whatever work you need done." Reeve tried to exude confidence in her voice, but even as she spoke she couldn't be sure if the woman would give her what she wanted.

"How much?" The woman didn't flinch or appear to pay any attention to what Reeve said. Reeve realized how fruitless the conversation was. Anyone who knew about horses could take one thorough look and know enough information about him to withhold all questions.

"Thirty-five," she heard Aurelio's voice behind her, his accent thick, but the sound of his offer unwavering.

"I'll give you thirty," the woman responded, her hands still resting on her hips as if she needed the support of her palms to keep her legs in place. "Thirty-four, and that's final," his voice was uncannily calm.

"Plenty of other horses in these parts," the woman said, trying to throw them off.

"Not like this one. He's ready to breed," As Reeve stood there, the woman holding the beginning of their future in her decision, she had an inkling that the woman had come to town looking just for this horse, that she had heard about it through another rancher or his wife, and that she had mares at home who would be ready, come the spring, to mate. She knew, too, that Stargazer would be perfect for any other work of her ranch, since he was already trained to run cattle. She knew that she didn't have to say any more, because Aurelio also stood with his hands on his hips in a defiant standoff with the woman. A pause lingered between them, the stubbornness palpable as the two locked eyes.

"OK, then, he looks like a good stallion. What's his name?"

"Stargazer," Reeve said. She felt as if she were letting everything from her past go, as if this was her last chance to hold on to what she had spent her life surrounded by, as if the dark eyes of the stallion could lead her back to the life she had given up.

She held her head down as the woman walked into the only bank in town to retrieve the money. Aurelio grabbed Reeve's hand and squeezed it in his large palm, but it felt sticky and hot to her. The sun beat down on their already burnt necks, and the sweat created a home on their backs. Reeve felt the moisture drawing a part of herself away from her body. But no clouds came to cover the sky.

After two days of an un-air-conditioned bus that stopped in every little town that existed on the map between western Texas and Houston, Aurelio bought a newspaper at a tiny newsstand in the station to cover their heads from the downpour. Reeve tossed her head back and let the happiness fill her face as she looked back at her newlywed husband and ran out into the rain. She held her face to the sky, drinking the cool water, gulping it down through her esophagus and into her soul. It drenched her face, her hair, her clothes. She felt its wetness penetrate her body like the strongest painkiller available, targeting her every ache with a relaxed feeling of satiety. Everything that had happened to her for what felt like a lifetime but was only thirty-three days melted away in the floods of water down into the sewers of Houston. The tears she released from her depths cleansed her eyes as quickly as the raindrops washed them away from her face. She stood there for as long as she could stand before turning to Aurelio, who stood watching her under the overhang of the bus station.

When she was thirteen, she had grown an intense interest in her mother. She pestered her father every evening about everything that had to do with Georgia Finnegan, from where she grew up, to how they met, to her brothers and sisters. She had only one sister, Renee, who still lived in Houston and had never married. Reeve had written her three letters during her thirteenth year, and Renee had promptly responded; but, seeing no real connection besides blood relation to the aunt she had met at her mother's funeral when she was four years old, Reeve had lost interest in writing almost as abruptly as she had gained it. Now, she stood at the row of payphones that lined the wall next to the door and searched the phonebooks for Renee's number. She panicked when she saw the long list of Finnegans, cursing her mother for having such a common Irish name, but felt relief come over her again as she saw only one Renee.

The taxi reeked of urine and body odor. They sat together in the back seat, clutching each other's sweaty palms. A nervousness existed between them that Reeve couldn't explain. She wanted to say more to Aurelio than, "we're going to see my aunt," but she didn't know what to say. All she knew about the woman was that she was a high school science teacher. She didn't know her age, anything about where she lived, or why she wasn't married. Reeve felt displaced from any family member other than her father, with whom she had spent all of her childhood. Her lack of a mother stung her heart at moments like this, when she sat in the stench of a hot taxi unsure of her future with a man she hardly knew (yet had married). She felt achingly lonesome as the car bumped through the streets, its windows streaked with a greasy rain that would not let up. She wanted to talk in the car, to hear some other noise than the tinny country music that the cab driver played on his eight-track, but her mouth filled with dryness in her anticipation.

When they arrived at her aunt's house, Reeve knew right away that they wouldn't be able to stay. It wasn't a house, really, but a duplex. Renee owned one side, and its one story bore a single bedroom and a miniature backyard. The front yard was trimmed with colorful flowers, from marigolds to roses, and had a neatly-cut green lawn. The duplex had white aluminum siding and a dark gray roof that extended over the small front porch. The concrete floor of the porch held a single rocking chair with a brown and white afghan draped over the side. When Reeve saw the afghan, the aching feeling in her heart exploded into her ears. She remembered, with sudden pain, an afghan similar to it that her mother had woven for her when she was born. In the rush to escape from her father's hatred, she didn't think to collect it before she left. Now she and Aurelio stood on the porch as the rain plummeted against the roof, Reeve staring at the afghan and Aurelio waiting for her to make a move.

"Should we knock?" he finally whispered, and Reeve reached up for the doorbell instead. She heard a birdlike set of chimes ring throughout the interior. Then, as if she had been expecting them and waited by the window for their arrival, Renee opened the solid oak door.

She stood two inches shorter than Reeve, and had the same blond hair and gray eyes that Reeve had inherited from her mother. Her face, though, did not bear the freckles of Georgia. Instead, it was covered in old pockmarks, and her eyes drooped, as if casting dark circles underneath were part of their purpose. She had her hair pulled back into a loose bun at the back of her head, and silver and yellow strands dangled against her angular face. Her large nose sat like a dominant mountain in the center of her face, bearing a brown-rimmed pair of glasses with bottle-bottom lenses that overshadowed her thin, red lips. She wore a frumpy green housedress that hung on her chunky body like the sack of a jellyfish; it moved with her as a jellyfish glides through water, its thin rayon bouncing up and down in a mysterious illusion of purpose.

When she saw the odd pair standing on her porch in the dim light, she squinted her eyes and examined them head to toe. Reeve, wearing the raggedy jeans she had worn, but since washed, on her night with William, and a thin white t-shirt, was still drenched with rain, and pieces of her hair stuck to the side of her face. Aurelio, still somewhat dry, wore jeans and a button-down cotton shirt, though his curly dark hair bore the appearance of a restless sleep.

Renee had not seen Reeve in fourteen years, and didn't expect or recognize her.

"May I help you?" she tried to be as cold as possible, suspecting they were salesmen or Jehovah's Witnesses.

"I hope so," Reeve began. "I'm your niece, Reeve O'Reilly. And this is my husband, Aurelio Lucero. We've come here all the way from Daddy's ranch, and we have a little money, but that's all." She didn't know what else to say, so she stood waiting for a response.

Renee's eyes widened in surprise. She calculated how old Reeve could be, thinking that she must only be a teenager, and she looked again at the dark stranger beside her.

"Well, Reeve, Aurelio, come in. I'll fix us a cup of tea."

Renee rarely had visitors. Her parents had both died before Georgia, and she kept to herself. She had never planned on living alone, but her looks and her desperate bashfulness had kept her from many dates, and the years slipped by until she became a middle-aged woman, too old for a husband. Instead, she committed most of her time to teaching, working with students in the worst schools of the city, anxious to see the changes that took place in their learning from the beginning to the end of the school year. When Reeve and Aurelio appeared at her door, she was both pleased and disappointed, for she wanted to see her niece, but feared for the path she had chosen in what seemed to her a frantic attempt to get away from the bad-tempered Seth O'Reilly.

"I suppose I can offer you a bit of help," Renee began as she poured the hot water from the teakettle into the mismatched porcelain cups. "But you'll have to tell me the story. The whole story." Renee was used to dealing with other people's problems. She found them much more bearable than her own. Whenever her students needed help, she sat down with them and discuss all the factors in their lives that were causing them problems. Renee had a special talent for opening her heart and her eyes, so that when people sat across from her, they felt they could say anything to her.

When she sat across from Renee in her comfy housedress and green felt-trimmed slippers, Reeve had a sense of home. Though she hadn't spoken or written to her in years, she felt herself cracking open the truth that she thought she could never say aloud again. The story flowed out of her mouth like water released from a dam, flooding the vicinity with its devastation and power. Renee remained still as she sipped her tea, her eyes zigzagging between Reeve and Aurelio. She listened as Reeve laid out the details of William's arrival on the ranch, nodding her head slightly as she thought of the greed that could overcome men. She listened as Reeve described her date with William, as Reeve choked up and looked at her hands when she told about the rape. She listened as Reeve described how she and Aurelio had met in the loft, like some twist of fate had caused their hearts to come together for the first time. She listened as Reeve described the fury of her father, and the journey of the couple through Texas. She listened to the silence that consumed the room when Reeve closed her mouth, sucking in long breaths of air before she could respond.

"You have had a difficult journey," she began slowly, as if blessed with the powers of a great Irish crone. "You've been through too much for someone your age. You should be out gallivanting with your friends and drinking sodas at the local fountain. But life has asked something different from you, Reeve. Life is testing you now, to see if you're strong enough to keep going." She locked their twin pairs of gray eyes.

"Do you think you're strong enough?" She asked the question with the genteelness and confidence of one who can read minds, as if she expected a positive response, but was also not allowed to offer one.

Reeve looked back at her aunt and the longing for her mother, and all she had missed with her absence in her life, plagued her. In the moment between Renee's question and Reeve's answer, the love that had been buried in her heart for most of her life emerged into the light, and Reeve felt an involuntary smile enter her face.

"Yes, I am strong enough," she said as Renee squeezed her hand.

Aurelio sat stone-faced beside her. Like the bubbling of water coming to a boil, a thirst of loneliness simmered in his throat. He wanted a drink, but he couldn't say why.

Chapter 25

On their first trip to Kansas City to meet Carter's family, Luisa had picked out a sleeveless red floral dress with matching shoes. They drove the ten hours from Denver east on I-70, leaving at six in the morning to be sure to arrive at dinnertime. Luisa wore sweats and a t-shirt in the car, her hair pulled back in a low ponytail. Carter had selected John Grisham's The Rainmaker to listen to on tape for the ride: half for the way there, half for the way back. He didn't like to talk much while driving, but instead enjoyed soaking up the view of another place, the changing of the landscape according to the time of day and the season, and listening to music or books.

As they escaped from the congestion of a Friday morning rush hour in Denver, Carter slipped his pickup into cruise control at seventy-five miles per hour. The book narrator's voice filled the extended cab of the Chevy, and the only communication between the pair involved Carter's frequent glances in Luisa's direction, his hand reaching over to squeeze her thigh, and kisses that he blew in the air to her. Though they said little, Luisa would always remember the drive as one filled with happy anticipation.

The previous weekend, Carter had taken her to Glenwood Springs and asked her to marry him. He now decided that since she would be a part of his family, she had better get to know them. They took the Friday off before Memorial Day to make the journey, and the sky's blue penetrated the horizon as they moved along the flatlands of Kansas.

Just after Topeka, where they had stopped for gas, Luisa turned the tape off and decided to freshen up her knowledge of Carter's family. "So, what does your mother do for a living?" she began, wanting to be sure that she had enough information to appear knowledgeable and interested at the same time.

"She runs a beauty parlor out of the basement," Carter said.

"And your father?" Luisa knew the answers, but she was tired of listening to the sad story in the book and anxious about a family she would be a part of but had never met.

"Don't worry, Sweetie, they're going to love you," he patted her leg with the tips of his fingers. "They'll love you because I do."

Luisa couldn't be sure. When she had introduced her fiancé to Aurelio, he had nearly lost his mind in anger, appalled that someone could think of marrying her so young. "But you and Mom were that young!" she had protested, and he shot back, "Yeah, and look—" but hadn't been able to finish. Luisa knew the rest of the sentence, though she had the decency at the time to keep her mouth closed as well.

"How can you be so sure?" Luisa looked over at Carter, whose eyes were focused on the long stretch of road before him. The blacktop sucked up the heat of the day, sending greasy waves back into the blue-skied atmosphere.

The dimples on Carter's face shined in the light. "You'll see, Sweetie. You'll see."

He was right. When they arrived at the two story brick home on the Missouri side of Kansas City, Julia DaSilva, Carter's mother, came running out of the house with her arms open and a welcoming smile on her face. She had been searching the street for Carter's truck for over an hour.

"Is this my new daughter-in-law?" her voice carried across the yard in a singsong chirp. Luisa avoided a direct look from her soon-to-be-mother-in-law, stepped out of the car, overwhelmed by the enthusiasm of a stranger.

"Hi, I'm Luisa," she began, but was stopped short by Julia's warm arms wrapping around her.

"I know everything about you, Sweetie. Carter doesn't leave out any details." Luisa's face reddened and she looked at the ground as Julia said the words. "Oh, don't you be embarrassed, Luisa. This is just the beginning of our life together." She laid her arm across Luisa's shoulders and walked her into the house. Carter followed with the suitcase and backpack they had packed for the weekend.

When Julia opened the red front door, a waft of roast chicken, sweet potato casserole, broccoli and cheese, and sweet honey rolls tickled Luisa's nose and caused her stomach to grumble. The entryway was decorated with red, white, and blue streamers to celebrate Memorial Day and Carter's grandfather, George Carter, who had served in World War II and for whom Carter had been named. The living room had vaulted ceilings with skylight windows bearing streams of light from the setting sun across the hunter green suede couch, loveseat, and matching chair. Seated around the fireplace on the furniture was the remainder of Carter's family: his father, Salvatore, his brother, Sid, and his sister-in-law, Lila. They stood from their chatter, the red wine glasses still in their hands, and let out boisterous applause and laughter when the three entered from outside.

"Well, it's about time," Sal said, "I think we've been waiting for you for about as long as our son has. Give me a hug, little lady," Luisa felt small as the large, dark, muscular man picked her up. A warm, sweet taste filled her mouth as he put her feet on the floor. She looked at Sid and Lila, who returned her gaze with their eyes shining.

"Don't let that bear scare you away. I'm Sid, and this is my wife, Lila. We're so happy to finally meet you. Carter told us a long time ago that he had met his bride, and we're glad to see that he's finally making it a reality." Sid winked at his brother, who shook his hand after he had dropped Luisa's.

"You're going to love this family," Lila, too, beamed with happiness as her thin, manicured fingers touched Luisa's shoulder.

Luisa had nothing to say. Lila pinpointed her thoughts. She already did love this family because it was the way she had always wanted her own family to be. She wrapped her arm around Carter's waist as they went into the dining room to eat. She bubbled with pride and love when she saw the table, set with fine china on top of a white linen tablecloth.. She was a special guest and a regular member of the family at the same time, and couldn't imagine a better beginning to the life she would share with Carter.

Tepid rain dotted the tin roof over the concrete outdoor hallway of Reeve's apartment building. Luisa stood knocking on her mother's door, listening for the familiar stomp of Reeve's exasperated steps coming to answer. Alejo stood beside her. She clutched his wrist in her palm, holding him back from his strong desire to run up and down the hallway.

"Don't you want to see Grandma?" Luisa cooed, forcing niceness into her tone. She knocked again. It was nearly six-thirty, and her mother should have arrived home from her office half an hour ago. Water dripped from the roof onto the blacktop below the second floor apartment, and then a loud thunderclap struck with shocking force. Alejo covered his ears and whimpered. "It's OK, sweetie, we'll go inside now." Luisa rustled through Alejo's diaper bag for her keys. She had a copy of the one to her mother's apartment for emergencies.

When she opened the door, the odor of rotten garbage and unchanged cat litter infiltrated her nostrils. The shades were pulled tight, and the coffee table was covered with old fast food wrappers and pizza boxes. Luisa stopped for a moment, thinking that she must be in the wrong apartment. She scanned the scant furniture: the futon had been opened up, and the recliner next to it was covered in clothes. The kitchen counter had piles of dirty dishes that were coated with half-molded bits of food. The cat, Ray, scampered out from under the futon and let out a loud, wailing meow. He dashed over to his food dish when Luisa looked down at him, but the cat food bag sitting next to it lay on its side, empty.

Luisa hadn't spoken to her mother in over a week and hadn't seen her in nearly three. Reeve sounded distant on the phone when they last spoke, but the shock of the filth that surrounded Luisa now couldn't begin to describe what was going through her head. Reeve had always kept a spotless house, insisting that she and Byron do daily chores that involved vacuuming window blinds and waxing floors. Even when she moved away from their family home into the small apartment two years ago, Reeve had always kept it as clean as if it were the Brown Palace Hotel. Luisa expected to see a disaster like this in her father's house, but she didn't know how she could handle it in her mother's.

Alejo still stood beside her, though he tried to wiggle away from her grasp. She squeezed his hand and said, "No," as firmly as possible without sounding angry. She stood staring at the disaster and considered her options. Just when she was about to leave, she heard the toilet flush.

Reeve appeared in the doorway of the bathroom with her hair pulled back into a neat bun and her beige pantsuit cleanly pressed. She wore her usual red lipstick and layers of mascara and eyeliner, and her nails had just been manicured. She gave Luisa the usual loving-mother look, and Luisa looked back at her mother as if seeing her for the first time.

"I wasn't expecting you," Reeve said, "or I would have cleaned up a bit."

"Didn't you hear me knock?" Luisa asked, unable to think of anything else to say.

"Oh, I was listening to the radio I guess." Reeve's pleasant manner was the sugary icing on a poisonous cake, and Luisa didn't know if she wanted to cut through to the center.

"Mom, are you OK?" She tried to hide her suspicion.

"Why yes, honey, of course. What makes you think otherwise?" Her grin mocked Luisa's intelligence.

"Mom, come on. This place is a mess. It stinks. How can you stand it?"

"Oh, I don't know." She looked around the room, examining the various piles of filth. "Maybe I thought you might notice me for once if I made a mess of my life like your father has." Her saccharine introduction melted into the arsenic of truth.

"What are you talking about?"

Reeve had controlled the anger for as long as she could stand. She rushed toward Luisa in a fit of rage now, her finger pointing accusingly at her face.

"What do you think I'm talking about? I worked my ass off trying to support our family for all the years of my marriage to that loser father of yours. I worked full time, paid all the bills, cooked, cleaned, and took you and Byron to school every day. And just when I thought you might turn to your mother in your time of need, you turn to your father instead, and pull out that horrible manuscript? And then, as if that wasn't bad enough, you make this crazy decision to move in with your neighbor, some man you had never met, who could be a child molester, or worse? How could you betray me like that?"

Luisa walked over to the futon where she pushed a pile of clothes and balled up sheets to the floor. She pulled Alejo into her lap and sighed.

"Haven't we all been through enough?" she whispered, though she wanted to say more.

"Yes, we've been through too damn much. Everything is gone now, everything. All we have is this little boy—" she held back the tears, but Luisa, too, began to cry.

"I just wanted to help Papa. He said he'd go into a detox program, a halfway house, and clean himself up. I really believed him this time. He's a mess. But he still has a dream, and I thought maybe I could make it into a reality, once and for all. I needed something to look forward to. I can't find a job, I had to sell my house, my husband... Can't you understand, Mom? Can't you just give me a break?"

A silence hung between them that did not disguise the ticking of the wall clock or the traffic that zoomed by on the busy street in front of the apartment building. Alejo squirmed in her arms, and Luisa gave in and let him wander through the mess. Reeve still stood looking down at her daughter, her hands on her hips.

After holding the same perplexed look on her face until her cheeks began to twitch in the desire to move, she said, "Do you think you could help me clean this up? It's driving me crazy."

Luisa wiped her tears away. She walked into the miniature kitchenette and pulled several trash bags out from under the sink. "Why don't we just throw everything out and start fresh?" She moved through the room, gathering cups, plates, old tissues and crumpled up pieces of paper, then throwing them into the sack. Alejo, like a soldier following his sergeant, trotted in Luisa's shadow and picked up whatever pieces he could find, joining in on the game.

"What an angel," Reeve said, "aren't you proud?"

The rain had subsided and the tin roof outside now glistened under the bright hot sun. Luisa hugged her son and squinted her eyes against the light that shone through the window.

"I couldn't be more proud," she said, and continued to clean.

Reeve followed her to Warren's house. She hadn't seen it before, and wanted to be sure that Luisa had decided correctly, at least for now. As she drove her old Honda behind Luisa's Corolla, a twinge of familiarity struck her. She realized that, although Luisa had not asked her for help, she had done what was in her means to get her feet back on the ground. Guilt inundated Reeve. It swept over her in a monstrous stance, images of her past washing over her mind. The real reason she had allowed her apartment to fall into despair was that she felt her life had done so, and the physical filth symbolically reminded her of all that she couldn't offer to her daughter and grandson. Although she didn't grieve for Carter in the same way as Luisa, she grieved for the wonderful life that Luisa and Carter had, for all it represented (Reeve's own lost dream), and for all that it was (the happiest she had ever seen her daughter). She hated what she had become because of the death of her son-in-law and hated even more how well Luisa seemed to be handling the death. She drove behind Luisa now and felt as if she drove behind her always. How she wanted to catch up with whatever strength it was inside of her daughter that kept her going strong and with a smile. Instead she sat behind the wheel of her own broken dreams and mourned the loss of her foolish young ambitions. She was older now and wiser, but still found the border between what she wanted and what she had heavily guarded and difficult to cross.

When they arrived at Warren's house, Reeve could see the immaculateness of his lifestyle before entering the front door. The lawn was not only green with the lushness of one that was watered daily, but it was also edged perfectly around every sidewalk. The flagstone walkway between the main sidewalk and the door had been swept that morning. The two green bushes in front of the living room window were trimmed into perfect rectangles, and a line of marigolds along the front of the house had not a single weed to suck the water from their soil. The ash tree that shaded the entire center of the front yard acted as if it dropped no seeds or twigs, and its lively emerald leaves flourished under the setting sun.

Drinking in the perfection of the home, Reeve's heart filled with relief. At least, she thought, Luisa will be safe here. Reeve had seen Warren only once, as he was leaving with a stack of boxes to take from Luisa's house to the Goodwill, and hadn't thought, at the time, that anything but neighborly kindness would develop between the two. Now, as he opened the door with a proud grin, his rusty hair neatly trimmed and combed, Reeve was glad that her daughter had made such a sound decision.

"It's a pleasure to see you again, Mrs. Lucero," Warren held out his hand.

"Oh please don't call me by that name. Call me Reeve," she said, trying not to sound desperate at the ring of her ex-husband's permanent mark on her life.

Warren had lived alone for so long that he hardly knew how to accommodate guests, both physically, through the offering of food or drink, or verbally, through polite conversation about the weather or whatever else it was that he imagined people out in the world talked about. So when Luisa busied herself with putting Alejo to bed, he felt a quietness enter the room in its awkward solitude. He decided to get right to the point.

"I understand that you are probably a bit concerned about Luisa living with me," he tried to look into her eyes, but humility instead cast his eyes to the floor. "But I want you to know, I only want to help her out a little. I have no..." he didn't know how to explain his whole life, his whole purpose in all of this, in a few simple words. "I have no bad intentions," was all he could think to say.

Reeve looked around the living room, its white walls, hardwood floors, simple furniture, and plain decorations screaming boredom to her. Her breathing resumed its usual pace. "I think she'll be OK here. Thank you so much for your generosity. I don't know what we would have done otherwise. We really appreciate it."

"You know, I've been living alone in this house for thirty years. No one has ever come to stay with me even overnight. I guess I thought it was time to open up my home to someone. Maybe I'm just a lonely old man now," Warren's face reddened as he said the last words.

"Oh, don't say that. You never married?"

"No, I never had too much interest in being around people. I've always enjoyed keeping to myself, and I like to make plans on my own. It's easy to plan for things when the only one to worry about is yourself."

"Well, one thing I learned early on in life is that you can't plan everything. I learned that when I met Luisa's father, and when I found out I was pregnant with both of my children." Reeve's eyes glistened as she looked at Warren. "But of course, sometimes surprises can be blessings in disguise."

"Yes, I suppose they can. If Luisa's husband hadn't died, I wouldn't have this bit of happiness I have right now," Warren hid his smile from Reeve as he patted his knee.

Luisa reentered the room. She had been standing in the stairwell listening to their conversation which eerily reflected her thoughts. Just that afternoon, she had been thinking about her life with Carter, how they planned everything from the date, time, and location of their wedding, to when and how they could buy a house, to Alejo's birth. Their lives were so perfectly planned that it seemed nothing could change that; and in one day, everything changed, and Luisa felt as if she would never be able to make any plans again. Moving into Warren's house represented her lack of plans: she knew she couldn't stay forever, but she also knew that she had no idea when she would leave.

"You're right, Mom," Luisa said, "sometimes the things we don't plan can be blessings in disguise. The problem is, too often we don't see the blessings soon enough." She wanted to say more, to explain to her mother the magnitude of the manuscript in her life, to show her the initial drawings she had composed, to talk passionately about the subject that meant so much to her life right now. But instead, she sat next to Reeve on the couch and patted her thigh.

"Would you like something to drink?" She could have been offering a glass of lemonade, but Reeve only heard the word drink and her heart lifted inside its chest.

"No, Sweetheart, I think I'll be going now. It looks like you've found yourself a nice place to stay. Thank you again, Mr. York, for being so generous to my daughter. I can't tell you how much it means to me."

Warren stood and walked her to the door. "Oh, don't thank me," he said, "Thank Luisa for bringing me a new purpose," he looked at the doorknob as she left, still too shy to hold her face in his full view.

The sun had set behind the mountains and the air around her smelled of rain as Reeve walked to the car. She could hear the somewhat distant, steady noise of cars moving along a busy street. Crickets and cicadas sang out to each other in the moist grass. She dashed toward the Honda with the words, "Just make it to the car," repeating in a rushed whisper on her lips, and pulled her keys out with a shaky hand. She was unable to even start the engine before the failure of her life twisted itself inside her throat, and the tears blurred her vision as she drove away.

"How could a stranger offer more to my daughter than her own mother or father?" she screamed again and again, her voice echoing off the thin glass of the window, dimmed by the blasting air conditioner and the rumble of the old engine. She asked the question in the same way it disappeared into the night: without an ear or an answer.

Chapter 26

Frankie's mornings began at three-thirty, when his alarm clock buzzed, waking him and his three brothers, who rolled over and returned to the slumber of youth. In the cool, dark hours of the morning, he rode his bike twenty-three blocks tossing papers into people's driveways for sixty-three dollars a month. When the sun cast its early gray light over the skyscrapers of downtown, Frankie threw the black leather bag that contained various shoe horns, several shades of polish, and a multitude of soft felt rags over his shoulders and headed east. He spent the rest of the day meandering from office building to office building, begging if he could polish the shoes of businessmen who rushed into work each morning or tried to get a bite to eat at lunch hour. His best business always came around five o-clock, when he discovered that men who had rushed all day were in no rush to return home. But by then he was exhausted, the twenty-five-cent fees all jangling in his pocket to bring home to Mother.

After three years of hard labor from which he took no pleasure or monetary reward, Frankie shined the shoes of a Marine Corps recruiter who passed out flyers in his blues uniform. Frankie, who had become studious and quiet in the bitterness of his adolescent toil (he missed school as an amputee misses his lost limb), hardly noticed the difference between the navy blue, black-tied uniform with the four stripes on each arm from the hundreds of dark suits that whizzed before his dreary eyes each day.

"Son, you look like a good hard worker. I believe I have the perfect job for you," the recruiter patted him on the back as Frankie expertly shined his shoes in less than five minutes.

"I already have two jobs, sir. I don't think I need another."

"How old are you? You look awful young not to be in school."

"Seventeen. We're… kind of hard up for money at home."

"Have you ever thought of taking the GED?"

"What's that?"

"The Graduation Equivalency Diploma. It's a test you take that's as good as having a high school diploma. And once you take it, you can join the Marines, and make a lot more than you ever will shining shoes."

Frankie's face reddened. He stared at the layer of gray muck on the concrete sidewalk. "Oh, I don't think my mother would much like me going away like that," he said, his voice low and filled with humility.

"What your mother would like," the recruiter said, holding out his hand for a friendly shake, "is the money you'd be able to send home every month."

His nights, which had before that day meant preparation of dinner, a quick shower, and an exhausted plop into bed at seven-thirty, changed into a secretive study of the book from the library: Preparing for Your GED. He not only hid in the basement with a flashlight and the book, but also hid away extra money from his mother, working twice as hard as usual to earn enough to pay for the exam. Frankie became obsessed with his new dream of freedom, of getting away from the house, its memories, and his present life to escape to a world filled with the commitment and respect that came with wearing a Marines uniform.

One warm morning in May, just after Frankie's eighteenth birthday, he packed up his usual bag of shoe shining items and headed east on his bike, his lips sealed with the lie inside of him. Instead of going to his usual office buildings, Frankie had to report to a high school on the other side of town to take the GED. The stress of the lie, the test, and his two options for a future (to remain in his mother's house shining shoes and delivering papers like a slave, or to see the world), all melted away as he pedaled with the fury of a man going into battle. His eyes wide, his mouth filled with the moist air of the early morning, and his heart pumping with the blood of a new man, he felt confident and relieved as he arrived at the school.

Frankie, who had always excelled in school, found the test easier than he had imagined, and whizzed through the test booklet in half the time allotted. When he emerged from the front doors of the high school into the bright sun of midmorning, he hopped onto his bike and headed over to his recruiter's office.

"I took the GED this morning, and I'm sure I passed. It was a cakewalk!" Frankie's long legs and freckled face glowed under his crazy red hair. The recruiter, Sam Goodson, looked up at the boy.

"Well, that's great, Frankie. Now why don't you sit down here and begin to pick out some career fields?"

"Oh, there's only one career field I'm interested in. Sniper training."

"Becoming a sniper isn't the easiest thing to get into, Frankie. You have to pass a lot of tests, and you have to have perfect vision."

"I already have the vision. You tell me what I need to study and I'll pass whatever tests come my way. Where do I sign up?"

"Hold on, son. First let's wait and see the results of your test. How long did they say it'd be?"

"Six to eight weeks," Frankie's voice lowered as he said it, the time period looming over him like an interminable torture.

"Well, then, think of a few alternatives to becoming a sniper in that time. Here's a list for you to take home and look over." The recruiter handed him a small brochure that listed all the career fields with brief descriptions after each.

When he arrived home later that afternoon with only a few quarters in his pocket from the brief time he had spent shining shoes, he tried to hide his eyes and his happiness from Mother. But as he looked to the floor and avoided her glare, Warren, who sat studying for his finals at the dining table, could see the light in his eyes. Although they hadn't talked about it, Warren knew that

Frankie had been studying each night, and that secrets surrounded him now everywhere he went. Warren, the expert at keeping secrets from Mother, felt offended and appalled that Frankie, too, had developed the technique, and he feared the outcome of what he planned. As Frankie prepared dinner, Warren's eyes skidded back and forth between his books and Frankie's face, searching for answers beneath the happy flush that he carried on his red cheeks.

Doris, who sat in the living room most of the time now in front of the television they had purchased a year ago with the younger boys' lawn money, wandered into the kitchen when the food was almost ready. Frankie frantically tried to avert his eyes from her, but when she asked him for his money, he had to look up.

"I didn't make too much today, Mother," he said, trying to sound sheepish and like a failure. "I'm sorry, but I think a lot of businesses were closed today. I didn't see too many men downtown." Frankie's eyes glistened with a combination of pride and deceit.

"Wipe that smirk off your face, boy!" Doris moved across the hardwood floor in a rage, the backside of her hand aiming for Frankie's cheek. But just as quickly as she made her move, Frankie made his. He reached out with his own arm, muscular from carrying and throwing newspapers for four years and shining thousands of shoes, and clenched her wrist in the palm of his large hand. He twisted her arm and pulled it behind her back, pushing her up against the wall.

"You will not hit me or any other person in this house ever again, or I will call Social Services on you so fast that you'll be in jail before you can blink." The words oozed out of him as if ridding himself of a poison that had swirled in his mouth for a decade.

Warren, unable to focus on his work, stood in the doorway of the kitchen taking in the scene. Though it was a warm evening, he shivered as he stood watching, fearful of the inner anger that might explode from his mother's depths.

"Let go of me, boy, or I'll have you thrown in jail! Who do you think they're going to believe, the poor, weak housewife and mother of six, or the strong, strapping, abusive son of an abusive father?"

"Don't you even think for one moment that my father was abusive! He did the smartest thing of all—got the hell away from you and your hatred!" Frankie held her face against the wall as her body squirmed beneath the weight of his, her legs wiggling like snakes.

"If your good-for-nothing father had stuck around, maybe you wouldn't have to quit school to support your family. You ever think of that, you little bastard? Let me go!" Doris masked the tears that streamed from her eyes. The mint green paint on the wall had darkened from the moisture of her face.

"My father may have been weak, but at least he did what he could to try to get Warren away from you. And he loved him! He loved us all, equally, boys and girls. But you, Mother, wouldn't know love if it slapped you in the face." Frankie's voice lowered and he loosened his grip.

Doris fell to her knees, her bitterness engulfing her like a swarm of bees. She began to rise again, but caught a look of Warren standing in the doorway. Well-fed and now thirteen, Warren had grown taller than she and stood with his arms crossed and a solemn look on his face as she stared at him.

"This is all your fault, you rotten seed," she glared at him. He didn't move.

"Stop it, Mother! Stop!! When is it ever going to stop? I can't wait to get the hell out of here." He hadn't meant to say the last part, but Doris shot a frightened look up at her eldest son.

"What do you mean? You're not leaving until I say so."

"I'll leave whenever I damn well please," Frankie began, "because I can do better than this, all of this. I wasn't meant to deliver papers and shine shoes for the rest of my life. I'm better than you, Mother, and your goddamn slave labor."

"Oh, and how do you suppose you're going to get a job or an apartment? Who would hire you? You have no boss and no real work experience. You're just a waste." In her fuming voice, Warren could hear the fear rise, though she tried to hide it behind the fury. Frankie, too, saw the fear in her eyes, and he tried to hide the smile that crept to his lips.

"In six weeks, I'll be enrolled in the United States Marine Corps, and I'm going to be far away from here." With deep satisfaction, Frankie rolled the words out of his mouth. Just as he did so, fire returned to Doris's eyes, and Warren turned on his heel and ran outside, slamming the door behind him and not returning home until long after everyone had gone to bed.

The morning of Frankie's departure, Warren sat bug-eyed on the living room couch, his head resting between his knobby knees to gather some momentum for the good-bye. Frankie surfaced from the bedroom wearing a white t-shirt, a faded pair of blue jeans, plain white tennis shoes, and white socks. His red hair dangled around his face like the sloppy strings of a mop, and he rubbed his eyes as he adjusted to the dim gray light of early morning.

"So you're really going, then," Warren's voice was hoarse from exhaustive tears that had streaked his face throughout the night. He looked out the window, onto the street where a new boy delivered newspapers, his inexperience obvious as most of the papers landed in the moist grass rather than the concrete walkways.

"Yeah, I really am." Frankie paused, thinking of all the things he wanted to say to his brother, the speech he had prepared the night before now escaping his memory.

"You know, it's going to be all right. Freddy and Kenny can look after you now. They're big enough to stand up to her. And you're getting pretty strong yourself."

Warren averted his eyes, still examining the dilapidated route of the new delivery boy, his bicycle zigzagging around the street as if he were on drugs. He felt a knot in his throat, and feared speaking because he didn't want Frankie to see him cry. The songbirds had awakened and whistled their morning greetings to each other as they swooped through the air, but the silence between the boys was palpable enough to swallow the noise from outside.

"And anyway, it's only a few more years. Soon you'll be out of here yourself." Frankie knew he was beginning to sound desperate. "Hey," he started again, walking over to Warren and patting him on the back, "I get thirty days of leave every year. I'll be back before you know it."

"No you won't," Warren's anger erupted from his chest, "you're never coming back. Why would anyone ever want to come back to this god-awful house anyway?" The emptiness of Frankie's absence had already consumed him. He twitched with emotion, his eyes still focused on the growing light from outside. He tried to keep the moisture inside his eyes, but he found himself releasing it, the salty, bitter tears streaming down his face in a waterfall of anguish.

"I will come back, and soon enough, in a couple of years, I'll make enough money to be able to get a little place of my own. And then," Frankie hadn't meant to tell Warren this yet, for fear that it might not come true, but seeing the pain of his brother, he wanted to do all he could to relieve it. "And then I'll be able to have you come live with me, away from her," he reached for Warren now with his arms wide, waiting for a hug.

"I have to catch my bus. Come on, Warren, give your old brother a hug," he pleaded now, in his heart at least, for a look in his direction. Warren sat like a statue with his face toward the window.

"Go on, get out of here," he mumbled, and limply held out his hand. Frankie squeezed it and rushed to the door. Warren remained on the couch with his eyes focused out the window and watched as Frankie walked down the street. He carried his shoulders like a confident, grown man, his head up and looking forward. Warren watched as he reached the corner, looked both directions, and crossed the street. Then Frankie disappeared into the depths of the city, and Warren sat alone on the living room couch as Doris crept into the room with her bathrobe slung loosely over her shoulders.

"He gone?" her voice cracked with the dust of the night still sitting in her throat.

Warren nodded a reply, his eyes still on the view from the window.

"Well get your ass up and fix me breakfast, you lazy little bastard."

His face twitched as the hand that hadn't touched it in years created a fresh red mark.

Chapter 27

For three weeks, a torrential downpour pounded the roofs, faces, and streets of Houston each afternoon. The summer rains were unusually strong, and many of the side streets flooded, causing cars to choke up and sputter to a halt. The power went out nearly every evening, just before dusk, and Reeve and Renee would sit in the two wingback chairs reading books by candlelight while Aurelio sat in the kitchen watching the tiny black and white television that Renee kept on the edge of the old metal table. Like sisters, the aunt and her niece discussed the books they loved, the authors they had read, and the reasons they loved to read. Their late afternoons became a comfort zone of common interest. Reeve, after her strenuous encounter with the reality of adult life, felt herself sinking back into adolescence as she sat with her legs hanging over the arm of the chair.

Aurelio knew that their stay couldn't last. He spent each morning walking the streets, going into shops, restaurants, and department stores and filling out job applications. By their second day in Houston, he had memorized Renee's address and phone number, and was able to complete the applications with speed and efficiency. After a brief lunch in Renee's house, which often consisted of strange items like peanut butter and fluff sandwiches, oily potato chips, and moist brownies, Aurelio and Reeve searched the want ads for apartments, calling some and visiting others.

Renee always stood in the background to their plans, making comments only when she wanted to tell them something about a neighborhood they looked at or a good way for Aurelio to get a job. ("It's always a good idea to call the store manager so your name will stick out from the pile of applications when he sifts through them," or, "You don't want to live over there. They have a real gang problem.")

Aurelio disliked Renee, though he couldn't say why. She seemed sloppy and plain to him. Each room in her house had random piles of books, magazines, and newspapers. The walls, a sticky yellow, hadn't been painted in years, and the gold shag carpet reflected styles from a decade before. The single small bathroom had soap scum as thick as frosting on a bittersweet cake, and the kitchen was disorganized, the countertops cluttered with plastic containers full of various food items and recipes, the drawers filled with miscellaneous receipts, twisty ties, old phone books, and an occasional piece of silverware. Renee represented to Aurelio exactly what his mother was not: she was sloppy, nonchalant, and purposeless. He hated staying there, where he and Reeve had to sleep in separate quarters since Renee's tiny spare bedroom had only a twin-size bed. Aurelio slept on the lumpy plaid couch that had probably been in the same position for twenty or more years, his nights haunted by restlessness and nightmares.

When a month had slipped by, the rain subsided, and Aurelio was offered a job. The sun shone on their luck for two days. Just after they found a job, they found a decent one-bedroom apartment in a nice part of town, not far from where Renee lived. Aurelio began working as a bagger in a grocery store. Although it wasn't his dream career, he socked away money right from the start, asking that Reeve prepare tuna fish sandwiches for dinner three times a week, turn out all the lights in the apartment during the day, and try to live on the money they had earned from selling Stargazer. For six months, Reeve clipped coupons, ran her errands by taking the bus throughout the city, and read countless books from the library for entertainment.

Reeve visited Renee about three times per week. Once the school year began again, Renee didn't return home most days until six o'clock, her afternoons filled with science club meetings, staff development, and class planning and grading. Reeve would often be waiting on her doorstep when Renee pulled up in her old Jeep, anxious to hear about her day and to talk away her loneliness. Aurelio's shift at the grocery store was twelve to eight, so she didn't have to return home to fix a simple meal for him until well after seven. She and Renee would sit at the kitchen table drinking cold glasses of lemonade and talking about what they had missed in each other's lives for eighteen years.

Despite her frumpy appearance, Reeve loved Renee. She was the only living relative she knew of who cared more about her than her own father. She loved Renee because she had told her everything, and Renee hadn't turned her away, but instead had opened her heart and home to Reeve and her husband. She loved Renee because she understood Reeve better than anyone ever had, and she filled the emptiness of Reeve's days with a warm smile and interesting stories about the students at her school.

Aurelio would come home each night to a meal of rice and chicken stir-fry, bean burritos, or the tuna sandwiches he so loved for their frugality and taste. Each night, he would have in hand a small sack of groceries from the store, items that had been on sale or that had been discontinued. With his employee discount, their grocery bills never stacked up. Reeve almost always stood in the kitchen with the yellow apron tied neatly around her waist, trying to play the perfect housewife that she had imagined her mother must have been. She offered him a kiss and a hug. Aurelio, his heart still flooded with the hopes that his dreams would come true and he could return to Mexico soon, would reach for his wife with the gentle touch of a comfortable lover.

One morning, as Aurelio still slept on the old full-sized mattress that rested on the floor of their tiny bedroom, Reeve awoke with a strange rumbling in her stomach. She felt nauseous and had to rush to the bathroom. Aurelio, who slept like a hibernating bear, didn't hear her vomit or flush the toilet, but Reeve knew, as she felt the brief relief from the nausea enter her body, what had happened. They hadn't been careful in their lovemaking, the money being too tight to buy condoms, and Reeve not knowing enough about ovulation to predict when they shouldn't have sex.

The nausea returned almost at once, and Reeve spent the rest of the morning sitting and lying on the bathroom floor, staring at the plain white walls and ceiling. She turned over in her mind all the good and bad aspects of the pregnancy, but she couldn't spend much time on the good things without quickly returning to the bad. It was a Saturday morning, and by eleven she felt strong enough to move from the floor of the bathroom to the old floral couch that Aurelio had purchased at a garage sale. In a groggy state, Aurelio came out of the bedroom rubbing his eyes and wondering why his beautiful young wife wasn't next to him in the bed when he awoke.

When he saw her curled with a book in her hand, but her eyes out the window, her knees pulled against her chest, he knew something must be wrong.

"Que paso, Chiquita?" he whispered, sitting beside her on the couch.

Reeve had debated with herself all morning about when she would tell him the news. She thought that she should wait until she knew for sure, but she didn't think a pregnancy test could prove it to her anymore than her own body already had. As she sat across from Aurelio, she focused her eyes on her book. The silence enclosed all the empty space in the bare room. Aurelio, nervous about what she might say, couldn't think of any other words to prompt her along, so he waited in anxious anticipation for her response.

"I think I'm pregnant," her voice was low, barely above a whisper. All she could hear was her heart thumping inside her, as if it had moved on its own from her chest into her eardrums.

Aurelio wanted to scream. He stared into his wife's face: in that moment, she represented everything he hated and loved about coming to the United States. He thought, before, that marrying her would be the ticket to his future, but when she told him the news, he saw nothing but failure enter his view. He imagined that he would work as a grocery store bagger for the rest of his days, and Reeve would stay home, surrounded by screaming children. They would have no money, no ways to advance from this rotten life they had created for themselves in the lust of their new marriage. He felt guilty and hateful all at once.

"Are you sure?" he heard himself say, though he didn't know how the words had entered his mouth.

"I'm pretty sure. I haven't had my period in about six weeks, and I was sick all morning." Aurelio's disappointment seeped through his question. Without even looking into his face, Reeve could feel his anger. It sat like a mosquito on his skin, sucking the blood dry in its haste for survival. She had wanted more than anything his happiness in this disclosure of news, but she knew, as she lay on the floor of the bathroom that morning and stared out the window waiting for him to awaken, that it would be too much to ask. Aurelio had presented her with the manuscript on their first night together, and he lived and breathed by its success. She didn't know how they could ever get it published now, or even move out of the small apartment, or even have the money to buy a crib.

Aurelio let out a long, disgruntled sigh and put his head in his hands. "How will we ever pay for a baby?" he murmured, blocking the tears that crept into the corners of his eyes.

Reeve had already thought of the answer to this question, and had it ready on her tongue like a jack-in-the-box waiting to jump out. "I'll get a job to save the money to pay for everything the baby needs. And we'll shop at garage sales and thrift stores for the clothes and the other stuff." Reeve thought about the ten by ten single bedroom in their apartment and its absence of furniture. A crib would take up most of the empty space.

"How can you work when you're pregnant? You need to take care of yourself, not work hard and hurt the baby." Aurelio tried to be logical, to think what his mother would have done (she never worked, but for taking care of all the children and the household), and he tried to hold back his appall at her suggestion.

"Lots of women work while they're pregnant. I can find an office job, like a receptionist, where I can sit down all day and answer phones or something. It's no big deal." She was lying now, because the thought of trying to find and keep a job in the next few months frightened her, but she didn't want Aurelio to be so disappointed by the pregnancy that he would leave, so she was willing to do anything. She didn't mention his manuscript; nor did he. She waited in the tangible awkwardness of his delay for any sign of hope to show itself in his eyes. But now, just as he had done moments ago, he averted his eyes from hers, and she felt a wall building up between them as they sat across from each other on opposite ends of the couch.

"I don't know if it's such a good idea for you to work. My mother never worked, and we had little money. But she was always there for our family." The sharpness of their cultural difference struck Reeve for the first time when he said those words. She knew it would be a struggle, that everything in their marriage would be a struggle, because of their opposing views on family, career, and everything else.

"I will be there for the child. I'm just talking about getting a job for now. Just to save money to buy the diapers and the clothes and stuff. I'll breastfeed the baby so we won't have to buy formula. I'll quit working when I have it." She hated the word it to describe what was growing inside her, but she couldn't think of a better term.

Aurelio didn't let the silence invade the room. Instead, he stood up and headed toward the bathroom.
"I have to go to work. I'm late." He went inside and shut the door.

It didn't take long for Reeve to find a job. With her pretty blond hair, unusual eye color, and patient smile, a young executive hired her on after just three days of looking. She had to buy new clothes, something she hadn't thought of before, as the office required that everyone wear suits, skirts, or nice blouses and pants. Her primary purpose at the financial planning office was to answer phones and transfer calls to the various businessmen. She sometimes had to make coffee or run to the local deli to purchase everyone's lunch. She picked up on the complicated task of operating several phone lines at once, and by the end of her first week, with her chipper voice and appropriate small talk being the first warm greeting to many new clients, her boss told her that she was the best receptionist he had ever hired.

Reeve began to feel like things were going to be OK, and that they would have enough money to pay for the baby and publish the manuscript. But right when she began working her eight to five position, for which she was still able to return home in plenty of time to prepare Aurelio dinner after his shift, Aurelio stopped coming home.

On the first night it happened, Reeve panicked. She called the grocery store where he worked ("He left two hours ago," the tinny voice of the cashier assured her), Renee ("Don't worry, sweetheart, I'm sure he's fine,") and finally, the police ("A person must be missing for forty-eight hours to file a missing persons report."). No one knew where he was, and Reeve felt her darkest fear being realized: he was going to leave her and never return. But, in the early hours of the morning, after rocking back and forth on the sofa in a whimpering slump for an interminable amount of time, Reeve remembered that the manuscript still rested in the satchel in the closet. She rushed into the bedroom and flung open the door to verify, and she knew Aurelio would return. She just didn't know when. She gave in to her exhaustion and crept into bed, falling into a deep slumber that was disturbed by the combination of the bright sun rising in the eastern sky and shining on her face through the small window, and Aurelio's heavy, labored breathing as he curled up, fully clothed, beside her.

Reeve raised herself and leaned into her husband, anxious to wrap her arms around the safety he brought to her life. But as she leaned forward, the bittersweet scent of tequila emanated from his mouth. His hair and clothes reeked of cigarettes, and his drowsy state confirmed where he had been for most of the night.

For years afterward, Reeve would think back to that moment that she discovered Aurelio had a problem. She would think, as she drove home from work one day with two screaming babies in the car, "Why didn't I leave right then?" She would think about that moment on nights when Aurelio wouldn't come home until well after his children were in bed, having not seen them all day, and her heart would twist inside of her with remorse. She would think about that moment when Aurelio would come home early from his shift on yet another blue-collar job, his pockets empty and his face sullen from the termination. She would think about that moment as they struggled to pay bills, her measly paychecks barely getting them from one week to the next.

But when she was in that moment, though a part of her wanted nothing more than to walk out of the apartment, close the door, and never return, all she could think to do was shake Aurelio awake.

"You're going to be late for work," she said in a flat voice.

Aurelio stirred, but did not move to get up. "No voy a trabajar hoy," he mumbled, the words slurred with the drool that dripped from the side of his mouth.

"You are too going to work today. It's not their fault you went out and got drunk last night, scaring the hell out of me." Reeve raised her hand to slap him in the face, but she found the words harsh enough and stopped herself.

"I'm too sick," Aurelio muttered, leaning over and vomiting on the olive green carpet.

Disgusted by the smell and the sight of it, Reeve had to rush to the bathroom herself. When she was finished, she crumpled onto the floor and sobbed. She had always pictured what it would be like to be married, to have a house on her Daddy's ranch and a husband who loved to work, to raise beautiful children who loved the land and respected their parents... and now, sitting in the cage of a bathroom in their tiny apartment, Aurelio sick with drunkenness and missing his only opportunity to improve their lives, Reeve felt the sting of her father's last words wrenching through her body.

Aurelio could hear her sobbing through the hollow plywood door. Although his body ached and his stomach churned, he forced himself to get up and followed his wife into the bathroom. Seeing her in a pile on the floor, Aurelio leaned over and wrapped his arms around her, sharing in her tears.

"I'm so sorry, Chiquita, I'm so sorry," he repeated again and again, trying to console her and relieve his own remorse. "I won't let this happen again. I was just so stressed about the baby, and us not having any money... I just needed a break from it all, you know? You understand, right?"

When Reeve didn't answer, Aurelio stood up to brush his teeth. Reeve raised her face and watched him as he moved through his morning routine. He brushed his hair with a wet comb and returned to the bedroom to pull his uniform from the closet. He dressed smoothly and silently, and then returned to the bathroom to relieve himself. He then went into the kitchen, where Reeve stood up and followed him.

"Do you know how worried I was? I called your job, I called Renee, I even called the police!" She rushed after him in a sea of rage, wanting to attack him, her hands in tight fists and held at her chin.

Aurelio ignored her, pulling several paper towels from their dispenser. He held the paper towels under the sink and wetted them, then went back into the bedroom and began scrubbing away at his pool of vomit.

"I have to go to work," was all he said as he stood up and threw the paper towels into the trashcan under the kitchen sink. A bitter taste filled his mouth as he returned his eyes to Reeve's. She didn't understand; had no sympathy for the stress he carried on his shoulders. Not only did he barely make enough money to pay their bills, but he also needed extra to be able to type up and send copies of the manuscript away to publishers. And she had to ruin it all for him by becoming pregnant. She didn't know how his heart ached for Mexico, how he couldn't go back there without the published stories, how shamefaced he would have to be, coming into the city with a wife, a child, and no money.

All of the bitterness swam into his eyes as she stood in the living room in one of his t-shirts, her hair a stringy mess around her puffy-eyed face.

"I'm going to be late," he mumbled, but he knew he was already too late to have a good excuse. He tried to think of one on the way out, but his mind was blank against the bright sun and the heat that surrounded him. He walked to work with his stomach churning and his head screaming at him in pain.

Reeve stood in the living room of the apartment with her face set in an expression of disbelief. She watched the door until the sound of his footsteps had disappeared from the stairway down onto the sidewalk below. She stood until the muscles in her calves ached and she felt faint. Then she sat cross-legged on the floor, like a little girl waiting for her father to come home. She didn't know what else to do.

Chapter 28

Though her father had abandoned the religion long before Luisa entered the world, Carter insisted that they marry in a Catholic church. For months prior to the wedding, Luisa had to take courses at the church with priests and nuns. They had to learn about Natural Family Planning and what makes a Catholic, about how and when she would be ready for her first Eucharist, and how to raise their children to be Catholic. Luisa, who had never had a religion, was at first zealous about her classes, and was so happy with Carter and his Irish-Italian heritage that she wanted to do anything to become a part of it. She didn't mind the strict conservatism of the church, at least not in the beginning. It wasn't until a week before the wedding that Carter approached her with some news that surprised her.

"I really appreciate all you've done to become a good Catholic," he began, "but the truth is, it's more for my family than for me. My mother would die if I didn't get married in a Catholic church, and, as you've probably figured out by now, they don't just let anybody in there to have a wedding. You really do have to be Catholic."

"What are you trying to say, that I've been wasting my time for the past ten months?" Luisa was offended by his fib.

"No… I don't think your time has been wasted. It's just—well, I don't really agree with a lot of things in Catholicism. And I don't expect to raise our kids Catholic anyway."

"What? What do you mean? Why didn't you tell me that before?" Luisa's feet were freezing now, fearful that this was the beginning of a lifetime of lies.

"Well, I didn't think you would go through with the conversion if you thought it would just be for our wedding day. And if you want, we can try going to church for a while. But I think you'll agree with me about it once you become a part of it."

"I just can't believe this," she muttered, and left the patio, where they had been sitting at the table going through the list of guests who had returned invitations so that they could give the caterer an exact number.

Carter followed her into the interior of his first floor apartment. Luisa had gone into the bedroom and sat on the bed thinking that she had made a mistake with her life.

"Sweetheart, I'm sorry I lied. I hated to do it. But I don't lie to you at all about anything else. And if you really want to try and be Catholic, we can. Maybe I'll have a change of heart. I just have trouble with people who force their religion on their children. I guess that's what I'm most afraid of doing. Maybe we could take our kids to church and see if they like it, and if they do, we can keep going." Carter had a way of touching Luisa on the small of her back that caused her to shiver and believe him. His fingertips gently skimmed the skin underneath her shirt, sending chills up and down her spine on the warm July afternoon.

"I just can't have you lying to me, Carter. You know I hate lies," she looked him in the eye, wanting to say more, to remind him of one of the first conversations they'd had in their relationship, when she told him about the endless lies of her father throughout her childhood, and how she despised lying more than almost anything else. "And this is a huge lie." Her voice solemn, she looked at her hands.

Carter took her hands in his and with his face begged her to look back at him. "I won't lie to you anymore, I promise." He kissed her on the lips and wiped away the tears that had gathered in the corners of her eyes.

When they were married a week later in the Catholic church, Luisa knelt with her rosary beads at the altar, praying for a happy, healthy marriage that would be filled with God.. When Carter kissed her for the first time as her husband, happiness emanated from the depths of her soul. They walked down the aisle of the church hand in hand, the beginning of their lives sealed with all the hope of a perfect life.

She hadn't been into the church in years. The door's click against its jam echoed as she entered, and the cool marble shaded the heat of the afternoon sun as she took tiny steps down the aisle. Built in gothic style, the flying buttresses created a triangular peak far above her head. The air tasted like moist water on her lips as she shuffled her feet alongside the multiple rows of cherry pews. Her Birkenstock sandals whispered on the burgundy marble floor, and her ankle-length floral summer dress swung from leg to leg, casting a tiny breeze around her, as she reached the altar. She knelt there, her knees shivering from the cold stone, and grasped the rosary beads between her sweaty palms as she whispered her prayer.

It was a Tuesday afternoon. The morning mass congregation had long since dissipated, but the church remained open to visitors. Luisa, too scared to pray to God, asked for Carter instead.

"I know you're here, somewhere, because I've looked everywhere else, and I can't find you. You didn't come home again. I couldn't figure that one out. I thought, since you put so much time and money and love into that house, that you would come there for sure. Well... now the house is gone. The new people painted over the murals in Alejo's room... and probably all the others, too. I'm living next door now, on the other side of the alley, with one of our neighbors. I don't know if you ever met him. His name is Warren York. I guess he's about my mother's age. Anyway, Alejo is doing OK. I think he misses his Daddy..." Luisa sucked in her breath, determined to continue despite the tears that drenched her face. "He started to walk about two months after... and he's drinking from a cup now, and learning how to hold a spoon. And I'm doing OK, too, considering. I still haven't found a job, but I'm doing the illustrations for the manuscript my father brought from Mexico. It's a relief, to draw and paint again. It's a good release."

Luisa stopped for a moment, not because the sobbing was keeping her from going on, but because she had come to say one thing, and found herself rambling about the small events of everyday life. "Carter, I know you're in this church. I know you can hear me. I came here to tell you... to tell you that I found your letter. I had no idea that you had written such a thing. It's almost like you knew... But of course you didn't know, right? And you knew I would never look in that old shoebox unless I was cleaning out the house. But anyway, I just wanted to say thank you. Because I was having so much trouble getting up every morning; like, the pain was always there. I would fix breakfast, and the pain would be between the spoon and my mouth. I would change Alejo's diaper, and the pain would be between the song I wanted to sing inside my head and the voice in my throat. And now, since I found the letter—well, I made a bunch of copies of it, and I carry it around with me, and whenever the pain gets in the way, I just open it up and read a few lines, and it's like the pain just evaporates, at least for a while. And I wanted to thank you for thinking of me..." she was running out of words and strength. "For always thinking of me, Carter. You were the best husband anyone could have ever asked for. And you said the happiest moment of your life was right here in this church, when you took my hand and made me your wife. So I know you're here. I just hope you're listening."

Luisa's words, which had barely been a whisper, had attracted the priest from the rectory. He sat in a pew several rows back and waited for Luisa to finish. When she stood up, the rosary in one hand and a soaked tissue in the other, he stood with a gentle solitude and his arms loosely at his sides, the palms open and facing Luisa.

"Are you in need of guidance, young lady?" he asked her in a steady, calm voice, his dark eyes locked with hers. As she moved closer, recognition came over his face. "Didn't I marry you to your husband several years ago?"

Luisa's smile seemed to dry the moisture from her face. She looked up at the hundred-foot ceiling and held her hands in the air. "I knew you were here," she called, her voice echoing through the church.

"God is always here, my child," the priest said. Luisa nodded, her heart filled with hope as she approached the priest who had sealed their wedding vows.

"I'm having a bit of trouble," Luisa began, "getting over my husband's death." She forced her face towards the floor, her hands at her back. Four months had passed now since that black letter day, and the aching inside her chest still crept into her throat, her mind, and her actions at every thought of Carter.

"I'm sorry to hear about your loss. Do you want to talk about it?" Priest Huxley sat down in the pew and laid his thin white hands on his lap. He held a tranquil expression on his oval face, his brown eyes glistening in the light that shone through the stained glass windows.

"Father, I'm sorry we haven't come to church. Carter… well, I didn't find out what his real reason was until we had been married for almost a year. He had a friend in high school, an altar boy, a kid who was not only baptized, went to church with his family every Sunday, and completed his Confirmation, but who was also gay. He was one of Carter's closest friends. And when he tried telling the priest in confession about his homosexuality, the priest admonished him for being a sinner against God. And when he told his parents when he was seventeen, they kicked him out of the house for not being a true Catholic… they were very strict. Well, the boy wandered from house to house, staying with different friends, but soon his luck ran out because most of his friends didn't approve either. Carter wanted to help, but his parents didn't think it was a good idea to encourage homosexuality. So… the boy killed himself after a few months of all this rejection. And Carter never felt the same about the Church after that."

Luisa had poured out the story as if she were serving Priest Huxley lemonade. She felt a weight come off her shoulders as she said it, as if she had instead told him what he wanted to know, probably how long it had been since Carter died, how he had died, and how she was dealing with it. But she found it so easy to spill the painful story of someone else, because her pain balanced with that of a stranger.

"I'm sorry that Carter rejected the Church based on such an unfortunate event. If the boy had come to me, I would have told him what I tell all the sinners who come to me every week: 'The Lord Jesus has sacrificed for us so that you may sin. If you ask for His forgiveness, He will grant it.' I'm sorry that the priest at their Church said the wrong things and the boy felt as if his sins were worse than any other man's. But that isn't true in the eyes of the Lord." Priest Huxley's voice flowed like a placid stream through a forest. It fed the wildlife around it with the luster of its waters, and asked nothing more than a bit of rain to help it along.

Luisa embraced the serenity of Priest Huxley as she sat next to him on the pew. She felt her heartbeat slow its pace and loosened her grip on her rosary as she lifted her face toward his.

"Carter died four months ago, in a car accident. After the investigation, they discovered it was a DUI—the other driver, I mean. Right in the middle of the day, too. We have a son, Alejo… well, Alejandro, but Carter wanted to call him Alejo. He's named after my paternal grandfather…" Luisa spoke in a quiet tone, carefully choosing her words. "I think I would be OK, or at least, I would be better than I am, if the other driver hadn't been drinking. Because my father—" her voice cracked, but she went on, "my father is an alcoholic. I feel like it's an ironic twist of fate that my husband, who never drank, should die by the same evil vice that I lived with my whole life."

"Perhaps God is asking something of you that He doesn't ask most people. Perhaps He asks that you become an advocate for the limitation of alcohol. You know firsthand how alcohol can ruin lives, probably more than most people who may have an alcoholic in their families. Perhaps you can begin speaking to our youth group about the dramatic damages of alcohol on people's lives. When God hands us tragedy, we must learn how to cope somehow, and giving to others is one of the best ways I know how to deal with grief." A small smile parted Priest Huxley's pink lips.

Luisa had always hated talking in front of people. Just thinking over the idea now, as she sat in the sanctuary of the Church alone with the priest, her hands became clammy and her throat constricted. She felt tiny and alone, regretting the decision to come here.

"I don't know, Father Huxley," Luisa could no longer hold her face to his, but instead returned her gaze to her rosary. "I'm not so good at talking in front of a group of people. Especially teenagers," she said, hoping he would offer her a better idea.

"It doesn't have to be a formal sermon at the altar, dear. You can just sit down with them at one of their meetings and talk about it in a casual, comfortable atmosphere. Our teenagers need guidance from someone other than their parents, someone who really knows the dangers of alcohol and drugs. You would be the perfect candidate. School starts again soon, and that means they'll be invited to many drinking parties. You can help them avoid falling too far into danger." Priest Huxley spoke with confidence, as if he wouldn't consider a negative response, and not only expected her to speak to the youth group, but planned on it.

Without processing the information too deeply, Luisa found herself saying, "OK," and thanking Father Huxley as she stood to leave. "My son is at home with my neighbor now, taking a nap. But he's about to wake up, I'm sure." Luisa jotted her phone number on a piece of paper from her purse and handed it to the priest.

"Call me when you think would be a good time to do the talk," she held out the paper, and Priest Huxley grasped her palm in his as he took it from her.

"God will be with you now, for you have come to Him. I hope to see you in church on Sunday."

Luisa could hear the echo of the door closing reverberating through the church as she trotted down the concrete steps of the exterior into the hot July sun. She knew she had marked the world that day as she heard the noise of the door closing behind her. She hadn't felt that way in a long, long time.

When she returned home, she looked through the back window and saw that Warren sat at the kitchen table feeding Alejo his strawberry banana yogurt. Warren's face, with the wrinkles around the eyes and the shiny, loose hair falling around his temples, glowed with a grin as he made airplane noises while putting the spoon into Alejo's mouth.

"Who's gonna catch the airplane?" she heard him say, "who's gonna make the airplane land?" Squealing in delight, Alejo threw his arms into the air. Luisa's face, which had hardened in the car as she stressed about what kind of talk she might do in front of a roomful of rowdy teenagers, softened now into a comfortable expression of relief as she watched the pair. The chessboard reentered her life for a moment; she hated feeling good about what she saw in the window, because it meant that Carter wasn't there to see this moment in Alejo's life, but she wanted to be happy and move on at the same time.

When she opened the back door and entered the kitchen, both faces turned toward her. "Mama!" Alejo cried, and held out his arm toward her.

"Hi sweetie," she said, and walked over to him, clutching his tiny palm in her own. "Are you having fun with Warren?"

"He's almost done eating," Warren said. "He woke up a little early today. I think he was hungry from playing outside all morning." Warren had closed his shop early and come home to watch Alejo when Luisa had called him and told him she had some important business to do downtown.

"Well, thank you for watching him." Luisa sat across from them at the table as Warren gave Alejo his last bites.

"Did you get everything you needed to done?" Luisa couldn't help but be amazed when she had conversations with Warren. Everyone else she had ever known always wanted to know the exact details of every situation. When she first told her mother about Carter, she had to go step by step into how they met, how long they had been dating, and his entire family history. If she ever asked Clara to do her a favor, Clara had to know everything about the task involved and why she needed her help. Even Carter had always been inquisitive, asking her how many credits she had left, how many hours were each class, or what she did each day with Alejo while he was at work. But Warren was a whole other animal; Luisa never had to explain anything to him. When she asked for something, whether it be for him to park his car in the back instead of the front or take care of Alejo, Warren would simply do it, no questions or comments involved. Luisa admired this in the man, but wondered, too, how he could never just want to know what was going on.

"Yes..." she pondered for a moment whether she should tell him about her afternoon, then decided to approach the subject in a different way. "Have you ever been to church?"

"My family always went to church. But I never started going with them until I was seven. My mother never even had me baptized like she did for my other siblings. But I still went through the motions of first communion and, later, confirmation. But I rarely go now. I'm not attached to it like some people. I think God works in mysterious ways... I know it's a cliché, but I can't imagine how going to church could make me believe more in God. Maybe I don't have enough faith because of the way things worked out for me in my life... I don't know." Warren looked at her as she busied herself with wiping Alejo's face. "I guess I took too long to answer your question."

"No... I went to the church where Carter and I were married. That's what I wanted to do this afternoon. I've been having more trouble adjusting than I've let on." She couldn't say anymore just yet, but she didn't have to, because Warren knew. He had heard her in her bedroom or the bathroom in the morning, weeping, unable to move. He had seen the passion come through in the paintings and drawings she had created for her father's manuscript, and he saw, often, that she watched the new people in her former house, her eyes fixated on the happenings so much at times that she would sit still for an hour or more.

"I thought that maybe going to the church... I know this is going to sound ridiculous to you, but I feel like Carter is still out there somewhere. And I thought, since I've looked everywhere else, that he might be there. Am I just crazy?"

"No, of course you're not. But don't you think that Carter is everywhere you go?"

"What do you mean?"

"I mean, Carter is always going to be in your heart, in your mind, in your thoughts, your actions... in everything you do for a long time. Do you think that he would only be in one place?"

"No... but sometimes I feel like I'm losing him. It seems like, even a month ago, I could wake up in the morning and be able to see his face in my mind, every detail, from the bright blue eyes to the stubble that he always let go for a few days too long... and now, it's like I have to look at a picture to be able to really see him. And I'm just so scared that—" Luisa stopped herself, because she was afraid of how stupid she would sound.

"You're just so scared that you're going to lose him forever?"

"I guess that sounds stupid, right? He's already gone." Luisa held Alejo in her lap now, and wrapped her arms around him for the comfort of his tiny love.

"But he's never really gone." Warren set his eyes on the view of his garden, which now flourished from his daily watering and the hot July sun. "Let me tell you something that I've learned about life from living it at a distance. If you try too hard to let go of what's most important to you, you lose yourself in the process. Trust me, I know."

Luisa wanted him to say more, to go into detail about his life, about what or whom he had let go, but she found her tongue stuck against the roof of her mouth.

"I think I'll take Alejo for a walk," she said at last, and closed the back door behind her as she left. Warren still sat at the table, watching her go, his heart aching for all the wrong turns he had made in his life.

Chapter 29

She drove across town to sit in the cool shade of a gigantic hundred-year-old cottonwood tree whose roots drank the water of the small lake on the south end of the popular park. The old blacktop walkway that encircled the lake was cracked whenever it met its match against the roost of the cottonwoods, the tallest trees in the metro area. Reeve loved to sit under this particular tree because the grass underneath was always just a little damp, and just cool enough so that when she lay her thin yellow sheet down, she could feel the coolness seeping through the earth into her thighs and the rest of her body. She loved to watch people speed by on high-tech touring bikes, clocking the two-and-a-half-mile loop around the park again and again. She loved to watch young families push their toddlers in strollers, pointing out the birds they saw in the sky or the carp they saw in the water. She loved to watch young lovers walking hand in hand, mesmerized by the beauty of the park and the love in each other's innocent eyes. When she came here, always with a picnic dinner from a local fast food restaurant, she could imagine that she lived in one of the luxurious homes across the street from the park, or that she lived inside one of the happy lives of the people who passed by. She could imagine that she didn't ever have to leave, that she might live in the nature of the world, and become fresh and in love again as she was in the early days of her marriage.

Reeve came to the park alone whenever she felt the sadness overtaking her. Since Carter's death, though he was neither her husband nor her son, she felt the sadness creep into her body two or three times a week. But, in the serene surroundings of the lake, the cottonwood trees, and the happy people who buzzed by, Reeve felt the pain loosen its grip on her life. With the divorce papers filed, Reeve felt that her life must be reaching a turning point. Since she had already faced the poor weather of misery for most of her adulthood, she assumed that, with the failure of her marriage, her motherhood (she hadn't heard from Byron in two months, and Luisa hardly spoke to her anymore), and her lackluster career, her life could be headed for a better place.

At forty-six, she waited in anticipation at the edge of her life, and then, as if she had been waiting for it all along, one day a registered letter arrived at her doorstep in the hands of the mailman, who held a pen out to her in his usual impatient manner.

Reeve had signed for the letter and slammed the door shut with one brief glance at the return postmark: Alpine, Texas. She had never heard from her father since the day she married Aurelio, though she had sent him various letters over the years. She stood behind the door of her tiny apartment gripping the letter between her clammy fingers. For the first time in twenty-seven years, a sense of hope engulfed Reeve, and she carefully pulled open the seal as she imagined a letter that asked for her to visit, or asked if there were any grandchildren, or asked for her forgiveness. Instead, as she should have guessed, inside the envelope was a formal letter from an attorney.

Dear Mrs. Lucero,

As per the will and testament of Mr. Seth O'Reilly, who passed away in July 2003, you are the beneficiary of ten thousand dollars. Attached is your cashier's check. Thank you.

Sincerely,
Hiram Franklin
Attorney

In a rage of tears, Reeve had rushed to her car with the check in one hand and driven first to the bank to deposit a portion of the check and then to a travel agent where she purchased two plane tickets to El Paso. She looked at the tickets in her hands now, moving her eyes between the detailed itinerary to the smiling faces of the passersby. How easily she found herself daydreaming about their lives again, but she knew what she had to do.

When she knocked on Warren's front door, she didn't expect him to answer. It was a Wednesday afternoon, and she figured it would be a good time to catch Luisa and Alejo alone. She wasn't prepared for his kind greeting and warm smile, the bitterness of his available generosity still burning inside her.

"Hello, Warren. It's nice to see you again," Reeve glanced about the immaculate living room. "So... not working today?"

"I decided to give in to corporate America and admit that I can't compete. I'm in the process of selling my shop."

Reeve had never even visited Warren's shop, though Luisa had gone on and on about the intricacy of his electric train set. "That's too bad. But you're not going to retire, are you?"

"Oh, goodness, no. I wouldn't know what to do with myself. I think I'll look for a low-stress, part time job. Just to keep busy. I don't much need the money." He couldn't look at her as he said it, feeling he had said too much. Luisa had told him about her mother's poverty.

"Well, that sounds like a good idea." Reeve stood in awkward silence for a moment, clearing her throat. "Is Luisa around?"

"She's up in her room painting. Alejo's taking his nap right now."

"Do you mind if I go up?"

"Of course not. Go ahead."

Reeve could hear the music blaring from behind the closed bedroom door when she stood at the bottom of the steps. Luisa played Joni Mitchell's Ladies of the Canyon, and as Reeve listened on the other side of the door, she had to wait before she knocked. She remembered playing the record again and again for Luisa and Byron when they were young, singing along with the music, dancing her children across the dining room floor. When they had become teenagers, they had developed tastes in music that Reeve couldn't fathom, Byron listening to hard rock and heavy metal, Luisa alternating, strangely, between hip-hop and country. But now, as if her childhood had revisited her adulthood as an effect of her grief, Luisa felt the desire to listen to the music her mother had played for her when she was young and innocent to the evils that surrounded most aspects of her life.

Reeve opened the door and watched her daughter paint for several minutes before Luisa noticed her. Engulfed in her work, she stroked with fiery passion on a canvas the size of the window that overlooked the backyard. She painted the vibrant colors of a Mexican dancer in traditional garb, the rainbow coming out in the hem of her dress and the ribbons in her hair. Luisa was so involved in the painting that she thought of nothing else, and when Reeve tapped her on the shoulder, she jumped up and screamed from being startled.

"Mom! What are you doing here? Aren't you supposed to be at work?" She tried to hide the irritation in her voice, but the disruption of her artwork disturbed her.

"I took the day off. I've come to ask you something."

"You took the day off and drove all the way across town to ask me something?" Luisa stood with the paintbrush in her hand, wiping some splattered paint from her empty hand on the smock that covered her clothes.

"Luisa, you know me. I don't do crazy things like take a day off work and drive across town to ask you a question unless it's something really important."

Luisa's face, which had been hard and suspicious, softened as her mother sat down on the bed, clutching her purse against her chest.

"Well, what is it?" she leaned over and carefully placed the brush on top of the drop cloth.

"I got a letter in the mail from Texas."

"From Aunt Renee?" Reeve hadn't spoken of Renee in years, but Luisa still remembered her, though she hadn't seen her since she was three.

"No, from your grandfather's attorney." Reeve looked up at Luisa now to examine the expression that came over her face, which held both confusion and anticipation.

"Your grandfather passed away last month. He left me ten thousand dollars. That was all that the note said. It came with a cashier's check."

"Oh, Mom, I'm sorry," Luisa's voice fell as if it were a balloon letting out air.

"Well, that's not the only reason I came. You're doing something great for your father now," she tried not to throw the words at her. "Now I want you to do something for me." Reeve bent her head to look into her purse. She pulled out the envelope from the travel agent. "I want you to go to Texas with me, so I can show you where I grew up. So you can know about where I came from. Because you never got to see it."

Luisa sat down on the bed next to her mother. "OK," she said in a soft voice, "When do we leave?"

Alejo had never been on a plane. He was fascinated by the window, and for most of the ride, pounded his palms against the plastic, looking out into the world. He eyed the people surrounding them on the plane as if they were a part of some intricate family of which he was suddenly a member, and squealed in delight when the captain came over the loudspeaker to welcome them aboard and announce their arrival in El Paso.

At the airport, Reeve rented a minivan because she thought it would be more comfortable for the three of them. Reeve had only been to El Paso a few times, and the years had erased any of the familiar street names and landmarks from her memory. The car dealership offered them a map and directions to Alpine, and when they stepped out of the cool air conditioning of the airport into the car rental lot, a wave of heat nearly knocked them over. Before they even arrived at the Dodge Caravan they had rented for two days, their foreheads and backs dripped with perspiration. The white van, with its immediate cool air tingling the moisture on their bodies, was one of the greatest feelings of relief Luisa had experienced all summer.

"How could you stand living in this climate?" she looked appallingly at her mother.

"Well, the difference between here and Denver is that there's always lots of shade. You'd be amazed at how much of a difference that makes. Plus, it actually rains here in the summer. Every summer." And, as if she had spoken to the sky, as they entered the highway out of the city, dark clouds from the west rolled in, their forecast a steady rain that would ride with them all the way to Seth O'Reilly's former ranch.

"This ranch was in my family for three generations. It would have been mine if—" Reeve had prepared the speech to share with Luisa on the two-hour ride for the past three days, going over it in her mind each morning as she packed and cleaned up her apartment in preparation for the trip, but now, as she began to speak, she found the words lost somewhere in the midst of all her nervousness and nostalgia.

"If you hadn't married Papa," Luisa finished her sentence for her. She knew more about Reeve's life than her mother realized. As a child, Aurelio would often tell her the story of how they met, how Reeve had saved him from a life of hard labor and solitude on a crazy man's ranch. Despite the fact that the crazy man was her grandfather, Luisa always loved to listen to the story, her father wrapping his arms around her as he sat next to her in bed, his love warm and complete and safe in those moments of truth.

"I know I haven't told you much about my past, Luisa. I had a lost of reasons, but mainly I wanted to forget it. I also wanted to protect you. I thought, if you didn't know about those things, you would be OK; you would be safe. But, the truth is, maybe I should have taken the time to describe to you what it was like for me growing up, what it was like when I met your father, and how we came to Colorado. If anything, it'd be nice if you knew more about my life than what your father may have told you."

Reeve surprised her. Luisa didn't realize that her mother knew anything about the stories Aurelio had told her, and she looked at her mother with an expression of bewilderment.

"Don't be silly. Aurelio is no good at keeping secrets. You should know that by now." The rain tapped the roof in a steady downpour, and the windshield wipers methodically wiped away semicircles of clarity as Reeve drove down the curvy two-lane road. The horizon was visible for miles, though, as Reeve pointed out, unlike the dry plains of Colorado, it was dotted with countless clusters of trees and shrubs. Luisa watched out the window, mesmerized by the storm as if she had never seen rain before.

"It doesn't always thunderstorm here; not like home," Reeve said, pleased by the tranquility of the water. Alejo slept in his car seat in the back, exhausted from the day's events.

"I guess that's what's so interesting, why I can't stop looking at it. I'm so used to hearing loud thunderclaps and seeing streaks of lightning flash across the sky. This is just so... calm." Luisa looked back at her mother now, whose face had tightened in preparation for what she was about to say.

"I want to tell you about it now," she began in a quiet voice, barely above a whisper, her eyes focused on the road. She didn't say what it was, but somehow Luisa knew not to ask, and waited with her heart pounding inside her chest for her mother to go on.

"My father, Seth O'Reilly, was a hardworking man. His whole life was our ranch. He rose at dawn each morning to complete his chores, and then went to bed just after dusk. He raised me to work hard for what I wanted." Reeve reached over to turn down the radio. "The ranch had been in the family since my father's grandfather, and since I was the only child, because my mother died so young, I was the only one to inherit it. My father was very anxious, once I turned eighteen, about making sure I married the right man so that the ranch would be in good hands."

"When you were just eighteen? Isn't that a little young? You didn't want to go to college or anything?" Luisa's mind filled to the point of overflowing with the questions she had been saving up for twenty-seven years.

"Well, it was still pretty common, in such a rural area and all, for girls to get married right out of high school, even in the seventies. Besides, I never did finish high school anyway, because Daddy needed me to cook for the men who worked the ranch. He had hired this Mexican woman, Paula, who became just like my second mother, and she taught me all I know about cooking."

Just thinking about the delicious meals Luisa had enjoyed as a child, from homemade tortillas to spicy tamales, the beef so tender it just about melted in her mouth, Luisa's mouth watered for the tastes of her mother's kitchen.

"I always wondered how you knew so well how to cook Mexican. I thought you just must have learned because of Papa."

"Anyway, Paula was a great woman. She was gentle and kind, patient and giving; she was everything I could hope for in a 'stepmother,' so to speak. And maybe that's why I felt like I was, in a way, Mexican myself.

"My father left every spring to find new workers, because in the fall, when the main season was over, a lot of them went back to Mexico or moved north to pick apples or do other types of migrant work. The spring was the main time for breeding the cattle, and even then, a lot of ranchers used artificial insemination, so that's part of the reason he needed so much help. That, and of course, raising all the crops to feed that cattle. So… the day of my eighteenth birthday, my father brought two men into my life." Reeve paused to catch her breath, the speech she had practiced reentering her mind. Her heart was in her throat with the pain of the story.

Luisa sensed her mother's discomfort. She turned to look at Alejo, whose head had toppled over to lean against the side of the car seat.

"And, looking back at it now, I often feel like both of the men became my worst enemies. If it weren't for you and Byron, I don't know how I could survive." Reeve reached over and squeezed Luisa's hand. She continued to drive, the collected rainwater sloshing under the tires now, and didn't say a word for as long as she could stand to keep her mouth closed.

"We'll be there soon," she went on at last, "and I'll show you where it happened."

As if trapped within a time capsule, the town showed no outward change as the minivan approached the single gas station. Even after all these years, the gas station had the same pumps, and hadn't modernized them as all of the other pay-at-the-pump stations that Luisa had ever seen. When she stepped out of the car, the heat had settled a bit under the rain, and didn't penetrate her body as the shock from earlier that day. Alejo, a very light sleeper who loved motion, woke when the minivan came to a stop. Luisa carried him inside to the single bathroom, which was coated in twenty years worth of gray, dusty grime, only to discover that there was no diaper-changing table. Disgruntled, she brought him back to the minivan, where she awkwardly maneuvered him in the seat while changing his diaper.

"Gosh, Mom, I had no idea that you lived in Boonieville. I mean, one gas station? Isn't there a city closer than El Paso?"

Reeve's face held a smirk as she moved her eyes up and down Main Street. The buildings truly were set in stone. The only new structure she witnessed was at the very end of the block, where a small wood shack had been thrown together and bore the sign, "Videos are Us." Reeve shook her head as she looked at the old stone courthouse, the two restaurants that stood across from each other, and the familiar pharmacy.

"No, there's not," she finally said. "And I used to love this town like it was my home. I guess that even a town this small is exciting to someone who spends most of her life around cows." Reeve went inside to pay the attendant.

As they pulled away from the gas station, it occurred to Reeve that she should get some information before making an appearance on the ranch. Though she hated to do it, she turned around and parked in front of the courthouse.

"What are we doing here?" Luisa looked perplexed. "I thought you said that your father's attorney already sent you the money from your inheritance."

"Well, I guess I bought those plane tickets without really thinking things through. I wanted to bring you here to see my father's ranch, but it's not my father's ranch anymore. So... I have to stop here to talk to the attorney. He's the same man who married your father and I."

Luisa's eyes widened. "You were married right here in this town?"

"Well yes, honey." Reeve turned off the engine. "I guess I never told you anything at all about how we met, now did I?"

Luisa shook her head. She wanted to elaborate about the magnitude of what her mother hadn't told her, but she couldn't. She could see the anxious anticipation in her mother's eyes as she stared at the tall oak doors of the two-story courthouse.

"Do you want to come in with me?" Reeve tried to smile at her daughter, but found her face puckering in a strange expression that combined fear and hope.

"Sure. I'll meet you in there in a few minutes. I have to get Alejo out and put him in his stroller."

As Reeve stepped out of the van, the heat singed her face and back once more. She took giant steps toward the courtroom door, pulled its heavy weight against her, and felt a rush of cool air relieve her body as she stepped into the atrium. She gasped at the sameness of the building; from the thin plastic chairs in the waiting area to the old wooden desks. It was as if the courthouse had captured the turning point in Reeve's life, and kept it here, untouched by the world, so that maybe she could come back one day and do it all over again.

Hiram's secretary still sat at her desk, though her hair had thinned and grayed, and her face bore wrinkles around the eyes and chin which she tried to conceal with foundation. She lifted her face now and took a moment to look over Reeve, whose figure had remained virtually the same since their last meeting, but whose hair was now cropped short above her shoulders, and whose eyes also carried the crow's feet of twenty-eight years.

"May I help you?" she asked in a raspy voice, trying to disguise her slight recognition of Reeve, because she couldn't quite remember where she had seen her before.

"Yes. I'm here to see Hiram Franklin." It was a Tuesday afternoon, and Reeve went over in her mind any possible reasons why he wouldn't be there, because if he wasn't, she didn't know how she was going to handle it.

"Do you have an appointment?" The secretary pretended to be polite, but Reeve could tell by the way she looked at her that she knew very well that

Reeve had no appointment, and Reeve grew irritated at the stupidity of the question.

"No, I don't have an appointment, but I flew down here all the way from Denver and I would really like a few minutes of his time."

Again, a spark of recognition flashed over the secretary's face when Reeve said Denver. She turned her wheeled chair to face the computer screen and typed something on the keyboard before looking back at Reeve. "He's meeting with a client right now," she said slowly, "but he should be able to see you in about ten minutes."

Reeve didn't reply, but instead took a seat in one of the plastic chairs, her eyes wandering about the expansive ceiling. Luisa came in with Alejo, sat down next to her mother, and whispered, "Is he here?" She reached into Alejo's bag and pulled out a bib, a towel, and a jar of baby food. "Do you want to eat, Baby?" she cooed to him before Reeve could reply.

"Yes. We're waiting about ten minutes." She sealed her lips then, not wanting to say another word in front of the suspicious secretary. She imagined that the woman was the town gossip, with all that she saw enter the courthouse every day, and even though she hadn't lived there in so long, it still bothered Reeve to even think about everyone in the town talking about her.

When Hiram stepped out of his office, Reeve felt as if her heart were imploding inside her chest. Always a large man, he was now gigantic. His stomach had multiplied two times since she'd seen him, and loose skin draped his face. His pant legs whistled together as he walked toward her, and his copper-colored hair had thinned so much that his round head shone under the fluorescent lights. Even his hand, as he held it out to her with a friendly, gap-toothed smile on his cleanly-shaven face, seemed larger than life.

"Well, I'll be damned," he drawled with a grin that spread his thick lips away from all of his teeth, "if it ain't Reeve O'Reilly. I was beginning to wonder if I'd ever see you again."

"Hello, Mr. Franklin." Reeve let his gargantuan hand squeeze hers until she felt her fingers go numb.

"And who is this little lady and precious child?" Hiram nodded toward Luisa, who now wiped Alejo's face with the towel.

"This is my daughter, Luisa, and my grandson, Alejo." Reeve was relieved to have something to say.

"Well, why don't y'all come on into my office and we'll have a talk." Hiram held out his arm as if he meant for all three of them to be wrapped inside of it. He turned to his secretary and said, "June, clear any appointments for the next hour."

Reeve felt immediate gratitude and relief. Her last meeting with Hiram hadn't left her feeling that he had any sort of respect for her. Now, a full-grown woman with a child and grandchild seemed to make him think that he owed her his full attention.

"Have a seat." Hiram said and motioned for them to sit in the two avocado green vinyl chairs that stood in front of his desk. He maneuvered his large body around the side of the desk, his actions taking up most of the tiny office.

"So, what brings you back to Texas, Reeve?"

"Well... I was hoping you could help me with that. I never did tell Luisa or her brother much about where I grew up, and I thought I might show her." She paused, trying to avoid eye contact. "Show her the ranch, I mean."

"Oh, yes, of course." Hiram's face reddened, as if mentioning the ranch embarrassed him. He rubbed his chin with his fingers, as he had done with his beard so many years before, and waited for a moment before saying anything else.

"Would y'all like a glass of water? June could—"

"No, that's all right. We just had some in the car." Suddenly anxious for him to continue, Reeve decided to get straight to the point. "Who owns my father's ranch now?"

"Well, Reeve, I hate to be the one to tell you this. Ted Dawson's grandson, William, got your father's ranch just before he died. He bought it from him, and not for the price it deserved. But your father was... he was a little bitter when he died, and just wanted to be rid of it."

In the instant that Hiram said William's name, Reeve's pale-skinned, freckled face morphed into the sultry color of her eyes. No air existed in her lungs. She sat as still as a stone in the chair, her jaw so tightly set together that no one could open it. The room dropped several degrees in temperature before Reeve, or anyone else, would dare to speak. Goosebumps crawled up Luisa's arms and back. Even Alejo sat motionless and quiet in his stroller. Hiram rubbed his chin again and again, unsure of how to go on. When the silence consumed his body so that his hands shook from the discomfort level in the room, he decided to fill Reeve in on what had happened since she left the town all those years ago.

"After you left, Seth was a different man. I've known Seth most of my life, and I had never seen him so heartbroken. When he came into town, he stopped saying hello to everyone like he used to. He never took a meal or even coffee with me for years afterwards, because I know he partially blamed me for... for marrying y'all, you know. Anyway, he would come into town with his hat pulled tight against his eyes; wouldn't look at nobody, and hardly spoke a word other than please or thanks. He kept going on down to Mexico in the spring to get his men, but I heard, from the ones who would come into town, and sometimes from Paula, that he never did treat any of them decently after you left. A lot of people in the town started to talk about how coldhearted he was, kicking you out of his life like that; but of course, some other people thought you deserved it. The truth is, no one ever really knew how Seth was, besides being a lonely old man. During the last twenty-eight years, I hardly saw or spoke to him at all. He always said he wanted to spend his life on that ranch, and he sure did, in the end. He didn't talk to me until a few years back, when he created his will. And even though I advised him against his choices, he was set in his ways. He left most of the money from the ranch to charity. You got your little piece, and William robbed him for the rest."

The last sentence caused Reeve's face to flinch. Air returned to her lungs and emotion rushed into her body. She stood, as if in the greatest hurry of her life, and spilled out in a flurry of tears, "Thank you for your time, Hiram." She turned on her heel, opened and shut the door, and rushed to the car.

Luisa sat, perplexed, in the awkward silence of her mother's absence. "We appreciate all of the information, Mr. Franklin. I don't know what's wrong with my mother." She searched the gold-colored walls for an answer, but saw only two diplomas in old metal frames that bore Hiram's name alongside undergrad and graduate degrees.

"I'll tell you something that maybe your mother never did," Hiram said, his voice low and cautious. "When she came in here to marry your father, she was beat up something awful, and looked as if she hadn't slept. I never did understand what had happened to her, but I'll be damned if I find out your grandfather had anything to do with it."

Luisa, shocked, stood in the same manner as her mother had. "Thank you again, Mr. Franklin." She held the door open with her palm as she pushed Alejo's stroller through, almost jogging to the outer doors of the courthouse.

When Luisa arrived at the van, heat waves surrounded it from the tires on the black pavement. Reeve sat in the driver's seat, her window rolled down, the engine not ignited. Her face and body drenched in sweat, she cried out long, emanating wails with her head against the steering wheel. "That dirty, rotten bastard!!" she screamed into the space between her lower and upper arm. "That dirty, rotten bastard!!"

Luisa rocked Alejo in the stroller, but he, too, began to collect perspiration on the sides of his face. She felt they would melt in the heat, so she put Alejo into his car seat and folded up the stroller to put it in the back of the van. When she sat down in the passenger seat next to her mother, she reached into the clenched fist and pulled out the car keys, starting the engine and turning the air conditioning to its highest setting.

"Mom, do you want me to drive?" She asked at last, confused about what to do, and more scared than she had been since the day she found out about Carter.

"Where?" Reeve murmured, her face still buried.

"Anywhere you want to go."

"Can you drive me back to where my life went wrong?" Reeve gave in now, and opened the driver side door.

As Luisa took the wheel and pulled the minivan away from the courthouse, Reeve pointed in the direction of the ranch. Luisa drove at the speed of a sloth, unsure of where they were going or why her mother was so traumatized.

After about ten minutes of dragging the wheels along the old two-lane highway, Reeve collected her tears inside of her and said, in a voice that threatened how serious and desperate she was, "Stop the car."

Luisa pulled over to the narrow shoulder and yanked up the emergency brake, putting the minivan in park but leaving the engine running with the air conditioning on. Alejo sat in his car seat in the back making small, chirpy sounds as he looked out the window.

"I should tell you, before we go, how I came to marry your father." Reeve began as if she were entering the beginning of a ghost story, her voice dark and mysterious. "It's not what you might think. It's not like Aurelio came into the country and swept me off my feet, carrying me away from the ranch and into another life. It's not like that at all." Reeve reached over and took Luisa's hand, clutching it within her own as she went on.

"My father had a neighbor, Ted Dawson, who owned a ranch about the size of his. All his life, he talked about somehow making enough money to buy out the Dawson ranch. I started to tell you this before, but... I didn't know how. Ted had a grandson who had gone to school on the east coast. He'd majored in something like agricultural engineering. He came to the ranch the same day your father did. My eighteenth birthday. My daddy didn't even have to say it—I knew. He had figured a way to acquire the Dawson ranch. By me marrying William Dawson."

Luisa began to picture in her mind the possible outcomes of the story. Her mother, always a bit rebellious, perhaps had fallen in love with Aurelio, and hated the fact that her father insisted she be with another. It made sense that she would run off with Aurelio to get away from all that.

"Well, I had feelings for your father, I can't explain why, from the moment he first spoke to me. I'll never forget what he said: 'How long must I work here before I can move on to better things?' It was like he spoke right to my heart. I had always dreamed of leaving the ranch, but I couldn't imagine how. Aurelio put the seed idea in my mind. I think that's what made me love him." Reeve paused, searching for the view out the window, as if the rolling fields and tree groves could guide her to the end of the story.

"Well, I wanted Daddy to be proud of me, and I knew he wanted me to be with William. So when he asked me to go out on a date with him, I agreed. William took me to dinner in one of the two restaurants in town. He was... very controlling. He seemed to think he knew everything about me. And on the way home—" she stopped to draw in a long breath of air. "He didn't take me home. He drove me way out to the corner of someone else's ranch. He turned off the engine of his pickup. We sat in the dark, so isolated, with no one around for miles. I was so scared. I didn't know what was going to happen, because he didn't say anything at all on the whole drive there. And then he raped me." The truth seeped from her lips like the great release of a dam breaking, the water rushing out and filling the river basin in a rage of freed entrapment.

Luisa now took her mother's hand within her own. The air in the minivan enclosed them, causing her body to constrict its muscles tightly against themselves. Her heart worked hard in her chest, and she could hear its beating in her eardrums. Her lips grew parched and her mind shot images before her, dark, violent images that she tried to brush away with her fingers, but could not.

"Oh my God," she repeated again and again, unable to answer with anything else.

"When we came back to the ranch, I went up to the hayloft where I always used to go to get away from it all." Reeve said as if she were a soldier who had to march into battle, like it or not. "And when I got there, there was your father, waiting for me."

Questions now inundated Luisa's mind. What did he do? What happened to William? What did my grandfather say? How did you leave the ranch? She saw the words splaying themselves in front of her, but her voice remained trapped inside her, aching to be ignited. Then, as if the recent events of the day had slipped her mind, she remembered what Hiram had said. "Oh my God," she repeated again, her whisper sharply cutting a slice in the thickness of the air.

"I think I can face him now. Let's go." Reeve spoke in a voice Luisa had never heard. She sounded like a different person had entered her body, taken over, and allowed strength to be a new part of her being.

Luisa turned on her blinker and looked behind her. She had seen no cars or trucks pass from either direction since they had stopped. She turned the wheel and pulled back onto the highway, her hands shaking in fear as they approached the ranch. She looked from side to side of the road for an answer, but all she could see was row after row of corn.

The house her grandfather built at the end of the long, straight, dirt driveway appeared to her the same as it had for all the years that it came into Reeve's sight from the passenger seat of her father's pickup. Looking at it now, a combination of remorse, anger, and happiness grasped her. She forced the tears to remain inside of her, determined to face the pain that met her head on. As Luisa pulled up in front of the house, Reeve could smell the familiarity of cow manure, and could see the men harvesting their first crop out in the field. They had a giant red harvester now that looked new. Next to one of the fields, Reeve could see another barn had been built, along with a grain silo.

The three sat in the minivan while Reeve caught her breath and tried to think through what she might say. She wore a look of deep concentration on her face. Luisa, still too frightened to speak, cast her eyes back and forth between the house and her mother. She had always pictured the ranch where her mother grew up, though Reeve had never described it, and the two-story farmhouse in front of her matched up well with what she had envisioned.

"I know it's hot," Reeve began, "but there's a nice oak grove in the back. Maybe you could take Alejo for a walk back there."

"But Mom—" Luisa found the words entering her mouth without her mind even placing them there.

"No, Luisa. Go around the back with your son. It's too hot to sit in the car, and I just can't have you witnessing this. Especially Alejo."

"OK," Luisa turned off the engine with a sigh, and then walked around to the back of the van to retrieve the stroller. The sun had inched to the horizon now, its fiery red ball relieving some of its earlier heat. Luisa could feel the temperature drop as evening approached, and she squinted her eyes toward the sun as it dipped behind a thin set of cumulus clouds. She set up the stroller on the somewhat muddy driveway, then unclipped Alejo's belt and carried him over.

"Grandma's got some stuff to do, so we're going to go for a walk. You want to go for a walk?" She tried to sweeten the bitter undertone in her voice, and Alejo seemed to buy it: he pointed to the stroller and squealed.

Reeve didn't expect an answer when she knocked on the front door. Her father had always worked dawn to dusk, and she couldn't imagine any other rancher doing differently. So when the tall, gangly William opened the door, his reddish hair now peppered with streaks of gray and his moustache shaved away, Reeve had to place her hand on her chest and take a few steps backward, nearly toppling off the porch.

As if someone from above controlled the expression on his face with invisible strings, William's cheeks moved from a broad, tight smile to a low, perplexed frown, and his eyes widened so much that he didn't seem capable of shutting the lids. He, too, placed his hand on his chest, letting loose a shocked whistle through his teeth, then opening and closing his mouth with the words, "I'll be damned."

So much inside of her wanted to explode, to jump on top of him and dig her fingernails into his skin, to kick him in the groin and punch his face until her rage was quenched by the violence she expunged. But, just as the night of the rape, she felt her body go limp and her desires not meet the reality she imagined.

"Hello, William." She crossed her arms over her chest now and stood in a protective stance. What she was protecting, she couldn't define.

"Hello, Reeve. I was wondering if you might come by here." His voice sounded different, as if he had been living in Texas so long that he had picked up a little bit of the drawl. He walked through the entryway and stepped onto the porch. He motioned for Reeve to sit in one of the white wicker chairs with the plaid cushions that bore a striking similarity to his red and white plaid shirt. "It's been a long time," he sighed as he sat down.

Reeve, too, sat, though she didn't plop into the chair with the casual comfort of William, but instead sat straight-backed on the edge, as if in anticipation of leaving at any moment. "Yes it has," she said, and moved her eyes about the covered porch, listening to the crickets come out for their evening song as the sun threatened to dip behind the cornfields.

"I've come to see, for one last time, my Daddy's ranch. I brought my daughter and grandson."

William's heart fluttered for a moment, and a look of disastrous terror crept into his blue eyes. "Oh," was all he could think of to say.

"I went into town first and talked to Hiram," Reeve felt herself trying to explain her actions. Then, as if something inside her bubbled up, she said, "And he about tore me to pieces when he told me you got this ranch. You damn well don't deserve it."

"I bought this ranch fair and square," a look of defiance fired up his freckled face now as he, too, crossed his arms and stared back at her.

"Doesn't sound fair to me. Bet my father was awful depressed if he was willing to sell it to your sorry ass." Reeve felt courageous as she swore at him, and she filled her mouth with the speech she had practiced in her mind in the car, amazed at the ease of the words that poured out. "What you did to me was the worst thing that ever could have happened in mine or anyone's life. You know, rape is worse than murder in some ways. When you kill someone, at least they can go on into Heaven and be in peace. When you rape someone, they have to live with it for the rest of their lives, its memory always present at the front of their minds. And the fact that you disappeared, got away with it, and never for one moment had to live with the torment I experienced for the past twenty-eight years makes me wish you were dead and gone."

She stopped for a moment, not because she didn't know what else to say, but to catch the surprised look that entered his face. "But you're not, and by some unlucky twist of fate, you landed here, at my childhood home, where all my happiness and sadness exist in one place. I don't know what to hate you more for—the rape or the robbery." Reeve's heart, which had echoed in her chest through the speech, now rested at a comfortable, calm pace. She dropped her arms into her lap and leaned back a bit in the chair, loosening her body as if she had just carried a sixty-pound pack on her shoulders and now rested from the release of the load.

William placed his elbow on the arm of the chair and laid his face inside the palm of his hand. He took a deep breath before lifting his face to hers. "I don't know where you ever got the idea that I raped you, Reeve. I never once heard you say no." His voice was even and remorseless, his eyes glued with hers as he said what he believed to be a reality.

The harvester, whose humming had been a background noise to their conversation, had now stopped. The crickets and cicadas raised the tone of their songs, and mourning doves had emerged from their quiet afternoon slumber to call to each other and pick at the ground for food. An occasional cow let out a long, slow, moan, and a tiny breeze whistled through the leaves on the two giant oak trees in the front yard. The sounds of the ranch flooded Reeve's ears as she tried with all the pressure in her jaw to keep it shut, and tried with all the pressure in her eyelids to keep them from widening. She realized, in the not-so-silent minutes that she sat across from the man who represented most of the hate she had carried around for so long, that, despite the bitter truth of his denial, she couldn't live one more day of her life in the way she had.

Reeve stood up, her back straight and her chin high. She didn't move once she had stood, but, with the confidence of a person who has just won the greatest election of all time, gazed into William's face. "I know what happened, you know what happened, and so does whatever soul may have been watching over me that night. If you cannot admit it, that's not my problem. But I didn't come all the way down here for you to admit what I already know. I came down here to forgive you, William. I'm moving on, and I'm going to have a better life now."

She turned without another word, leaving William on the porch with a look of bewilderment controlling every muscle in his face.

Chapter 30

The summer sun burned Warren's back and neck during its first week of unbearable heat, but then he had a layer of protection for the remainder of the season. Now with more yards to mow than ever before, Kenny and Freddy had used part of last year's earnings to buy a second lawnmower and weed eater. At last taking advantage of their secret, and with new desires that involved taking out girls and going out on the town with their friends during the school year, the two older brothers became more scrupulous with their money. Warren, who hadn't spent more than a dime in years, felt the weight of the bills in his pocket grow heavier each day, his workmanship so perfect that many of the people in the neighborhood offered him tips. To avoid home as much as he could, Warren would not only mow, edge, and weed-eat the lawn, but also offered gardening services such as planting seeds, watering, and weeding, and, for a high price, would sometimes trim the dead branches off trees or shrubs. His business consumed all of his time from April through September, with the summer months bringing in new customers and more extra work. Warren couldn't think of a better way to spend his time than the eight hours a day of backbreaking work. When he was busy, he didn't have to dwell on Frankie's absence or the dark atmosphere of his home.

Fearful that her other sons might turn on her and leave, Doris decided to be more lenient with Kenny and Freddy, allowing them to stay in school. She hoped that this allowance would bring more loyalty into her life, because as she aged and saw the growing opinions of her boys, she realized that they were all beginning to turn against her. She still couldn't decide what to do with Warren, because no matter how she tried, she couldn't bring herself to feel anything but hate for the boy. When he worked and worked and hardly spoke, his presence only apparent when dinner or breakfast were prepared, Doris felt that she could continue to have him in the house.

At first, Frankie's letters came once a week. He wrote about the strenuous workouts of basic training, the heat on Paris Island, and the other men in his platoon. Then he wrote about the special forces he was accepted into because of his high test scores and perfect behavior during basic training. Whenever Warren received a letter, he would take it into the backyard and sit underneath the old elm tree, his back resting against the gray knotty trunk, his body enjoying the cool shade of its outspread leaves. He would read the letters again and again, drinking up the words and trying to envision what it must be like to live somewhere else in the world. He kept the letters in an old cardboard pencil box underneath his bed. All of them were in their original envelopes and neatly folded in exactly the way Frankie had folded them.

When most of the summer had slipped away in a whirlwind of work, the letters came less frequently. When he didn't receive a letter in over two weeks, Warren feared that a telegram announcing Frankie's death could arrive at any moment. But then, at last, the mail brought news from Frankie, but it wasn't what Warren wanted to hear. When he opened the letter, he noticed right away that Frankie had just written part of one side of a page, when he normally wrote on the front and back of two pages. The handwriting was blurry, as if Frankie had been drunk or in a hurry when he wrote it. And what it said took all hopes away from Warren's heart.

```
Dear Warren,                    August 27, 1964

    I'm sorry I haven't written. You won't
believe it. The best thing in my life has
happened. I've met a girl, and I've received
orders, all within a month. The girl's name is
Darlene, and we met at the BX in San Antonio
where I was doing specialized training. Her
father is a retired pilot! We're going to be
married in two weeks. Can you believe it? And
in about three months, they're sending me to a
place called Vietnam. Maybe you could look it
up in the library. My whole troop is going.
They have been having a bit of a civil war, and
we're going in to help them out. I've got to go
now. I've been awful busy training and spending
all my free time with Darlene. You take care,
and remember I love you.

                            --Frankie
```

Warren's first instinct was to crumple up the letter and toss it in the dumpster. He imagined doing exactly that, but found himself mesmerized by the words so that he read the letter so many times that he had it memorized. When he felt he had read it enough, he leaned his head against the tree and squeezed out a few aching tears. He sat there well past the time he usually prepared dinner, unable to move his legs, until Doris came out to find him.

"What the hell are you doing out here, boy?" She stood over him in her yellow housedress, her hair a tangled mess. "Is that a letter from your brother? Let me read it." She leaned over to snatch the letter from Warren's hands, and as she did, Warren's body came to life with the ferocity of a lion who had been trapped in its cage far too long.

"You will not lay one finger on this letter, or on me, for the rest of your pathetic life!" Warren jumped up, the muscles in his face twitching, his strong arms showing off the power they had attained after a summer's worth of work. He now stood several inches higher than Doris, and far outweighed her physical strength.

Doris tried to appear brave, but her stout body swayed as he spoke, his size coming into her view as if for the first time.

"I'm not even a little bit scared," she said, but as she said it, her voice wavered, and she took a step back.

Warren raised his right arm into the air high above her head. Without realizing it, Doris flinched in anticipation of a painful blow to her cheek. Warren tried to keep the smirk from moving onto his face, but found the expression too suitable for his emotions in this moment of power.

"Do you think for one moment that I would sink to your level?" He caught her green eyes now, the fire he had seen for most of his life now gone. Instead, her eyes swam with a look of terror mixed with bewilderment.

"You wouldn't have the guts to hit me, 'cause you know what I'd do." Again, though she tried to sound strong and defiant, her voice instead spoke of defeat.

"There is nothing in the world you can do to me that you haven't already done. You will not destroy my life for one minute longer." Warren felt his body move closer to hers. She cowered like a frightened mouse until her back rubbed against the trunk of the tree. Seeing his chance, Warren put his large palms on both of her arms, pressing her against the tree with calm strength. "Now you listen to me, Mother. If you ever so much as think about laying a hand on me or anyone else in this house, or ever so much as think about saying one of your nasty little names to me or anyone else, I have a list of people I can call. Mavis, for one, who told me to call her if things ever got bad. The IRS, for making Frankie work all those years and never claiming it. Social Services, for making Frankie quit school when he was thirteen. I could go on," Warren's round face presented itself half an inch away from Doris's oval one, his eyes holding the fear of hers within the courage of his own. "But I don't need to, do I? Because you're going to change now or lose us all." He paused. "Even the girls."

Like a snake trapped under a boulder, Doris writhed against Warren's arms. Her jaw had dropped so that her lips were parted in preparation for speech, but no words came out between the cracked, crooked teeth. For the first time that Doris could remember, although thousands of words and images flashed across her mind, she had nothing to say. Warren held her for as long as he could stand to have his hands touching the skin he so hated, and at last let her go. Her back slid down the trunk of the tree and she plopped onto the rooted ground, putting her face into her palms. She cried into her hands and whispered, at first too quietly for Warren to hear, but then just loud enough for him to catch it, "I tried to love you, but I couldn't."

The truth arrived in front of Warren for the first time in his life. It hit him in the face with a blow that stung as painfully as the back of her hand. It clutched his heart so that he felt no beat inside his chest. It clung to his skin so that sweat remained trapped underneath, though the skin felt dry and hot like the ground of the driest desert. It broke into his muscles so that they flexed without control, bulging against the organs that kept them in place. The truth at last overtook him, and he found himself toppling to the ground next to his mother with a long, pathetic wail slipping from his lips.

He didn't know if he should hate her more or forgive her. They sat next to each other, not touching, for as long as he could stand, the only sounds distant lawnmowers and Doris's inconsistent sobs.

"Frankie's getting married. And he's being shipped out to Vietnam." He didn't mean to tell her what was in the letter, but he didn't know what else to say.

As the summer drew to a close and school started again, everything in Warren's life cooled down. The temperature of his morning walk was frigid enough to require a jacket even in early September. He couldn't remember a colder late summer. Both of his sisters now went to the elementary school, and it was Warren's responsibility to walk them to school in the morning and wait out front in the afternoon when they were finished. The girls loved Warren, especially Margaret. Every day after school she ran out of the front door with a drawing or a piece of writing or a book to show him from her first grade class. "Warren, look what I made for you!" were often the first words out of her mouth at the end of the day, her gap-toothed smile spreading across her freckled face. Rose, shier than her sister, would walk alongside Warren and hold his hand, then talk briefly about her day or something new she had learned.

Warren loved taking care of his sisters, though he knew what they represented in his life. Even Frankie promised that Kenny and Freddy would guard over his safety, they were too busy now with their active social lives at the high school. Both boys were on the football team, and though he was only a junior, Kenny was the starting quarterback. Freddy, still a sophomore, played junior varsity linebacker, and he was also very good. Both boys had somehow enough courage to talk to and go out with girls, something that Warren couldn't even imagine.

When he returned home from school each day after the fateful truth of Doris's hatred had been exposed to him, he no longer felt nervous or uncomfortable or bitter when he entered the house. As if the admittance had been more than she could handle, Doris now spent most of her waking and sleeping hours inside her bedroom, the door closed and the old radio playing big band music. She hardly ever dressed or came out, except to grab a few morsels of food or use the bathroom, and her housedress had thinned from wear so that it hung transparently over her shoulders. Doris, who had once been stout and strong, now had the body of a starving child, her arms and legs bone thin, her hips even with the rest of her body. Even her large breasts sagged so that they seemed to disappear into themselves. Doris's will, too, had weakened; she no longer cared what Warren did, or how the girls were dressed, or how to manage the five children on her own. She wanted nothing to do with any of it, and let her fear wrap itself around her cold body as she lay underneath three layers of blankets in her bed.

Warren, who had carried much of the household responsibility since Frankie left, flourished in Doris's absence. The heat of her anger towards him dissipated into a cool disregard, and he took on all that was necessary to maintain the home without too many wandering eyes from strangers. He learned how to keep the books and pay all the bills, tapping on Doris's door only to ask for her signature on the monthly checks. He learned ingenious ways to save money, like buying everything in bulk at the grocery store, or making all their clothes from fabric he bought at the Goodwill. He learned to manage his eighth grade studies with getting the girls bathed and ready for bed each night, cooking a meal for five hungry, growing children, and distributing chores so that each person contributed to the house's cleanliness, and, in his view, success.

Doris's apathy became Warren's strength. He had new confidence about what he could handle, and felt that the worst part of his life must be over, because the older he got, the closer he came to leaving the house forever. He thrived because of Frankie's love and the letter he had sent. Its presence in Warren's life had made everything different. It had made new things possible that had seemed impossible to him before.

Frankie wrote after he arrived in Vietnam, a brief note about the strangeness of the country, the never-ending jungle and humidity that allowed even the driest skin to drip with moisture. With Frankie's APO address on the outside of the envelope, Warren wrote to his brother twice a week. He told him about school, his teachers, how his brothers and sisters were doing, and how his life had changed. He always wrote at the end of every letter, "Thank you for taking care of me when I was small," because he didn't think he could say that enough times. He hoped that Frankie received the letters and read them when he had a chance, because Frankie didn't write back for over six months, though Warren checked the mailbox each day with a heart rate that couldn't be slowed from his high level of anticipation.

When a letter finally arrived, in the spring, nearly a year after Frankie had gone away, Warren clutched the envelope with the red white and blue border close to his chest as he ran into the backyard to read it.

"Go on inside and fix yourself a peanut butter sandwich," he haphazardly yelled to the girls, who stood at the mailbox looking perplexed by Warren's sudden zest. He almost climbed over the fence, he was so excited to see what the letter might say.

The handwriting on the outside of the envelope hardly looked like Frankie's, with the letters angled to the right as if he were trying to write with his left hand, but Warren recognized the large W of his name, which Frankie always tried to make much larger than the rest of the letters and with a curly-cue on the top right. When he sat down at the base of the elm, he could hear the songbirds of early spring sing to each other. He smelled the pungent scent of the daffodils whose bulbs he had planted in the fall. He focused his eyes on the envelope, which looked as if it had been folded and perhaps carried around in Frankie's pocket long before he mailed it. In the center was a strong crease mark. Warren tried to imagine what the letter might say. Would Frankie write to him about what it felt like to be married? Would he describe what it was like to be in the war? Would he go into more detail about the countryside and what his troop was doing? Warren had imagined for so long what Frankie did in Vietnam that he couldn't picture Frankie even writing anything that he hadn't already pictured in his head. In his absence, Warren had studied all about Vietnam in the library, learning everything from the religion to the government. The topic of Vietnam began coming onto the radio news more and more frequently. Now, hardly a day passed without Warren reading a newspaper headline about more troops headed that way or a news flash on the evening show about the rising death toll of American soldiers. While Warren felt uncomfortable with these stories, he never imagined that Frankie was in any danger. He figured that Frankie's intelligence would keep him away from what most of the regular infantry had to face.

He opened the envelope with the careful hands of a surgeon performing open heart surgery. As he pulled out the thin white stationary, his heart raced inside him. The letter was about the same length as the last one he had sent, but at the first sentence, Warren knew that it said much more.

Dear Warren,   April 7, 1965

    Death haunts me. It follows behind me like a
ghostly bird. I see it in the fires, the bombs
that take away the life. I see it in their
faces, so small and kind and innocent. I see
the death even in my sleep, creeping in on me
and taking away my breath. It is like a
disease, but worse. It doesn't stop or just
leave me in peace, but takes everything away
from me.
    Darlene writes as much as you. But she is
worse to hear from because she expects a baby.
How can I be a father when I'm a killer?
    A killer, a killer, a killer.
    I'm here in Vietnam. Defending my country.
Defending… hmmm. They look so small and
innocent, like they just want to go on working
in their rice paddies. Not like they would ever
want us here. Are they death, or is it me?

                          --Frankie

Warren refolded the letter and put it back into its envelope. He folded the envelope along its crease and put it in the back pocket of his jeans. Every night from then on, he took the envelope out of his pocket, put it on the dresser, and returned it to his pocket the next morning. He didn't write Frankie back. He no longer imagined what it was like in Vietnam. He no longer listened to the radio news or read the headlines of the newspapers in the newsstand at the corner. He went on with his life like a mechanical soldier, trying to imagine what it would be like to face death, but knowing all too well that he had, once, and couldn't do it again.

He didn't hear from Frankie until a phone call six months later. He was home.

Chapter 31

She could feel the baby moving now. She hadn't seen a doctor yet, but Reeve figured out that she must be about five months pregnant. She began to pray for the baby, spending each early morning on her knees at the edge of their mattress, her heart open to whatever God could hand her next. She remembered sitting with her father in the Baptist church as a child, the ranchers and their wives and families all taking part in the sermon of the preacher, shouting out, "Amen, father," or, "Praise the Lord." How ridiculous it had seemed to her then, her own father sitting upright, his lips sealed. Now, she longed for the church and the strong faith of the people who were part of it.

Renee took her to the library and showed her all the books available for new mothers. One of the books had drawings showing each stage of a woman's pregnancy. When she checked it out and took it home, Reeve spent the better part of one evening examining the pictures as if she were looking at the scrapbook of her life. The illustrations intoxicated her so that she didn't want to look at anything else or even move from the dinette where she sat, the book open under the flickering fluorescent light.

When Aurelio stumbled in late that night, hours after his shift had ended at the grocery store, she wanted to forgive him. She wanted to show him the pictures and point to her belly and say, "Look, this is what the baby looks like now," and smile at his excitement. But as soon as he stepped in the door, he carried the same sullen look on his face that he had worn for four months, and wobbled just enough to make the acrid hate bubble up inside her at his presence.

Not expecting her to be awake at eleven thirty when he knew she had to work at eight the next morning, Aurelio's ears reddened in embarrassment. "I—" the sound came out of his mouth in what sounded almost like a Texan drawl, and Reeve's heart flipped inside her: he sounded, in that one brief second, like her father. Aurelio stopped himself before going on, not willing to admit that he hadn't thought of an excuse.

Reeve sat at the table with the book in front of her. She rose to greet him, but instead of lifting her arms to offer him a hug and a cup of coffee, she found herself picking up the book instead and throwing it towards him. It was a large hardcover book with over a hundred ten by ten pages, and it flew through the air like a broken-winged bird, landing just in front of where he stood.

Aurelio said nothing, but went into the bathroom and closed the door. Just then, the baby kicked, tickling and startling Reeve. She stood staring at the bathroom door, feeling life move inside her for the first time in the same moment that it occurred to her that she could put everything to an end.

The next morning, though the sun shone through the window with its usual glorious brightness, Reeve felt the darkness of the night before linger in her soul. She forced herself to rise with the rays of the sun and went into the kitchen to fix breakfast, leaving Aurelio snoring on the mattress. She scrambled eggs and cheese next to bacon in the eight-inch frying pan, as she had done every morning since she became pregnant. She moved perfunctorily, as if her actions were commanded by some other force besides her own mind.

When she arrived at the office, she realized right away that she had forgotten something, but she couldn't say what. Her boss Ron looked at her strangely as she took her seat next to the phone. "Is everything all right, Reeve?" he asked, the look of bewilderment blinding her.

It was too hard a question to answer. "Yes, I'm fine," she said. Then, "May I please use the bathroom before work?" she asked in a little-girl voice, his strange look penetrating her and frightening her down to her bones.

"Of course, darling, you know I don't have rules about that," he patted her on the back and went into his office.

When Reeve saw herself in the mirror above the porcelain sink of the bathroom, she gasped at the astonishment of her ugliness. Her face, streaked by tears from the night before, had bled mascara down her cheeks, and the skin beneath her eyes drooped in dark purple circles. Her long blond hair, which she usually spent a good twenty minutes combing and working into a neat braid or ponytail, had remnants of yesterday's work, the hair rubber band dangling at her shoulder blades. Strings of hair had fallen out and rested in tangled chunks around her shoulders.

Reeve didn't know what to do. She stood in the bathroom replaying in her mind her morning routine. She remembered fixing and eating breakfast and dressing in the navy blue suit she had purchased at the Goodwill, but she didn't remember even going into the bathroom to look in the mirror. Shocked by her appearance, Reeve's face reddened under her freckles at the thought of her boss seeing her like that. Not wanting to cry anymore onto the already-tearstained face, Reeve turned on the faucet and filled her palms with the ice-cold water. She splashed her face, stinging it into reality. With her fingertips, she scrubbed at the black mascara marks until her cheeks were pink from the pain. She wet her hands again and attempted to work her fingers through her hair. She had no purse with her today, no brush or comb. How ridiculous she felt as she stood in the office restroom attempting to prepare herself for the day, and she prayed that no one would enter and further her humiliation. She managed to detangle enough of her hair to twist it into a bun at the nape of her neck, but the rubber band broke when she tried to wrap it around the large ball of hair.

Reeve went into one of the stalls and sat down on the toilet. The baby moved inside of her. She wished it would stop. She tried to think of what she would say when she went back out into the office, but her mind was as blank as the movements of that morning. She didn't know how much time passed as she sat in the stall, but at last she heard the door creak open and Ron call into the restroom, his deep voice echoing against the high ceilings and porcelain fixtures.

"Reeve? Are you OK?"

The last thing that Reeve wanted to hear was the sympathetic tone of a man, a man other than her own husband. It was then that she gave into the tears, her sobs now filling the empty space in the room. Ron heard her and closed the door. He called the only person Reeve had put down as a reference: Renee.

They sat across from each other in the wingback chairs again. Still cluttered with piles of books, the room was exactly the same as it had been when Reeve first entered it a year before. Renee had fixed sweetened iced tea and held it between the palms of her chunky hands as she looked over at Reeve.

"Do you know why your mother named you Reeve?" Renee held a coy smile, and Reeve looked up at her, surprised. She hadn't expected the conversation to begin this way.

"I didn't know my mother picked the name. I always thought Daddy did, because it seemed like he had control of everything."

"Not everything. No one could control Georgia. She had that name picked out the moment she found out she was pregnant. She was so sure it was going to be a girl. Your parents didn't even have a phone yet, can you believe it? She made Seth drive her all the way into town to use the phone in one of those little cafes. She called me right up and said, 'I'm having a daughter, and I'm going to name her Reeve after Grandma Reeve.' I told her, 'What an honor.'"

Reeve was interested in something for the first time in days. "Who was Grandma Reeve?"

"She was our mother's mother. She came here all the way from Illinois because she heard about a seamstress job, and she wanted to live near the ocean. Her husband had died the year before and she was on her own. She knew how to make the most beautiful dresses you've ever seen."

"Her first name was Reeve?" Reeve had never heard of anyone having it for a first name.

"No, that was her husband's name, but she always had us call her Grandma Reeve out of respect. Her first name was Lucille. She was a fighter. She somehow raised my mother and her sister all on her own, and they both became wonderful, loving women. She never did remarry. She always used to say, 'I've survived this long without a man. Why do I need one now?' That may sound pretty simple to say nowadays, but back then, she really stood out. A lot of people respected her, but a lot of people didn't like her independence. Either way, it didn't matter to her. She could always win them over with a dress design they hadn't seen before. She retired when women began to wear pants regularly. She said, 'if women were meant to wear pants, then men were meant to have babies.' She was a riot." Renee said, caught up in the reminiscence.

"I never knew anything about her. Thank you for telling me." Reeve felt relieved. Renee always knew exactly what to say to make her feel comfortable.

She waited a few moments, pondering how to put into words all the things that had been racing through her mind for months. There were so many ways to say it, and so many elaborate problems that had developed in her life since the pregnancy. But she could say anything except, "Aurelio has a drinking problem."

Though it was a simple sentence, she felt that it was the hardest thing she had ever said to anyone. In its five words, she summed up all that was wrong with her life, from not trying to prosecute William, to allowing her father to disown her, to giving in to the impulse of marrying a complete stranger, to the mistake of her pregnancy. She felt a great release as she said the words, but she also felt a terrible sense of loss.

Renee, too, waited to respond. She sat in the wingback chair with her legs dangling over the side, mostly hidden beneath her green housedress. Her expression spoke of calm acceptance. "How long?" she asked, when the silence seemed too strong.

"Since I found out I was pregnant." Reeve broke down then, putting her face into her palms, the tears hot against her skin.

"There's no easy answer to this. Is he still going to work every day?"

"He manages to make it in, but sometimes he's late. I'm sure he's had several warnings by now."

"If he's still working, then there's hope. There are lots of programs. Detox centers, halfway houses…" Renee's voice faded off. She focused her eyes on a pile of magazines on the floor. The top one was a National Geographic with a picture of an African princess on the cover. "The best thing is for him to go to AA meetings. Does he drink every day?"

"Almost. Maybe once a week he'll come home on time and act like he's married to me." Reeve cracked her palms open to speak, but couldn't say much amidst the sobbing.

"Then he'll have to go to meetings every day." Renee paused again, mesmerized by the exotic eyes of the princess, her head wrapped in a red and gold scarf that sparkled in the light of the camera's flash. "But you should know," she leaned over and lifted Reeve's chin, "that no one can help him but himself. Nothing you can say or do is going to convince him to stop unless he's ready to stop of his own will."

Reeve's eyes looked almost black, as if the moisture of her tears had stained them into the darkness she felt within. "But surely he'll want to stop because of the baby," she whispered.

"You've been through too much this year for a girl your age. And I know you're not going to believe me now, but you will once you see it play out. Aurelio is not going to quit drinking because you ask him to. He has to be ready on his own." Renee's voice was strong and knowledgeable, as if she had gone through this with her own husband. Reeve knew she had never married, and she questioned her judgment now, unwilling to admit that Aurelio wouldn't listen to her or give up on drinking for the sake of the baby.

"There's no one in the world who would judge you for leaving him now. I could help you out until you get back on your feet."

Reeve played the image in her mind of the night in the loft, when Aurelio's strong arms seemed the only thing connecting her to the living. How she fell in love, and so quickly and passionately! Nothing in the world, no drinking problem or hatred or ignorance on his part could take away the burning love she held in her heart for him.

"I just couldn't leave him. He was there for me when I needed it the most, and I ought to be there for him."

Renee's eyes had moved back to the picture of the princess. "African Royalty," the caption below her hands read. The beauty of her patient eyes helped Renee to say what she had to. "You have a long road ahead of you, Reeve. And it may never end."

"I guess that's what marriage is all about," Reeve whispered, but even she knew the deceit behind her words.

She lingered outside of the grocery store that evening. She meant to stop him before he walked past their apartment and on to the life he drank away each night in the small Irish pub. When he emerged from the double glass automatic doors of the grocer, his eyes widened in surprise. Reeve stood in a loose-fitting summer maternity dress, her face and hair freshly washed from the shower she had taken that afternoon, her mascara and lipstick in perfect condition on her rosy-cheeked, freckled face. She looked at Aurelio, trying to be casual and comfortable so that he wouldn't sense the purpose of her visit.

"Hola, Esposo," she cooed, her accent perfectly mimicking his.

"Hola, Esposita," he said, taking in her glowing beauty and reaching down to give her a hug. "I'm happy to see you."

As they walked, his sober presence, with his gentle touch and loving eyes, captivated Reeve. He held her hand in the palm of his own, his fingers stroking the back. "Have you thought of any names?" he asked.

"No, not really. Do you think it's a boy or a girl?" Reeve's happiness could not be expelled at his sudden interest in the baby.

"Oh, a girl, of course. Would it be all right if we named her Luisa, after my mother?"

Reeve had never met his mother, and wasn't sure about naming her daughter after a stranger, but wanted Aurelio to be in a good mood before she delved into the purpose of her arrival. "I suppose so. Luisa. That's a pretty name." She said and Aurelio squeezed her hand. They walked at a slow pace and arrived at their apartment as the sun disappeared over the horizon. Reeve had a pot roast, one of Aurelio's favorite meals, cooking in the crock-pot, surrounded by onions, carrots, and potatoes. She had made sopapillas for desert, and now served up two glasses of cold lemonade. Aurelio plopped down onto the couch and took off his shoes. He walked into the bedroom to change out of his uniform. When he returned to the living room, he wore the same clothes he had bought on the day of their wedding.

"To what do I owe this pleasure of handsomeness?" Reeve cooed to him, her voice singsong and happy.

"I wanted to look nice for my bride." Aurelio said and sat down at the small round pine table, where the smile drained away from his face as he clasped his hands together and rested them on the table.

"I want to apologize to you, Reeve," he began in a different tone, his voice wavering now as he spoke. "I haven't been myself these last few months. I've been so stressed out about having to take care of a family. And..." his voice trailed off as he gazed out the window, his eyes averting hers. She stood at the crock-pot, scooping the vegetables onto a plate, her body half turned towards him. "And maybe I haven't been dealing with my stress in the best ways." Reeve held her breath as he said, "After you went to work this morning, I saw the book you checked out from the library. I think I looked at every picture two times. They are incredible. The baby is so real... Maybe before I couldn't understand. I didn't think of it as being alive yet. But now, I feel different. And I want to have the baby. And I want to be a good father and husband, and come home from work every night to spend time with you."

It took every muscle in her face to keep the grin away, so that finally she gave in to it and turned, her cheeks red and her heart filled with relief. She turned back to him and wrapped her arms around his neck. "Oh, Aurelio," she whispered between kisses, "everything is going to be fine."

Chapter 32

Aurelio's therapist had been sober for thirteen years, though he was not ashamed to admit that he drank for an equal amount. When he called Luisa and asked her to come have a meeting with him at the halfway house, he introduced himself as Dante Jarvis. On the phone, his voice sounded raspy, and Luisa questioned whether anything from his mouth could help her father. But he spoke with confidence and wouldn't take no for an answer.

"Your father tells me you're not working now, and you even have someone who can baby-sit. So I don't want to hear any excuses of why you can't come, because I've heard them all before."

Luisa disliked his cockiness, but had to admit to herself that she didn't have an excuse, and reluctantly said yes. She asked that they meet during Alejo's naptime, not wanting to bother Warren with the possibility of dealing with a crying baby for two hours, and she lay Alejo down just before she left. The halfway house was in the Capitol Hill neighborhood, just a ten-minute drive, though she felt as if she might as well be driving cross-country. All the lights along the one-way avenue were red when she came to them. Though she didn't believe much in signs, she found it ironic that she just couldn't seem to get there on time when she was usually early.

The halfway house was in an old mansion built at the turn of the twentieth century. In the back, it had its original carriage house that in recent years had been converted to a garage. It was a three-story brick building built in the Victorian style that represented numerous remaining mansions in the neighborhood. A decent sized yard surrounded its wraparound porch, but on either side, three story brick apartment buildings stood, their flat roofs and square windows mocking the magnificence of the mansion. A green roof complemented the green trim painted around the large windows of the mansion, and Luisa even noticed that the railings along the steps leading up to the porch were the same shade of mint green. As she walked up the flagstone walk, she saw two men sitting in rocking chairs on the front porch. They smoked cigarettes and were having some kind of discussion about what was going on in Iraq. One of them was a Vietnam vet and brought up the similarities between the wars. Trying not to eavesdrop, Luisa avoided eye contact with the men as she held the railing and walked up the stone steps, but their voices carried out into the street, so that even passersby looked up to see where the noise came from.

One of the men noticed her, her beauty entrancing him. "Can I help you find someone, little lady?"

She had been here once before, but hadn't seen either of these men, and figured they must be new arrivals. "No thank you, I know where his room is." She felt her face redden as the men looked her over, and she took large steps toward the door.

The receptionist at the front desk, where the men had to check in and out before leaving the house, recognized her from her previous visit. "Your father and Dante are waiting for you in the back conference room." She said, her blond curls dancing around her face. She was reading The Bell Jar, and leaned back in her padded office chair and put her eyes back on the book before Luisa could even speak.

The foyer of the mansion, where the receptionist's desk sat, had vaulted ceilings and darkly stained oak moldings along the corners. Two round windows cast the afternoon light in crisscrossing circles at her feet. The floor, too, was a dark hardwood, and a narrow oriental rug led Luisa toward the back. She walked past two six-paneled doors that were labeled with the names of the people whose offices were inside before reaching the closed door marked Conference Room. She hadn't been there before, and expected it to look like a conference room in an office building with a long, rectangular table and padded office chairs on wheels pulled up on all sides. What she saw when she opened the door surprised her.

As if to mock the Victorian era, someone had decorated the room in modern style. Three seats lined three of the walls, each with its own design. One was a hunter green suede sofa, with overstuffed pillows that bore artistic lines of various colors to complement the green. Its coordinating partner was a love seat bearing the design from the pillows of the first, its own pillows bearing the hunter green suede. And to match, an overstuffed chair had hunter green suede cushions, but arms and pillows with the same artistic design. The walls were painted a complementing paler shade of green, and three paintings with a similar artistic pattern were framed above each piece of furniture. Two large square windows stood in between paintings, and a small oak desk with a computer sat along the same wall that held the door to the room.

Aurelio sat with is feet propped up on the ottoman and his body relaxed on the cozy arms of the chair. His leather sandals were on the floor next to him. Though he looked relaxed, he also looked thin, and his muscles twitched without him even realizing it.

At the computer desk, a large African-American man with arms as thick as Luisa's thighs typed rapidly, not even flinching when Luisa entered the room. On his large, round head, a goggle-eyed pair of glasses rested on his wide nose. A neatly trimmed moustache grew over his thick pink lips. His hands, which seemed like those of a monster attacking the tiny keyboard, had short, thin nails and dots of hair on the backsides. He sat erect, the shoulders of his six-foot-three frame rising far higher than the back of the chair. His head, absent of all hair, partially from balding and partially from shaving, shone under the yellow recessed can lighting.

Luisa stood for more than a minute before anyone spoke. The silence of the room engulfed her, and she felt awkward and out of place.

"Well, Aurelio, are you going to introduce me to your daughter?"

As if he were a television and Dante the remote, Aurelio came to life, stepping out of his seat and putting his feet into his sandals.

"Of course, Dante. This is my daughter, Luisa." Aurelio said, holding his arms wide as if presenting a prize to a group of anxious contestants.

Dante stood up from the desk and walked towards her, holding out his gigantic hand and taking hers within it. "Hello Luisa. It's a pleasure to finally meet you. Aurelio talks about you all the time."

Luisa didn't reply.

"Please sit down so that we can talk." Dante motioned to the suede sofa and Luisa put her purse on the floor as she sat. She didn't lean back against the softness of the cushion, as she would at home, but sat at the front edge, her back straight and her eyes forward.

Dante could sense her discomfort. He opened his palms toward her and beamed. "Relax. This isn't the Spanish Inquisition."

Luisa still had no response. She didn't move.

"I asked you to come here today because I want you to realize that alcoholism is a family problem. It is not just Aurelio's problem. It affects everyone in Aurelio's life. And part of Aurelio's therapy involves working with his family to help overcome the disease." Dante paused, waiting for Luisa to soak in the information or to ask any questions.

Luisa still felt uncomfortable. The way Dante spoke of her father, she realized, because she couldn't admit it before, that Aurelio had an illness. Though she and her mother and brother had always assumed that he could stop drinking if he just wanted to, they couldn't grasp the physical need to drink. As if it weren't true to her until Dante said it, the reality of her father's problem struck her in a way it never had before. She hated to think of her father as being sick, but in the moment of truth, she realized there was no better word to describe him.

"Whatever I can do to help," Luisa said at last, her voice shaky with nervousness and fear.

"I'm glad you want to help Aurelio, but it's very important that you realize that you also need help. You have been dealing with this problem for your entire life, and I'm sure it hasn't been easy."

Her discomfort turned instantly to hate. She hated sitting there, listening to a stranger tell her that her life hadn't been easy. The images of her childhood began to flash before her mind's eye: the time when she was in a school play and her father had remained at home, too drunk to leave his bed; the time when she had a slumber party and all the girls had to go home because her father had been arrested for a DUI, and the frantic look on her mother's face as she tried to come up with a better excuse to tell the girls' parents; the time when Byron had become so angry with Aurelio that he started attacking him in his drunken state, knocking his father down the steps, where he hit his head against the wall and had a concussion; the time when Luisa had her high school graduation party and Aurelio had become so drunk that he started slurring his words together and making fun of her in front of all her friends...

The hate bubbled inside her stomach so that she felt nauseous with its presence. Her face stiffened and the muscles in her thighs and biceps tightened. She wondered how long she would have to sit there and listen to someone tell her that her life hadn't been easy. She wanted to stand up and scream at him for pointing out the most obvious thing, and she wanted to slap Aurelio across the face and run out of the room, the mansion, onto the street and never look back at him again. She wanted to expunge him from her life as her mother had tried to do.

But she couldn't. Beneath the hate, she still had love for her father. She wanted him to get better. She wanted their relationship to get better. She wanted their lives to get better. All she could hope for was that everything would be better one day, and if she had to sit here uncomfortably on this comfortable sofa, then that was the first rotten step she knew she had to take. .

The silence of Luisa's thoughts consumed the air in the room. No one spoke, but Dante sat back on the sofa next to Aurelio and placed his hands on his knees, waiting for a response. Aurelio's eyes examined Luisa as if she were a creature he had never seen before. He studied her face with an expression of curiosity.

"No, it hasn't been easy for me at all," Luisa finally said.

Aurelio let out a long-awaited sigh that released itself like a summer breeze, gently touching the faces of the others in the room. Luisa could feel the tension loosen inside her, and her muscles relaxed. She found herself leaning back against the pillows and letting her arms fall comfortably into her lap.

"Let's begin by talking about how Aurelio's drinking makes you feel," Dante said.

"I couldn't begin to describe the complexities of my emotions when he drinks."

"That's not an answer, Luisa. Try me."

"How does it make me feel? You mean, when I bring my son to see him and he's passed out on his bed, too drunk to realize that we've come for a visit? I feel nothing but rage. It's been too long to feel much else. Except... except sometimes I just feel sad when I think about all the things he's missed out on because of it, all the opportunities he's passed by. I'm sure it's not easy being him, but it isn't much easier being related to him either. Sometimes I just feel sorry for him." Luisa avoided her father's eyes. She felt as she had during much of her life, like she was the parent and he the child. She wondered what he was thinking, but he said nothing.

"Do you ever feel sorry for yourself?" Dante asked.

The tension crept back into Luisa's body like cancerous cells multiplying and taking over all her healthy organs. Cold chills collected on her arms as she considered the question. Since Carter had died, she hadn't gone a single day, let alone more than an hour, without feeling horribly sorry for herself. She hated feeling the way she did, but didn't know how to stop the feeling from overtaking her. She felt far sorrier for herself than she ever had or would for her father, because much of her still believed that he had put himself in this situation, whereas her situation was an unfortunate circumstance and the un-chosen family she was born into.

Dante could see her back stiffen after he asked the question. He opened his mouth to explain, but Luisa stopped him, standing up and holding her hand in the air.

"Did you know that my husband was killed by a drunk driver in the middle of a weekday afternoon?" Her voice reflected the rage she had previously mentioned, and she bent over to pick up her purse, avoiding the surprised stares of the two large men. She rushed to the door, slamming it as she left the room, and jogged down the hallway to the front door of the mansion. She stepped out into the bright heat of early September, the sun blinding her eyes after half an hour in the depths of the dark mansion. She rushed to her car, where she got in and allowed herself to spill all the hot, desperate tears she had been holding inside.

When she started the engine, all she wanted to do was go home. She just didn't know where it was anymore.

Warren could tell she had been crying. Her eyes were swollen with redness and the whites were bloodshot. Her nose, too, was red, and her mascara had been wiped away with tissues, the white fuzz from the paper still tickling her cheeks. She came into the kitchen where he sat reading Consumer Reports, Alejo banging on pan lids at his feet. He stood to greet her, but she shook her head and went straight up to her room. He remained in the kitchen, the only noise being the muffled sound of her CD player bolting out Metallica from the other side of her closed door.

Luisa painted with a passion she had never felt before. She paid no attention to what she was wearing, but instead opened every tube of acrylic paint that she owned, squeezing the colors onto the palette as if it were her last chance to ever create art. She worked well into the evening, forgetting all else, her hands furiously moving the paintbrush over the canvas, stopping only to rest her arms and to breathe. When the natural light had faded into the mysterious pink and gray twilight, she sat down in front of her creation and drew it into her soul.

It had begun with the hundred-foot-tall Texan oaks, a grove that stood at the edge of a farm. The trees she had painted in a flash, their trunks mere streaks of brownish-gray paint drawn up to blotted clusters of dark green leaves. The sky above, painted a deep shade of navy blue, was dotted with little white stars and a silver crescent moon. A tiny ray of silver light from the moon shone down on the scene in the tall grass at the roots of the oaks. Some of their trunks had been splattered with blood. A dark figure, indescribably un-human but with the red freckled face of a man, cast a frightening shadow over the small, thin, blond girl over whom he stood. The girl, whose clothes had been stripped and lay in a pile next to one of the trees, also had streaks of blood on her face, arms, and between her legs. Though her body had been painted simply, with little attention to detail, the expression on her face was mesmerizing. Her gray eyes seemed too large for her small cheekbones; they so widely held a look of disbelief. The thin red lips of her mouth parted as if she were simultaneously trying to take in air and say something. The nostrils on her thin nose flared up, and the blond hair around her face was a tangled mat of knots. Her face and body were covered partially by the shadow of the figure above her, and the pale green grass around was also dotted with spots of blood.

Luisa sat staring at the painting until she could no longer see it. The music had stopped playing and the room grew dark. Then she heard a slight tapping on the door.

"Luisa? May I come in?" Warren's voice was as gentle as a violin in her ear.

"Yes, of course." She stood, covered in paint, and walked toward the light switch. Her senses came back to her as Warren entered, taking in her appearance.

"Is Alejo in bed?"

"Yes, I put him down an hour ago," Warren nodded, looking at the paint on the palette and the paint on Luisa and the paint on the painting as if he were examining a strange foreign exhibit in a museum. He sat down at the edge of the bed and smiled in the only way he knew how, his muscles tight on his face as if he were unfamiliar with the expression.

"I got a call from my brother today. He's having a barbecue this weekend for Labor Day. He invited all of us." Warren paused as Luisa adjusted her eyes to the brightness of the light. "Did I tell you that I have two brothers, two sisters, and about twelve nieces and nephews?"

Luisa felt happy for the first time that day. She had feared his entrance, feared what he might say when he saw splashes of paint on his immaculate hardwood floor, feared that he would give her a lecture about parental responsibilities or what it was like to have an alcoholic father... but he knew just what to say.

"Can I bring my father?" she asked, and Warren nodded.

He stood up and began the process of cleaning up Luisa's mess as she headed toward the door to take a shower. "We all have pain in our lives, Luisa. At least you've learned a good way to deal with it. I've learned so much from you." Warren bent over the drop cloth, unable to look into her eyes as he said it, for tears were brimming in his own. She said nothing, but closed the door behind her, allowing Warren to sit cross-legged on the floor and drink in the beauty of the art she had created. It was the most passionate, colorful, and truthful piece of modern art in his home. He wondered what price she might ask, and another idea brewed in his head.

Dante insisted on coming to the barbecue as well. The meeting with Luisa had shaken up Aurelio, and he was not allowed to leave the house alone for fear that he might take a plunge into alcohol. Luisa's Corolla was packed with potato salad, deviled eggs, and Alejo's booster seat in the trunk, Warren in the passenger seat, and Aurelio, Alejo, and Dante squeezed into the backseat.

She picked up Aurelio and Dante on their way to the west side of the city where Freddy lived with his wife, Carly. It was Labor Day, and the sun still screamed of summer, with the temperature rising well above eighty degrees by the time they reached their house at one o'clock.

The house was typical of the neighborhood, a small ranch with tiny bedrooms at the back, an eat-in kitchen, no dining room, and a partially finished basement. The outside was blond brick, and Luisa could see the resemblance between Warren and his brother immediately, before even catching a glimpse at him, just by looking at the perfectly green and neatly trimmed lawn with a row of blooming rosebushes lining the front of the house. When they entered the house that was filled with strangers who all bore at least a twinge of Warren's red hair, Luisa felt out of place, as if she were trying to take part in someone else's family. She stood next to Warren with Aurelio and Dante behind them, and realized that Warren, too, looked uncomfortable.

She had forgotten to ask, between their hurried conversation and the barbecue, when it was that he had last seen his family, but from the looks on their faces as they entered, she could tell it had been a long while. The eyes of all the adults in the room lit up, and as if programmed by a machine that operated a remote to their jaws from somewhere across the room, their mouths opened and were unable to close at the initial shock of Warren's appearance and his accompanying guests.

"Well, I'll be damned," a tall, gangly man who had to be Warren's brother came and slapped him on the back. "You came, and you brought people?" He said the word people as if he were speaking of aliens.

"Well, yes," Warren's face reddened as he reached for his brother's hand. He seemed nervous, as if he were unsure of what to say next.

"Please pardon my husband," Carly, Freddy's tall, thin, blond wife stepped into the living room from the adjacent kitchen and squeezed her husband's arm. "I'm Carly, and this is my crazy husband, Freddy. Pleased to meet you."

Luisa stepped up in the midst of Warren's silence. "I'm Luisa, and this is my son, Alejo, my father Aurelio, and his..."

"His therapist, Dante," Dante spoke up, proud and verbal, holding out his hand to Freddy.

Luisa felt flushed and cast her eyes to the floor.

"I'm a recovering alcoholic," Aurelio said, and plastered an artificial smile on his face.

In the brief moment between Aurelio's words and the response of the people in the room, who had all silenced themselves at the introductions, Luisa swore that her heart leapt straight out of her chest and was now flopping around on the floor like a fish out of water.

"Well, we know all about that in our family, don't we Warren? I'm sure glad to see someone who's actually trying to change, rather than just running away." Freddy held out his hand to shake Aurelio's. He had grown into a tall, muscular, confident man. He kept his red hair cut short, in military style, though he refused to shave away his trimmed moustache and goatee. His green eyes shone above the freckles on his cheeks, and the strawberry blond hairs on his arms shone under the light from the window. He showed a perfect set of white teeth between his narrow lips and round dimples on each cheek. He looked more like he was thirty-five rather than fifty-four, and it was hard for anyone to believe that he had three grown children.

"Please come in and have a seat. What an adorable little boy. How old is he?" Carly motioned to the couch, where Luisa gladly sat, though with a straight back as she had done at the halfway house.

"Thank you. He's a year and five months."

"Oh, what a wonderful age," Carly's eyes appeared misty, and she looked up at Freddy, who had become busy showing the men to the backyard grill. "I wish I could have a grandchild." She said. "Would you like some iced tea?"

Luisa nodded, then leaned against the soft cushion at the back of the plaid couch. She found it strange that no one had asked who she was, what she was doing there, or what her relationship to Warren was. She felt relieved and at home, with only one question burning inside her: why on earth would Warren turn his back on this family?

Carly returned with two tall glasses of amber colored iced tea. She sat down in the coordinating sofa that was across the gray carpet from the couch. Luisa knew that Carly must be her mother's age, but she didn't look it. Her blond hair shone in the light from the window, and her constant expression of happiness bore hardly a wrinkle around her eyes and mouth. She had a thin, well-worked-out body and walked with the confidence of a woman who knows what she wants in life. Her blue eyes dazzled all who looked upon them, and her painted lips were as thick and lush as a supermodel's. When she sat on the chair, she held perfect posture and crossed her long right leg over her left, showing off her pedicured toes inside her shiny white leather sandals. She wore a slim-fitting floral summer dress with spaghetti straps that displayed a golden tan on her arms and shoulders.

"We're so glad that Warren finally came. I haven't seen him in years." When she spoke, she held no grudge in her voice, but instead acted as though Warren's arrival was simply a treat meant to brighten her day.

Luisa admired Carly for everything she was: she loved how well she carried herself, her natural beauty, and her kind spirit. Luisa felt safe and at home. "Yes, I was surprised when Warren mentioned it. Do you have a barbecue every year on Labor Day?"

"Yes, and Memorial Day and Fourth of July. Then of course we all get together at Christmas, but usually we keep to our immediate families for Thanksgiving and Easter."

Luisa felt as if she were taking part in a dream, the dream she had always had of an extended family. It sounded so nice to have a large family in town who took the time to see each other several times during the year. She just couldn't imagine letting a family go. Warren had told her about what happened to him as a child, but she wondered how much his brothers had to do with it.

"It's too bad Warren doesn't come by more often." She felt herself trapped in an awkward moment with nothing more to say.

"Warren's had a pretty rough time. Not like his siblings. It was hard enough what his mother did to him, but when Frankie died, he just shut down."

Having given her no specifics, all Luisa had gathered from their conversation about his family was that Warren had once had three brothers, and now he had two. She was anxious to know more, but hadn't the courage to ask Warren.

"When did that happen?" She tried to sound as if she were making a casual remark, as if the answer were of no importance to her, when in reality she wanted to know more than anything.

"Oh, he died over thirty-five years ago, on his second tour in Vietnam. Warren never really got over it, because Frankie always took care of him when they were kids. He was like a father and a mother to Warren."

"Did you know Frankie?"

"Not really. Freddy and I have been together since high school, and I met Frankie when he first came back from Vietnam. But I don't think I met the Frankie who everyone loved and spoke so highly of. He was different... distant, I guess. War can really mess with your mind. He had a young wife and a little baby, Joey. They lost touch with the family after Frankie died. I guess Darlene never wanted to be part of what reminded her of Frankie's death. Kind of like Warren." Carly paused, examining Luisa's expression. Luisa looked studious, as if she were listening to a lecture, but had forgotten her notes, and so she was trying to memorize every detail of what the professor said.

"I'm surprised you don't know all this already... though maybe I shouldn't be surprised. We all know how Warren likes to keep to himself. How did you meet him?" The question had crossed Carly's mind of whether they were dating, but given Luisa's age and situation (having such a young child), she second guessed herself and figured there must be another circumstance.

"We were neighbors across the alley. But we didn't meet until after my husband died in the spring. Then Warren offered to help me and Alejo out for a while. We're living with him now." Luisa looked down; she didn't want to have to be the one to explain what would probably look like a strange situation to an outside observer, but she had no choice.

Just then, the front door opened and a young man and woman entered, both tall and with strawberry blond hair, each carrying a large bowl of salad. The woman, whose hair was a shade lighter than the man's, had the same full lips and voluptuous legs of Carly, and bore the round dimples of Freddy. Her hair, which had a shiny wave to it, hung down her back, and her straight nose and round cheeks had a sprinkling of freckles. Her voice, too, sounded like Carly's as she looked up at her mother and held out the salad, her slim arms dotted with bleach blond hairs and freckles.

"I spent all morning on this Waldorf salad, so everyone better eat it," she said.

Luisa had taken a moment to view the woman, but only a moment. Instead, her eyes moved like the lens of a photographer, taking in pictures of the tall, muscular man who stood beside her. With his hair cropped in military style like Freddy, he too bore the family dimples, and had thin red lips under a neat red moustache. His heart-shaped face carried high cheekbones and deeply set blue eyes that sparkled beneath the reddish-blond eyelashes and eyebrows. He had the perfect white teeth of Carly, and the thin frame of his hips seemed to sink below his broad shoulders and thick arms. He wore a blue polo t-shirt that reflected the color in his eyes and tight-fitting blue jeans. When he spoke, his voice had the smoothness of butter, and Luisa felt herself shivering, though she sat with her back to the sun.

"No one's going to eat your Waldorf salad because they're going to be full from my fruit salad," he patted his sister on the back and winked at his mother.

The two were so busy bragging about their salads that at first they didn't notice Luisa, but when Carly stood up, both siblings saw her, their expressions that of curious wonder.

"Luisa, please pardon the manners of my children. This is my son, Tyler, and my daughter, Jennifer."

Luisa stood. Fear, infatuation, and extreme guilt ran through her, but at last she held out her hand. "Pleased to meet you. This is my son, Alejo. I'm a friend of Warren's."

Tyler's eyes lit up. "Uncle Warren's here? I can't believe it. Nice meeting you, Luisa."

"Hello. It was nice of you to get Warren to participate," Jennifer said, and then followed Tyler out back to put their salads with the other food and to see Warren.

Carly, still standing, followed her children, and then motioned for Luisa and Alejo to come. "You might as well meet the rest of the family," she said, and led Luisa, with Alejo tagging along at her side, to the backyard.

Again, Luisa could see the similarities between Freddy and Warren. All along the back fence, and taking up a large portion of the yard grew a vegetable garden with rows of corn, tomato plants, pumpkins, lettuce, squash, raspberry bushes, strawberries, spinach, beans, and an herb garden with everything from garlic to parsley. On the opposite end of the trimmed and weeded yard, rosebushes, peonies, lilac bushes, snow-on-the-mountain, helios, and rhododendrons bloomed in the sun of the early afternoon.

Carly led Luisa through the family line, where she met all of Warren's nieces, nephews, grandnieces, grandnephews, his brother Kenny, his sisters, Rose and Margaret, and their spouses. The men, including Aurelio and Dante, who seemed right at home, clustered around the oversized grill while Freddy and Kenny flipped burgers, and the children took turns playing foursquare on the driveway that led to the garage from the alley. Carly, Jennifer, and Margaret hurried in and out of the house, bringing out plates and bowls of buns, potato salad, cooked beans, and condiments, and then setting them up along one of the four long wooden picnic tables that took up all the space of the covered brick patio.

Luisa, unsure of what to do, offered her help to Carly, but Carly insisted that, being their guest, she take one of the chaise lounge seats at the back of the yard. Luisa sat in the shade of the tall corn stalks that had just been hulled, and Alejo sat in the grass at her feet playing with his plastic truck set. Time after time, he pushed the fireman's head down on the fire engine, which caused the hose to spin and the engine to go, "Whooooo---ooooooooo," a noise so familiar to Luisa's ears that she hardly noticed it.

Just before the burgers and hot dogs were ready, as Luisa sat comfortably in the chair, her sandals in the grass beside her and her feet up and crossed in front of her on the padded chaise lounge, Tyler broke off from the men and came over to her. He sat down in the other chaise lounge and put his feet up, sipping at the can of Dr. Pepper in his hand.

"I have to say, I admire you," he said, relaxed and comfortable in his chair.

"Admire me? You don't even know me."

"No, but I know Uncle Warren. I can't tell you how many times I've gone over there and tried to get him just to come out of his house. I've spent more money than I should have in his shop, just so I could talk to him. I can't even remember the last time he came to one of these, but it must have been ten years ago or more, because I was still in high school. But I guess all it took was a little taste of a family in his own house to get him to change. He's talked more today than I've ever seen." Tyler nodded in the direction of the men at the grill. Most of them were silent, with an occasional laugh rising up at something Warren said. They encircled him as if he were the main act at a circus, and had their eyes locked on his mouth as if he were speaking a foreign language.

"Well, I hope you don't have the wrong idea." Embarrassment flooded Luisa's face again.

"Oh no, Luisa, Warren told us all about it. I'm sorry to hear about your husband. Sounds like he was a great guy. I can't imagine meeting the perfect person for me and losing her so soon. It would be like a dream come true, and then the worst nightmare."

Though he tried to look at her as he said it, Luisa turned her head the other way. She thought of her trip to Texas, and what her mother had said about Aurelio speaking right to her heart the moment they met: How long must I work here before I can move on to better things? She looked up at Aurelio now, sharing a conversation with Warren, Kenny, and Dante. His body, though thin and drained from years of drinking and weeks without it, still showed signs of vitality as he stood alongside the men. When her mother had told her about she and Aurelio's first meeting, she had longed to know what it was like to hear someone speak so directly to her heart. Now, not six months after she had lost the only man she thought she would ever love, she heard another putting into words just what she couldn't. She held her jaw still and pulled air in and out of her lungs with the caution of a spy trying to keep silent in the significant moment between life and death. She felt the lump in her throat constrict, and she knew that if she spoke everything would flood out of her. Her body stiffened for a moment that may have lasted ten minutes or thirty seconds. She couldn't tell, because time had stopped between desire and guilt.

"I'm sorry if I upset you, Luisa. That's the last thing I would want to do."

Tyler stood up then and walked toward one of his cousins who leaned down over a cooler sitting next to the house. Just as his cousin reached in to retrieve a beer, Tyler touched his arm and whispered in his ear, barely motioning in Aurelio's direction. His cousin returned the beer to the cooler, and Luisa watched as Tyler lifted up and carried the cooler inside and downstairs into the basement. She smiled then, unable to control the tears from dripping down over her lips and into her mouth.

Chapter 33

He only had two and a half weeks before he had to return to base, and he also had a young wife and baby. Warren vied for his time, but Frankie wasn't the same person who had taken care of him as a child. He didn't stay with them, but stayed in a motel close to downtown with Darlene and Joey. Having inherited Frankie's bike when he left, Warren zoomed across town each afternoon when school ended, hoping to get some time with his brother before he was gone. The weather was unusually warm for April, with the afternoon temperature reaching seventy degrees or higher most days. Warren was in ninth grade now, and took all honors courses upon recommendations from his eighth grade teachers. Though he carried a heavy homework load, he couldn't resist strapping on his backpack and speed pedaling on all the back streets that led to downtown from his junior high school. His desire to visit with Frankie burned in him like a raging forest fire amidst no rain. Nothing could keep him from spending what little time he could with his brother.

When he met Darlene for the first time, he knew right away why Frankie had fallen for her. She matched Frankie's six-foot height, and she had long black hair that fell down her back like the shiny mane of a horse. Her pale white skin looked as if it had been cut from a porcelain doll, and her painted red full lips couldn't hide the glistening smile of her straight white teeth. She had eyelashes that were so long Warren thought they must be artificial, but when she blinked in the slow, casual way that she did, he couldn't focus on their length, but on the royal blue eyes they tried to cover. Her petite nose curled up just a bit at the tip, and her high cheekbones contrasted the demureness of her tiny chin. She wore silver teardrop earrings that almost touched the thin shoulders of her svelte frame, and when she held out her hand to shake his, he felt as if he were reaching into the delicate, long fingers of a velvet glove.

"Hello, Warren. It's nice to finally meet you." When Darlene's lips moved, the language poured out of her mouth like sweet juice filling a parched throat.

"And you as well," Warren tipped his head a bit, trying to hide his reddened face from her.

Darlene had invited him into their room, where there were two queen-sized beds, a small round table, and two chairs. Frankie sat in one of the beds and stared at the TV while Joey slept in the center of the other, pillows lined up on either side of him.

When Warren entered, Frankie looked up at him and forced what little happiness he had to enter the expression on his face. He didn't fool Warren. He moved to get up from the bed, but Warren held his hand in the air, remembering the letter and not wanting to disturb him.

"It's OK," he said, and walked over to his brother, holding out his hands. "I'm glad you're safe," he whispered in the midst of their awkward hug.

Frankie broke away soon and put his eyes back on the tiny black and white TV. "Do you guys have one of these yet?"

"No. Mother likes to listen to the radio. I don't think she'd be too interested in a television." Warren didn't want to say too much, thinking of Doris at home in her thinned housedress, hardly leaving her room and only nodding when Warren had told him that Frankie was home from the war.

"I got hooked on it back at the base. It was the only thing to do in the beginning when we didn't have weekend or evening passes. But then I met Darlene." Frankie put on another weak smile and tried to look at his wife, but she was on the phone with the front desk, asking for the room service menu.

"You wouldn't mind if we just had dinner in the room, would you Warren? Frankie hasn't much felt like leaving the room just yet."

"Oh, of course, that's fine. I've never had room service before," Warren sat down on the bed next to Frankie and watched the TV. Leave it to Beaver was on. Warren immediately became engrossed in the friendly mannerisms of June Cleaver, who gently touched her husband and smiled when her boys came home, her dress ironed and the meals prepared.

They watched the program for about fifteen minutes when the baby stirred, then began screaming. Darlene, who had been sitting in one of the chairs skimming through the newspaper, walked over and put her face close to his. "Hello, pumpkin," she cooed, and ran her long red fingernails along the sides of his face.

Frankie stirred, too, as if coming out of a coma. He sat up higher on the bed and looked at Darlene holding Joey, and then looked at Warren. "Would you like to meet my son?" he asked with pride.

"Of course."

Darlene carried the chubby Joey over to Warren, who sat with his back straight and his legs on the floor at the side of the bed. He had never held a baby before, and the thought of doing so scared him to his bones.

"Could you hold him while I fix his bottle?" Every time she spoke, Warren became transfixed with Darlene's sweet voice, and he nodded now without a word.

When Darlene was in the bathroom waiting for the water from the faucet to warm, Frankie got up to turn off the TV and returned to the bed, sitting beside Warren. "He's four months old already. I can't believe it." He paused, as if thinking of what to say next, and then said, "I wish I could have been there when he was born," in a voice that, to Warren's ears, reflected the tone of his second letter from Vietnam.

Warren looked down into his nephew's face. It looked like a giant round ball. His cheeks were so chubby that they seemed to cause his blue eyes to squint. He had a little pug nose that wrinkled up when he made a noise. His tiny red lips were just a shade darker than his pink skin. He had pale blond hair, so blond that it was almost white, that sprinkled his head no more than the fuzz of a peach. His ears stuck out from the sides of his head just a bit, and he held his hands in the air, randomly flinging them about in tight fists.

"Hi there, little guy," Warren said, and Joey gurgled in response. A quick smile flashed over his face, but ended almost instantly when Darlene returned to the room with the bottle. Joey twisted his head, his eyes fixed on his mother, and let out a small scream.

"Come here, Pumpkin," Darlene cooed, and gently took Joey out of Warren's arms.

Once Darlene began to give Joey his bottle, Frankie lost interest in his surroundings again and stood up to turn on the television. He plopped back down on the bed, his pillow behind his back, and didn't say another word for over an hour. Warren began to wonder why Frankie had even bothered to come home at all, if this was how he was going to act. He didn't recognize his brother, the boy who had been so gentle and kind, and who now sat like a half-dead lump on the bed, caring nothing for the people in the room who loved him.

When Warren left that first evening, he assured himself that Frankie would be better if he just took the time to visit him each day. But rather than getting better, Frankie seemed to get worse. He hardly moved from the bed and wore the same white t-shirt and jeans every day. By the end of the first week, he had a full orange beard and his hair was as greasy as a kitchen rag. Darlene, who too had at first been optimistic about Frankie's change in behavior, looked upon Warren with tired eyes when he entered the room on Saturday morning.

"Hey, Warren," she whispered, holding a squirming Joey in her arms. "Frankie's not feeling too well today," she sighed, nodding her head in his direction.

He looked as if he hadn't move since he'd arrived. He sat with his legs crossed in front of him on the bed, his eyes glued to the glow of the television. He did not acknowledge him, other than a slight nod, when Warren entered.

Warren sat next to him on the bed and held his palms in tight fists at his knees. His emotions pulled him in two directions. He blazed with a desire to take his fists and use the strong muscles in his arms to jump on top of Frankie and punch him in the face, punching the life he now lived out of him until he returned to the young, innocent boy he was on the day he left for the Marines. But another part of him was drenched with the desire to walk out of the room, close the door, and never look back, not wanting to remember Frankie for who he was now, but instead hold close his safe arms when Warren was a child.

Fighting with the emotions that rushed through him, Warren looked between Frankie and Darlene, his head moving back and forth like a cat watching a toy move in front of its eyes. Neither of the actions he wanted to take seemed reasonable, and he sat watching The Andy Griffith Show for about five minutes, when he suddenly stood up.

"My brothers and sisters have been asking about you all week, Darlene. They sure would like to meet you, since you've come all this way."

Darlene's eyes lit up for one brief moment. She had spent too many hours inside the motel room, and couldn't understand why they had driven for three days to see his family when all Frankie wanted to do was stay inside. She had never before been out of Texas, and had been so excited about the trip, about seeing the mountains, visiting a new city, and meeting the family of the man she loved. But after sitting in the dark room with the television blaring for six days, every doubt she had ever had about marrying Frankie after so short a time got the better of her, so that she felt nothing but sadness when she looked at him and thought about the rest of her life by his side. The light that entered her eyes when Warren asked the question quickly flickered into a thundercloud of worry.

"I don't know, Warren. What do you think, Frankie?"

Frankie hadn't been listening, but pretended to laugh at something Gomer Pyle did on the show. When he heard his name, he turned his head just a tad in her direction. "Hmmm?" He moaned, his voice rough and absent of emotion.

"Warren would like for us to go see your family today. I haven't had the chance to meet your other brothers and sisters, and I would like to see the city where you grew up. What do you think?" Darlene tried to candy-coat her voice, but the dark undertone was strong enough for anyone to hear.

Frankie took in a long breath that he held in his lungs for several seconds. When he finally let the air out, it seeped from his mouth like the last sputter of a car that had just run out of gas. He stretched his arms behind his back and interlaced his fingers behind his head, looking up at the ceiling. His eyes darted from side to side, but he looked at neither Warren nor Darlene. The two sat, each at the edge of a bed, their feet on the floor, waiting for his response.

"I suppose we could," he said at last, causing Darlene to nearly jump up in excitement.

"Oh, Frankie, thank you so much!" she squealed, and rushed toward the bathroom. "Let me just go freshen up.

When she was inside, Frankie looked at Warren and said, "I guess I'll have to take a shower as well, though I don't know why. Mother would never notice."

"But Freddy and Kenny and Rose and Margaret, they'll be happy to see you. They've been talking about it all week. 'When is Frankie coming over?' 'When are we going to see Frankie?' It's all I've been hearing." Warren, too, tried to sound chipper, but he didn't know what he could say that would make Frankie feel loved and wanted and safe, and more like himself.

Frankie attempted to smile, but the muscles on his face twitched into a strange smirk. Joey lay on the bed next to them making gurgling noises, and the television still blared in front of Frankie's face, but the room felt eerily silent. Warren, who had been pushing the question from the forefront to the back of his mind all week, decided he couldn't hold it in anymore, and seized the brief moment of Darlene's absence from the room. "Frankie, are you ever going to talk about the war?" He rushed the words out, afraid that if he spoke too slowly he would never finish the question.

187

Frankie, whose face had at least softened into an acceptable blankness from earlier that week, now turned his head towards Warren with dark, stormy eyes that said one thing: hate. "No," he said, and placed his glare back on the television screen.

When they stepped out of the cab at Frankie's childhood home, Darlene held her hand to her chest as she looked at the perfection of the lawn. Still green in late October and neatly edged and weeded, Warren had been watering it every other day in preparation for Frankie's arrival. The summer before, he had planted two evergreen bushes along the front of the house, and they too looked like they had been trimmed in even squares just for Frankie. Darlene carried Joey in one arm and held an overstuffed diaper bag on her other shoulder. At midmorning, the sun shone down on them from a royal blue sky. Warren took a deep breath of air and grinned alongside Darlene; even if Frankie had slipped into a depressive slump, he could at least be proud of his new sister-in-law and nephew.

Frankie's once-high shoulders now sloped towards the ground as he walked. His tall, muscular, red-freckled arms glared in the brightness of the sun, but the pale skin of his face reflected nothing but the darkness he felt inside. His hazel eyes carried large purple semicircles underneath, and the red lashes pointed toward the ground. His straight nose also aimed at the ground, and his thin pink lips and cheeks drooped from his bones. His red hair was chopped short against his round head in the traditional military cut, and his long white neck glowed in the sun like the backside of a sea lion. He wore a loose fitting pair of navy dungarees and a plain white t-shirt that too hung loosely on his back, as if his body were unable to carry the weight of the clothes. Though stronger than before he had left, he was just as thin, weighing no more than one seventy at six feet tall. He dragged his white p/t tennis shoes up the concrete sidewalk toward the house, barely lifting his head to notice the magnificence of the yard.

Warren averted his eyes from Frankie and instead chatted with Darlene. "Freddy just turned sixteen, and Kenny is going to graduate this year. He's the starting quarterback on the high school football team. Rose is ten, and Margaret, the baby, is seven. She was born on my birthday, the first day of spring." Warren rambled on as they took the steps up the walk. Frankie's slow pace kept them from moving quickly, though Warren was very anxious to bring them inside. He had assured himself that once the entire family surrounded Frankie, the girls hanging on his legs, the boys telling them about their football team, that he would melt back into the loving patriarch of the family once again.

Margaret was in the window, pointing and jumping, her mouth open in a joyful scream. "They're here! They're here! They're all here, even the baby!" They could hear her screams from outside.

Rose opened the door before they even stood before it. They had all gathered on the porch, and Rose squealed when she saw Frankie and the tiny baby in Darlene's arms. "Oh, I can't believe it! How cute!"

Darlene's eyes sparkled as she looked at her young sister-in-law, and she entered after Warren while Frankie lingered on the porch for a moment before stepping inside. Rose and Margaret stood at Frankie's legs, their heads coming up to the bottom of his ribs. They clung to him like babies cling to their mothers, and Frankie had no choice but to put his arms around his baby sisters. "Hey, girls," he said at last, and patted them each on the back.

Warren showed Darlene the couch and asked her to sit down. She placed the diaper bag on the floor next to her and held Joey against her chest as she sat down. "Well, are you going to introduce me to your family, Frankie?" Again, she forced her voice to sound as pleasant as she could manage, though even the young girls sensed the cool undertone.

Frankie plopped down next to her on the couch and sighed. "Margaret, Rose, come meet your new sister, Darlene, and your nephew, Joey."

Just as the girls in their long-sleeved velveteen dresses walked over to Darlene, Freddy and Kenny came in from the backyard where they had been tossing the football. Both boys had grown several inches since Frankie had last seen them. Kenny, taking after Doris's side of the family, had large bones, and because of football practice, the muscles to match. His strawberry blond hair was moist around the edges from perspiration, and his freckled face glistened from the moisture. Although Kenny's complexion was a bit darker than Frankie's and Freddy's, he matched his brothers' looks in height, body type, and facial structure. His round head bore a nose as straight as Frankie's and a set of hidden cheekbones that seemed to disappear beneath his aqua eyes. He stood in gym shorts and an ash-colored t-shirt next to Freddy, who held the football under his arm. His hair, which matched the shade of Kenny's, was buzzed almost completely off because of a dare he had accepted from one of his defensive linemen. He showed off the nice teeth and dimples that he had inherited from his father when he saw Frankie, Darlene, and Joey. He, too, was as tall as his older brothers, but carried a thinner set of bones than either of them, again taking after his father's side of the family. When the boys spoke, almost saying the same words at the same time, their deep voices intertwined so that, to a stranger, it would be nearly impossible to tell one from the other.

"Well it's about time you came by," both boys said, then walked over to Frankie, who still sat on the couch, immobile except for his eyes, which darted from one brother to the next.

"And who is this beautiful lady? And a baby, Frankie? I can't believe it." Kenny said, then held out his large hand to shake Darlene's. She placed her thin, feminine fingers inside of his, and her hand became engulfed in his palm.

Frankie didn't move, but attempted to plaster a smile on his face, though his eyes remained dark and he showed no teeth, but barely lifted his lips into his cheeks. The boys tried to pay no attention to Frankie's behavior, and sat down in the two wingback chairs opposite the couch. The girls sat at the floor in front of the baby making cooing noises and squeezing his hands and feet. Kenny and Freddy talked with Darlene, casually asking her about where she had grown up, how she had met Frankie, and telling her about their own recent adventures on the football team and with their girlfriends. Darlene, her southern charm shining through despite her anxiety after a week with her depressed husband, managed to laugh alongside the boys and talk to the girls about their favorite subjects in school. By late morning, Freddy and Kenny's girlfriends, Carly and Suzy, stopped by. Darlene felt relieved to be able to sit down with girls her age, though Frankie still showed no interest in meeting or talking to the girls. The morning passed by, and Warren went into the kitchen to prepare a pasta dinner when Darlene asked if there was a place to put Joey down for his nap.

It was a simple question, but all the eyes in the room avoided hers, and instead tried to catch glimpses from each other. And, as if summoned by the question, a door creaked open and Doris emerged from her bedroom. She traipsed into the living room at a snail's pace, her slippered feet dragging along the hardwood floor. Her shoulders, once thick from her large bones and held high, now slumped farther to the floor than Frankie's. Everyone in the living room could smell her before hey saw her; Warren ran over in his mind the last time he had seen her shower, but he couldn't remember. She reeked of sweat and urine and feminine smells, all combined to emanate an odor that caused everyone's nose to twitch. When she stepped around the corner from the small hallway, her long, blond, greasy hair hung in tangled clumps around her sallow face and wrinkled neck. The pale, freckled skin of her face drooped as if her skin were trying to pull her head to the ground. Her blue housedress was nearly transparent, and loosely draped her body, where her age-spotted arms rested at her sides like great weights that she couldn't lift.

The living room, which had moments before been filled with chatter, now carried a creepy silence that would not be broken. Doris's children sat with straight backs and worried looks, and the only other sound besides Doris's dragging feet was Darlene's sudden sucking in of air, her eyes wide with a look of frightened wonder as she saw her mother-in-law for the first time.

"Well, you're home and didn't take a moment to see your mother, huh? You good-for-nothing—"

Frankie stood then, his hunched body coming to life at her appearance and her tone, and took Darlene's hand inside his own. "Let's go. Now." When he spoke, he left no room for argument, his voice definitive and demanding. Darlene stood up with Joey in her arms and awkwardly bent over to pick up the diaper bag. Frankie pulled her to the door with such force that it looked as if he might pull off her arm, and before anyone could speak, they had slammed the door behind them.

As he pedaled across town that afternoon, Warren's fury took over his legs so that he arrived at the motel in half the time it usually took. He pounded on their door with the force of a sledgehammer knocking over a wall, but no one answered. He wondered if Frankie had actually taken the time to show Darlene around the city like she wanted, but he doubted it. He went to the front desk and asked the clerk if the Yorks were still checked in. The clerk sighed and looked back at him, his small, pimply face scanning Warren's as if he were trying to determine something.

"Are you Warren York?" he asked.

"Yes."

"The Yorks checked out earlier this afternoon. About an hour ago. They left this note for you."

His thin hand placed the note in Warren's, and Warren snatched it, and then ran out of the hotel. He shoved the note in his pocket and rode his bike over to a nearby park. He threw his bike to the ground and tore open the envelope. Inside, there were two folded notes on the stationary from the motel. One was from Darlene and one was from Frankie.

```
Dear Warren,

    I'm sorry we had to leave so quickly. Please
tell everyone I was very happy to meet them
all. They were all so nice. Thank you for
taking me to meet your family.

                              Love,
                              Darlene


Warren,

    I just can't take another minute of her. I
had to go. Will write when I get settled on
base.

                              --Frankie
```

In two fists, Warren crumpled the notes. Then, the hot tears of rage burning his cheeks, he tore them to pieces and let them float away on the cool autumn breeze. He didn't know then that it would be the last piece of writing he would ever receive from Frankie. He sat in the park until long after dark, and then rode home to fix dinner for his broken family.

Chapter 34

They had lived there for over a year, and by then knew Houston well enough to navigate the streets in the old station wagon Aurelio had purchased. They arrived at the hospital with plenty of time to deliver the baby. Reeve had gone into labor in the dark hours of the night. She kept a card by her bed that Renee had given her that listed the early signs of labor. It was a short list that included continuous cramping in the lower abdomen, contractions that were regular and lasted for an hour or more, or the bag of waters breaking. After she was unable to sleep for two hours, timing the contractions until they were seven minutes apart, she turned to Aurelio and squeezed his shoulder. "It's time," she whispered, and Aurelio jumped out of bed as if a spider had bitten him.

"OK, I'll get the bag and start the car. It might be cold outside."

Reeve enjoyed a brief moment of happiness. Aurelio thought that seventy degrees was cold, and she knew that the September weather in Houston reflected temperatures that most of the country would consider summery.

"OK," she said, and wrapped her arms around his neck. She loved him then as much as she had when he first spoke to her. Since their talk on the night she met him at the grocery store, Aurelio hadn't come home late one time, and had instead been saving money and spending time in the library researching how to get published.

Since they didn't have insurance, they had to use the remainder of the money from selling Stargazer on the delivery costs, which added up to about a thousand dollars. Reeve hated to use the money, but Aurelio was working hard, as she was, to make up for it. They had searched Goodwill stores and garage sales to buy the necessary items for the baby, including a secondhand stroller, several outfits, and as many cloth diapers as they could find. Since they were scrimping, they decided not to buy a crib right away, but then Renee surprised them with one just before Reeve was due. It was used, but Renee had repainted it a nice cream color, and had taken the time to crochet a blanket that coordinated with the white crib sheet. Because the baby had hardly any clothes, they were able to use just half of one of their own dresser drawers to keep them. Just days before she went into labor, Reeve had washed and neatly folded the clothes and diapers and straightened out the bedding on the crib. She told Aurelio that it could happen at any time, but he didn't seem to believe her until he was awakened in the middle of the night.

When they arrived at the hospital, the nurse at the counter in the emergency room kept running her eyes between Aurelio and Reeve as if she didn't believe that they were together.

"Have a seat and fill out these forms," she said, and they found themselves waiting for over an hour on the uncomfortable vinyl chairs.

Reeve, whose contractions had moved from discomfort to pain by the time they reached the hospital, pretended not to notice as she saw two other couples, both white, come in and be led to labor and delivery rooms before them. She felt discouraged and restless, but didn't know what to do. Using one of the courtesy phones in the lobby, they had called Renee upon entering the hospital. When Renee arrived and saw the two still sitting in the waiting area, Reeve hunched over in the midst of a painful contraction, Aurelio trying to rub her back with his gentle hands, she stomped over to them.

"Why on earth haven't they put you in a room yet?" she asked, appalled.

"I…" Aurelio didn't know how to answer. He had lived in the United States long enough to know two things: first, that it was the land of opportunity, and, second, that it was not the land of opportunity for everyone.

Renee stormed over to the counter and kept a low tone as she spoke to the nurse, motioning towards Aurelio and Reeve. The nurse, whose large round face at first looked defiant and ready to respond, slowly melted into an expression of bewilderment as Renee continued to speak. The nurse picked up a phone and spoke into it, then placed her look again on Reeve and Aurelio.

"Mrs. Lucero?" her whiny voice called out, "Fiona will take you to your room now."

The nurse's aide, Fiona, emerged from behind the counter with a grin on her face. "Hello, Mrs. Lucero. How long have you been in labor?"

"I think about four hours now," Reeve mumbled, her body in too much pain and her discouragement from the long wait weighing on her mind.

When they were almost to the room and out of earshot from the nurse at the counter, Fiona whispered, "Don't worry about Nurse Mitchell. She won't be bothering you anymore." Fiona helped Reeve out of her clothes and into the hospital gown, then asked Aurelio if there was anything he needed. She kept the smile, which to Reeve looked sincere, on her face the whole time that she was with them.

"At least she was nice," Reeve said to Aurelio, who stood at the side of the bed squeezing her hand.

"It's going to be all right," Aurelio said, and began his job of coaching Reeve through her contractions, which were now less than five minutes apart. Renee waited in the family waiting room, anxious to hear the news, but knowing that the baby might not arrive for several hours.

Reeve had only been to the clinic to see a doctor three times during her pregnancy, but was still able to have a normal delivery, though it took longer than she had hoped. After thirteen hours of labor, more than an hour of which she had been pushing, the nurse laid a wet, screaming little girl with black curly hair on her chest. Both Reeve and Aurelio had tears in their eyes, and Aurelio looked down at his wife and daughter and said in Spanish, "Welcome to the world, Luisa Maria. We love you."

Though the pain seared her body with a stronger force than any pain she had ever experienced, Reeve felt nothing but love in its purest form during the moments after birth. She moved her eyes back and forth between the puffy face of her daughter and the exhausted but grinning face of her husband, and her heart swelled inside her chest. Her face beamed; her cheeks were rosy and her eyes wide, and her smile couldn't be replaced with any other expression. She clutched her daughter close to her, the warmth of her body seeping through the blanket she was swaddled in, and whispered again and again, "I love you, I love you, I love you." She couldn't think of a time in her life when those words had ever meant more to her.

The nurse came too quickly to take Luisa to the nursery. Reeve wanted to hold her for the rest of the night, the rest of the next day, the rest of... she never wanted to part from her from the moment she first laid eyes on her, and she let out a gasp of disappointment when the nurse said she had to bathe her in the nursery.

"Esposo, go with her, stay with her," Reeve called to Aurelio, and clutched his hand within hers as a fresh set of tears welled up in the corners of her eyes.

While they were in the nursery, a doctor came in to suture her episiotomy and help her deliver her placenta. The pain crept into her happiness and stayed there until she was able to see Luisa again. The doctor wasn't gentle, but placed both hands on her abdomen and with great strength pressed down, forcing the placenta's delivery. He didn't look at her, or even bother to speak, as he went to work on her body. Embarrassed and alone, she felt herself too full of pride to cry in front of him. The violation of her past crept into her mind, and as he walked out of the room, his white coat garish under the fluorescent lights, she let the tears flow down her remorseful cheeks.

She didn't know how long she sat in the room alone, but it was enough time for her to release the tears and dry her eyes, and for her to realize that she was starving. She scanned her eyes around the room, as if a meal would suddenly appear, when at last a nurse came in.

"We're going to take you to your postpartum room now. Your husband will meet you there." The stout nurse helped her off the bed and into a wheelchair, then strolled out of the room and down the whitewashed corridor towards the other section of the hospital. They passed the nursery, and Reeve pleaded with the nurse to stop and let her look. She peeked into the glass and saw Aurelio standing next to a nurse who held Luisa's head under a faucet. Aurelio held a look of calming love despite the obvious screams emanating from the baby. Reeve's face, which had been set in stone after her release of tears, now softened as she watched the pair.

"You need rest, sweetheart," the nurse said, pushing the wheelchair past the window. "It's almost eight, and you've worked pretty hard today."

Renee was waiting in the room. She gave Reeve a hug and helped her into bed, an old Nikon camera dangling around her neck. "I just got back from looking in the nursery. Congratulations! What did you name her?"

"Luisa Maria, after Aurelio's mother," Reeve beamed, thinking in the back of her mind, What about my mother? And realizing that there was a possibility she would never meet Aurelio's mother just as he would never meet hers.

"Oh, what a beautiful name. She's gorgeous, and you look wonderful," Renee's crow's feet wrinkled up around her eyes.

"I can't wait to take her home. I'm ready to leave the hospital now. But we have to stay two days, and they want to keep her in the nursery and only bring her to me for feedings. I just want to hold her," Reeve could feel her voice cracking as she said the last sentence.

"Don't worry, sweetie. You'll have plenty of time to hold her. The nurses have to monitor her in the nursery to make sure she's OK. You want her to be healthy, don't you?"

"Yes, of course." Reeve cast her eyes into her lap.

"I brought some flowers for you," Renee's voice was chipper. "I know how you love daisies."

"Thank you, Renee. For everything." Reeve felt too emotional to say anymore. Her body was torn between laughter and tears, though she couldn't say why.

"You get some rest. I'll come by tomorrow to hold that little angel." Renee squeezed Reeve's hand and left just as Aurelio entered the room.

After two days in the hospital, Reeve held the tiny Luisa in her lap as they drove across town to their apartment. When Aurelio stopped the car, he got out and walked around to the passenger side to open the door for his wife and daughter. Reeve again felt so emotional at the unusual gesture that she found herself balanced between happiness and sadness. Aurelio held his arm out and helped Reeve lift herself, her body still in great pain, and Luisa out. Then he gently took the baby in his arms and carried her up the stairs to the apartment while Reeve leaned against him.

She had met with several nurses, in addition to reading through two books at the library about breastfeeding, but she still found it to be more difficult than she had imagined. Luisa was slow to latch on and didn't suck for very long. Reeve worried that she wasn't getting enough. She also slept almost all the time, and Reeve found herself struggling to wake her so that she could eat. She desperately wanted help, but she didn't know how anyone could help her with the thing only she could do. For the first week, she spent most of her afternoons and evenings crying. Aurelio came home each night to see the pair on the couch, the baby nestled against her mother's chest in a fitful sleep, the mother tearstained and looking exhausted as she held her.

After two weeks had gone by, Aurelio, tired of eating cold cut sandwiches for dinner and trying to figure out the complicated washer and dryer at the Laundromat down the street, came home from work one night in a sour mood.

"Are you used to taking care of her needs now?" he asked Reeve as he sat next to her on the couch.

Reeve looked up at him with curious eyes. "What do you mean?"

"I mean… has it become easier, now that it's been a while?"

"Well, I suppose it has. But honestly it's been a lot harder than I thought it would be."

"Reeve, you're a homemaker now. You need to learn how to balance everything. When are you going to start taking care of the home?"

A light flashed across Reeve's eyes, and though she tried to suppress her anger, she found it difficult to maintain a level tone of voice. "I've been a little busy and a little exhausted. I don't know if you've noticed, but she still wakes up three times in the night to eat. I'm so tired during the day that it's all I can do to feed her."

"My mother was able to take care of all her children as well as the baby, and still cooked dinner and kept up the house. I saw her do it several times." Aurelio wasn't trying to be mean. He just wanted Reeve to follow the example of the woman he so admired.

"Well good for your mother. I don't know how she did it." Reeve looked across the room. She didn't want to cry again, not when she was so angry.

"I just think that maybe you can work out a schedule with her. You know when she sleeps and when she eats. You can do laundry and clean and cook when she sleeps."

"But if you know anything about babies at all, or even paid attention to your own daughter, you would realize that they don't eat and sleep regularly. I never know how long it's going to be before she wakes up from a nap wanting to eat. Sometimes it's two hours, but other times it's only twenty minutes. It's exhausting just trying to take care of her." Reeve pleaded now, wanting him to understand how difficult it was for her. Her wide eyes searched his face for some sign of compassion, but Aurelio just turned his head away from her.

"I believe that in a marriage, a husband and wife each have their roles. I work hard every day at my job and bring home the food and money. I pay the bills. And I spend what little free time I have in the public library renting a typewriter to type up my manuscript. I think it's only fair that you do your part by taking care of the home that I provide for you." Aurelio spoke in an even tone but averted his eyes from Reeve until the final sentence of his speech.

She could only picture one thing as he spoke: a warm bed at the top of a tower, down comforters surrounding her, and the comfort of Luisa lying on the soft mattress beside her. She would be safe there, alone, away from the world, and she could sleep when she wanted to sleep, eat when she wanted to eat. She could care for Luisa in the way that she knew best, and not have the disowning of her father, the rape of William, or the control of Aurelio weighing on her shoulders. She could be free and live her life as she pleased.

She held the image of the tower in her mind for as long as she could, then turned her face toward her husband's and said, "You and I have different ideas about marriage." She couldn't think of anything else to add, so she went into the bedroom and curled up under the secondhand set of sheets and cried. She listened as the front door of the apartment opened and closed. She was still listening hours later when Aurelio stumbled back through the door in the darkness of early morning.

Reeve didn't know what to do permanently, but she knew that she couldn't stay with Renee forever. By Thanksgiving, Luisa did begin to maintain a schedule of eating and sleeping, and Reeve found herself sorting through the clutter of Renee's house, organizing it, and preparing delicious meals each night. The bittersweet irony was that she was doing everything Aurelio had asked her to do, only not for Aurelio. He came by on the weekends to visit with Luisa, and after a few weeks had passed, Reeve could see the longing and regret in his eyes. But if she was anything she was stubborn, and she would not give in to him even when he began to beg her. She had to come up with an alternate plan to her life. It came to her one day on the back page of the newspaper, in a tiny ad in the bottom right-hand corner. "Train to be a midwife and help pregnant women through the beautiful birthing process. Financial aid available for those who qualify." At the bottom of the ad was a telephone number. Reeve clipped the ad and carried it over to the phone. During her pregnancy, she had read about midwives in the public library, and though she didn't use one herself, she disliked the coldness of the doctor who had delivered Luisa, and knew in her heart that a midwife would have been kinder and gentler. She had an aching inside of her to reach out to others, and couldn't think of a better way. She knew that she would have to find a job somehow, and this seemed like the perfect opportunity.

That weekend, when Aurelio came to see Luisa, he had a large bouquet of roses for Reeve. "I know I made a mistake," he pleaded, "and I want to be better to you."

Reeve wanted to forgive him, but she wanted to hold out even more. She had spoken to a midwife on the phone and discovered that there were several training opportunities available, but none of them were in Houston. Midwives were common in the smaller towns in the northeast segment of the state, where teenage mothers were becoming more and more common. Most didn't have the means to pay the hefty medical expenses that came with using a doctor. The midwife, Lorraine, had spoken to her on the phone for over half an hour, and Reeve had written down all of the important information on a torn-off page of a yellow legal pad. Now, as Aurelio pleaded her forgiveness, she held the folded up paper in her pocket, her hand opening and closing around it as she looked up at her husband.

"I'm going to be a midwife." She spoke with confidence and held Aurelio's eyes.

A look of confusion came over his face as he looked back at her. "A midwife?"

She realized that he didn't know the English word, and she tried to explain what it meant, but found it difficult to put into words. At last, he nodded, and told her that his whole family had been delivered by midwives.

"What does that mean, exactly? Will you go to school?"

"Yes, but first I have to get a GED, which is like a high school diploma. I have to take a test. And then I have to move to the northeastern part of the state where they have a training center." Reeve paused to examine Aurelio's reaction. He held a stony look, as if he expected her to say more. She went on. "I'm taking Luisa with me. You can come on two conditions. You stop drinking and you don't tell me how to run the household." Her voice didn't falter as she spoke, and she held his brown eyes within her grays.

Aurelio waited before he spoke. He hesitated for two reasons. First, he had always been raised to respect women, but also to control them. Second, he knew, somewhere in his soul, though he would never admit it aloud to Reeve or anyone else, that not drinking would be a near impossible task. His eyes scanned the room after she was finished staring him down, and he noticed that many of Renee's cluttered piles had been organized and redistributed to shelves and other places in the house. He drew in a long breath and let the air come out between his teeth in a slow whistle.

"I think we should both make decisions about how the household works. And I won't drink anymore."

Reeve's face softened, and she moved towards him. He reached for her, wrapping his strong arms around her waist. She felt safe again, as she had the night in the loft, and allowed her body to fall limply into his grasp. They stood there for as long as their legs would allow before weakening under the pressure of immobility, and when Reeve shifted away, Aurelio lifted her chin with his palm and pressed his lips against hers with gentle passion.

When Luisa awoke from her nap moments later, both her parents stood over her crib and cooed down to her, their arms around each other's waists. She squealed and flung her arms in the air, happy at the sight of their happiness. It was the last time she would ever see them together with expressions of love towards each other and her. Luisa, still an infant, would never remember it. For the rest of her life, she would always hope to hold such a memory in her mind and in her heart.

Chapter 35

They had been fighting for a week, and Carter thought Luisa was being unreasonable. She wouldn't speak to him, and when he came home from work, she purposely went out, or stayed inside their bedroom with the door shut and locked, listening to her CD player and sifting through her art books. She wouldn't cook for him or fix his lunch or give him his goodbye kiss in the morning, and he was torn up inside over it.

The previous week, his friend Greg from high school had been in town for two days on business. The night before he was going to fly back, after a day filled with boring meetings, he had begged Carter to come out with him to one of the bars downtown. Carter, reluctant, hadn't seen Greg since he and Luisa's wedding over two years earlier.

"I can come, but I can't drink," he told him on the phone.

"Why not? You're not an—"

"No. Long story. I promised Luisa."

"Oh, she's got you whipped that bad, huh?"

Greg's mockery stung Carter's ears on the drive over to his downtown hotel. Greg, a stocky five foot seven with black curly hair clipped short around his square face, got into the car. "I thought this day would never end. Sorry I didn't get any time to visit with y'all."

"Oh, it's all right. Luisa has been studying for her finals. She's just about done with her master's degree, thank God. She's been in school the whole time I've known her. It'll be nice when she doesn't have to study anymore."

Greg still couldn't understand Carter's desire to settle down at so young an age. Whenever he traveled to consult new clients in the software business, which happened about two times a month, his ultimate goal was to find a pretty lady in a bar and take her back to the nice suite that his corporation put him up in. He loved the excitement of chasing down women and then letting them go the next day. How Carter could stand to wake up to the same face every morning for the rest of his life perplexed him.

He slugged him in the shoulder and said, "By the way, the drinks are on me. Luisa will never be bothered if you at least don't waste any money on the shit."

Carter didn't want to get into a semantic discussion about why he couldn't drink, but he hadn't had a sip of alcohol in over three years, and he had to admit to himself, though he wouldn't say it aloud to the cocky Greg, that Luisa had him by the reins.

"I'll be all right. Someone's gotta drive us home, you know." He tried to sound like he didn't care one way or the other, and was relieved when Greg changed the subject and started talking about the meetings he had led all day.

When they stepped out of the car in the LoDo neighborhood, Greg scanned his eyes over the two story nineteenth-century warehouse that had since been renovated into a restaurant and bar. By the time they arrived, the sun had set behind the mountains, and the glow of twilight reflected itself against the yellow lights that poured out of the windows. Greg squinted his eyes as he moved them from the first to the second floor windows, then punched Carter again in the arm and said, "Looks like all the action is upstairs. Let's go."

Wearing a tight polo t-shirt and khaki shorts that showed off his muscles, Greg trotted up the stairs at the pace of a thirsty horse coming in from the fields to drink from the trough. Carter followed, his steps slow and reluctant. He, too, wore a polo t-shirt, but had chosen loose jeans to go along with it. The bouncer at the door checked their ID's, and as soon as they entered the smoky bar, they went straight up the stairs.

On Fridays, the business men and women who worked downtown came to the bar for happy hour, and many of them stayed long after the cheaper drinks had turned into overpriced concoctions of water and alcohol. By the time Greg and Carter arrived, just after eight o'clock, the bar held a number of men wearing button-up white dress shirts, the ties left in the car, and the pants of a suit, while the women wore silk blouses and skirts with high heels and pantyhose, their hair falling loosely around their faces from the low ponytails or buns they had kept during their jobs.

After just one drink, Greg ordering a martini and Carter a glass of water, the late-night crowd began streaming in, and the men wore jeans and polo shirts while the women wore nice pants and simple cotton shirts or polyester blouses, their hair and makeup done up just as carefully as if they were preparing to go to a wedding rehearsal dinner. Greg, not wanting to get mixed up with a starchy businesswoman, kept his eyes focused on the newer, younger crowd, their faces wrinkle-free and bragging of the recent history that bore their twenty-first birthdays. People crowded around the three bartenders at the bar, yelling out their drink orders over the noise of the crowd and the music that blared from speakers all around the room. Tables lined the perimeter of the second story, some high with barstools and ashtrays in the center, some regular size with velveteen booths and vases of fake flowers, where people sat munching on appetizers or even dinner.

Carter, who hadn't been to a bar in a couple of years, became mesmerized by the chipper faces of the people he saw, the men flirting with women and buying them drinks, the women reaching out to touch the men's arms or place kisses on their boyfriends' cheeks. So much seemed to be going on all at once, and in so many different, miniature circles within the room, and yet it also seemed to be one conglomeration of people together for the same purpose. He sat next to Greg and tried to hold a conversation about how his work had been going, how his marriage had been, and asking Greg about his own recent success, but found it difficult to concentrate between the intoxicating noises and views. In the midst of a sentence, Greg's eyes wandered and he told Carter that he was going to have to take a moment to meet the lady behind him.

For the next hour, Carter sat in silence as Greg flirted with the long-legged blond who wore tight-fitting jeans and a button-down silk blouse that was hardly buttoned at all, exposing her large breasts pushed up by her bra. Every few minutes, Greg would catch Carter's eye and wink or offer to buy him a drink, and Carter listened to the mundane conversation between the two. It involved discussions about football and their jobs and the spring weather in Denver compared to Kansas City. When Greg, after three beers, got up to go to the bathroom, Carter found himself with the responsibility of entertaining his lady friend as she sipped at the second amaretto sour that Greg had bought for her. From the dazed look in her green eyes and how she giggled at everything that came out of Carter's mouth, he could tell that Greg picked women only for looks, and secretly thanked Luisa for being intelligent and quiet, and for staying away from places like this. At the same time, seeing the buzz of the alcohol take over her movements, as well as watching the comfort of the people surrounding them, who all seemed at peace with themselves, their faces bright with drug-induced happiness, Carter had a craving for a drink that he couldn't deny.

When Greg returned from the bathroom, Carter said, "How about a couple of tequila shots?"

"Now there's the Carter DaSilva I grew up with. You wouldn't believe it, Marie, but Carter used to drink me under the table when we were in high school."

Greg ordered the shots, and the warm, bitter liquid stung Carter's esophagus as he swallowed. He felt its warmth enter his stomach, burning it up, the heat of the drink rising to his skin and his face. When he took a breath after the drink had settled, he couldn't keep the smile from taking over his mouth. He immediately felt buzzed, and the bar, which before had looked foreign with its people clinging to each other in rapturous wonderment, now offered him the comforts of home. He patted Greg on the back and said, "Are you ready for another?"

Because Greg wanted to take Marie back to the hotel and he knew he wouldn't be able to drive, Carter spent the only money he'd brought that night on the taxi ride home. He didn't arrive until well after midnight. Luisa was already in bed, though she pretended to sleep, her eyes wide open in the dark. Not wanting to disturb her, Carter used the bathroom and pulled a blanket over his shoulders as he settled in to the discomfort of the living room couch. Luisa dozed off at last, though her anger, and Carter's frequent visits in the middle of the night to the toilet to vomit, kept her tossing and turning.

The next morning, through his harrowing hangover, he tried to explain to her what happened. She sat at the dining table moving her spoon in circles through her bowl of Cheerios, keeping her eyes focused on the bowl as if it were filled with sparkling gems. She listened as he relayed the events of the night before. She said nothing. She didn't want to speak because she thought that she might scream or run out of the house or, worse, take her long fingernails and dig them into his face. The anger inside of her ate at every capillary in every vein. She could feel her blood throbbing beneath her skin as she opened and closed her fist. She carried her bowl to the sink, tossed it in with the flippancy of a careless slob, and went upstairs to take a shower.

It was a Saturday morning and she drove east, not sure of where to go. She had her wallet and a light jacket, and the temperature was eighty degrees by the time she moved from the skyscrapers and ongoing housing developments into the stark expanse of the plains. She wanted to see forever, to look at the roundness of the horizon beneath the perfect blue sky and let the howling wind take her pain away. But before she could reach the total absence of civilization, she felt nauseous and knew she must stop to eat. The evening before, she had discovered that she was pregnant, and had waited as long as she could to break the news to Carter, but he never came home in time to hear it.

After she left, Carter remained on the couch, his body aching from alcoholic dehydration and the night of vomiting. He kept the tears from creeping out of the corners of his eyes by taking large breaths and trying to swallow the painful lump inside his Adam's apple. He thought about all the promises he had made to Luisa over the years and how many he had broken. The promises, like the way his heart felt now, were shattered into pieces. He hated himself for the stupidity of his decisions, for allowing himself to be influenced by a man who he hardly spoke to any more, and who had no direction to his life. He wanted to stop Luisa as she left, to stand in front of the door and force her to stay inside, to force her to talk to him, to force her, at least, to say that she loved him before she left. But he felt weak and sickly and disgusted with himself, and he couldn't think of the right words to say to her. Instead, he allowed the morning to pass as he dozed in and out of sleep, his stomach ailment fading away as the sun beamed hotter on his back from the easterly window.

At last he got up to use the bathroom, and, discovering no toilet paper, opened the drawer and saw the pregnancy test lying flat, in plain view. Two purple lines filled the circle and the square, both definitive and bright. He stared at the test for a long time, the contrast of the purple and white blazing his eyes. He sat on the toilet, feeling dizzy and hating himself even more. He used the bathroom and then went downstairs.

He started with the kitchen. Luisa always complained that when he did the dishes, he never cleaned the sink. Now, he cleared away every item from the counter, from the porcelain canisters to the breadbox, and wiped clean all the spaces against the wall. He got out a scrubbing sponge and the special liquid cleaner created just for the ceramic stovetop and shined away until it was spot-free and glowed beneath the light above. He retrieved the 409 and scrubbed every stain out of the microwave and took out the plate to wash in the sink. He loaded and started the dishwasher, then took the toaster oven out to the birdfeeder and knocked all the loose crumbs inside, and scrubbed it until the white exterior glared at him under the bright sun.

When he returned to the kitchen, he quickly fixed himself a turkey sandwich, careful not to drop one crumb on the countertop, and he even washed and put away the plate and knife when he was finished eating. He got out the vacuum cleaner and vacuumed every room in the house, taking off the tube to get into the cracks along the baseboards and the cobwebs along the upper corners. He straightened up the office, filing away old pay stubs and bills, and then dusting off the desk and computer. He then dusted all the surfaces in the house, from the mantel over the fireplace to the television. He took another brief break to drink a large glass of ice-cold water, and then retrieved the steam cleaner from the coat closet by the door. While he boiled water on the stove, he swept and mopped the kitchen floor, then took the steam cleaner upstairs and made perfect columns of cleanliness in the hallway and the bedrooms. After removing his sopping wet socks, he took the roll of paper towels from the kitchen, along with the 409 and Windex, and cleaned every surface in the bathroom.

Exhausted from the afternoon of work, he plopped down on the couch and sighed. He hadn't seen the house so clean since his parents last came from Kansas City. Luisa became obsessed with spotlessness whenever guests came to visit, and would spend hours each day picking at every piece of dust in the furniture and vacuuming, scrubbing, and organizing everything from the books on the shelves to the DVD's in the entertainment center. Now, proud of his work and hopeful for her forgiveness, Carter took a shower, and then went to the local department store to pick out an outfit for their unborn child.

Luisa drove until she reached the Pawnee Buttes. She had come here on a class camping trip in eighth grade and had always wanted to return. She loved how the white stone, irregularly shaped buttes stood out against the plains, their height and width a strange vision under the never-ending vastness of the grasslands. The dirt path leading up to the buttes hadn't changed, and the knee-high green grass tickled her exposed legs as she walked toward the buttes. Wildflowers, ripe in late June, bloomed all around her, and their varied scents moved into her nostrils with the passing breezes. She wore a t-shirt and shorts with gray trail running sneakers and white socks, and the sun tinged her back with its early afternoon heat. She had stopped at a gas station in the closest town and picked up several granola bars and a thirty-two-ounce bottle of water, all of which she wrapped inside her jacket and tied around her waist. Her back ached from the weight of the water, and she stopped frequently to take large gulps, partially from thirst and partially from the desire to release herself from the extra weight.

When she arrived at the base of the first butte, she examined the structure as an engineer examines a building during an inspection. In the thirteen years that had passed between her first visit here and now, the buttes had given in to the whipping winds that crossed the plains. When she came before, she and her classmates had climbed up the sides and found a path midway, and were able to walk around the circular exterior of the butte, though the path was narrow and often slippery with loose dirt beneath their feet. Luisa could see that there was no possible way to climb up the butte at all, and any path that had previously existed was now washed away into the dirt of the plains.

She could feel and hear the wind. It stung her face with bits of dust from the butte and pulled out pieces of her hair from the low ponytail she had tied at the nape of her neck. She could taste the cleanliness and dryness of the air when she opened her mouth and faced the gusts of wind that came from the west. She sat down at the base of the butte and focused her eyes on its mate, about a hundred yards farther down the trail. Without approaching it, she could see that it, too, had eroded with wind and water, and no longer bore a trail around its center. She watched it for a long time, letting the wind sweep across her body, her eyes moving from the butte to the grasslands and back again. She couldn't think of a time in her life when nature amazed her more. She had no idea that these large structures could change so much in a matter of years. She wondered how long it would be before the buttes would disappear entirely. She thought about the child inside her and what the buttes would be like when she returned one day with him or her. Would they still be four stories tall, or small mounds of white clay that one could scramble over on all fours?

Tears seeped into her eyes as she thought of the change that had taken place. She had imagined, on the two and a half hour drive, that she could still climb to the path and encircle each butte, looking out over the plains from a higher point, drinking in their beauty. Now, sitting at the bottom edge, she felt tired and weary from her lack of sleep and the long drive. She pulled a granola bar out of her rolled up jacket and began chewing it slowly. She moved the pieces around in her mouth, in no hurry to eat, swallow, or move. She didn't know how long she sat there, but the heat of the late afternoon infiltrated her skin. Beads of sweat shone in the sun between the dark hairs on her arms. She felt weak and listless and decided to go home. She wondered if Carter had discovered the pregnancy test that she purposely hadn't thrown away.

He had learned to cook only two meals in his time as a married man: spaghetti and meatballs and chicken quesadillas. He shredded the cheese now over the flour tortillas as the square pieces of chicken breast meat simmered in the green chili on the stove. He poured medium hot salsa over the cheese and looked at his watch: almost six. Luisa always had dinner ready by six. He spooned pieces of chicken and green chili onto the first tortilla, shredded more cheese over the meat, and placed another tortilla on top. He put the quesadilla into the microwave and set the cook time at three minutes, then turned to look at the half dozen roses and the small wrapped package on the table. He'd found a yellow set of pajamas that had a duck on it, and, as it seemed to be the only item in the baby department with a bird, he bought it and wrapped it up. On top of the package was a card that had a long, mushy poem about how sorry he was. He had also said his own short apology at the end.

She came in just as the microwave beeped and hung her jacket and put her shoes in the coat closet next to the door. Luisa could smell the quesadillas and see the nice table he had prepared, and she knew, from the wrapping paper that bore pink and blue rattles, that he knew of the pregnancy. She could see that he had spent the better part of the day cleaning the house, something he always did when they fought. Luisa could almost taste the forgiveness that she so badly wanted to give, but instead went into the kitchen, took the plate with her quesadilla off the counter while Carter heated up his in the microwave, and walked up to their bedroom, shutting the door and locking it.

He'd waited all day, and had little patience left. With a red face and hot tears in his eyes, Carter stormed up the stairs after her and banged on the bedroom door.

"Are you ever going to talk to me? Are you ever going to forgive me?"

Luisa didn't answer. She had mastered the silent treatment in her early years when she and Byron hid in the basement of their parents' home and listened, without words, to their parents' vicious arguments. She could go days without speaking, letting her parents know that there were other, crueler ways to express anger than by cussing each other out and throwing books across the room. Carter, too, knew that she could be silent for long periods, but she had never closed him off for this long. He had also never gone out drinking before and come home late at night in a taxi.

Three days passed before Luisa found it inside herself to speak to him. In the meantime, she spoke to Clara on the phone, who told her she was being unreasonable. Carter, who rarely spoke to his friends about his personal problems with his life, took a different route. On Sunday evening, he went into the office and wrote Luisa a letter.

During the course of their relationship, Carter had written Luisa exactly six letters. One, he wrote from Kansas City soon after they'd met and he had been visiting his parents. Two more he had written in response to letters Luisa had written to him. The other three letters were true love letters that he had shared with her in the early days of their relationship, letters that told her why he loved her and that he wanted to spend his life with her.

Now, Carter wrote Luisa a letter that he wouldn't give her. After two days of reflection and regret, he felt an urge to put into words what he couldn't say aloud or with any action. He spoke from his heart and shared with Luisa all of his darkest fears, his fears about the future and what life might be like for him if she were gone. At the end of the letter, he told Luisa the most important things he wanted her to remember about him after he was gone.

When he finished, he put the letter inside an envelope and sealed it, writing on the outside, "Luisa: Please do not read until after I die." He wondered if Luisa would be an eighty-year-old woman when she discovered the letter, and how his life, and his memories, would be so different then. But he knew, as he climbed up on a stepstool and put the letter in a shoebox at the back of the top shelf in the closet, that he couldn't give her the letter now. He just couldn't explain to himself why.

When she returned from class on Monday afternoon, Carter was still at work. The package still sat on the edge of the dining room table, the shadows from the roses dancing in the afternoon light on its paper. She opened the card first, and finally let the tears flow from her eyes. They dripped down onto the blue and pink rattles and trickled into the white background of the wrapping paper. She pulled apart the pieces of paper as if she were a surgeon opening up a patient's chest. She put her hands on the soft terrycloth fabric, and then picked up the sleeper and pressed it into her face. She cried and cried and cried, thinking of all that had gone wrong in her life and all that had gone right.

When he returned home, Carter saw Luisa standing in the kitchen with her "Kiss the Cook" apron on and a set of chrome tongs in her hand. She was making beef tamales, his favorite Mexican meal. She flipped her hair back and turned towards him, then told him to sit down.

"So you know we're pregnant," she said after a moment of silence.

"I couldn't be happier." Carter tried to smile, but felt he must keep a cautious distance.

Luisa drew in a few breaths before she spoke. She had been thinking about her words for three days, choosing them carefully, rearranging them in her mind, until she had prepared the perfect speech. She not only wanted him to take her seriously, she wanted him to think of what she said as the turning point in their marriage.

"I don't like to give ultimatums," she began, catching his eye before he looked away. "But now that I am pregnant, and we're bringing another life into this family, it is more important to me than ever before that you never, ever drink. Now, I know you don't think it's a big deal to have a drink once in a while with your buddies. I know you may think that just because my father has a problem doesn't mean you will. I know all the things that you probably might think about it. But you need to realize one thing above all else. You not drinking is the absolute most important thing I will ever ask of you. I care more about this than anything else. And even though I would hate to break up a family, I will divorce you if you ever drink again." Luisa's heart pounded inside her eardrums. She couldn't keep eye contact with Carter for fear of what he might say.

"I won't. I promise. Having a baby means more to me than anything. I would never do anything to hurt our family. And I'm so sorry, Luisa." Carter stood and reached for her. He wrapped his arms around her tiny waist and pulled her close.

She cried into his shoulder and whispered, "I forgive you."

It was the last fight they ever had.

By mid-October, when the leaves began hanging limply from their branches, ready to fall, Luisa had finished her paintings and sent away professionally bound copies of the manuscript to several writing agents. Aurelio, who now lived in a three-quarter-way house and worked the night shift at UPS, couldn't be more proud. He kept one of the copies for himself and read one of the stories each morning when he returned from work. With ninety days of sobriety behind him and a lifetime ahead of him, he felt the publication of the manuscript was the turning point in his life. His heart ached for Mexico, for his family, for his home. Over the years, he had maintained regular contact with his parents and siblings through phone calls and letters and sent home pictures of his children as they grew. His mother always ended each phone conversation and returning letter with the same question: "When will you make me proud enough to see you again?"

Aurelio could never admit to them that he had a drinking problem. For years and years, he couldn't admit it to himself. But Dante insisted that he discuss his problem openly with his family and friends. Aurelio called Mexico in early September and talked for three hours, the words filled with sobbing on both ends of the receiver. After he admitted the truth to his family, Aurelio felt that he could admit it to everyone, including himself. He became more determined to stay sober, and, for the first time in his life, began attending AA meetings. Each night before work, and other times in between when he felt a burning urge to drink, he attended a meeting. At first, he didn't speak much, but listened to the stories and problems of the other people. After a while, he realized that it wasn't going to do him any good just to listen, so one night he opened up and began to talk. He found the words coming easily out of his mouth, pouring out of him like the drinks the bartender had once kept flowing for him at his local dive, and soon he was one of the longest talkers in the group, telling them everything from why he started drinking to the newest thing Alejo had learned to do.

With the worst of his past behind him and the possibility of the manuscript's publication ahead of him, Aurelio wore his hopes and dreams on his smiling face in a way he hadn't since his youth. He felt in love with life again, and, though his body and spirit had been battered by years of abuse, he could feel the healing power of his new life begin to take over.

Luisa, who had used painting to release herself from the sharp puncture of Carter's death, felt the opposite of her father. On her way home from the post office after dropping off the last copy to be mailed away to an agent, Luisa felt a great weight coming onto her shoulders. For seven months, she had barely caught a breath as she worked, first on clearing away the loose items from her house, then adjusting to life in Warren's home, then to helping her father and mother work through the problems of their past, and all the while pouring out the pain that seeped through her veins with a canvas, relentless colors, and a paintbrush. Now, with her father walking on his own two feet, her mother moving away from her past, and the manuscript on its way to publication, Luisa felt the reality of her current life hit her hard in the face.

She began to wake each morning with a mantra in her head: I have no money, no home of my own, no job, no husband, and a child to support. The words that she repeated to herself each day kept her lying in bed longer than she should have, when she could hear Alejo crying from his crib, anxious for milk. She felt out of breath as she stepped into her slippers, trekked across the hallway, and found herself cradling him in her arms and crying as she had done when Carter had just died. She would repeat the mantra as she fixed his milk, changed his diaper, and got him dressed; she would repeat it as she ate her own breakfast, took a shower, and took him on a walk. The words made her hate her life, though they also pushed her forward. She knew that she had stayed in Warren's house too long and that it was time to move on.

She began to search the classifieds for any kind of job, having given up the possibility that she could find a job in an art museum or a community college. She skimmed through the ads each morning as she drank a cup of Earl Grey. Warren, an early riser, would be out in the yard or running errands. The efficiency of his life remained the same even after Luisa and Alejo moved in, so Luisa always had most of the morning to herself. She loved and hated this. She knew that she needed the time to get her life into order, and much of that involved trying to find a job and then an apartment, tasks that could be daunting, but were manageable with a decent resume, a few phone calls, and a deposit (which she already had in the bank from the sale of her house). But she also knew that getting her life in order meant much more than just arranging for her financial security. It meant that she had to get in order every other aspect of herself. Without a specific task to complete, as she had with the painting for the manuscript, Luisa let her emotions run wild. In one moment she would be so happy that she had lived, that she was here to see Alejo grow, to see that he would have a good life, and to continue her own. In the next moment, she would feel bitter guilt for allowing herself a moment of happiness. She would often cry in these moments. After her tears had fallen, her body would fill with rage, rage at everything from the man who had driven drunk and killed Carter, to Carter himself for leaving her so early in life. Then, she would stomp around the house, pulling things out of drawers and closets and throwing them across the room, only to turn around and pick them up again, rearranging them in an even neater manner. Her whirlwind of emotions carried her through the mornings until she finally would settle down to the reality of her position.

She was circling ads with a red pen in the paper one late morning when someone rang the doorbell. Alejo, who wandered around at her feet picking up random pan lids that she had spread on the floor for him, widened his eyes and squealed, "Din-don!" It was one of the new sounds he had picked up in the last few weeks. Luisa and patted his head. "That's right! Ding-dong! Who do you think it is?"

As she walked towards the door, the thought occurred to her that she would never walk towards a door again after hearing a doorbell without dread and apprehension overcoming her. She felt the muscles tighten in her jaw as she reached the door, her hand pausing for a second before turning the knob to open it. As she did so, all air escaped from her lungs, as if the hand of an absent angel had pulled it out of her body to hold on to until she could recover her eyes.

There in front of her was the handsome, dimpled, smiling face of Tyler, who held a sack from Dunkin' Donuts in one hand and two covered cups of coffee in another.

"I thought you might like some company," he said, and Luisa could hear the nervous waver of his voice.

A moment of true happiness engulfed her, though it was wrapped inside the ever-penetrating feeling of guilt. She held open the door. "Well that was nice of you. Come on in." She hadn't seen him since Labor Day, and now, in his button-down collared white shirt, blue tie, and black dress pants, he appeared more handsome than ever. His hair, which must have been freshly cut when she first met him, now draped itself around his ears. He still had the moustache, and had grown a goatee whose red hairs shone beneath the light of the kitchen lamp as they sat down at the table. His muscular arms looked tan from a summer of being outside, though the tan was beginning to fade with the season.

Tyler sat across from her and placed the tray with the coffee cups on the table and reached inside the bag and pulled out two bagels and small plastic containers of cream cheese.

"I didn't figure you were the type to eat donuts," he said, examining her thin frame beneath her long-sleeved blue cotton shirt and jeans.

"And how did you figure that?" Luisa's tone was flirtatious, though every part of her insides tried to keep it from being so.

"Well, at the barbecue, you ate only the meat of the chicken, not the skins, you stayed away from the potato salad and had the spinach salad instead, you drank water instead of pop, and you only ate the strawberries from the strawberry shortcake. I figured you must be a health nut." He paused, a nervous smile on his lips. "Well, I'm kind of a health nut myself."

"I guess I do try to watch what I eat. But sometimes I just have to have a candy bar. My husband—" she caught herself saying the word out loud, and her face reddened, but she decided to continue. "My husband would always stop by the store on his way home from work whenever I called him with a candy bar craving."

"He sounds like a great guy."

"He was. He really was."

Tension hung in the air between them for a moment, and then Tyler placed his hands, palms down, on the newspapers. "It looks like you're looking for a job. Any luck?"

"Not yet. I've only sent out about ten resumes. And there just aren't any jobs for art historians right now. I've been having some trouble." Luisa glued her eyes on the newspapers that were sprawled out on the table, too embarrassed to look up.

"Well, that's just what I'm here for. Warren told me that you're a pretty great artist. I just might know of a job for an artist."

Her embarrassment turned to humiliation. She felt not just her face, but her entire body redden with heat. Though she tried to suppress it, she could not keep the large, painful lump from burgeoning inside her throat. She didn't want to admit it to herself, and would never think of admitting to him, that she wanted him to come here for a different reason. Carter's absence had left her with all kinds of longings, many of which she tried to hide, but couldn't. Since the moment she had met Tyler, her most regrettable longing of all came out: the longing to be loved, to be held, to be touched by a man. In the six weeks since he first appeared in front of her, he had appeared many times in her dreams, both sleeping and awake. She imagined him coming into her life and carrying her away from all her pain, rescuing her from the depths of her grief. Though she knew that he couldn't do such a thing, that for the rest of her life she would always feel a tinge of pain as she awoke each morning and went to bed each night, she loved imagining that it was possible. But now, as she held her stare on the newspapers, all she could do was call herself stupid and force the tears to remain inside her eyes.

"I suppose I am." When she spoke, her voice carried in the air like a feather being blown away on the breeze.

"I guess you don't know much about me. I'm a headhunter for various corporations. I know what you mean about finding a job. The economy's not the greatest right now. But there are jobs out there, if you look in the right places. And I know all the right places to look." Tyler tried to catch her eye, but she remained focused on her task of avoiding his look. "Anyway, I've become good friends with the CEO of one of the companies I work for. He's filthy rich, of course, and has somehow managed to invest his securities in all the right places, so even when the stock market doesn't do so well, he always stays ahead of the game. Well, he's a huge art collector. He started his collection when he met his wife, who also loves art, and he's been filling every room of his house with art for twenty years. He always has his eye out for what's new in town, and when I told him about you, he asked me to invite you over to his house, and for you to bring some work to show him. If he likes what he sees, he'll pay you a salary to paint for him. It may not be a permanent job, but the money will last you a good long while."

Luisa didn't know what to say. She couldn't imagine a more perfect opportunity. When she was in college, she had wanted to become a fine art major, but both her parents strongly suggested she choose a more practical field that would actually produce a job. Seeing how they struggled in the early years of her childhood, Luisa had wanted a different kind of life, and had taken their advice, though she just couldn't keep herself away from the field of art. All through college, with her fine arts minor, she heard professor after professor tell her how talented she was, all of them pleading with her to change over, but her need for security was as strong as her need to create each painting. Once she had begun her master's degree in art history, she had little time to paint, and then she became pregnant, so her palettes and paints remained in the closet until after Carter's death. Now, as she listened to Tyler's speech, her childhood dreams of becoming an artist seemed to blossom into a beautiful reality.

"It sounds like an opportunity I can't let pass by." Luisa's pale brown skin glistened under the kitchen light. Alejo whined at her feet, tugging on her pants and pointing to the refrigerator. "Do you want your milk, Alejo?" He nodded and Luisa stood up, thankful for the distraction away from Tyler's blue eyes.

"That sounds great. I'll give Bill a call and we'll see when we can meet. You don't mind if I come along too, do you?"

"No, of course not." Luisa said and finally looked into Tyler's face as she warmed the milk in the microwave. His eyes held a softness that looked to her like two calm pools of water. She wanted to jump in and swim in the warmth of his offer, in the warmth of him.

Tyler paused before he spoke. He cleared his throat. Luisa busied herself with putting the lid back on the sippy cup and bent over to give the cup to Alejo.

"Well, good, because I was hoping to be able to take you out to dinner first."

When she heard the proposal, her heart leapt inside her chest as it did when she sped down the highway and saw a flash of police lights behind her car. She felt that she had been caught, that he must have known what she was thinking, and she turned shamefaced toward her hands, again unable to look at him.

"That is," Tyler said in haste, his voice now nervous and anticipatory, "if you don't think it's too soon."

Alejo wandered around the kitchen, standing up and then sitting down, tilting his sippy cup, and his chin, toward the ceiling. Luisa now focused her eyes on her son, her mouth parched, the words escaping her mind. She had her back to Tyler now, but felt him come up behind her and touch her shoulder. He turned her around and lifted her chin toward his. He had one hand on her shoulder, barely touching her with his long, thick fingers. Luisa's breath quickened and she clenched and unclenched her fists at her sides. When he spoke again, she felt her hands go limp and her muscles relax.

"It's OK to say no. I'll still try to get you the job." His voice had calmed, and he still held his hand under her chin. She wanted him to demand that she go, to profess his love to her, to pull her close to him and kiss her passionately.

"I don't want to say no," she finally said, "but I don't want to say yes either."

"How about I call you in two days and see how you feel. Do you think you could have some paintings picked out by then?"

"Yes, of course."

"Well, I need to get back to the office. I'll talk to you in a couple of days."

Luisa walked him to the door and watched him from the front window as he walked to his car. She watched him get into the driver's seat of the silver

BMW and watched as he started the ignition, adjusted the radio, and pulled away from the curb. She didn't know how she would ever be able to say no when he called.

Chapter 36

If it weren't for Rose and Margaret, who still clung to his legs when he returned from school each day and often called him, "Daddy," when they chose household roles for their dolls, Warren would have moved out of his mother's house at the age of sixteen. For years, he had saved almost every dime and dollar he made, and had enough to make a deposit on an apartment and pay a year's rent in advance. Warren was tall and lanky like his father, and because of the lawn mowing business had upper body strength. He looked more like a young adult than a teenager. He knew he wouldn't have any problems lying to a landlord about his age. In the spring of his sophomore year, he began to form a plan in his mind of how to escape, but Rose and Margaret always blocked his vision of a one-bedroom apartment or walking to school by himself. Kenny had escaped the draft by receiving a football scholarship to the University of Oklahoma, and he never wrote. Freddy, whose talents didn't quite match Kenny's, played his hand at acing all the most difficult courses available at their high school. He still planned on attending college in the fall, though he knew an athletic scholarship was unlikely. Warren watched as his brothers grew and left the house, knowing that their mother would fall into an even deeper depression once they were gone, though she would never admit why.

The certified letter from the U.S. Marine Corps became the breaking point in Warren's life. The mail carrier, wary of bringing such letters to more and more families as the war escalated, held his head down when Warren answered the door. His stout frame beneath the blue and white, sweat stained uniform was a stark comparison to Warren's height and thinness. He wore a large beige sunhat that helped him hide his beady black eyes from the look on Warren's face when he saw the return address. Warren took the cardboard envelope in his palms and used it for a backboard as he shakily signed for the letter. Except for his mother, he was the only one home. Freddy was still at school, as were the girls, and his mother was encapsulated between the plain white walls of the bedroom.

When the mailman walked away, Warren took the letter in his hands and walked out to the elm in the backyard. Though he knew from the neatly typed address that read "Mrs. Francis York" that Frankie hadn't written the letter, he still hoped that if he opened it here in the familiar place where he'd read all the letters from Frankie, the news wouldn't be as bad as he imagined. For two years now, the black and white television that Kenny had purchased with his lawn mowing money bore deathly images of the war, from land mines exploding in the distance to fiery bombs that fell from the air. Warren had watched the images increase with each nightly newscast, and every time he saw them, his stomach flipped with fear and discomfort. Even now, though he was older and no longer taking the abuse he had as a child, he felt young and innocent, and still couldn't understand Frankie's desire to join the military and commit his life to his country. The more he read about the war, the more it sounded wrong to him; not because the Vietnamese didn't need help from the Americans, but because they didn't seem to want it. He began to form an opinion in his mind of how conflicts should be resolved, and he couldn't imagine, thinking of the time his mother stood over him as he licked the floor, that violence was the best solution.

Warren had kept his opinions to himself, but realized as the months went on that many others felt the same as he did. But he was not a joiner; he was an outsider, and knew he always would be. Even in his own family, with his athletic, popular brothers and bubbly younger sisters, he felt like a weak middle child who just couldn't fit in. The only place he had ever felt at home was in the warmth of Frankie's presence when he guarded him as a child.

Now, as he slid his index finger under the cardboard, images of Frankie as a young boy flooded Warren's mind. Frankie, with his sloppy red hair and gangly legs, who spoke with the knowledge of a man though he was only a child. Frankie, who took care of the whole family single-handedly as their mother's mind began to slip away, and who had the courage to stand up to her and leave, thinking it was best. Frankie, whose first tour of duty in Vietnam had left him a broken man, half of what he was, and frightened Warren into a sorrow that he hadn't yet been able to escape .

The thick paper felt rough between his moist fingertips. It was clean and white and had never been folded. Warren admired the perfection of the typist who had laid the letter so neatly in the envelope—even the edges showed no signs of wear.

```
Dear Mrs. Francis York and Family,   13 May 1967

     It is our sincere regret to inform you that
your son, Staff Sergeant Francis Henry York,
passed away when his troop was bombed on 10 May
1967. Sergeant York committed three years of
his life to the service of his country in the
United States Marine Corps, and we thank you
for this contribution to the defense of our
countrymen's freedom and rights. Please
remember, in your time of grief, that his death
was an honorable one.
```

Warren folded the letter before reading the signature. He creased the paper between his palms again and again, resisting the urge to tear it to pieces. A robin pecked about in the yard, searching for worms as the sun set in the western sky. He focused his eyes on the robin because his body was numb. Her small black head bobbed up and down from the air to the earth as if she were going underwater and coming up for air. Her orange legs bounced about with quickness and accuracy, and her black eyes examined each place she dug with her yellow beak. At last, she found a worm, and clutching it under her bill, she effortlessly rose up into the air, chirping a song of success. A breeze tickled her feathers and Warren heard her swoop into the neighbor's ash tree, where she rested on a branch among the budding leaves and enjoyed her meal. From a distance, amidst the shadows of the tree and twilight, Warren watched as she tore apart the worm with her claws and beak. Her actions were simple and disciplined and showed the commonality of her everyday life. He tried to imagine, as he focused his mind on the bird, what it would be like to have such a simple life, where gathering food and flying into the sky were your main concerns, and death was always hiding around the corner in the form of a cat or a fast car.

As he watched, he folded and refolded the letter in his hands so that the crease was worn enough to tear the paper easily into neat rectangles. The robin flew away into the setting sun behind the pink clouds, and Warren tried to stand. He still couldn't move. He clicked his jaw and chewed on his inner cheeks. His back rested against the rough trunk of the elm, and his knees bent just below his eyes. The sky darkened around him, and soon he sat under a night sky, though the stars were faint against the glow of city lights.

Rose found him there. She had been calling his name to come for the pasta dinner she had prepared and finally took the time to step outside. Even when she stood over him, he didn't move. He didn't lift his face to see hers, and he didn't offer her a smile or a flower under his palm as he often did. He was so still that, if it weren't for his wide-open eyes, Rose would have thought that he was dead.

"Warren, it's time to eat. What's wrong?"

She had turned on the patio light, and a small triangular stream of yellow flooded Warren's position like a spotlight against the darkness. He squinted his eyes for a moment as he lifted his chin toward her, but then his eyes widened again and his head returned to its straightforward look, almost as if he wasn't sure she was there.

"Warren, are you OK?" Rose's eyes centered on his face, but as she stood with no response, her head turned toward the rest of the body. She saw the cardboard envelope on the ground beside him, though there wasn't enough light for her to read the return address. She saw the letter folded inside his right palm.

"What is it Warren? Is it Frankie?" It was the only thing she could think of that would make him so upset, and her heart leapt inside her chest as she mouthed Frankie's name.

Warren, hearing the name spoken aloud, allowed his brain to flash before him the bright images of his youth: Frankie carrying him up the stairs of the basement when he was too weak to walk; Frankie grinning under the garish sun as he tossed Warren the baseball; Frankie wrapping his arms around Warren's cold body in the bed he kept open for him; Frankie sneaking bits of steak and potatoes in a napkin down to Warren's basement abode; Frankie standing up to Doris when he announced his departure for the Marines; Frankie's face softening as he looked into the eyes of his son.

Warren shook his head and closed his eyes. Rose watched his head move back and forth like the pendulum of a clock that would never stop. She crouched down beside him and picked up the envelope, reading the return address. "It is Frankie, isn't it?" she whispered, but Warren continued to keep his eyes closed and his head moving. Rose reached out to him, at first with the idea of taking the letter from his hand, but as she moved her arms closer to his, she wrapped them around his neck instead. Warren felt the weight of his head rest against her shoulder, and he let out a long, slow moan, the tears soaking her high collared white shirt. He didn't think he would ever be able to move from that spot, and their tears intermingled until the remainder of the family, excluding the reclusive Doris, discovered the pair, and, without having to ask, joined in their pain.

Darlene had decided that Frankie would be buried at Arlington, but she told Freddy over the phone that her family would be holding a memorial service in Texas if they were interested in going there. Freddy told her how sorry he was, and how awful it must be for her and the baby, and offered to help in any way he could. Darlene told him that he didn't have to worry about that since she would be moving back in with her parents after everything was settled.

When he got off the phone, Freddy turned to his family, who had gathered around the red-faced Warren on the couch. Warren still had the tired, numb look from the night before, and his clothes, now wrinkled and stinking of sweat, clung to his thin frame. His red hair drooped around his round face and his eyes hadn't moved from the floor. He hadn't spoken a single word since Rose's discovery of him in the yard, and Freddy began to worry about what he might do. An obscurity had taken over his pale white face so that he appeared to be half alive, half dead. His eyes hung loosely in their sockets as if one could reach down and grab one, pulling it away from his head like a child taking a gumball from the machine. Freddy walked over to the couch from the phone and sat down in a chair across from Warren. He thought about Darlene's flippant tone on the phone, and tried as hard as he could not to expose to Warren or the rest of the family how clearly she sounded as if she weren't even disappointed by Frankie's death. He thought about the last time they had seen Frankie, in his state of deep depression, and had to admit that if he hadn't improved in the months they spent together before his deployment, he couldn't blame Darlene if she felt a sense of relief to be free of him. But Darlene's relationship with Frankie had been so short lived. She didn't know him like the rest of them, and certainly had no idea of Frankie's effect on Warren's life. He looked at his younger brother now, and, though his hairstyle hung into his face in a stark contrast to Frankie's military cut, his round face and droopy eyes resembled Frankie's. The way he hung his shoulders like a forsaken animal was a striking similarity to Frankie's last presence on the couch.

"I spoke with Darlene. She's pretty upset," Freddy felt his face redden as he lied. "She said they're going to hold a memorial service in Texas if we want to go there. I don't know if you guys want to have one here or not." Freddy's eyes scanned the room, looking over the pink tearstained faces of his family members. They all held different focal points on the floor, stealthily averting their eyes from the truth that Freddy bore.

Freddy had told Doris the night before. She had fallen so far into the depths of depression that, when Freddy first said, "Mother, there's something I have to tell you about Frankie," she had looked up into his face with an expression of bewilderment, whispering under her breath, "Frank? He's long gone, isn't he?" Freddy had to sit down with her on the bed and explain that he wasn't speaking of her husband, but her son. Recognition had filled her eyes once she realized whom he spoke of, but she still seemed perplexed by the circumstances of Freddy's visit to her room. The smell from her unmade bed that reflected a body that hadn't been washed in weeks engulfed his nostrils as he spoke.

"Mother, Frankie joined the Marines, remember? He became a soldier. And they sent him to the war in Vietnam. He went once, and came back to see us with his wife and baby, remember?"

Doris's face, which had stiffened into a permanent stone frown over the last years, bearing crow's feet around the eyes and loose skin under the chin, now softened a bit as she recollected her eldest son. "Oh, yes, of course. What's wrong?"

"He got sent back to Vietnam, Mother. And his troop was bombed. And he died." Freddy didn't know how else to say it. He took his mother's hand. For many years, he had hated her, hated what she had done to Warren, hated her for causing his father to leave, for lying to the police and the social worker, for trapping herself in her room and not taking an inkling to raise her own family. Now, as he saw her withered, weak body slump on the edge of her bed as the sadness crossed over her eyes, he felt nothing but sorrow in his heart. He wanted to hold her and run away from her at the same time, because already a part of him blamed her for Frankie's departure. Frankie had always been bright and should have gone to college, but she denied him that. She had denied them all so many things, and he could never understand why. All he could understand was that she didn't know how to change.

"He died?" she whispered at last, and her voice creaked as someone who hadn't spoken in a long time. "Are you sure?"

"Yes. We received a registered letter from the Marine Corps."

Doris's red hair hung in greasy strings around the face that she buried in her right palm. With her left arm, she reached for Freddy, but not to hug him. She pushed him away, causing him to stand. Then she lifted the mess of covers and pulled them over her, curling into the fetal position.

"Please go away," she moaned, and Freddy stood before her wishing to speak but finding no words.

The image of Doris's small, twisted body flooded his vision now as he looked at his hunched-over family.

"The church will probably want to hold one for him, like they do every week for another poor soul who died in that God-forsaken war," Warren's baritone voice shook the silence in the room. Rose and Margaret lifted their tired eyes, suddenly coming to life in their surprise. "But I'll be going to Texas to see my sister-in-law and nephew."

Without another word, Warren stood up and walked to the room he shared with Freddy and emptied his school bag of its books. He let the pencils and notebooks fall to the floor as he packed underwear, socks, t-shirts, and blue jeans into the bag. He opened his closet door and looked at the one suit he owned, a hand-me-down from Kenny who had told him he probably wouldn't have time to go to services while he was at school. Warren stood for a moment examining the navy blue, high collared suit with the white shirt and red and blue striped tie. Knowing he didn't have a garment bag, he slipped off his socks, shoes, pants, and shirt, and then walked across the hall to the bathroom in his white underwear, carrying the suit on its hanger and placing it on the towel rack. He showered and dressed quickly as his family waited in the living room.

When he emerged from the steaming bathroom with his hair parted in the middle and his tie tight around his neck, Margaret ran up to him and wrapped her arms around his waist. "Can I come with you, Warren? I want to see them, too."

Warren had said all he wanted to say. He shook his head and peeled Margaret's hands away from his waist. He clutched his school bag on his right shoulder and headed for the door. He turned to look at the perplexed faces of his family members before he left. Freddy stood and tried to say something, but he couldn't think of the right words to stop Warren from going.

"Be careful," he said at last, and said, "I called Kenny. He's going to come in on the Greyhound tomorrow. I'm going to call Priest Ferdinand to see if we can arrange a service." Warren nodded and reached for the door handle. A desire burned in him to open the door, walk out, and never return, as Frankie had done. But he knew he couldn't; he knew that the strings of his siblings pulled too tightly at his heart, and that he would come home and finish school and take care of his sisters until they were grown enough to look after themselves.

A cold May rain stung his face when he walked down the porch steps onto the sidewalk, and he had to stop as soon as he'd begun his journey to reach into his bag and pull out an old yellow secondhand parka he'd purchased at the Goodwill. He pulled the string tightly around the hood. His gray breath floated in the air as his shiny black shoes sloshed in the moisture on the concrete walkway. He had to walk three blocks to the nearest bus stop that would take him to the station downtown. After the city bus, it would be another seven blocks to the Greyhound station.

When he paid his fare, he took a seat in the very last row of the half-filled bus. It was midmorning and most of the commuters were already at work.

He watched the rain fall greasily down the tinted windows, blurring the passing cars and bobbing umbrellas along the sidewalks. He held a look of stoic discontent. His lips were perched slightly downward, but his eyes were bright and observant. He slumped against the hard plastic of the seat, his body aching from a night without sleep. The large engine of the bus was the only sound. The other passengers sat listlessly flipping through newspapers and magazines or staring out the window. He felt cold and alone. As the bus navigated the partially flooded streets, he tried to imagine what it had been like for Frankie during his last moments. Was he scared? Did he want to die? Was he relieved? Questions engulfed his mind, along with more images of Frankie's face, Frankie's open arms, his smile, and his look of depression and fear when Warren had last seen him.

He searched his mind for a plan, but nothing seemed correct now. He wanted nothing more than to stay on the bus, to ride on it as it moved back and forth along its route, until its driver changed and the night fell and the bus had to sleep for the night, gas up in the morning, and continue its mundane life the next day. The circular route that stopped at so many places and took so many people where they needed to go had no end and no beginning and was in itself aimless. He felt like the bus; he knew that he could serve a purpose in people's lives but not his own. He wondered what it would be like to be truly alone, to not have to deal with the everyday problems that came with a family. He began to imagine a different kind of life, where he could escape it all and live on his own, and only have himself to take care of. The safety of the vision satisfied him enough to keep himself from crying every time Frankie's image crossed over his mind. Maybe Frankie wanted the same thing when he returned from Vietnam the first time. Maybe the responsibility of his young family was too much for him to bear after all he'd been through. But Warren didn't even know what he had been through, because Frankie had never told him. He was angry at the same time that he mourned; angry at Frankie for leaving and for coming back a different person; angry at the government for sending troops into such a deathly and pointless war; angry, most of all, at Doris, who he believed had caused every ounce of pain he had experienced in his life. Now Frankie's death twisted Warren's emotions together like he was wringing the filthy dishwater out of a rag. He wanted the rag to be dry and the water to rinse down the drain, but no matter how many times he wrung it, moisture still remained between the threads and the stench of the water crept into his nostrils.

Lost in thought, Warren realized suddenly that the bus had been stopped for more than its usual thirty seconds, and all the passengers had disembarked. The driver stood, and, leaving the engine running, went outside to smoke a cigarette. Warren got out of his seat and walked to the front of the bus. He took the two steps down quickly and, pulling his parka tight against his ears, held his face down as he briskly strolled the seven blocks. The chilly, humid air bit at his lungs and by the time he reached the Greyhound station his once-neatly-pressed pants were drenched and wrinkled. He bought a ticket to San Antonio from the wad of dollar bills he had pulled from his sock drawer. As he read the print on the ticket, he realized for the first time that he had never left the city or the state. It would take three days to arrive in San Antonio. Warren wondered what images his mind would create as he stared out into the countryside he had never seen. He put the ticket in his interior jacket pocket and waited for the announcer to call his bus.

Again, Warren chose a seat at the back of the bus along the window. He craned his neck toward the wet parking lot, where other buses rumbled in their designated spaces. He avoided eye contact with the passengers who entered after him. He held his school bag in his lap as a mother would hold her child. His arms were wrapped around its bottom loosely and his fingertips gripped the thick cotton fabric. Not many people spoke as they filled the seats of the bus, but he heard bits and pieces of a few conversations. He wondered what final destinations each of the passengers had, and wondered if anyone would be following him to San Antonio. At last, though he felt he had been sitting in the gray polyester seat for a decade, the bus driver announced that they were departing, and the first stop would be Castle Rock, thirty miles down the road. Surprised that the bus would stop so soon, Warren realized then why it would take three long days and nights to make the journey. He wondered if they would stop every thirty miles for the rest of the trip. The thought tugged at his already restless state.

When the bus stopped in Trinidad for dinner at a small diner, it occurred to Warren that he hadn't contacted Darlene or her family, and that she didn't know he was coming. He dialed his home number and spoke with Freddy, whose voice was hoarse from crying and talking to everyone he knew, relaying the news of Frankie's death. He reassured Warren that he had spoken with Darlene's parents that afternoon and that Darlene would be arriving from Tennessee at about the same time.

The rain had stopped, though the clouds hadn't dissipated, and the sun now set as the bus moved eastward, away from the mountains. Purple, pink, and orange streaks of light glistened on the feathery clouds against the shadowy sharp peaks of the mountains along the New Mexico border. The sun was a bright red and had already hidden itself halfway behind a pass when Warren moved his eyes from their focus on his school bag to the window. The beauty of the colors contrasting the snowy peaks stirred his emotions. He wondered what it would be like to fly into the sunset, to see the sky surrounding him and be a part of the glorious color. Touched by the beauty, a small smile came over his face.

A middle-aged woman had chosen the seat next to him at Trinidad where she entered the bus for the first time. She had graying light brown hair pulled back into a loose bun at the nape of her neck, and strands of hair fell in curls around her plump round face. She wore a high collared, button-down, floral short-sleeved dress that showed the aging spots on her pale white arms. She held a paperback romance novel in her hand, but her brown eyes shifted toward the window to gather the view of the twilight. When she saw the smile sneak onto the face of the boy who had looked so sullen as he dragged his feet to the back of the bus in front of her, she couldn't help but speak up.

"It really is a pretty sunset, isn't it?"

Warren, startled by the woman's high-pitched voice, shifted in his seat. He nodded and mumbled, "Mmm-hmm," but refused to turn his head fully toward her.

"I've seen lots of sunsets in my day, but I must say, that's one of the best I've ever seen. We get great sunsets in Trinidad. What about you? Do you see any pretty sunsets where you're from?"

"Not really," Warren's neck muscles stiffened as he tried to keep his face toward the window.

The woman, determined to keep a friendly conversation to pass the time, persisted. "Where are you headed?"

"San Antonio."

"Well, I guess we have something in common. I'm going to San Antonio myself. My son is graduating from Air Force basic training on Saturday. What brings you there?"

Startled before, now Warren felt strangely disturbed. He wanted to get up and move to another seat, and he lifted his head just a bit to scan the seats surrounding him, but the bus was full. More passengers had come on than left, and he felt trapped and without breath. The last thing he wanted to do was share his life story with some stranger on a bus. But he saw no way around her question.

"My sister-in-law and her family live there. They're holding a memorial service for my brother. He died in Vietnam."

The woman gasped and reached over to clutch Warren's wrist in her soft, thick hand. "Oh, sweetheart, that's terrible. I pray every day that my son, Jeffrey, will be safe, and lucky enough not to go into the war, though I know it isn't likely. It must be so hard on your family. Are you traveling alone?"

The woman's skin felt like silk on his arm, and he wanted her to wrap her arms around him in the safety of her love, the way he had always imagined his mother might do, if she had loved him. He felt his heart opening up just a bit, and he turned to look at her. She held an empathetic expression on her face, and the wrinkles around her eyes and mouth stood out in her mixture of concern and ☐ranquility. Her thin pink lips pointed upward into her cheekbones just a bit. She held in the smile of warmth that she so wanted to give him.

"Yes. My family is holding their own service at our church in Denver. But I wanted to see my nephew again and make sure my sister-in-law would be OK. When my brother came back from his first tour of duty in Vietnam, he just wasn't himself. He was lost, and depressed, and couldn't seem to open up to anyone, even his wife and young son. I think Darlene really suffered while he was home."

"War does that to everyone involved. When my husband left for the South Pacific during World War II, I don't remember a day passing during that year and a half that I didn't cry or pray or wish our lives were different. And when he came home, he wasn't the same jovial prankster I had married. He was… drawn into himself, as if he wasn't sure what his place in the world was anymore. It was a hard time for our family for a few years, until his wounds began to heal. I imagine your sister-in-law never got to see your brother's wounds heal, and that's probably the hardest part for her. I can see why you would want to be there for her."

The woman still held Warren's wrist, and now her fingers stroked it a bit. Warren, not used to gentleness of any kind, felt his body relaxing under her motherly touch.

"I just hope I can help her out somehow. Even if I have to move down there. She said she's going to move back in with her parents, since she was living on base in Tennessee before, and I guess that might help, but I would love to be involved in my nephew's life. He never got to know his own father." Warren found himself confessing to the stranger the secret he hadn't shared with any of his family members and had not admitted to himself. He didn't know how Darlene would react to his arrival or his pocket full of money, but he hoped that she would hold open her arms and welcome him into her life. He was putting everything within himself into that hope.

"Let me give you some advice. Even though I didn't lose my own husband, I saw plenty of other women lose theirs while I waited for mine to return. The fate of a war widow is hard to determine. Every day, she expects to hear the bad news, and when she does, it still shocks her to pieces. It is the worst kind of pain imaginable; that the person you love the most in the world and have committed your life to is now gone forever. I know it must be hard to lose a sibling as well, but when you lose your spouse, you feel like you've given everything to someone who couldn't give it back." The woman paused and looked over Warren's face. His hands rested lightly on his school bag and he looked at her with calm expectancy.

"So when you see your sister-in-law, try to be as sensitive as you can. She has lost everything she hoped for in life, and nothing you can offer her will be able to make up for it. She may deny help from you now, out of grief and pride, but as time passes, she'll need your help. So you'll just have to be patient, son." The woman squeezed his wrist. The wrinkles around her eyes moved together as she raised her lips.

The sun had set and darkness was the only view from the bus window. They drove several hours before stopping in Albuquerque, where the driver got off and switched with another. Most of the passengers had fallen asleep. Some awoke as the bus came to a stop and got out to stretch their legs and relieve themselves. Warren and the woman kept a steady conversation going until she got off to use the bathroom inside the bus station. Warren stayed in his seat, anxious not to lose it or have his bag rummaged through. When the woman returned, she said she was tired and was going to try to get some sleep.

For most of the next day and part of the next evening, as the bus rumbled along from one small bus stop to the next, Warren shared intermittent conversations with the middle-aged woman. He found himself opening up to her more than he had to anyone, perhaps because she was a stranger and would carry his story to no one he knew, or perhaps because a part of him had been longing to share his story for a good part of his life. He spoke of his mother, but not in great detail. He still feared what could become of his family, who had managed to hold themselves together all these years, if anyone really found out the truth behind the closed doors of their household. He spoke of how his father had left when he was a young boy, and of how much he loved his baby sisters. The woman, too, told him about her family, her two sons, both in the military, and a daughter who was a junior in high school. As she told him stories about her family, Warren drew a picture in his mind of what a family could really be like, a family with two functioning and loving parents. He ached to be a part of it, but knew that his fate led him elsewhere, and the longer he listened to the woman talk, the further he looked inwardly at himself, thinking that his life would be most complete if he lived it solitarily.

When they reached San Antonio on the morning of the third day, the woman turned her body towards him and reached out her arms.

"It was so nice meeting you. With all I see on the news about where the youth of this country is taking us, I'm glad to see that there are bright and shining stars like you to lead us into the future. I'm sorry about your brother, but I want you to stay strong. Cherish your happy memories of him, and remember that he died in the most honorable way: serving his country. Can you remember that?" The woman had tears at the corners of her almond eyes, and she reached up briefly to brush them away, and then pulled Warren into a hug.

"Yes, I can remember that," Warren felt a hard lump tug at his throat. He wanted to say more, but he was afraid of sobbing too heavily into her arms if he spoke.

The bus pulled into the station and the woman pulled away. She looked out the window and let out a squeal. "Oh, there's my Tom!" She jumped out of her seat, putting her oversized purse onto her shoulder. "Goodbye, son. I never did get your name."

"It's Warren, Warren York," he said, relieved at her touch's departure. "And yours?"

"Doris Smith," she said and waved, then followed the line of people off the bus as all the color faded from Warren's face.

Darlene's beauty came from a perfect combination of her mother and father's features. Both were tall with dark hair, though neither as dark as Darlene's, and her mother's high cheekbones and miniature nose complemented her father's narrow chin and blue eyes. Darlene and Joey had arrived just an hour before Warren, and, along with her parents had eaten a small meal at the bus station delicatessen while waiting. They stood in front of the bus expectant of Warren, who was the last to emerge from the folding doors. Darlene stood next to her mother, who held Joey in her arms. When she saw Warren, she rushed forward with her arms wide open. He walked toward her and pulled her into him. She smelled of a soft floral perfume, and her eyes, though puffy from lack of sleep and crying, glistened in the gray-skied light.

"I'm so glad you came. I knew you would," she whispered as she pulled away, and Warren could see that she was thinner than the last time he had seen her. "These are my parents, Jack and Fran." She motioned toward her parents with a hand that seemed to dangle on its bony wrist as if it were just attached by a thin string. Her cheeks were hollow and the high cheekbones cast shadows on her thin skin. She wore no makeup now, and her shoulders slumped much like Frankie's had the last time he'd seen him. Her white button-down cotton shirt draped her body and fell nearly to her thighs, which were loosely covered in navy blue twill pants. She looked like a skeleton of the figure he had seen before, as if the life had been slowly draining out of her from some secret abyss.

"Nice to meet you. I hope I won't be too much of a bother," Warren averted his eyes from Darlene and looked up into the faces of her parents, both ruddy and smiling back at him.

"Don't be silly, sweetheart," Fran said, "this is a hard time for us all. Family needs to be together. I'm just sorry that we didn't get to meet the rest of your clan. But I'm sure it would cost a fortune that y'all don't have to bring everyone down here." Fran put an arm around Warren's shoulders, and Jack reached out his hand. Warren shook it, his grip weak and small in Jack's strong, large palm.

They drove across town with Warren, Darlene, and Joey in the back seat of the double cab of Jack's pickup, though Joey squirmed in Darlene's arms and had to be passed to Warren several times. Now almost two, Joey had grown dark hair like his mother's, though Warren could see a reddish tint, and he already bore the freckles so common in the York family. He had blue eyes like his mother, though his weren't as bright, and his pink skin was still pudgy with baby fat. He was learning how to talk, and Darlene repeated the phrase, "Uncle Warren," again and again until at last he looked up into Warren's face with a grin and said, "Un!" Warren held his warm body close, the safety of his innocence keeping all other thoughts from his head.

When they arrived at the large ranch home where Darlene had spent most of her childhood, Darlene's two older sisters, Ruth and Janice, who were in the process of preparing a large lunch for everyone, welcomed them. Fran showed Warren where he would sleep, in the guest bedroom in the basement, while Jack insisted on carrying his small bag downstairs. Warren, tired and mangy from the days and nights on the bus, felt ridiculous for wearing the suit, which was now wrinkled from the walk in the rain and smelled of body odor. He asked if he could go downstairs and change. The family had planned the memorial service for the following morning at their Baptist church, and he hoped to wash the shirt and iron the pants and jacket before then.

He stepped into the small bathroom at the foot of the basement stairs while Darlene's family carried on mixed conversations above him. Their voices, though muffled, carried through the floorboards. He stood in front of the bathroom sink and leaned over to wash his face. When he lifted his head, pushing a hand towel into his skin and wiping the moisture away, he stared at the reflection in the mirror as if he didn't recognize what he saw. Though he had hardly slept in days, his blue eyes were alert and white, and he bore no dark circles or puffiness under them. His red hair, neatly trimmed, was only a bit out of place around his round face. He couldn't describe to himself the stranger who stood before him. He was neither his past nor his future, but lived in this moment as if his face would remain this bright as long as he opened his eyes. He thought about the woman named Doris on the bus, who had the kindest heart of anyone he'd ever met, yet bore the same name as his depressed, cruel mother. He thought about Darlene's family, their warmth and functionality, and all that Frankie would miss out on now that he was gone. He thought about Frankie again, the images of his thin, muscular body dancing in front of his mind's eye. Warren held so much sadness inside his soul as he glanced at the reflection in the mirror, yet... he couldn't help but feel that, at the same time, his life was just beginning. Frankie's death represented so many ideas in his mind, but the one that stood out among all the loss and grief and anger was freedom: he knew, looking at the young, once-innocent face, that in four days he had changed from a boy into a man.

When he went upstairs, Darlene greeted him at the top of the steps. She spoke in a hushed tone as she asked him to come to the back bedroom with her so they could talk. She reached for his hand, but Warren shirked from her touch as he followed her long legs and hair down the hallway past the kitchen. The room, which belonged to the still-single and slightly overweight Ruth, was painted in a blue that matched the color of a noonday sky. A handmade blue and pink quilt adorned the bed, with matching pillow shams and a bed skirt in the same shade of blue as the walls. A small window allowed the vivid light of midday to shine a rectangular ray on the gray carpet, and an oak student desk, scattered with papers, stood next to the window. Framed prints of landscapes decorated the walls, and a double-mirrored closet reflected the room back onto itself. Darlene sat on the bed, putting her feet up and leaning against two pillows that she propped behind her back on the oak headboard. She patted the edge of the bed and motioned for Warren to sit down, but he shied away and pulled the small wooden chair away from the desk.

Once the door to the room had closed, Darlene's expression, which before had glided between polite smiles and pain-stricken grief, changed to one of power and acceptance. She waited until Warren was seated and looked directly into her eyes before she spoke. "I wanted to talk to you about all of this because maybe you're the only one who could understand."

"OK," Warren felt stupid for not being able to think of a more intelligent response.

"You can hate me for saying what I am about to say, because I know how you loved your brother. But that's what I want you to know. I did love him. I've lived in this town all my life, and seen thousands of boys come out of basic training in those cute little blue and white uniforms. I've seen them wandering through the town on their last weekend before graduation, showing their families all the touristy sites. I thought I could get away from all of it by moving away from here. But when I saw Frankie for the first time—" Darlene put her hand on her chest and took a long breath, her eyes welling with tears even though her facial expression looked happy, "I just loved him. It seems so simple and easy, but I think love can be like that sometimes. I knew, right from the moment that he first walked into that soda fountain with a couple of other Marines who were at the base on a special training mission, that I was going to marry him. And I did, just a few weeks later, even though everyone thought I was crazy. But Frankie was so open, so benevolent, and so gentle... I never had any doubts." Darlene paused again, moving her eyes from their weary vision back to Warren's face.

"I knew he was a soldier, and I thought that he'd be OK when he told me he was going to this little war in Vietnam. When he described it, it sounded like America would just send some planes with some bombs, then a few ground troops, and the whole thing would be over. But of course we all know that isn't the case. They wouldn't tell him how long he would be gone, but said to expect to stay at least a year. Oh, Warren. That was the hardest year of my life. I found out I was pregnant, which in itself was the most bittersweet thing I could have imagined. I never pictured that my family would begin without my husband being there to welcome his child into the world. I stayed here with my parents for as long as I could, but I knew that I had to be an adult, and so I moved on to the base housing. Having the baby was so wonderful, yet so sad. I wrote letters to Frankie every day telling him all about every little thing that Joey did, from spitting up to smiling for the first time. At first, Frankie would write back, and his letters sounded optimistic and sincere. But after about six months, he didn't write as much, and when the letters came, they were short and emotionless. I really started to worry, but my mother told me that war was hard, and he would be better once he came home.

"But he wasn't better. You saw him when we went up there. Oh, Warren," her voice wavered and she clutched a pillow against her chest. "He only got worse after that. I thought that moving to the new base might help, and the training exercises he was doing would keep him busy. I thought he would change once he got to know Joey, or once we... really got to be on our own. But he just became this depressed, self-absorbent stranger. He hardly spoke to me at all. He sat on the living room couch watching TV every moment he was home. I thought that his absence from my life had been hard, but his presence was worse. I tried talking to him about the war, or getting him to go to a counselor about what he was going through, but he wouldn't do either. By the end of the year, when he told me he had orders to go back, I was relieved. I couldn't stand to be with him anymore." Darlene avoided eye contact as she said the last sentence. She let silence hang in the room between the two.

At last, Warren cleared his throat and spoke. "There's something terribly wrong with my family," he said. "I don't know how much Frankie told you." He wouldn't continue until she responded.

"He told me all about his siblings, but not much about his parents. He said your mother liked to keep to herself, and that she didn't have a lot of friends, and that your father left when he was just a boy."

"That's part of it. But only a small part." Warren crossed his arms over his chest and sighed. Several times he opened his mouth to continue before words actually came out. "The truth is, my mother abused me when I was a kid. Not like normal discipline. Abuse." He stopped, the word vibrating in his mind. "And my father was a drunk, and my other brothers were too young. Frankie was the only person in my life who I could trust. He used to sneak food down into the basement, where I slept, and he would often sneak me into bed with him after Mother had gone to bed. He was so kind to me. He was the person you fell in love with. But, even before he left, when my mother made him quit school to run a paper route and shine shoes, he started to become more and more depressed, as did she. It's like, neither of them really knew what their place in the world was, and they were always trying to figure it out. My mother didn't want to be our mother, and Frankie didn't want to be her son. Going over to Vietnam probably made Frankie lose himself even more. I can't imagine what it must be like over there." His eyes scanned the room. For years afterwards, he would picture this room and its dull representation of his heartstrings letting loose in front of a near-stranger who happened to be somewhat related to him.

"I guess what I'm trying to say," he said after several moments, "is that maybe I could understand how you feel. Though most of me still burns with a love for Frankie that could never be quenched." Warren dropped his hands onto his lap as he finished. He couldn't go on because the tears had formed in the corners of his eyes, and the lump in his throat constricted his voice.

Darlene lifted her face from its purposeful concentration on the pillow she held. She moved her look towards Warren, whose eyes focused on the small window. "I'm so sorry about what happened to you when you were a child. I think the worst thing anyone can do is abuse a child. But I think you're right. I think your mother and Frankie were lost souls. I just hope Frankie found his way..." her voice trailed off. Warren stood and walked over to the bed. He sat at the edge and took her palms in his hand.

"It's too hard for me to be a part of your life," he whispered. "But I have money to give you. I've been saving for years. And I will continue to send it to you and Joey, until he's eighteen. But I have to go now."

Darlene's eyes widened and she raised her back away from the pillows she leaned against. "What? But you came all this way, and the memorial service isn't until tomorrow, and... what about Joey? And his father's side of the family? And..." she was crying now, her voice panicky, but Warren stood, determined to leave.

"I'm so sorry, Darlene, but I have to go where my life takes me." He held out his arms, and she ran into them, wanting to punch him and hold him close at the same time.

He left the room, went downstairs and quickly gathered his things. He returned to the bedroom where Darlene cried on the bed and threw down a thousand dollars. Darlene's sisters were just laying out the plates for lunch as Warren walked out the front door. The earlier clouds had cleared, and he squinted his eyes against the dazzling sunlight as he looked out onto the street. He began to walk, at first without purpose. Then he pulled his school bag tight against his shoulders and took the first steps toward home.

Chapter 37

She awoke with a start. She hadn't thought about that in a long time. His image haunted her mind from minute to minute, but, after seven months, had become little more than an image. Her memories of his daily presence in her life had begun to fade, so that now, she only had the distant, specific memories to hold on to. But the dream that awakened Luisa before Alejo awoke for his milk would creep into her mind for the rest of the day, the week... maybe longer.

It was just after they had met, after Luisa had tried to scare him off with her threat of no drinking and no sex until she was ready. She had visited his apartment only once, and, scanning the refrigerator, pointed out to him its barren reality of bachelorhood.

"Not a single candy bar or a gallon of milk? And no cereal to go with it?" It had been late. They'd been up watching a movie, and she wanted something to eat before she drove home. The next day, when Carter picked her up from her last class at the college on the other side of town, he held a huge grin on his face.

"You want to come over for a little while?"

"Don't think you're gonna get lucky," she told him, to which he said, "No, but you might."

They had driven in silence. When they entered his apartment, a small vase with a daisy sat on the counter. Surrounding it were twelve candy bars, all of varying brands. Luisa dashed over to munch on one, but Carter's grin was stronger as he held open the cupboard and refrigerator doors simultaneously.

"I wasn't sure which kind to buy, so I got them all." The once-empty cupboards now resembled the cereal aisle of the grocery store, and inside the refrigerator were a gallon each of skim, one percent, two percent, and whole milk.

Luisa jumped into Carter's arms and gave him her first passionate kiss. His lips were as soft as silk pillows, and she knew, without a doubt, that she was in love with him and would never love anyone else in the same way or with the same undying passion.

Now, she rose from her bed, examined her puffy, sleepy eyes in the mirror, and walked across the hall to Alejo's room. It was time for them to get up and go grocery shopping. They were out of cereal, and she had a craving for a candy bar.

Warren sat at the table drinking his tea and sifting through the headlines when she entered the kitchen with Alejo in her arms. "You're up early today," he said, though he didn't lift his eyes from the paper. "Do you ever think this war is going to end?"

"I thought it did. At least, that's what they were saying six months ago. It's turning into Vietnam." She caught herself on the last word, but it was too late. Warren lifted his eyes from the newspaper and looked into hers. Alejo became too heavy to hold on her hip, so she set him down, but he tugged at her sweatpants and pulled her over to the refrigerator, anxious for her to fix him his milk.

"I'm sorry, Warren. I guess I don't really know much about it."

"And I know way more than I should." Though he hadn't joined his counterparts in growing out their hair and burning draft cards, Warren had attended many protests during his latter years of high school. To all of them, he had carried a handmade poster with Frankie's basic training photograph in the center, and words on the top and bottom that read, "How many brothers and sons must die before we realize the truth: violence isn't the answer," in bold blue and red writing. He thought about these protests now as Luisa poured Alejo's milk into a sippy cup and handed it to him. She then poured herself a cup of tea and sat across the table from Warren.

"Anything horrible happen in the world today?"

Warren folded each section of the paper and stacked them neatly on top of each other, pushing them to the edge of the table.

"My brother Frankie died in Vietnam." After he said it, his shoulders sank and he leaned back in his chair. He felt as if he were in a confessional, because it had been thirty years or more since he had said that sentence aloud, though it traipsed through his mind daily.

Luisa looked at her hands. "I know," she whispered, "Carly told me."

"But she doesn't know much, really, because she never went through it. Even Kenny and Freddy and Rose and Margaret—I don't even think they know what it was like for me. Frankie wasn't just my brother, he was the only person in my life who ever truly loved me, right from the beginning, even though I was sickly as a baby, first with pneumonia, then with shingles … he never cared that I wasn't the girl my mother wanted or that I had weak lungs and couldn't run as fast as my brothers. He just loved me, and took care of me when my mother and father wouldn't, or couldn't. He took care of all of us. He brought home the only money we had besides welfare checks, and fixed us dinner every night, and taught me how to budget and clean the house. He kept my mother in line after the social worker suspected child abuse so she wouldn't return and we could stay together. He was so important to all of our lives, but most of all to mine." Warren sipped the last of his tea and took a long breath through his nostrils before going on.

"I wouldn't be here today if it weren't for Frankie. I'm sure of that. And before I met you, I often wondered why I was the one chosen to stay, and he was the one chosen to go." His voice cracked as he finished, but he managed to hold the tears inside.

Luisa couldn't hold in her tears. Her cheeks were moist before he could end his story. She reached for his hand and whispered, "Maybe God chose you to stay and save our lives. Because that's what you've done."

A palpable silence hung between them, and then Alejo whined and tugged at Luisa's pants. Happy for the distraction, she reached to pick him up. "We're going to the store today. Do you need anything?"

"I know you have your own parents, and I know that they love you. But I want you to know that I love you just as much as I would my own daughter, if I had one." Warren rushed the words out of his mouth, spilling them onto the counter

"I know, Warren. And I can't tell you how much it means to me. Frankie looks down on you from Heaven, and I bet he's so proud." She stood in the doorway with Alejo on her hip. He needed a diaper change, and she didn't know how long she could stand there holding him. At eighteen months, he weighed twenty-four pounds, and his weight sunk into her hipbone.

"How could he be proud? Look at the life I've led. I spent my whole life hiding from the world. My family hardly knows me, and I don't know how to begin a relationship with any of them. All my nephews and nieces are grown. I missed their entire childhoods, without so much as a single card for any of their birthdays. What kind of person am I?"

Luisa pulled Alejo into her lap and sat down again. "You're the kind of person who realized that you'd made some mistakes, and now you're trying to change them. Remember the night when I came home and painted that picture of my mother's rape and you told me that at least I knew of a good way to release my pain? Well, maybe you just didn't know any other way but to close everyone out of your life. But that doesn't have to stay that way. Did you ever think, a year ago, five years ago, ten years ago, that you would ask a perfect stranger and her young child to come live in your house?"

Warren's look of uncertainty melted into a small smile. "No, of course not."

"See how much you've changed just in the past few months? You've still got a lot of living to do, and your family's still alive, even if they're all grown up. You can still be a part of their lives. They want you to be a part of their lives."

"How'd you get to be so smart for such a young woman?"

"You met my father, Warren. You ought to know I grew up a little faster than most. And tragedies make you grow up even faster. You ought to know that."

Warren stood and put the teacups on the counter next to the sink. He pulled the teakettle off the stove and ran it under hot water, scrubbing it with a soapy sponge. "I used to send money to my nephew and sister-in-law in Texas. She finally remarried, and we lost touch. Joey's thirty-eight now. I can't believe it. Seems like he's the same age as me. I wonder if he goes by Joe. I wonder a lot about them."

"Where in Texas?"

"In San Antonio. I wonder if they still live there."

"Why don't you look them up? I bet they aren't too hard to track down. Did your nephew have your last name?"

231

"Yeah, but I'm not sure if he changed it when Darlene remarried. And the person she married was named Johnson. Pretty hard to find, there must be a thousand of them in that town alone."

"One thing I've learned in the past year," Luisa spoke as she stood up and pushed her chair under the table, carrying Alejo up to his room, "is that family is more important than anything."

At the grocery store, Luisa dawdled over the produce, trying to choose the best avocados for her mom's famous recipe of guacamole. That weekend, she and both her parents were celebrating the sending off of the manuscripts. Reeve had agreed to come to Aurelio's house because the manuscript had affected her life almost as deeply as his, and she wanted to congratulate him on his sobriety. Luisa dawdled as well in other parts of the store, trying to act like she cared which brand of rice she bought or which type of milk to buy because she feared returning home. It had been two days since Tyler came to her house, and she had frantically spent the previous evenings, after Alejo went to bed, sifting through her canvases to decide which ones to take with her to the meeting. She feared Tyler's call, its presence or its absence. Either way, she couldn't bear to sit at home next to the phone. She hadn't told Warren about Tyler's offer, fearful that saying it aloud to anyone would make it untrue; fearful that speaking of Tyler would bring a tone into her voice that she didn't want anyone to hear.

She chose whole milk for Alejo and two percent for herself, then moved into the candy bar aisle and picked out a couple of Heath bars to snack on later. Alejo sucked on a cookie he had received from the bakery department. The crumbs were all over his chin and chubby fingers. "Coo-ie" he gurgled, to which Luisa said, "Mmmm, was that a good cookie?" Dragging her feet, she paced through the aisles of the store until Alejo became restless in the cart and she knew she had to return home.

A short, brown-skinned woman with glistening black hair that dangled loosely around her shoulders stood in line with her three small children in front of Luisa. She had a handful of coupons that she held from the beginning of the transaction, but she didn't speak a word. When the bagger asked her if she wanted paper or plastic, she simply pointed to the plastic bags. In Spanish, the children carried on a conversation about the variety of candies available before their eyes. The cashier, a short, overweight, balding man with pale white skin and greasy strings of black hair, didn't see her hand full of coupons, but told her the amount when he had finished ringing her up. She looked at the number on the screen and shook her head, then held out the coupons for the cashier.

"I wish you would have given these to me at the beginning," he said, "because now I have to void out my total." He snatched the coupons out of her hand, but she still didn't speak. A new price came up on the screen, and the woman began to count the bills from her billfold. The cashier crossed his arms and sighed, then repeated the amount out loud. Luisa could see that the woman wasn't going to have enough money. She touched her on the shoulder and

232

whispered in Spanish, "Here is twenty dollars more. Feed your children," and slipped her the bill from her hand. The woman, whose face had grown panicky, jumped at Luisa's touch and looked up into her face. "Gracias, gracias, gracias." She clutched both her palms, and then pulled away and paid the cashier.

After Luisa had paid for her own groceries, she heard the cashier mumble to his bagger as she pushed her cart away, "That's all we need is someone helping out another good-for-nothing illegal alien who can't speak English." She spun on her heel and looked the man in the face, her arms crossed, her stance defiant.

"If you think this country was founded by anything but immigrants, it's clear to me why the only job a man your age can get is being a cashier in a grocery store." She turned around just as quickly and marched up to the manager, and then filed a complaint against the cashier.

As she drove home, she thought about what it must have been like for her father when he first came to the country, and how difficult it must have been for him to face prejudice in so many places. She thought, too, about Carter, whose bashfulness would have kept him from making a move, whose fear of dealing with others' problems would have kept Luisa's mouth closed as well. She felt free of that now, of him standing next to her in the store and avoiding confrontation at all costs. She felt alone, but strong, as if she could touch others in a way she hadn't been able to before. She knew that what she had done in the store was the right thing to do, and she knew she never would have done it if Carter had been there. The thought disturbed her, but she felt as if she was moving toward the next part of her life: the part without him.

As she pulled into the driveway off the alley after the short drive home, she turned off the engine and hung her head to cry. The tears began to drip out of her eyes like the first drops of slow rain at the beginning of the storm. They darkened her olive green shirt with semicircular marks, and she remained silent. But the longer she sat there, the stronger the storm became, and soon her face, hands, and shirt were drenched with the moisture of her release. Alejo squirmed in his seat and whined to be let out, but Luisa's body throbbed beneath her sobs as if she knew no other place than what she pictured in her mind. She began to whisper her thoughts, but then said them aloud, first in a normal tone, and then screaming against the interior of the closed car. "I don't want to have a life that isn't a life with him! I don't want to have a life that isn't with him!" But she knew, the more she said it, that she had already begun that life, and nothing could keep her from continuing it.

Alejo began to scream in response to her, and at last she reached into the glove compartment, retrieved a small travel pack of tissues, and wiped her nose and eyes. She opened her car door and went to get Alejo out. Before she even touched it, he pointed to the buckle of his car seat seatbelt. "You want me to unbuckle you, Mi Hijo?" she cooed, then held the lump in her throat back and the tears inside, thinking that those were the exact words her father had always used when speaking to Byron as a child. She reached in and lifted Alejo out of the car, clutching his body close to hers. "I love you so much," she whispered into his cheek. She put him down next to her and opened the trunk, beginning the chore of carrying in the groceries as Alejo toddled around in the backyard. She knew, in the first steps she took toward the door, that she would never be finished crying over Carter's death.

Clara, Reeve, and Aurelio were the only ones who ever called Warren's house, so he didn't even bother to answer the phone when it rang. He had one of the original touch-tone phones that he had purchased years ago at a garage sale for fifty cents. It was beige, corded, and sat in its place in the phone nook in the dining area. It was the only phone he had, and he had never bothered to buy an answering machine to go along with it.

When Luisa walked in the door with her first handful of groceries, Warren stood up from his seat in the wingback chair in the living room, where he had been reading Consumer Reports, and took the groceries out of her arms.

"The phone rang three different times," he said, and then, as a look of worry came over her face, "in a row. So I finally answered it. It was my nephew Tyler." He could see that she had been crying, and he hoped nothing had happened to her in the store. He felt too embarrassed to relay the message Tyler had left.

"Oh?" Luisa responded, trying to sound naïve. "What did he have to say?"

"He wanted to know if you were still going to go to dinner with him before he took you to meet his client. Did he come by here on Monday?"

"Yes, when you were out looking for a new part to your lawnmower." Luisa turned in the kitchen and went outside to gather more groceries and bring Alejo in. The temperature was just fifty, and clouds loomed in the air. Warren followed her.

"He said he might have a great job offer for you. He told me all about it. Why didn't you?"

Luisa didn't want to have the discussion just yet, but she realized she had no choice. They each lifted several more bags out of the trunk as she said, "I don't know. I guess I wanted to see if it would work out."

"If it would work out with the job, or with Tyler?" Warren had stopped in the middle of the sidewalk, and Alejo tugged at his pants, holding his arms out for him to pick him up.

Luisa stopped too, her legs and her heart. Her face reddened and she looked at the ground. A small black spider moved across the sidewalk toward the yellowed grass. She sucked in a long breath before she said, "I don't know. Both, I guess," and she walked into the house.

After not working and wearing jeans and sweatshirts for almost two years, choosing an outfit caused her almost as much grief as choosing a set of canvases. She had given away or sold most of her nice clothes, saving only the ones she felt were most appropriate for job interviews. She chose one of these outfits now, a beige suit with a knee-length skirt and matching jacket with a wide neck and collar. Normally, she wore a sleeveless polyester white mock turtleneck with the semi-low-cut jacket, but tonight, she wore nothing but a bra underneath it. She wanted to look good for two circumstances: making Tyler want her and making his client hire her, so she pulled her hair into a French twist at the back of her head, allowing two curled tendrils to fall behind her ears. She dressed her face with a thin layer of eyeliner under the eyes and mascara on the lashes, then just a touch of blush on each cheek and some red lipstick that Clara let her borrow (she wasn't accustomed to wearing makeup). She wore white pantyhose and white, open-toed leather shoes with one-inch heels, and white pearl earrings, a gift from Carter's mother on their wedding day, to coordinate. She shaved her legs in the shower and afterwards put on layers of lotion scented of lilacs, her favorite spring flower.

When she came out of the bathroom, Warren and Alejo were eating some leftover chicken and peas from one of the chickens Warren had roasted on Sunday. Alejo looked up at his mother and held a questioning expression on his face, almost as if he didn't recognize her.

"I guess you've never seen me dressed up before, have you?" she said, and patted him on the cheek.

When Tyler rang the doorbell, Luisa feared that Warren and Alejo could see her heart pounding inside her chest. She felt it penetrating her sternum as she walked towards the front door. When she opened it, she nearly sank to her knees at the sight of him. She was out of breath and said nothing. She couldn't move her eyes away from his—it would paralyze her.

"Hello, Luisa. You look gorgeous," he stepped inside. "Hi, Uncle Warren. Hey, Alejo, whatcha eating, little guy?" He strolled over to Alejo's highchair and examined the bits of chicken and semi-smashed peas on the tray. "Mmmm, looks delicious," Alejo said, "Hiiii," the newest drawn-out word he had learned.

Luisa motioned to the five canvases that leaned against the wall next to the door. "Thanks for watching him, Warren. Tyler, would you help me carry these to the car?" She tried to sound professional, but her voice cracked as she spoke and sounded to her like that of a small girl. She couldn't remember a time when she had felt such a burning twist of guilt and anxiety. It wrenched in her gut as she hurried to the car, loading up Tyler's trunk with two of the canvases while he placed the other three gently on top.

"Wow, Luisa. You're amazing. There's no way you're not getting a job tonight." He placed the tips of his fingers on her right shoulder for just a second. The cold chills raced down her arms and spine, and she sucked in her breath, unable to answer.

Once inside the luxurious interior of Tyler's BMW, he turned to her and asked, "Do you like Italian food?"

"Yes, of course, doesn't everyone?" she said.

"I made reservations at a real Italian place on the west side of town. My parents used to go there. It was an Italian neighborhood, back in the day. Now it's mostly Hispanic, but this restaurant is so good that it's survived all these years."

Luisa nodded, her face staring down at her hands. She couldn't think of anything to reply.

"You sure are quiet tonight," Tyler said at last. "Are you nervous about the interview? Don't be. I'm sure everything will work out. You deserve it more than anyone I know." He moved his head between the road and her face, unable to keep his eyes away from her for more than a few seconds as he drove across town. Luisa averted her gaze from him, causing him painstaking discomfort in the silence that filled the car.

"Do you like the Beatles?" he asked, slipping a CD into the player.

"Of course. Who doesn't?" Luisa forced a smile while the Beatles' One collection roared through the speakers. She was relieved to be free of talk, and before the third song was through, Tyler pulled into the back parking lot of a restaurant that stood in an old pre-war neighborhood. It wasn't on a main street or surrounded by other franchises, like so many of the restaurants she frequently saw. It hid itself in the midst of small brick ranches, its adobe walls and red tile roof bearing no bragging rights except for a flashing neon sign on top that, if a driver was really looking, he could see from the nearby interstate.

Luisa was about to open her door as they pulled into the parking space, but Tyler put his hand on her arm. The hairs stood up at his sudden and gentle touch, and she found herself lifting her face and looking directly into his blue eyes. They were bright and anxious, and he moistened his pink lips before he spoke.

"I don't want to scare you off, Luisa," he said, his voice quiet and gentle, touching her skin with the softness of a feather, "but I haven't gone a day without thinking about you since I first laid eyes on you at my parents' house." He paused, examining her wide-eyed face. Her bottom jaw dropped just slightly, and he could see the shimmering white teeth behind the glistening lipstick.

"I hope you have a good time tonight. You deserve it."

Luisa released the balloon of air that had expanded in her chest as she listened to him speak. He was so honest and straightforward that she didn't know how to reply. She expected sweet talk or inadvertent charm piled on her, not the plain truth that most men would say to scare off a woman. She wanted so much to say that she, too, hadn't stopped thinking about him. She wanted to tell him about how she saw him take the cooler of beer down to the basement at the barbeque, and how much that simple gesture had meant to her. She wanted to tell him that she was falling for him, but that she still clung to Carter's love and probably always would. She wanted to reach for the hand that touched her arm and pull it around her, releasing herself into his warmth and love...

Instead she froze and held the smile on her face for several moments before finally answering, "I know I will. Everything is wonderful." She turned from him then, opened the door, and stepped out of the car.

Once seated in the tall booths of the dimly lit restaurant that played Italian love songs in the background, Luisa began to feel as if she had entered a dreamland, and her life from this moment forward would be played out in front of her like some surrealistic fantasy. Tyler, his strong arms and broad shoulders apparent even beneath the black jacket and white shirt, looked too good to be true. He's nice, rich, and good-looking; how could that be? Luisa asked herself again and again, unable to grasp the reality of the situation. And he wants me... me of all people, when he could have any single, gorgeous, childless woman in the world. She didn't know whether to hold back tears or suppress her smile, because her emotions were tearing her up inside.

After eating the salad and minestrone that came with every meal, Luisa found herself picking at her ravioli, too nervous to eat. Tyler kept the conversation going by talking about his job and the many interesting people he met, especially now when so many people were looking for jobs. He told her about a guy who had been laid off from one telecommunications company, where he made twenty dollars an hour, only to be hired as a contract worker through a temp agency, doing work for the same company that laid him off, but earning fifty dollars an hour. "If these companies just realized how idiotic that sounds, maybe they wouldn't have to lay off so many people. I tell you one thing: if I were a CEO, I would find more effective ways to cut costs."

Luisa listened intently, drawn in to a world that she knew nothing about. Not only did she not have a career in corporate America, neither did her parents or Carter, so she had never heard stories of the intricacies of large corporations. She couldn't understand why it interested Tyler so much to be involved with businesses that operated in such idiotic ways, but it took most of the meal for her to finally say something.

"If you hate these companies so much, why are you in this profession?"

Tyler's expression, which had peacefully carried him through his ramblings, changed from comfortable to surprised.

"Well, I don't like the companies, but I like helping people, and since I know how to deal with the idiots in the companies, I can help the good guys get the jobs. It's that simple." He waited for a moment before adding, "No one's ever asked me that before," with a tone of confusion in his voice. "I guess I never even thought about it myself. Isn't that weird?"

"It must be the job for you then," Luisa said, her heart flipping inside her.

The waitress returned with Tyler's credit card receipt, and Tyler looked at his watch. "Bill and his wife are expecting us for dessert at eight, so we'd better get going. Are you ready for a change?"

"Ready as I'll ever be," Luisa stood and slid her arm into his as they walked out of the restaurant. She couldn't help but smile for the remainder of the night.

Chapter 38

He stood examining the multicolored lights on the trees with his arm nearly touching the navy blue sleeve of the salesman's polo T-shirt.

"They make Christmas trees that come with the lights attached?" Warren's mouth was dry as he spoke. Though the question inched out of his mouth as slowly as a snail, his mind raced. He tried to remember the last time he had bought a Christmas tree. He racked his brain. He knew it hadn't happened at all during his entire adult life. It must have been in high school, yes, that was it, he had taken the girls to a Christmas tree setup in the mall of the grocery store. What had he paid then, all those years ago? It must have only been $5.

"Here's our top-of-the-line Douglas fir. Just touch the needles. You'd never know it wasn't real. And it comes not only with these gorgeous yellow lights, but a pine scent and a one-year warranty." The excitement in the salesman's eyes reflected the intermittently blinking lights. Warren reached out his right hand and wrapped his fingers around some of the needles. With his left hand, he flipped over the inconspicuously-placed price tag.

"$399!" He yelled, and in the moment that he realized how loud his remark was, a few passing shoppers turned to stare.

"Yes, but it comes with a stand." The young, dark-haired salesman's expression had moved from pride to panic. "And let me tell you, sir, that you're not really buying just a Christmas tree here. You're buying years of happy memories with your family."

"Does the price include installation?" He found himself smirking at his own little joke, but the salesman didn't seem to think anything was funny. His face went blank and he looked down at the floor. Warren's face reddened in embarrassment.

"I'll take it," he said quickly, his heart flipping inside of him. He couldn't remember a time that he had spent so much money on a single small item.

"There's no excuse for this, you know," Clara was saying as Warren opened the front door. "I mean, you practically live in the same place, and we haven't missed our tea in all those years, even when you first started dating Carter..." Her voice trailed off.

Luisa sipped her cup and raised her eyebrows at Warren.

Clara looked up at Warren briefly but held up her hand before he could speak. "I just want to know what's going on. I want to help you. I want to know if you're OK. Are you OK? I haven't heard from you in weeks. Did you find a job? Did you start talking to that youth group you told me about? Am I still your best friend?" She threw in the last question as a joke, but she could tell it had pained Luisa. That same grief-stricken look that Clara had seen on her face so many times that year now entered it again.

"Of course you're still my best friend! Do you think that's ever going to change? I've just been... busy."

"Oh come on, Luisa. You're not going to get away with that."

Warren cleared his throat. "Ladies, do you want to help me carry in this Christmas tree? It's in a box, but since it's so big, I had to have a salesman help me put it in the trunk. Or did you want Ty—"

Luisa's eyes flashed in anger before Warren could finish the sentence. Tyler was coming over for dinner that night, but Luisa wasn't sure she was ready to tell Clara about him.

"Did we want to tie what?" Clara's eyes moved from Warren's face to Luisa's, trying to read the secret between them.

"She's going to find out anyway, you know," Warren said, and his tone reflected a father talking to his daughter. Luisa almost said aloud, "I know, Dad, but I don't want to tell her." Instead, she caught herself and looked into Clara's eyes.

"Well," she sighed, reluctant to continue. "It's just, Warren's nephew, Tyler." Her pale brown cheeks darkened to a crimson red.

Clara looked across the table at her for a moment, unsure of what she was saying. As realization crept into her mind, she widened her eyes in surprise.

"Have you---Did you two—What's going on?"

Just then, a door opened from upstairs and they heard Alejo's feet plodding down the steps. "Mama, Mama!" he called, and Luisa stood to greet him at the bottom of the stairwell. She reached over and picked him up, nestling her face into his warm neck. His dark hair was tussled and sticking out in random places around his head. She pulled him onto her lap as she sat across from Clara. He immediately grabbed at her teacup, but Luisa's hand was faster as she pushed it to the center of the table. "Tea! Tea!"" He yelled out, but Luisa shook her head and told him he could have his milk.

Clara watched the scene take place, all the time, her mind wandering, trying to answer the questions that Luisa wasn't answering. She hadn't heard from her in weeks. Luisa wouldn't return her phone calls, and she had truly begun to worry. She arrived on her doorstep on a Saturday afternoon, hoping to catch her at home.

"I'll tell you the whole story, but you have to promise not to freak out."

"How bad could it possibly be?" Clara asked her.

"Pretty bad," Luisa lowered her eyes now, holding back the tears. She didn't know how to begin. She thought about all those paintings she had done over the summer. She though of Aurelio, who now had held a job for longer than any job he'd had in years. She thought of her mother, whose smile came to her face more easily now than ever before. She thought of the church, and Father Huxley's warm hands around hers as he thanked her for coming every Sunday. She thought of the youth group, and the grinning faces of hope that the kids had when she talked about her life.

Most of all, she thought of Carter. His blue eyes dancing with light as he surprised her on her birthday with a porch swing. His hands moving up and down her side as he lay next to her on a lazy Saturday morning before Alejo was born. The grin on his face, so enduring, as he said his vows to her. His deep voice making easy conversation on one of his daily calls home. His high-pitched yell when the Chiefs scored against the Broncos. His soft footsteps on the stairs as he carried Alejo up to bed.

"I think I'm in love," Luisa whispered, and Warren dropped the keys he had been holding in his hand. Luisa kept her eyes in her lap.

"Oh, thank God," Clara said matter-of-factly. "I thought it was something terrible again. You can't go scaring me like that, Luisa. What would I ever do without you?"

Clara's kindness swept over Luisa. Nothing but pure relief lifted her head as she looked across the table at her best friend. "Do you remember in tenth grade when we went to Homecoming and nobody at the dance would dance with us and you spent the night at my house and my Dad was all drunk and I had to tell you the truth about him even though I had never told anyone before?" She rushed the words of the sentence together, afraid it might not all come out if she broke it up.

"Yeah?" Clara looked perplexed again.

"I knew, then, when you told me, 'Everyone's got skeletons, Luisa,' that we'd be friends forever."

"OK, OK, stop changing the subject. Do I get to hear about this Tyler or what?"

"Not until you help me carry this tree in," Warren interrupted.

"Geez! It's like having a whole other father!" Clara said.

"I know," Luisa said, and opened the front door as she began her story.

Chapter 39

On the morning of his fifty-third birthday, Warren opened his eyes in the gray light of predawn, examining the strange shadows in the strange room where he had spent a restless night. The room was cool and the sheets itchy. He could hear the motel air conditioner buzzing at the window, where the curtains were drawn tight against the night. Outside, the interstate hummed with life, from speeding cars to the methodical diesel engines of giant semis. Warren listened for some time before he moved, and then pulled the floral bedspread away from his chin, put his feet on the floor, and groped along the wall until he reached the bathroom.

When he returned to the room, he began a pot of tea; though their singular pot came without Earl Grey. He determined that plain black tea would be enough to satisfy him until the continental breakfast. Having no newspaper, he turned on the television and sat at the small table flipping through the channels until he found CNN. He didn't have cable TV at home, and enjoyed catching up with the in-depth reports of CNN when he had a chance, which wasn't often. He sipped his tea from the small white Styrofoam cup, watching flashes of men in desert uniforms drive by in tanks while the morning business news rolled across the bottom of the screen. When he finished his cup, the bitter taste of the tea left his mouth feeling parched, and he walked into the bathroom to fill a glass with cold water. He came back into the room and opened the shades. The sun had risen and flooded the room with the garish light of early morning. Now sipping at his water, he stared out into the neatly landscaped lawn, and then out onto the interstate's increasing traffic. He had never been here before; had never even been to a motel, or taken a road trip for years and years. As he observed the cars and trucks whiz by, he wondered where the drivers' destinations were, how far they were going, and how far they were from where they'd come. He hadn't lived a life where he wanted to travel, but now he felt the urge as he looked at the open expanse of the highway. Already, in the past twenty-four hours, he had seen so many new things, from the mountains south of Denver to the desert in New Mexico, and that was just the view from the interstate. He wondered what it would be like to travel home on two-lane roads, the roads that had existed before the four-lane mega-highways, to see where they curved, what sights and small towns they led to. He told himself that he would. Then someone knocked on the door.

"Warren? Are you ready to go down to breakfast?" Luisa called through the door. She had a plan to get through the one-year anniversary of Carter's death, and it involved nothing more than focusing all of her attention on getting to San Antonio before nightfall. Alejo stood at her hip and cooed, "Unc! Unc!" in his slurred and happy language.

Warren quickly pulled on some pants and went to open the door. "Unc!" Alejo squealed again, and Warren reached for his open arms, lifting him into his own. "You're up early," he said to Luisa, and she said, "I know. I'm anxious to get on the road."

At breakfast, Luisa fixed herself a waffle on the self-serve waffle iron, and then broke off pieces to give to Alejo alongside his small bowl of fruit. Warren made buttered toast and a bowl of cereal and enjoyed his cup of Earl Grey as he ate. Only a few other guests ate alongside them at the high tables. Warren turned to Luisa halfway through the meal and said, "Today's my birthday," and then looked down into his hands.

Luisa raised her eyebrows. "Really? Well, happy birthday. Is that why you wanted to come now?"

"Yes, though I can't say why. I've never thought much about birthdays. Of course, when I was a kid… well, no one really paid attention, especially since my youngest sister has the same birthday as me. We always tried to celebrate hers, if you can count dinner and a cake a celebration."

"Your birthday is on the first day of spring, the season of renewal." Luisa spoke in a low tone and allowed the tears to well up in her eyes. She had thought about this date too much in the last year, but now its reality hit her. She was shocked to hear that Carter's death fell on Warren's birthday, and the irony twisted inside her like a snake trying to escape from the pit of her stomach.

Warren reached for her hand and squeezed it. "Yes, it is the season of renewal. For all of us." He paused, and then said, "Do you think Joey will look like me? I always did take after Frankie."

"Of course he will. Everyone in your family looks alike. I'd never seen so much red hair in my life until I met all of you." Luisa was happy that the conversation had shifted.

Outside, the New Mexico wind blew their hair into their faces as they loaded the back of the rented minivan with their two suitcases. The gusts came from the west, and Luisa listened to the roaring wind, glad that, even though they'd be driving, the wind would be behind them, pushing them forward. The sky's dark gray clouds hung over the distant mountains like great menacing monsters threatening rain. The cool morning air created goose bumps up and down Luisa's bare arms, and she hurried to strap Alejo into his car seat before pulling the door closed.

"Do you want me to drive?" she yelled to Warren over the sound of the wind, and he nodded in return, holding the newspaper he'd retrieved from the lobby.

"I still don't know how you have the patience to sift through all of those articles. Don't you ever get bored? I only read Ann Landers and my horoscope every day. But you even take the time to do the crossword puzzle."

"When you've lived alone as long as I have, you find things like this to keep you busy. This is the first trip I've taken since coming here almost forty years ago, and Jesus, I'm coming to the same damn place."

"That I'll never understand either. I've always loved to travel. I hope I'll always be able to, but it depends on how things work out for me, I guess," Luisa held in her smile, but Warren saw the corners of her mouth move up just a bit before he focused his eyes on the first article of the day.

They drove in silence for over an hour when Alejo began to fuss. "I think he needs a diaper change," Luisa said, pulling off at a rest stop just over the Texas border.

"I was born in Texas," she said as she stepped out of the car, "and I spent a few years here as a child when my mother trained to be a midwife. But I don't remember much. Just the birds. We used to see all kinds of birds. I miss that sometimes, even though I must say, you sure have been able to attract so many varieties in your feeders. I guess it just takes time and patience, something I've never had much of."

"You could have the time if you made it," Warren said, heading for the men's bathroom as Luisa carried Alejo into the women's.

Warren drove next while Alejo dozed off in the back and Luisa looked through her Audubon Bird Society book of Texas birds. Though they couldn't see much on the highway, she planned on sneaking away in the early morning to see what she could find in the outskirts of San Antonio where Joey and his family lived. Watching the birds, a hobby she had let slip behind her other passions during the last year, became renewed with the coming of spring. She wanted to tell Alejo about the birds, to teach him how to identify different species, to determine which were male and which were female, and to love their beauty as she did. The bright photographs in the book jumped out at her now, and she scanned her eyes along the grasslands in search of a hawk or a starling.

They drove in front of the storm with the wind at their back as Luisa had hoped, and Warren, though fifty-three, was not so cautious that he couldn't keep up to the seventy-mile-per-hour speed limit, where he had set the cruise control. In front of them, I-10 opened up to rays of sunshine that dotted the landscape between passing cumulus clouds, their puffy whiteness a stark contrast to the obscurity of the storm clouds behind them. Luisa loved road trips. As a child, her parents had little money, and any trips they took as a family meant loading up the old Chevy Nova with camping gear and heading for the mountains for a weekend getaway. She loved the freedom of the open road, the ability to move at your own pace and not have to depend on schedules that were made to accommodate all the passengers on an airplane or a train. She loved to see the different landscapes and structures along the highway, to watch as the countryside whizzed by, offering her sights of snowcapped peaks and endless prairies. She loved to crack the car window open and listen as the wind stung the sides of the car, fighting its motion or helping to move it along.

Now, she rested her head against the headrest and started to doze off. A dream came to her, though she wasn't wholly asleep. She dreamt that she was in the car, just as she was, only Carter was driving and Alejo was a young boy, not a toddler. Carter sang along with the radio as he drove, as he always had. His favorite song, "Against the Wind" by Bob Seger, came on, and he turned up the stereo, waking Luisa. He sang each memorized word with the exact tune and passion of the artist, and then turned toward Luisa, who had sat up in her seat, and squeezed her thigh just above her knee, causing her to jump. "We're almost there," he said, and Luisa nodded, though she didn't know where she was going. She looked out the window and saw the flatlands of eastern Kansas, the grasses and cornfields leaning against the fury of a harsh westerly wind. "How much longer?" she asked, and Carter's face softened as he glanced over at her. "As long as it takes, Luisa," he told her, and looked back at the open expanse of the highway in front of him. Alejo sat in the back seat and said, "You're always asking how much longer, Mom! We'll be there when we get there, like Dad always says." Luisa looked back and forth between her pale skinned son and husband, grinning and crossing her arms in a self-hug, happy for the first time in as long as she could remember.

"Luisa," Warren placed his hand gently on her shoulder, "we're about a hundred miles out. Do you think you can drive?"

"How long was I asleep?" Luisa sat up and looked around. The car was now flooded with rain so that the windows bore a blurred gray version of the landscape on either side of the van. The dream stung at the center of her vision, and she had trouble focusing on the present moment. She looked at Warren and at Alejo, not yet two, who now had his eyes open at her, holding out his hand. The dream's happiness danced around her body now, and her skin tingled as a smile came over her lips.

"Yes, I can drive," she said at last as Warren pulled under the overhang of a gas pump just off the interstate. She stepped out of the car and walked to the other side, the question, "How much longer?" on the tip of her tongue. She took the keys from Warren's hand and slipped into the driver's seat without another word. After he filled up the tank, Warren leaned his head against the window and soon began to snore. The rain pounded on the roof as Luisa drove east, whispering to herself, "As long as it takes." She couldn't answer the questions inside her head with a better response, and thanked Carter for giving her one last gift before she journeyed to Mexico.

Darlene met them at Joey's house for drinks before dinner. The rain had stopped, and Joey and his wife, Sylvia, had already prepared margaritas and chips and salsa, both of which were placed on the rectangular glass table on the backyard patio of their ranch home. Warren and Luisa pulled into the driveway of their suburban home just as the sun set in the west. Joey kept a neatly trimmed lawn that Sylvia lined with rosebushes that bore three glorious colors in the early spring: red, pink, and yellow. They were just beginning to bud, and the plate glass window at the front of the house reflected the dark green leaves and colors that hid beneath the outer petals. The house, built by a developer when they bought it, was sided in beige vinyl siding, and had a two-car garage on the left side. To Luisa, it appeared to be just like all of the suburban homes she saw outside of Denver, with its limited windows and mimicry of so many other houses on the same block. To Warren, it looked like his childhood home, except that it had siding instead of brick. They both stood staring at the house for a moment before getting Alejo out of the car and heading toward the front door.

Darlene answered, and though she had aged, she looked just as beautiful to Warren as when he'd first laid eyes on her nearly forty years before. She now kept her black hair cut short, and had the ends curled around her pale white face. The warmth of love was in her eyes as held the door open, and then held out her thin arms toward Warren, who had grown in his late teens to surpass her long legs.

"We're so glad y'all came," she breathed into his neck as he bent to hug her. "It's been too long." When she pulled away, she already had tears in her eyes, and her mascara and eyeliner began to run down the sides of her cheeks. She held out her hand to Luisa and squeezed it in her narrow palm, her long red fingernails tickling the back of Luisa's hand.

"You must be the angel that has come into Warren's life and brought him back from his reclusive lifestyle. I couldn't wait to meet you. And who is this little sweetheart?" She lowered her body towards Alejo's face, whose shyness had overcome him as he buried it in Luisa's legs.

"This is my son, Alejo."

"Oh, Alejandro? That's a real popular name down here. I've had many students named Alejandro, but only a few who went by Alejo. Hi, sweetie. Do you want a cookie?" Alejo's eyes lit up, and Darlene led him into the kitchen, where Sylvia stood at the sink washing lettuce for the salad and Joey prepared the meat for the grill.

Joey, too, had surpassed his mother's height, and stood a muscular six foot two. His hair, reflecting both the darkness of Darlene's and the red tinge so familiar to the York family, he wore in military style. He had no facial hair on his angular face, and his green eyes were set deep beneath his reddish eyebrows. When he smiled and held out his hand to his uncle, he showed off his even white teeth, and his handshake was one of a man with power as Warren's hand was squished between his strong fingers.

"I finally get to meet my famous Uncle Warren," Joey's deep voice echoed through the kitchen, which was as spotlessly cleaned as the rest of the house.

Joey wrapped his arm around Sylvia's small back and led them outside, where the warm Texas spring bragged of seventy degrees. Sylvia, a small, blond, mousy woman, looked more like she was Joey's doll than his wife. When she spoke, her voice carried in the breeze so that anyone listening would have to lean in to hear what she had to say. She was no taller than five foot two, and her curly golden ringlets bounced around her thin neck and heart shaped face. She too had green eyes, and a face filled with freckles that seemed to penetrate the skin of her tiny round nose. She had thin pink lips that she tried to keep closed over her crooked, yellowing teeth, and she kept her arms crossed over her floral patterned summer dress. Though she hardly spoke for most of the evening, no one seemed to notice. Joey's loud voice echoed against the backside of the house with one story after another about his childhood, his long enlistment in the military, and what it was really like to be a drill sergeant for the Air Force basic training.

Joey and Sylvia had two children, Frankie and Diane, who were ten and eight years old and took after their mother, saying little, eating quickly, and then disappearing from the table. Darlene, proud of who her son had become, also sat back and listened for most of the night as Joey's eyes lit up with each tale, and smiles and laughter erupted onto the happy faces of Warren and Luisa. Towards the end of the night, Darlene took Warren's hand and pulled him into the living room, where she sat down on the couch and got out her purse.

"After you left San Antonio the last time I saw you, I still had to go through all of Frankie's personal things that were sent home from his base in Vietnam. He never carried much with him when he was deployed, because he was always afraid of losing everything. I was hoping, back then, that there would be a love letter to me, one in which he would apologize for being so cold, for hurting me so much… But there wasn't. I searched through all of his things again and again, but I only found one letter."

Warren's heart flipped inside his chest, hoping that the letter was for him, because he, too, had had the same feelings of loss and regret whenever he thought of Frankie's coldness when he last saw him.

"When I first saw the envelope, it had already yellowed, and it had been folded so many times that there was a line of dust along the crease. I held that envelope in my shaking hands for so long before I dared to open it. I thought about all the things it might say, all the people it could have been written to… I hoped, maybe, that he would have written a letter to Joey, to tell him he loved him and that he'd wait for him in Heaven…" Darlene had just begun the long story that she had been saving up in her mind for thirty-six years, but the tears still came into her eyes now that she was finally face to face with Warren.

"But the letter wasn't for me, or for Joey, or for his mother, or for you, Warren. It was for the man and child in this picture." With the cautious touch of someone trying to take apart a bomb, Darlene reached into her purse and pulled out a wallet-sized black and white photo with slightly frayed edges and faded Vietnamese writing on the backside. She held it in her palm towards Warren as if she were offering him a precious jewel, and he took the picture into his hand and fixed his stare upon it, mesmerized by its combination of simplicity and complexity. A young Vietnamese man with a thin, angular face and neatly trimmed black hair stared back at him, the smile missing from his perfect complexion. In his arms he held a chubby-faced baby with a tuft of black hair on the top of his head and a grin that caused his eyes to squint and his cheeks to bear two round dimples. He had two teeth. Though the picture was in black and white, the image was clear and entrancing as Warren held it in his shaking palm. He could think of no words, but stared at the picture for as long as he could stand. When he looked up at Darlene after several minutes had slipped into the night, he, too, had tears in the corners of his eyes.

"Who is it?" he whispered, though his heart told him that he shouldn't ask, because without even hearing her response, he knew the answer to his question.

Darlene had drawn a miniature pack of tissues out of her purse, and she held one to her nose. Her eyes were red and her face streaked with moisture and what was left of her makeup. She sobbed into her tissue for a moment longer before she responded, the letter still inside the envelope in her other hand.

"I have never shown this to anyone, although I've read it probably a thousand times. I could read it to you with my eyes closed," she closed her eyes then, and more tears rolled down her cheeks. She wiped them away with the soaked tissue and reached for another one. "Jesus, I can't believe I'm going on like this after all these years. Seeing you... gosh Warren, you look so much like Frankie. Losing a husband is something you never really get over."

She handed him the envelope, and before he could open it and pull out the letter, he turned it over and looked at to whom it was addressed. In small black, perfectly practiced print were the words: "To the man I killed and the father his child lost."

Warren's breath slipped out of his chest then, disappearing into the air like a fog streaked with the burning sunlight of midmorning. More tears crept down his cheeks and he opened his mouth, afraid that if he didn't he would no longer be able to breathe. With the delicacy of an artist painting a fragile eggshell, he turned the envelope over and pulled out the folded stationary, which at one time had been thick parchment paper, but was now thin and marked with Darlene's fingerprints along the edges of the letter. Warren opened the one-page letter, his hands still shaking as he read.

```
Dear Sir,                              9 May. 1967

     Your picture has had a place in my wallet
for two years now. I don't know how long I will
carry it, but each night, I am unable to sleep
until I spend a good deal of time looking at
it. You haunt me, both in my daydreams and my
nightmares. I sit here now in a tent with
twenty other men who are all writing letters
home to their wives and girlfriends and parents
and siblings while they listen to the bombs go
off and the planes go down in the distance that
is not so distant. I, too, should be writing to
my wife, or to my little brother who has no one
in the world to love him but me. But I can't. I
have nothing to say to them that would make
them feel any differently, or make me love them
anymore, or make me into the person I was
```

before I came into this war. It is my second tour of duty here, and I hate it no more than I did before. I hate the heat, the mosquitoes, the close quarters, the constant filth, the smell, the reason we're here, the death… the fear of death. I guess you know what that's like even more than me.

The Marines' whole purpose in life is infantry training. Beaten into our brains from the first moment of basic training until the moment we depart this earth, we are prepared for war. I came to Vietnam with six months of war training in my background, everything from how to aim an M-16 to how to dig a hole for my shit. Despite all of this, when I arrived, I realized right away that I was not prepared at all.

I could see women in the rice paddies, children clinging to each other in the doors of the huts. I could smell your food cooking and taste the fear of the people whom we fought for and against. But when I came upon you that night on the trail, I never realized how part of something I really was until I saw how alone you were. You wore the Viet Cong uniform but you didn't look like a Viet Cong to me. You looked like a little boy, so frail. Your chin shook and you spoke one word in Vietnamese, a threat maybe, or a plea, I couldn't tell. The full moon cast a white light on your face, and I knew you were too scared to pull the M-16 high enough to aim at me. We stood there for what seemed like the entire night but was probably only a moment or two, and then I took out my pistol and shot you square in the forehead. Your eyes widened as you fell, and your arms plopped around you like sacks of water. Without thinking, I reached down and sorted through your pockets. You had cigarettes and a lighter and some old letters and this picture.

I have a son at home whom I haven't taken the time to love, because every time I look at him I think of yours, who will never see his

father again. I wonder sometimes, if you and I
had met in another time or place, if our kids
would play together, if we would share a beer
on the front porch, if we would be friends. But
I know this could never be true: you were the
enemy, and I was just doing what I was trained
to do. Now I must live with your life in my
mind for the rest of my days, however long that
will be. I just wanted you to know that I'm
sorry your life had to end at my hands. I'm
sorry we met under the circumstances that we
did. I hope, when I return to the United
States, that I can be a better person, having
had a taste of your life on my palms through
this small black and white picture. I want to
thank you for giving me your life and the
opportunity to live my own.

               Sincerely,
               Sergeant Francis York, Jr.

Warren read the letter three times when at last Darlene spoke. "Look at
the date," she whispered, as if he couldn't help but see. "He died the next day,"
and a new wave of tears flowed from her eyes, her makeup now completely
washed away, the blackened tissues resting in her lap.

Warren leaned over and placed the letter on the coffee table, then
reached for Darlene, wrapping her in his arms with his strength and warmth.
"Thank you for sharing this with me," he murmured into her shoulder, "even
though it was written to neither of us, it still helps me feel like there was a
chance, had he lived, that Frankie learned to forgive himself, and would have
come home a better person, more like the person he was before the war. It's
just awful to think that he never had that chance."

They held each other on the beige couch for several moments, their
sobs interlinking finally Warren decided to speak some more. "I'm sorry for
leaving you that day, for traveling all that way and not even attending the
service. I'm sorry about not ever coming to visit again, and for the pathetic life
I've led. I've been thinking a lot about my life lately. I look at Luisa, who had
the most perfect life I can imagine, with a loving, well to do, supportive
husband, a young baby, and the beautiful youth that would last her for years.
And she, too, comes from an abusive situation, though a different kind. Yet...
and it's hard to admit. She's so much stronger than me, and so much more able
to handle her grief. I wish I had that wisdom when I was young. Maybe my life
would have turned out differently." Warren's face was red as he pulled away
from Darlene, using one of her tissues to blow his nose and look away from her
in shame.

"I always wondered why you left so suddenly. You never said."

"I just wanted to be alone. I figured if I was alone, no one could hurt me. In a way I was right, because I have scarcely spoken to my family members for over thirty years now, and I haven't been bothered by any of their problems. But I also haven't been showered with any of their joys, and that's what makes me the saddest."

"It's not too late, you know," Darlene clutched his palm, trying to get him to turn his face towards her.

"I know. If Luisa has taught me anything, it's the importance of staying dedicated to family. You ought to see the book she made." Warren's tone had changed from sadness to pride, and he wiped the last tears away from his face.

Luisa had come in from the backyard soon after Darlene pulled Warren into the living room. She was in the bedroom adjacent to the living room changing Alejo's diaper and getting him ready for bed, and found herself eavesdropping on the greater part of their conversation. Darlene's words, "Losing a husband is something you never really get over," had struck her so that she couldn't leave the room, but had to listen in to the talk as if her life depended on it, her own tears washing away the tiredness of the long two-day drive. Alejo had fallen asleep on the bed where she sat at the edge, her mind burning with questions about Frankie's picture and letter. When Warren spoke so kindly of her, she cried even more, because she felt that she hadn't dealt with grief the way she should and that Carter wouldn't have wanted her to fall in love with someone else so quickly, and that her days of mourning were endless because they would always be tinged with guilt.

"I want you to have this letter. I hope it brings you many days of peace, and allows you to have closure, at last. You deserve it, Warren."

That was the last thing she heard, and she found herself, exhausted, lying down next to Alejo and closing her eyes, falling fast into a deep sleep. She awoke the next morning with Tyler standing over her.

"I thought you weren't coming until tomorrow," she sat up, groggy and surprised. "I have your ticket information..." but she couldn't think of where. Alejo still slept beside her, though he stirred when she spoke.

"I couldn't wait. I left the same night you did, and drove like a maniac thinking I could catch up with y'all. I just couldn't wait."

"Oh, Tyler," she felt fresh tears come with the new day. She had survived the one-year anniversary of Carter's death, but she still had so far to go. "And my parents?"

"They're still coming on tomorrow's flight. This way we can just take my car all the way down to Jimenez and not have to worry about renting one."

They stood next to the bed and Alejo sat up, rubbing his eyes and squealing, "Mama, Mama, milk, Mama!" Tyler sat down next to him and lifted him into his arms, throwing him into the air.

"Are you excited to meet your great-grandparents, Alejo?" Alejo giggled in delight as Tyler threw him again and again. Luisa watched the two for a moment before taking Alejo's sippy cup out of the bag and heading for the kitchen, hoping there would be milk for her to pour.

Chapter 40

Aurelio's body, thin for years and pale due to his lack of proper nutrition, had transformed into that of a robust, healthy man. Though he couldn't disguise the wrinkles around his eyes and mouth nor hide the strands of gray in his dark brown curls, the mornings he now spent in the gym showed off curvy biceps and a six-pack of muscle, not beer, on his stomach. His skin had returned to the ruddy color of youth that Reeve remembered when she had first laid eyes on him, and he no longer carried his shoulders with the hump of an aimless man, but high and proud, the world's opportunities in front of him. His brown pupils sparkled against clear white retinas, and when he smiled underneath trimmed moustache, he showed a set of teeth and gums that had finally received some attention and serious cleaning. He no longer looked tired and thin, but vivid and strong as he faced the world with the new aura of hope that surrounded his every move.

He had driven across town a month before with the letter from the publisher, and stood at the bottom of the steps that led to her apartment waiting for her to return from work. He hoped she wasn't on call, because he had been waiting for too many years to share this news, and hadn't told anyone, not even Luisa. At last Reeve walked up, a look of surprise on her face.

"What are you doing here? Is Luisa OK?" She tried not to sound accusatory, but her tone reflected her distaste for his arrival. She stood in front of him with her long blond hair pulled into a tight ponytail at the nape of her neck. She wore Birkenstocks with a purple floral pattern over her thin feet and a summer dress that mimicked the design, with orchids interlocking over pale lavender rayon. Her gray eyes appeared dull and hid themselves under her eyelashes. She couldn't fully look at the man she had sworn her life to all those years before. Her thin fingers gripped the strap of the purse that dangled on her shoulder, the long fingernails clawing at the brown leather.

"As far as I know, she's fine. I'm here for a different reason."

When he spoke, his voice was smooth, unslurred, and almost without any trace of the heavy accent he had carried on the back of his English words for his adult life. His voice surprised her. Its calmness touched her inside and her heart fluttered. She forced her eyes and face to look directly into his eyes. He didn't fidget or stand with his hands in his pockets or try to be anything he wasn't. He stood straight and tall, his face patient and expectant as he held an envelope in the palm of his right hand.

"I always dreamed of the day I would receive this letter. I imagined us living in a nice house on a hill overlooking the mountains… I imagined Luisa and Byron, tiny children at our feet, screaming with joy at their father's success… I imagined that you and I would go out to a fancy dinner at our favorite Mexican restaurant, and then we would come home and make love on the balcony that opened up off of our master suite... I imagined it so many ways, and it was always perfect. But I never quite imagined that I would be standing here, sober as dawn, in front of an apartment building where my wife lives without me." Aurelio cast his eyes toward the black pavement of the parking lot as his voice softened. He waited a moment before speaking again.

"But it is just as well. Because the news is as sweet in my mouth as it always was in my dreams, like honey flowing from my throat as I say these words. They're going to publish my manuscript." Two clear tears met in the corners of his eyes as he looked into Reeve's face. The dullness evaporated and her eyes shone with the brilliance of love and acceptance as she looked back at him.

"Does this mean that I can finally meet the bearer of my daughter's name?"

Aurelio's relief swept over him as he sat down on the bottom step and wept.

At fifty, Aurelio had never before been on a plane. Though Reeve had laid down the law a month earlier, informing Aurelio that there was no chance that she could ever forgive him for thirty years of the alcoholic abuse that she considered the ruin of her life, she found herself holding his hand as the plane took off, trying to calm the nerves and diminish the desperate look on her former husband's face.

"It's more dangerous to drive than it is to fly, you know," she told him, but the beads of sweat still gathered at his high-cut sideburns, and his eyes examined the window as if he had never before looked outside.

"I drive every day. It makes sense. Getting into a huge metal object that supposedly can float in the air doesn't make sense. If I had known Tyler was going to drive anyway—" Aurelio drew in a breath and released it with caution. He didn't want to say anything bad about the man who had returned the smile to Luisa's face.

"It's only a two and a half hour flight. Tyler got us the best tickets. You can survive two and a half hours, Aurelio." When she said his name, it rolled off her tongue with the gentleness of a mother consoling her forlorn child. He looked into her face and forced a smile.

"You are more beautiful now than the day I first laid eyes on you," he whispered, unable to contain his love for her any longer.

Reeve pulled her hand away and shifted in her seat, leaning more toward the stranger next to her than to him. "You can't sweet talk me, Aurelio. It's too little, too late." Her tone changed from gentle to cold, and Aurelio again fastened his gaze on the window, mesmerized by the smallness of the farm fields below.

Neither of them spoke for the remainder of the flight.

On the morning of their arrival, Luisa awoke to the sound that haunted her everywhere she traveled in her life: mourning doves. Their calls to each other echoed in her memory and in her presence: the sad, longing, "Whoo-oo, woo, woo, woo" repeated again and again, so that the smaller songbirds and the morning breeze that swept across the window were numb and meaningless. She lay awake next to Tyler listening to the song, remembering the first time she had heard it. They were living in a small cottage in the northeastern part of Texas where her mother trained to become a midwife. They lived on the outskirts of town where all she could see if she looked in either direction were the plains that endlessly engulfed the earth in a curving, rolling landscape. Their cottage had two bedrooms, a tiny kitchen, a living room with a wood stove that served as both heater and range, and a tiny lean-to bathroom adjacent to the kitchen. They had to go outside to access it. The cottage walls were made of wood paneling and the owner, a friend of the midwife whom Reeve studied under, had decorated them with bits and pieces of Native American art that she had acquired at roadside stands and garage sales.

Luisa was five when she first heard them. Byron had just been born in the very next room two weeks before, and his presence in her life troubled her. He took so much of his mother's time, and her father seemed to be gone even more often. Luisa often woke early in the morning, before her mother even had a chance to rouse her, and listened to the mourning doves. She loved and hated the sound. She thought that they sounded sad and lonely, but she didn't understand why, because they were together. Always there was more than one dove calling out to another, and their sad calls echoed each other in perfect harmony.

She had asked her mother what they were one morning at breakfast, to which she had said, "Those are mourning doves," while she fixed herself a cup of coffee and sat down across from her, Byron in her arms, at the old wooden card table.

"Are they called that because they sing in the morning?" Luisa wanted to know.

Her mother had looked out the window then, as if searching for their pale brown feathers to verify her words. "No, sweetie. It's a different kind of mourning. Mourning is something you do when you are very sad, and you have lost something very important to you. You mourn what you have lost."

Though her mother's voice was distant and her mother's face had turned far away from hers, Luisa had to know more. "What are the doves mourning, Mama? What did they lose?"

"I don't know, sweetie. Maybe they just like to remind us every day of what we have lost." She stood up from the table and emptied her coffee down the sink.

"It's time to get dressed. I laid your clothes out on your bed." She said nothing else, but placed Byron on the couch and began to wash the dishes.

Luisa returned to her room and sat on the bed, listening to the mourning doves again. She thought about how they were sad together, and how being together didn't seem to make them feel happy. She often felt that way at home, when her parents were together. Always they fought, and Byron seemed to scream all the time, and she couldn't understand any of it. She wondered what the birds were looking for, but she also wondered what her parents had lost, because they seemed to be mourning as well.

She listened to those birds sing together everywhere they lived throughout her childhood. For a long time, she thought the same two birds had flown with her family from place to place. When she was older, she realized the truth, but couldn't shed the irony of their presence in her life.

"Do you know why I think I always hear mourning doves?" she had once said to Carter as they lay in bed listening to the birds.

"No, why?"

"I just feel like they're my parents, always mourning for each other and everything they have each given up to be together, and everything they've lost along the way. I think I'll hear those mourning doves until my parents are happy... I think I'll hear them everywhere I go for as long as I live, because I feel like I'm just surrounded by mourning."

Carter had wrapped his arms around her then, spooning her in the warmth of their newlywed bed, kissing her neck. He whispered into her ear, "Maybe they're not really mourning at all. Maybe that's their call of happiness, and it's been following you, trying to catch up with you, for your whole life." He had kissed her then, passionately on the mouth, and as the doves continued their song, they had made love in the coolness of early morning.

She turned her body towards Tyler now, feeling the heat seep across the sheet from where he slept. She wanted to tell him about the doves, but their presence and her memory of Carter was a secret she wanted to keep. The sun rose higher in the sky and at last he stirred, rubbing his eyes and turning his face toward her.

"How long have you been awake?" he asked.

"Not long."

"Are you excited?"

"Nervous, mostly. I never thought I'd be twenty-eight years old and meeting my grandparents for the first time."

"I'm sure they'll welcome you with open arms. Don't you think they're as excited as you?"

"I don't know. Does it seem normal to send your son away and ask him never to return unless he's successful?"

"Well, maybe you'll see why when we get there. I've been to Mexico a few times... if you saw how they lived, and the poverty in that country, maybe you could understand why it was so important to them. They put all their dreams on his shoulders. It might have been a bit too much pressure."

"I can't imagine what it must have been like for them. In some ways, my parents' beginning was like a fairy tale. My dad was the gallant knight who saved my mother the dame from a horrible life with a horrible man, and their love was so deep that it lasted all these years... But at the same time, their life began as a nightmare, with my mother's rape and then the disowning from her only family... When I got married, I thought I had escaped all of that. I thought I could be safe from that kind of pain. But it's scary how life will creep up and remind you."

Alejo stirred in his playpen, and Luisa closed her mouth to listen.

"You can't live without pain, Luisa," Tyler said, direct and forward as he stood from the bed.

"Hey, boy, you ready to get up?" he said and bent over to pick up Alejo, carrying him out of the room and shutting the door behind them.

Luisa sat up in bed, intending to get up, but their calls echoed across the yard and she lingered for a moment longer: "Woo-oo, woo, woo, woo." She loved the simplicity of their song. She didn't know how to face the day without their music in her ears.

At breakfast, Warren's face glowed with a happiness that even Luisa had never seen. He looked as if he had fallen in love. For the past day, he had carried Frankie's letter in his pocket. He'd shown it to Tyler and Luisa the day before, and had finally taken the time to tell them some of his favorite memories of his brother Frankie. He spoke with candor and pride, as if he had changed his mood from gloomy regret to happy reminiscence, and Luisa was more than thankful that she had planned this part of the trip to begin her journey to Mexico.

"When does your parents' flight arrive?" Sylvia asked as she served up bacon and eggs.

"At ten-thirty. We hope it's on time, because we're going to leave straight from the airport. We hope to get to Jimenez by noon tomorrow. I don't know where we're going to stay tonight."

"I'm sure we'll be able to find a place. It'll be an adventure," Tyler broke up pieces of bacon for Alejo.

The conversation danced around the table with a light air, making Luisa ease into the comforts of Joey and Sylvia's home. Warren, though his smile was bright, kept stealing glances of Luisa's face, trying to read her emotions. He had dreaded this day for months now, because he feared he would hardly see her bright eyes and cheery smile anymore. When she and her family would return from Mexico, she planned on moving into Tyler's condo. All of their things were packed in boxes that lined the walls of she and Alejo's rooms, and already, as he had closed the door the morning they left, he could feel the house echo with their absence. He felt safe here, in Joey and Sylvia's house, but he knew the safety wouldn't last, and though his contentment and long-awaited feeling of closure regarding Frankie had satisfied him, a thin layer of darkness rested in his eyes as he looked at Luisa's always-hopeful face.

After breakfast, Darlene drove over and met Luisa, Alejo, and Tyler at the door, where they stood next to their three suitcases passing out teary-eyed goodbyes. After saying a brief hello to Darlene, Warren took Luisa's small hand into the sweaty palm of his own and pulled her into the hallway. He looked down at the carpet as he spoke, fearful of what would come if he held her face in his eyes.

"I hope your family is everything you've ever wanted, because mine has been, thanks to you. I never thought—" even with the steady view of the neutral-colored carpet, he couldn't choke back his emotions. "I never thought, when I saw the happiness and love that you, Carter, and Alejo shared, that I would ever know such happiness myself. I had lived so long with the pain that I didn't know any other feeling. Luisa, you have brought me everything I could have hoped for, and I want to thank you for that. I want to ask you not to forget me when you go." He whispered the last sentence, terrified of her response, but before he could even finish she had wrapped her arms around his neck and pulled him close to her.

"I'll come by every day if you want, Uncle Warren. Because that happiness you saw looking into Alejo's room… I never thought I could have it again either, and in just a year, I feel like you've been central in putting the pieces of my life back together. Your presence in my life is priceless, and I will never forget you."

They stood together in the hallway until Tyler came to pry them apart.

"Luisa," he whispered, "we have to go or your parents will wonder what happened."

Luisa grasped Warren's hand as she pulled away. She didn't say another word as Tyler buckled Alejo into his car seat, and looked out the window, her mouth unmoving, on the drive to the airport. The sky, which had promised the day with a luminous blue, now teased the sun with large cumulus clouds and a gray rain shower in the distance. Tyler played a collection of Queen songs on his CD player, but the closer they came to the airport, all Luisa could hear was the ongoing call of mourning doves. She kept their song in her mind and behind her closed mouth as they pulled into the passenger pickup lane of the San Antonio airport, wanting to say something but not knowing what to say.

Her smiling parents, including a very relieved Aurelio who had just survived his first flight, loaded their small suitcases into the trunk and piled in on either side of Alejo in the back seat of Tyler's BMW.

"Are you ready to begin the journey of our lives?" Aurelio asked as he pulled the door closed.

All the faces in the car turned toward his, unable to respond.